The Snake Stone

Jason Goodwin fell under the spell of Istanbul while studying Byzantine history at Cambridge University. Fifteen years ago, following the success of *The Gunpowder Gardens: Travels in China and India in Search of Tea*, he made a six-month pilgrimage across Eastern Europe to reach the city for the first time, a journey recounted in *On Foot to the Golden Horn*, which won the John Llewellyn Rhys/*Mail on Sunday* Prize in 1993.

Intrigued by the enduring influence of the Ottoman Turks on Eastern Europe, Jason went on to research and write *Lords of the Horizons: A History of the Ottoman Empire*. Jan Morris called it 'a high-octane work of art', and the *New York Times* praised its 'dazzling beauty . . . the rare coming together of historical scholarship and curiosity about distant places with luminous writing'.

In *The Janissary Tree*, his first novel, he returned to Istanbul and the history of the Ottoman Empire. Michael Bywater in the *Daily Telegraph* praised it as 'a tremendous first novel, born of a deep engagement with the culture', while for Michael Arditti in the *Daily Mail* it 'brilliantly conjures up the exoticism of Istanbul'.

He is married to Kate, his companion on the walk to Istanbul; they live in rural Sussex with their four children.

JASON GOODWIN

The Snake Stone

ff

faber and faber

First published in 2007
by Faber and Faber Limited
3 Queen Square London WC1N 3AU

Typeset by Faber and Faber Limited
Printed in England by Mackays of Chatham, plc

A CIP record for this book
is available from the British Library

ISBN 978-0-571-23640-4

2 4 6 8 10 9 7 5 3 1

For Izaak

The king commands us, and the doctor quacks us,
The priest instructs, and so our life exhales.

Lord Byron, *Don Juan*

The voice was low and rough and it came from behind as dusk fell.

'Hey, George.'

It was the hour of the evening prayer, when you could no longer distinguish between a black thread and a white one in ordinary light. George pulled the paring knife from his belt and sliced it through the air as he turned. All over Istanbul, muezzins in their minarets threw back their heads and began to chant.

It was a good time to kick a man to death in the street.

The grainy ululations swept in sobbing waves across the Golden Horn, where the Greek oarsmen on the gliding caiques were lighting their lamps. The notes of prayer rolled over the European town at Pera, a few lights wavering against the black ridge of Galata Hill. They skimmed the Bosphorus to Uskudar, a smudge of purple fading back into the blackness of the mountains; and from there, on the Asian side, the mosques on the waterline echoed them back.

A foot caught George in the small of his back. George's arms went wide and he stumbled towards a man who had a long face as if he were sorrowing for something.

The sound swelled as muezzin after muezzin picked up the cry, weaving between the city's minarets the shimmer of a chant that expressed in a thousand ways the infirmity of man and the oneness of God.

After that the knife wasn't any good.

The call to prayer lasts about two and a half minutes, but for George it stopped sooner. The sad-faced man stooped and picked up the knife. It was very sharp, but its end was broken. It wasn't a knife for a fight. He threw it into the shadows.

When the men had gone, a yellow dog came cautiously out of a nearby doorway. A second dog slunk forward on its belly and crouched close by, whining hopefully. Its tail thumped the ground. The first dog gave a low growl, and showed its teeth.

Maximilien Lefèvre leaned over the rail and plugged his cheroot into the surf which seethed from the ship's hull. Seraglio Point was developing on the port bow, its trees still black and massy in the early light. As the ship rounded the Point, revealing the Galata Tower on the heights of Pera, Lefèvre pulled a handkerchief from his sleeve to wipe his hands; his skin was clammy from the salt air.

He looked up at the walls of the sultan's palace, patting the back of his neck with the handkerchief. There was an ancient column in the Fourth Court of the seraglio, topped by a Corinthian capital, which was sometimes visible from the sea, between the trees. It was, perhaps, the lingering relic of an acropolis which had stood there many centuries ago, when Byzantium was nothing but a colony of the Greeks: before it became a second Rome, before it became the navel of the world. Most people didn't know the column still existed: sometimes you saw it, sometimes not.

The ship heaved, and Lefèvre gave a grunt of satisfaction.

Slowly the Stamboul shore of the Golden Horn came into view, a procession of domes and minarets which surged forwards, one by one, and then modestly retired. Below the domes, cascading down to the busy waterfront, the roofs of Istanbul were glowing red and orange in the first sunlight. This was the panorama that visitors always admired: Constantinople, Istanbul, city of patriarchs and sultans, the busy kaleidoscope of the gorgeous east, the pride of fifteen centuries.

The disappointment came later.

Lefèvre shrugged, lit another cheroot, and turned his attention to the deck. Four sailors in bare feet and dirty singlets were stooped by the anchor chain, awaiting their captain's signal. Others were clawing up the sails overhead. The helmsman eased the ship to port, closing in on the shore and the counter-current that would bring them to a stop. The captain raised his hand, the chain ran out with the sound of cannon fire, the anchor bit and the ship heaved slowly back against the chain.

A boat was lowered, and Lefèvre descended into it after his trunk.

At the Pera landing stage, a young Greek sailor jumped ashore with a stick to push back the crowd of touts. With his other hand he gestured for a tip.

Lefèvre put a small coin into his hand and the young man spat.

'City moneys,' he said contemptuously. 'City moneys very bad, Excellency.' He kept his hand out.

Lefèvre winked. '*Piastres de Malta,*' he said quietly.

'Oho!' The Greek squinted at the coin and his face brightened. 'Ve-ery good.' He redoubled his efforts with the touts. 'These is robbers. You wants I finds you porter? Hotel? Very clean, Excellency.'

'No, thank you.'

'Bad mans here. You is first times in the city, Excellency?'

'No.' Lefèvre shook his head.

The men on the landing stage fell silent. Some of them began to turn away. A man was approaching across the planked walk in green slippers. He was of medium build, with a head of snowy

3

white hair. His eyes were piercingly blue. He wore baggy blue trousers, an open shirt of faded red cotton.

'Doctor Lefèvre? Follow me, please.' Over his shoulder he said: 'Your trunk will be taken care of.'

Lefèvre gave a shrug. '*A la prochaine.*'

'*Adio*, m'sieur,' the sailor replied slowly.

That same morning, in the Fener district of Istanbul, Yashim woke in a slab of warm spring sunshine and sat up, drowsily rubbing his hands through his curls. After a few moments he cast aside his Korassian blanket and slid from the divan, dropping his feet automatically into a pair of grey leather baluches. He dressed quickly and went downstairs, through the low Byzantine doorway of the widow's house, and out into the alley. A few turns took him to his favourite café on the Kara Davut, where the man at the stove gave him a nod and put a small copper saucepan on the fire.

Yashim settled himself on the divan facing the street, beneath the projecting upper windows. He slipped his feet under his robe: and with that gesture he became, in a sense, invisible.

It was partly the way Yashim still dressed. It was several years since the sultan had begun to encourage his subjects to adopt western dress; the results were mixed. Many men had swapped their turbans for the scarlet fez, and their loose robes for trousers and the stambouline, a curiously high-necked, swallow-tailed jacket, but few of them wore European lace-up boots. Some of Yashim's neighbours on the divan resembled black beetles, in bare feet; all elbows and pointy knees. In a long cloak, some-where between deep red and brown, and a saffron-coloured robe, Yashim might have been a ruck in the carpet which covered the divan; only his turban was dazzlingly white.

But Yashim's invisibility was also a quality in the man – if man was the proper word. There was a stillness about him: a steadiness in the gaze of his grey eyes, a soft fluidity to his movements, or an easiness of gesture, that seemed to deflect attention, rather than attract it. People saw him – but they did not quite notice him; and it was this absence of hard edges, this peculiar withdrawal of challenge or threat, that comprised his essential talent, and made him, even in nineteenth-century Istanbul, unique.

Yashim did not challenge the men who met him; nor the women. With his kind face, grey eyes, dark curls barely touched, at forty, by the passage of the years, Yashim was a listener; a quiet questioner; and not entirely a man. Yashim was a eunuch.

He took his coffee propped up on one elbow, and ate the corek, brushing the crumbs from his moustache.

Deciding against having a pipe with his coffee, he left a silver piastre on the tray and walked down the street towards the Grand Bazaar.

At the corner he turned and glanced back, just in time to see the café owner pick up the coin and bite it. Yashim sighed. Bad money was like poison in the bowels, an irritant that Istanbul could never rid itself of. He hefted his purse and heard the dry rustle of his fortune susurrate between his fingertips: this was one of those times when currency seemed to melt like sugar in the hand. But sugar was sweet. The sultan was dying, and there was bitterness in the air.

In the Street of the Booksellers, Yashim stopped outside a little shop belonging to Goulandris, who dealt in old books and curiosities: sometimes he stocked the French novels which Yashim found hard to resist.

Goulandris fixed his visitor with his one good eye and ground his teeth. Goulandris was not one of your forward, pushy Greeks; his job as a bookseller was to watch, not speak. One of his eyes was filmed with cataracts; but the other did the work of two, recording the way a customer moved, the speed with which he selected a certain book, the expression on his face as he opened it and began to read. Old books, new books, Greek books, Turkish books – and precious few of those – books in Armenian and Hebrew and even, now and then, in French: Dmitri Goulandris stocked them as and when they came to him, pell-mell. Books did not interest him. But how to price a book – that was another matter. And so, with his one good eye, he watched the signs.

But the eunuch – he was good. Very good. Goulandris saw a well-set gentleman in early middle age, his black hair faintly touched with grey beneath a small turban, wearing a soft cloak of an indeterminate colour. Goulandris believed that he could penetrate any of the ruses that people used to throw him off the scent – the feigned indifference, the casual addition, the artfully contrived and wholly careless impulse. He listened to what they said. He watched the way their hands moved, and the flicker of their eyes. Only the damned eunuch remained a constant puzzle.

'Are you looking for a book?'

Yashim straightened and looked round. He had been far away, revisiting the agonies of love unfulfilled with his old friend Benjamin Constant; now he found himself in the familiar cubby-hole in the grand bazaar, the walls lined with books from floor to ceiling, the dim lamp and Goulandris himself, the bookseller, in a dirty grey fez, cross-legged on his stool behind a Frankish desk. Yashim smiled. He was not going to buy this book: *Adolphe.* He closed it softly and slid it back into its place on the shelf.

Yashim smiled and bowed, one hand to his chest. He liked this place, this little cave of books: you never knew what you might find. Goulandris, he suspected, had no idea himself: he doubted if he could do more than read and write in Greek. And today, hugger-mugger with the Frankish textbooks on ballistics, the old imperial scrolls bearing a sultan's beautiful calligraphic tugra, the impenetrable Greek religious tracts, the smattering of French novels which Yashim so enjoyed – there, bizarre as it was, a treasure that caught his eye. It had not been there last month. It might not be there the next.

Yashim drew down three books which interested him. He hesitated a little over the third – he wanted it badly, of course – and then slipped it to the bottom of the pile as he placed the books on the desk. Goulandris sucked his lips. He did not haggle, or offer arguments. He suggested prices. Yashim barely suppressed a flicker of disappointment as Goulandris solemnly priced the third book just a shade beyond his reach. That left him two books: he put one back, reluctantly. He delved into his purse. Goulandris pulled a notebook from his desk drawer and made a little entry.

And finally, with a nod to the old man in his dirty fez, Yashim stepped out into the alley of the booksellers, clutching volume 1 of Carême's *L'Art de la Cuisine Française au 19me Siècle* under his arm.

At the bottom of the hill he turned towards the market.

Yashim saw the fishmonger staring stonily at his scales as he weighed out a bass for an elderly matriarch. Two men were haggling over a bunch of carrots. Bad money bred suspicion everywhere – though George would be reliably immune, Yashim thought. He kept the stall which Yashim liked best, and always had good ideas for supper. George would growl and say the money was shit.

He looked ahead. George wasn't there.

'He's not coming in no more, efendi,' an Armenian grocer explained. 'Some kind of accident's what I heard.'

'Accident?' Yashim thought of the vegetable seller, with his big hands.

The grocer turned his head and spat. 'They come up yesterday, said George wouldn't be here no more. One of the Constantinedes brothers to get his pitch, they says.'

Yashim frowned. The Constantinedes brothers wore identical pencil moustaches and were forever on the move behind their piles of vegetables, like dancers. Yashim had always stuck with George.

'Efendi! What can we do for you today?' One of the brothers bent forward and began to arrange a pile of aubergines with quick flicks of his wrist. 'Fasulye today at last year's price! One day only!'

Yashim began to assemble his ingredients. Constantinedes weighed out two oka of potatoes and tumbled them into Yashim's basket, replacing the scoop on the scales with a flourish.

'Four piastres, twenty – twenty – twenty – eighty-five the potatoes – five-oh-five – and anything else, efendi?'

'What's happened to George?'

'Beans today – yesterday's prices!'

'They say you're going to take over his pitch.'

'Five-oh-five, efendi.'

'An oka of courgettes, please.'

The man picked the courgettes into his scoop.

'I heard he had an accident. How did it happen?'

'The courgettes.' As Constantinedes tilted the scoop over Yashim's basket Yashim gripped it by the edge and gently raised it level again.

'I'm a friend of his. If he's had an accident, I may be able to help.'

Constantinedes pursed his lips thoughtfully.

'I can ask the kadi,' Yashim said quietly, and let go of the scoop. The kadi was the official who regulated the market. The courgettes rained down into the basket. 'Keep the change.'

8

The man hesitated, then scooped up the two coins without looking at them and dropped them into the canvas pouch at his waist.

'Five minutes,' he said quietly.

4

Yashim stirred his coffee and waited for the grounds to settle. Constantinedes tilted the cup against his lips. 'We all got a choice. We don't want aggravation, see?'

'Yes. Is George all right?'

'Maybe. I don't ask.'

'But you'll take over his pitch.'

'Listen. This was between them and George. Keep us out of it. I'm talking to you because you was his friend.'

'Who are they, then?'

The man pushed his coffee away, and stood up.

'A little piece of everything, that's all.' He bent down to pick something off the ground and Yashim heard him whisper: 'The Hetira. I'd leave it, efendi.'

He walked back to his stall, leaving Yashim staring at the shiny thick dregs in his coffee cup, wondering where he had heard that name before.

5

Some cities in Europe were now bigger than Istanbul, and more industrious, and lonely; for Istanbul was a city in which every-one, from sultan to beggar, belonged somewhere – to a guild, a district, a family, a church or a mosque. Where they lived, the work they did, how they were paid, married, born or buried, the friends they made, the place they worshipped – all these things were arranged for them, so to speak, long before they ever balled their tiny fists and sucked in their first blast of Istanbul air; an air freighted with muezzins, the smell of the sea, the scent of cypresses, spices and drains.

Newcomers – foreigners, especially – often complained that Istanbul life was a sequence of divisions: they noticed the harem arrangement of the houses, the blank street walls, the way trades-men clung together in one street or a section of the bazaar. They frequently gave way to feelings of claustrophobia. Stambouliots, on the other hand, were used to the hugger-mugger atmosphere of warmth and gossip which surrounded them from the cradle and followed them to the grave. In the city of belonging, Yashim well knew, even the dead belonged somewhere.

He ran his thumb along the table's edge: it occurred to him, not for the first time, that of all Istanbul he might be the excep-tion which proved the rule. Sometimes he felt more like a ghost than a man; his invisibility hurt him. Even beggars had a guild that promised to provide their burial at the end. The ordinary eunuchs of the Empire, who served as chaperones, escorts, guardians – they were all, in that sense, members of a family: many belonged to the greatest family of all, and lived and died in the sultan's service. Yashim, for a spell, had served in the sultan's palace, too; but his gifts were too broad to be comfortably con-tained there, between the women of the harem and the secrets of the sultan's inner sanctum. So Yashim had chosen between free-dom and belonging: and a grateful sultan had bestowed that freedom on him.

With freedom had come responsibilities which Yashim worked hard to uphold: but also loneliness. Neither his condi-tion, nor his profession, such as it was, gave him the right to expect to see his own reflection in another pair of eyes. All he had were his friends.

George was a friend. But what did he know about George? He didn't know where he lived. He didn't know where he'd met his accident. But wherever he was, alive or dead, someone in the city knew. Even the dead belong somewhere.

'George? I never asked,' the Armenian stallholder said, scratching his head. 'Yildiz? Dolmabahçe? Somewhere up the Bosphorus, I'm pretty sure – he walks up from the Eminönü wharf.'

One of the Eminönü boatmen, resting his athletic body on the upright oar of his fragile caique, recognised George from Yashim's description. He took him up the Bosphorus most evenings, he said. Two nights ago a party of Greeks had spilled out onto the wharf and asked to be rowed up the Horn towards Eyüp; he had dithered for a while because he had not wanted to miss his regular fare. He remembered, too, that it must have been after dark because the lamps were lit and he had noticed the braziers firing on the Pera shore, where the mussel-sellers were preparing their evening snacks.

Yashim offered him a tip, a pinch of silver which the boatmen palmed without a glance, politely suppressing a reflex that was second nature to most tradesmen in the city. Then Yashim retraced his steps towards the market, wondering if it were in one of these narrow streets that George had had his accident.

The sound of falling water drew his attention. Through a doorway, higher than the level of the street, he caught a glimpse of a courtyard with squares of dazzling linen laid out to dry on a rosemary bush. He noticed the scalloped edge of a fountain. The door swung shut. But then Yashim knew where George might most likely be found.

Almost ten years after the sultan had told his people to dress alike, George stuck to the traditional blue, brimless cap and black slippers which defined him as a Greek. Once, when Yashim had asked him if he was going to adopt the fez, George had drawn himself up quite stiffly:

'What? You thinks I dresses for sultans and pashas all of my life? Pah! Like these courgette flowers, I wears what I wears because I ams what I ams!'

Yashim had not asked him about it again; nor did George ever remark on Yashim's turban. It had become like a secret sign between them, a source of silent satisfaction and mutual recognition; as between them and the others who ignored the fez, and went on dressing as before.

The door on the street gave Yashim an idea. A church stood on the street parallel with the one he was strenuously climbing towards the market. A group of discreet buildings formed a complex around the church, where nuns lived in dormitories, ate in a refectory and also ran a charitable dispensary and hospital for the incurably sick of their community. If his friend was found on the street after his accident, it was to this door, without a shadow of doubt, that he would have been brought, thanks to his blue cap and his black Greek shoes.

But the door remained closed, in spite of his knocking; and in the church, when he finally reached it, he had to overcome the suspicions of a young Papa who was doubtless bred up in undying hatred for everything Yashim might represent: the conqueror's turban, the ascendancy of the crescent in the Holy City of orthodox Christianity, and the right of interference. But when at last he passed beyond the reredos and through the vestry door, he met an old nun who nodded and said that a Greek had been delivered to their door just two nights past.

'He is alive, by the will of God,' the nun said. 'But he is very sick.'

The wardroom was bathed in a cool green light and smelled of olive-oil soap. There were four wooden cots for invalids and a wide divan; all the cots were occupied. Yashim instinctively put his sleeve to his mouth, but the nun touched his arm and told him not to worry, there was no contagion in the ward.

George's black shoes lay on the floor at the foot of his cot. His jaw and half his face were swathed in bandages, which continued down across his shoulders and around his barrel-shaped chest. One arm – his left – stuck out stiffly from the bedside, splinted and bound. His breathing sounded sticky. What Yashim could see of his face was nothing more than a swollen bruise, black and purple, and several dark clots where blood had dried around his wounds.

'He has taken a little soup,' the nun whispered. 'That is good. He will not speak for many days.'

Yashim could hardly argue with her. Whoever had attacked his friend had done a thorough job. Their identity would remain a mystery, he thought, until George recovered enough to speak. The Hetira. What did it mean?

While the nun led him out through the tiny courtyard, Yashim told her what he knew about his friend. He left her with a purse of silver and the address of the café on Kara Davut where he could be found when George regained consciousness.

Only after the door had closed behind him did he think to warn her of the need for discretion, if not secrecy. But it was too late, and probably didn't matter. For George, after all, the damage was already done.

 6

Maximilien Lefèvre stepped lightly from the caique and made his way up the narrow cobbled street, carefully avoiding the open gutter which ran crookedly downhill in the middle of the road. Here and there his path was barred by a tangle of nets and creels, set out to mend; then he would vault over the gutter and carry on up the other side, sometimes stooping to pass beneath the jettied upper floors of the wooden houses which tilted at crazy angles, as if they were being slowly dragged down by the weight of the washing lines strung between them. Old women dressed from head to toe in black sat out on their steps, their laps full of broken nets; they regarded him curiously as he passed by.

Ortaköy was a Greek village, one of a dozen or so Greek villages strung out along the Bosphorus between Pera and the summer houses of the European diplomats. They had been there when Alexander the Great took his helots on their legendary campaigns in the east; Greeks from the Bosphorus had manned the ships which sailed against Xerxes, and four hundred years after the Turkish conquest they still drew a living from the sea and the straits. Long ago, Lefèvre recalled, an Ottoman pasha had blandly explained that God gave the land to the Ottomans, but to the Greeks he left the sea. How else? Agamemnon had assembled his war fleets against Troy when the Turks were still shepherding flocks across the deserts of Asia. The thought made Lefèvre frown.

Foreigners seldom visited the Greek villages, in spite of their reputation for good fish; before long, Lefèvre found himself with a tail of curious small boys, who shouted after him and pushed and shoved one another while their grandmothers looked on. Some of the smaller boys imagined that Lefèvre was a Turk, and all of them guessed that he was rich, so when Lefèvre stopped and turned around they drew together, half curious and half afraid. They saw him pull a coin from his pocket and offer it with a smile to the smallest boy among them. The boy hung back, somebody bolder snatched the coin, and pandemonium erupted as the whole pack of children turned as one to chase after him down the street.

Lefèvre took a turn onto an unmade lane. Swarms of tiny flies rose from stagnant puddles as he approached; he swept them from his face and kept his mouth shut.

The café door stood open. Lefèvre made his way rapidly to the back and took a seat on a small veranda which overlooked the pantiled roofs and the Bosphorus below. After a while another man joined him from the interior of the café.

Lefèvre stared down at his hands. 'I don't like meeting here,' he said quietly, in Greek.

The other man passed his hand across his moustache. 'This is a good place, signor. We are not likely to be disturbed.'

Lefèvre was silent for a few moments. 'Greeks,' he growled, 'are nosy bastards.'

The man chuckled. 'But you, signor – you are a Frenchman, no?'

Lefèvre raised his head and gave his companion a look of intense dislike. 'Let's talk,' he said.

❧ 7 ❧

In the palace at Beşiktaş, with its seventy-three bedrooms and forty-seven flights of stairs, the Shadow of God on earth, Sultan Mahmut II, lay dying of tuberculosis – and cirrhosis of the liver, brought about by a lifetime's devotion to reforming his empire along more Western, modern lines; and bad champagne chased down with spirits.

The sultan lay back on the pillows of an enormous tester bed hung with tasselled curtains, and gazed through red-rimmed eyes at the Bosphorus below his window and the hills of Asia across the strait. He had, he dimly knew, a world at his command. The fleets of the Ottoman sultan cruised in the Mediterranean and the

Black Seas; the prayers were read in his name at the mosques in Jerusalem, in Mecca and Medina; his soldiers stood watch on the Danube by the Iron Gates, and in the mountains of Lebanon; he was lord of Egypt. He had wives, he had concubines, he had slaves at his beck and call, not to mention the pashas, the admirals, the seraskiers, voivodes and hospodars who governed his far-flung empire in trembling – or, at least, respectful obedience to his will.

In his thirty years as sultan, Mahmut had presided over many changes to the Ottoman state. He had destroyed the power of the Janissaries, the overmighty regiment which opposed all change. He had adopted riding boots and French saddles. He had told his subjects to stop wearing the turban, if they were Muslims, and blue slippers, if they were Jews, and sky-blue hats, if they were Greeks: he had meant all men to receive equal treatment, and to wear red fezzes, and the stambouline, a cutaway coat.

The results were mixed. Many of his Muslim subjects now reviled him as the Infidel Sultan – and many of his Christian subjects had developed unrealistic expectations. Those Greeks in Athens – they had actually rebelled against him. After seven years of fighting, with European help, they had created their own, independent kingdom on the Aegean. The kingdom of Greece!

As for the champagne and brandy, they had eased some of the anxiety that the sultan experienced in his efforts to update, and preserve, the empire of his forefathers.

And now, at the age of fifty-four, he was dying of them.

His hand moved slowly towards a silken cord whose tassels brushed against his pillows, then it fell again. He was dying, and he did not know who he could ring for.

The sun pulled slowly round, now slanting from the west. There were others he remembered, not just names, but the faces of men and women he had known. He saw the old general Bayraktar, with his furious moustaches, and the astonishment on his face when he burst into the old palace all those years ago, and hoisted Mahmut out of a laundry basket, to make him sultan. He saw his uncle Selim dead, in a kaftan stained with the blood of the House of Osman, and Fatima alive: fat, cheerful, the one who rubbed his feet the way he liked and expected nothing. He remembered another general who had fallen to his death, and the faces of men he had seen in crowds: a sufi with a gentle smile, a student in the grip of loyalty, clutching the Banner of the Prophet; a black eunuch, down on his knees; a Janissary who had cocked his fingers at him, like a pistol, and winked; the pale whiskers of Calasso, the Piedmontese riding master, and the downcast eyes of Abdül Mecid, his son, who had a chest like a girl's waist; and the beard of the Patriarch – what was his name? – who took the cross of office from his hands, and died twirling at the end of a rope in the hot sun.

There was another face, too . . . His hand moved out, his fingers groped for the tassel.

But when the slave arrived, bowing, not looking up, Sultan Mahmut could not remember who it was he had wanted to see.

'A glass . . . the medicine . . . there, that's it,' he said.

'Doctor Millingen –' the slave began.

'– is my doctor. But I am sultan. Pour!'

'Take care on these stairs, monsieur. They are very worn – I've slipped on them myself.'

'But only on the way down, Excellence! I'm sure of that.'

Stanislaw Palewski, Polish ambassador to the Sublime Porte,

frowned and carried on up the stairs to Yashim's apartment. Was the Frenchman implying that he got drunk?

He put a hand to his cravat, as if the touch would reassure him: impeccably starched and properly tied, the cravat was not, he was vaguely aware, in the latest fashion; like his coat, like his boots, like his own diplomatic position, it belonged to another age, before Poland had been wiped from the map by the hostile manoeuvrings of Russia, Austria and Prussia. Palewski had arrived in Istanbul twenty-five years before, as the representative of a vanished country. Elsewhere, in other capitals of Europe, the Polish ambassador was only a diplomatic memory; but the Turks, the old enemy, had received him with good grace.

Which was, he thought with a frown, in the days before Istanbul became positively overrun with mountebanks, schemers and dealers of every nationality and none. Before visiting Frenchmen buttonholed you and invited themselves along to dinner.

But also before he had come to know Yashim.

How they had become friends was still a matter of debate, for Yashim's memory of the event differed in emphasis from Palewski's; it involved more broken glass, and less enunciated French. But they had been firm friends ever since. 'Together,' Palewski had once declared, weeping over a blade of pickled bison grass, 'we make a man, you and I. For you are a man without balls, and I am a man without a country.'

It was an appeal of friendship which Palewski now threw Yashim, as Lefèvre advanced past him into the room, flinging out his hand.

'*Enchanté*, m'sieur,' he said. 'It's most kind of you to have us! Something smells good.'

It was not Yashim's habit to shake hands, but he took Lefèvre's and squeezed it politely. Palewski opened his mouth to speak when the Frenchman added:

'I was quite unprepared for such a generous invitation.'

He was a small, stoop-shouldered man, delicately built, with a few days' growth of white stubble and a voice that was soft and sibilant, close to lisping.

'But I am delighted, monsieur –'

'Lefèvre,' Palewski cut in, finally. 'Docteur Lefèvre is an archaeologist, Yashim. He's French. I – I felt sure you wouldn't mind.'

'But no, of course not. It's an honour.' Yashim's eyes lit up. A Frenchman for dinner! Now that was a decent challenge.

Palewski set his portmanteau on the table and clicked it open. 'Champagne,' he announced, drawing out two green bottles. 'It comes from the Belgian at Pera. He assures me that it belongs to a consignment originally destined for Sultan Mahmut's table, so it's probably filth.'

'I am sure it will be excellent.' Lefèvre smirked at Yashim.

The ambassador looked at him coolly. 'I rather think the sultan's illness speaks for itself, Lefèvre. It defeats all the best doctors.'

'Ah, yes. The Englishman, Dr Millingen.' Lefèvre's hands fluttered towards his head. 'Who I consulted recently. Headache.'

'Cured?'

Lefèvre raised his eyebrows. 'One lives in hope,' he said sadly.

Palewski nodded. 'Millingen's not too bad for a doctor. Though he killed Byron, of course.'

Yashim said: 'Byron?'

'Lord Byron, Yash. A celebrated English poet.' He reached into his bag. 'If the champagne's no good, I have this,' he added, drawing out a slimmer and paler bottle which Yashim immediately recognised. 'Byron was an enthusiast for Greek independence,' he went on. 'Never lived to fire a gun in anger, as far as I know. He died trying to organise the Greek rebels in '24, at the siege of Missolonghi. Caught a fever. Millingen was his doctor.'

19

They drank the champagne from Yashim's sherbet flutes.

'It sparkles,' said Lefèvre.

'Not for very long,' Yashim added, peering into the glass. 'Dr Lefèvre, I welcome you to Istanbul.'

'The city ordained by Nature to be the capital of the world.' Lefèvre fixed his dark eyes on Yashim. 'She calls me like a siren, monsieur. I cannot resist her lure.' He drained his glass and set it down silently in the palm of his other hand. *'Je suis archéologue.'*

Yashim brought out a tray on which he had set a selection of meze – the crisped skin of a mackerel rolled loose from its flesh, then stuffed with nuts and spices – uskumru dolmasi; some tiny böreks stuffed with white cheese and dill; mussel shells folded over a mixture of pine nuts; karnıyarık, tiny aubergines filled with spiced lamb; and a little dish of kabak cicegi dolmasi, or stuffed courgette flowers. They were all dolma – that is, their outsides gave no hint as to the treasures that lay within; and all made to recipes perfected in the sultan's kitchens.

Palewski was brooding over his champagne. Lefèvre picked up a courgette flower and popped it into his mouth.

'How shall I explain?' Lefèvre began. 'To me, this city is like a woman. In the morning she is Byzantium. You know, I am sure, what is Byzantium? It is nothing, a Greek village. Byzance is young, artless, very simple. Does she know who she is? That she stands between Asia and Europe? Scarcely. Alexander came and went. But Byzance: she remembers nothing.'

His hand hovered above the tray.

'One man appreciates her beauty, nonetheless. Master of Jerusalem and Rome.'

Palewski buried his face in his glass.

'Constantine, the Caesar, falls in love. What is it – 375 AD? Byzance is his – she suits him well. And he raises her to the imperial purple, gives her his name – Constantinople, the city of Constantine. The new heart of the Roman Empire. Nothing is too good for her. Constantine plunders the ancient world like a man who showers his mistress with jewels. He brings her the four bronze horses of Lysippos, which now stand above the Piazza San Marco in Venice. He brings her the Serpent Column from Delphi. He brings her the tribute of the known world, from the Pillars of Hercules to the deserts of Arabia.'

'And his mother, too. Don't forget her,' Palewski added.

Lefèvre turned to the ambassador. 'St Helena, of course. She came to the city, and unearthed a portion of the True Cross.'

'They should make her patron saint of archaeologists, Lefèvre.'

The Frenchman blinked. 'All the holy relics of the Christian faith were brought to the city,' he added. 'Relics of the earliest saints. The nails that fixed Jesus to the cross. The goblet and plate that Jesus used at the Last Supper. The holy of holies, gentlemen.'

He held up his hand, fingers outspread.

'Two centuries later, Emperor Justinian builds the church of churches. Aya Sofia, the eighth wonder of the world. She has come a long way from the fisher-girl, Byzance.' He paused. 'What to say? The centuries of wealth, monsieur. The perfection of Byzantine art. Ceremony, bloodshed, the emperor as the regent of God Almighty.'

Palewski nodded. 'Until the Crusaders arrive.'

Lefèvre closed his eyes, and nodded. 'Ah. Ah. 1204, yes, the shame of Europe. I would call it a rape, monsieur: the rape of the city by the brutal soldiers of western Europe. Her diadem flung into the dust. It is pain for us to speak of this time.'

He selected a delicacy from the tray.

'And yet she is a woman: she recovers. She is a shadow of her-self, but she still has charm. So she seeks a new protector. In 1453: the Turkish conquest. Let me say: she becomes Istanbul. Mehmed's whore.'

It was Yashim's turn to blink.

'The Turks – they love her. And so, like a woman, she becomes again beautiful. Is it not so?'

Lefèvre peered into a silence. 'But perhaps my little analogy displeases you? *Alors*, it can be changed.' He spread out his hands, like a conjuror. 'Istanbul is also a serpent, which sheds its skin.'

'And you collect those discarded skins.'

'I try to learn from them, Excellence.'

Palewski was studying the tray, a scowl now plainly on his face. 'Good meze, Yashim,' he said.

'All dolma –' Yashim began; he meant to explain the theory behind his selections, but Lefèvre leaned forwards and tapped Palewski on his knee.

'I have travelled, Excellence, and I can say that all street food is good in the Levant, from Albania to the Caucasus,' he remarked.

Palewski glanced up. Later, he told Yashim that the sight of his face at that moment had brought him the first pleasure of the evening.

Lefèvre licked his fingers and wiped them on a napkin. 'The singular contribution of the Turks – I believe this is correct – to the *dégustation* of civilised Europe – you'll forgive me, monsieur, I am merely quoting – is the aromatic juice of the Arabian bean: in short, coffee.' He gave a laugh.

'I shouldn't believe everything you read in books,' Palewski said, with another glance at his friend.

'But I do. I believe everything I read.' Lefèvre wetted his lips with the tip of his tongue. 'A professional habit, perhaps. Letters. Diaries. Travellers' memoirs. I choose my literature carefully. Trivial information can sometimes turn out to be very useful, wouldn't you agree, monsieur?'

Yashim nodded slowly. 'Certainly. But for every useful scrap of information, you must reject a hundred more.'

'Ah, yes, perhaps you are right.' He leaned back, touching his thumbs together. 'Have you ever heard of Troy?'

Yashim nodded. 'Sultan Mehmet once laid claim to Trojan ancestry,' he said. 'He presented the fall of Constantinople as a revenge on the Greeks.'

'How interesting.' The Frenchman pinched his lower lip. 'I was about to suggest that one day we will uncover the ruins of the city that Agamemnon sacked.'

'You believe it exists?'

Lefèvre laughed softly. 'More than that. I think it will be found exactly where legend has always placed it. Scarcely a hundred kilometres from where we sit – in the Troad.'

'Are you to dig for it yourself?'

'I would, if I could get permission here. But for that – and everything else – one needs money.' He smiled pleasantly and spread his hands.

A breath of air stirred the curtains, and a ring chinked softly on the rail.

'Of course,' Lefèvre continued, 'sometimes these things may just drop into your lap, if you read carefully and learn where to look.'

He took a sip of champagne. Palewski got up and opened the second bottle with a pop.

'I'm afraid you must find us very careless with the past,' Yashim said. 'We don't always look after things as we should.'

'Yes and no, monsieur. I do not complain. Carelessness of that sort may be a godsend to the archaeologist. One has only to go to your Atmeydan – the ancient Hippodrome of the Byzantines – to see that all its monuments remain, intact. With the exception of the serpent column, of course. The column has lost its heads, which is no fault of the Turks.'

Palewski suddenly picked up his glass and drained it.

'Nobody remembers any more, I shouldn't think,' Lefèvre

went on. 'But the bronze heads were wrenched off the column little more than a century ago. To think what their eyes had witnessed, in the centuries since they stood beside the Delphic oracle!' He half-turned towards Palewski. 'It was foreign vandalism, excellence.'

'Disgraceful,' Palewski murmured.

'Yes.' He frowned and leaned forwards, pointing at Palewski. 'Do you know, I recall a story that it was perpetrated by compatriots of yours! Young bloods in the Polish diplomatic, a century ago. I am sure I am right. Still, as I say, you never know what may drop into your lap unexpectedly. And profitably, too, for all concerned.' He paused. 'I think it so often pays to believe what you read.'

In the silence that followed this remark, Yashim produced his main dish, a succulent *agro dolce* stew of lamb and prunes, followed by a buttery pilaff. Lefèvre rubbed his hands together and pronounced it excellent. He had seen – and smelled – it cooking on the brazier. They drank off the second bottle while he outlined his plans to leave Istanbul and make a tour through the Greek monasteries in the east. 'Trabzon, Erzerum. Wonderful men, ignorant men,' he told them, shaking his head.

'I must say, Excellence, this has been a delightful evening. They say a visitor is starved for good company in Istanbul these days, but I see no sign of it. No sign at all.'

He left shortly afterwards, when all the champagne was gone, insisting that he could see himself home. Yashim took him down to the alleyway, led him to the Kara Davut and found him a chair.

'One of these days –' Lefèvre called out, with a wave; and then the chair-men hoisted him onto their backs and trotted away, and Yashim didn't catch the end of his farewell.

He turned and made his way back up the alley, thinking over the evening's conversation. For a moment he had the impression that something had moved at the top of the alley, where a small votive candle burned in a niche; but when he turned the corner the alley was dark, and he heard only the sound of his own footsteps. Once, before he reached his door, he turned his head involuntarily and glanced back.

Palewski whipped the door open as Yashim reached the top of the stairs. He had the vodka bottle by the neck.

'It wasn't the first time he mentioned those serpent's heads, Yashim. He was like that when we met.' Palewski seemed struck by a thought. 'Do you know, if he ever asks to see me again, I'll say no. I certainly won't let him out of my sight,' he added paradoxically, uncapping the bottle.

Long ago, in a moment of exuberance, Palewski had led Yashim to a vast armoire that stood at the head of the stairs in the Polish residency. Turning the key in the lock, he had swung back the doors to reveal two of the three bronze heads which had once adorned the Serpent Column on the Atmeidan. They had goggled at them in horror for a few minutes, before Palewski abruptly closed the door and said: 'There. It's been eating me up for years. But now you know, and I'm glad.'

'Even Lefèvre isn't going to look into that big cupboard for the serpent's heads, my friend.'

Palewski jerked at the bottle so fast that a splash of vodka landed on his wrist. 'For God's sake, Yash!' He glanced wildly at the door. 'That Frenchman would be through it like a dose of salts.' He licked his wrist. 'Profitable for all concerned, my eye. He smells them, and I've got no idea how.' He poured two shots and knocked his back. 'Ah. Better. Cleans out the system, you know. It's my guess that the man's some sort of thief, Yashim. He knows too much. I'm sorry I brought him. I just couldn't shake him off.'

'My dear old friend, we need never see him again.'

'I'll drink to that,' Palewski said.

And he did.

9

'You are not what I had expected,' Madame Mavrogordato said. It was not a reproach. It was a statement of fact.

She sat bolt upright in a carved wooden chair, her jet-black hair piled up and stuck with pins. She had the face of a Cappadocian god, with straight black brows and chiselled lips. Yashim blinked, and swayed a little on his feet. Madame Mavrogordato was not what he had expected, either.

On balance that was a good thing; but today the balance was fine. Yashim's temples throbbed. His mouth was dry. Palewski was probably right, and the sultan was really dying from that champagne. He wished he had ignored the note, and gone to the hammam first – he should at least have eaten some soup. Tripe soup, best. Palewski, having gone off cautiously down the stairs in the middle of the night, would still be comfortably asleep in bed.

The note had been delivered by hand, very early. While men consulted Yashim about money in one way or another, and sometimes about death, women summoned him more rarely. Women were usually worried about their husbands, their servants – or a mixture of the two; and sometimes they wanted nothing more than to satisfy a curiosity about Yashim. He was attached to the palace; he lived in the city; so they invented little troubles and called him in to brighten up their day. In normal circumstances, even the Christian women would have thought twice about summoning a man to their apartments; but Yashim was above suspicion. They called him, politely, lala, or guardian. In a city of a million people only a handful of men deserved the title, and most of those worked in the women's apartments in the sultan's palaces.

Madame Mavrogordato did not call him lala. She would never have servant trouble.

The Mavrogordato mansion stood alone behind high and fire-blackened walls in the Fener district of Istanbul, halfway up the Golden Horn. Yashim lived in the Fener, too, but that hardly made them neighbours: his home was a small tenement apartment above an alley. During the Greek riots eighteen years ago, the district had been ravaged by a fire; beyond the blackened walls, the mansion itself was entirely new. So, too, were the Mavrogordatos.

Quite how new, it was hard to say. Certain old Greek families of the Fener had for centuries provided the Ottoman state with dragomen, governors, priests and bankers; but many had been linked to the Greek independence movement, and after the riots this so-called Phanariot aristocracy all but disappeared. The Mavrogordatos belonged to a circle of wealthy families who did the same sort of business the Fener aristocracy had done, and even their name seemed quite familiar. But it was not quite the same name, and they were not the same people.

Yashim bowed. Madame Mavrogordato's black eyes flickered towards an enormous German grandfather clock which stood against the wall of the dark apartment.

'You are late,' she said.

Yashim glanced at the clock. Beyond it, another clock stood on an inlay side-table. Behind Madame Mavrogordato an American clock hung on the wall, with a little glass panel through which you could see the pendulum rhythmically reflecting back the subdued light in the big, closely shuttered room. Between the windows stood another grandfather clock. Its hands showed a little after ten.

'Why don't you wear the fez?'

'I am not a government employee, hanum. I am almost forty years old and I believe I am old enough to choose what I find comfortable. Just as I like to choose who I work for,' he added coolly.

'Meaning what?'

'I live modestly, hanum. I would rather be busy than idle, but I can be idle, too.'

Madame Mavrogordato picked up a silver bell at her elbow and shook it. An attendant appeared noiselessly at the door. 'Coffee.' She glared at Yashim for a moment. 'I do not permit smoking in these rooms.'

She indicated a stiff French chair. The attendant returned with coffee, in a silence measured out by the ticking of Madame Mavrogordato's four clocks. Yashim took a sip. It was good coffee.

'It may or not surprise you to learn that I, too, have lived modestly in my life,' Madame Mavrogordato began. She picked up a string of beads from her lap and began to thread them through her slender white fingers. 'That time, I hope, is past. Mr Mavrogordato and I have worked hard and – we have sometimes had the good fortune that others lacked. I am quite sure you understand what I mean – as when I say that I will not allow anything to jeopardise that good fortune.' The beads slipped through her fingers one by one. 'You may have heard that Mr Mavrogordato is a Bulgar. It is not true. He comes from an ecclesiastical family, formerly in Varna. I am related to the Mavrogordato family by blood, and Mr Mavrogordato by his marriage to me. Early on, I recognised his talent for finance. He is good at figures. He enjoys them. But he is not a bold man.'

She looked Yashim squarely in the eye. Yashim nodded. Mr Mavrogordato obviously was a Bulgar. Yashim didn't mind. Left to his own devices, he supposed, Mr Mavrogordato might yet be totting up the church accounts in some provincial viyalet. Instead, he had become a merchant prince in the capital of the Ottoman Empire, steered by the woman whose slender claim on the Mavrogordato legacy had provided the necessary leverage. A woman whose boldness was scarcely in doubt.

'My husband is a moderate man, of thoroughly regular habits. It falls to me to maintain a household that is quiet, orderly and appropriate. Anything that disturbs Mr Mavrogordato in his work, also disturbs us here.'

Madame Mavrogordato, Yashim noticed, had not touched her coffee.

'I know very little about business,' Yashim said.

'It is not necessary that you should. What I require is a certain – intelligence. And discretion.' She paused. Yashim said nothing. 'Well?'

'I hope, hanum, that I am discreet.'

Her lips tightened. 'Yashim efendi, my husband was visited last night by a Frenchman. He asked for a small loan. In the course of the discussion, the man made certain offers which were in some sense disquieting to my husband. Later, I was able to detect his agitation.'

Yashim blinked. 'Offers, hanum?'

'Offers. Promises. It is hard for me to say.'

'You think that your husband was being blackmailed?'

Madame Mavrogordato's face remained impassive, but she twisted the string of beads in her hands so tightly that Yashim half-expected them to break. 'I do not think so. My husband has nothing to be afraid of. I believe that the Frenchman was proposing to sell him something.'

'You believe – but you're not sure?'

'My husband keeps nothing from me, but he found it hard to recall exactly what the man said. If, indeed, he said anything at all. It was more a question of – of the tone. As if he were hinting at something.'

'Maximilien Lefèvre,' Yashim said.

Madame Mavrogordato looked at him sharply. 'That's right. What else do you know?'

Yashim spread his hands wide. 'Very little. Lefèvre is an archaeologist.'

'Very well. I – that is, my husband and I – would like you to find out a little more. If possible, I would like you to encourage Monsieur Lefèvre to conduct his – research – elsewhere. I resent disturbance.'

Yashim put out his lower lip. 'I can try to find out something about Lefèvre. But I should speak to your husband.'

Madame Mavrogordato's eyes were iron black. 'It is enough that you have spoken to me.'

She picked up the bell, and tinkled it. A servant appeared, and Yashim rose to leave.

'One thing,' he added, as he reached the door. 'Did your husband give him that loan?'

Madame Mavrogordato worked her jaw, and glared. 'That –' she began; and with that hesitation Yashim realised that she was far younger than he had originally thought; not yet forty. 'I – I never asked.'

As Yashim followed the footman down to the hall a door opened and a young man stepped forwards.

'One moment, you,' he said. 'Go along, Dmitri. I'll see the fellow out.'

The young man was in his early twenties. He had a thick mop of black hair and was strongly built, with broad shoulders and a big jaw which hadn't lost its puppy fat. He was dressed in a well-cut stambouline, a starched collar with a silk cravat, black stovepipe trousers and a pair of slim, black leather pumps. He was almost as handsome as his mother – the resemblance was very striking – but his eyes were smaller, harder; and there was a contrasting softness around his mouth which Yashim liked rather less.

'Good morning,' he said, politely.

The young man scowled, and stared at Yashim.

'I saw you come in. You were talking to Mother.'

Yashim raised an eyebrow, and made no reply.

'Did you talk about me?' the young man asked abruptly.

'I don't know. Who are you?'

'My name's Alexander. Mavrogordato,' he added bullishly, as if he half-expected Yashim to deny it.

Yashim thought for a moment. 'No. No, we didn't discuss you at all. Should we have?'

The young Mavrogordato gave him a suspicious look. 'Are you being clever?'

'I hope so, Mr Mavrogordato. But now, if you will excuse me –'

The young man reached out and grabbed Yashim's sleeve. 'Why are you here, then?'

Yashim looked down slowly at the hand on his sleeve, and frowned. There was a pause, then Mavrogordato let go. Yashim brushed a hand across his sleeve.

'Perhaps you might wish to discuss it with your mother. Please don't detain me again.'

He stepped round the young man. As he passed, he felt his breath on his face, sour like a tavern.

⟨ 11 ⟩

Holding the lamp in one hand, Goulandris surveyed the shelves which lined his little cubbyhole in the Grand Bazaar. Now and then he reached out to knock the books into line, and close the gaps. Satisfied, he returned to his stool, set the lamp on the desk, and blew out the flame.

A shadow fell across the desk. Goulandris glanced up, without enthusiasm.

'The shop is closed,' he said. He moved his head to see better, but the figure in the doorway stood against the light. 'Come back tomorrow.'

He turned his head again, hoping to identify the man at the door. If he came tomorrow, it would show that he was eager: Goulandris wanted to be able to recognise him again.

'There was a book,' the man said slowly.

The bookseller sighed. He opened the drawer and dropped the little account book into it. He closed the drawer with both hands.

'There are many books,' he said querulously. 'Tomorrow.'

The shadows deepened: it was Goulandris's impression that the man had taken a step closer, into the room. But for him, with one eye, it was always hard to tell.

But yes, the voice seemed closer now.

'Not many books. Just one. A Latin book, no? I am sure you can remember.'

Goulandris swallowed. He leaned away from the desk, allowing his hand to move towards a little bell that stood on a low shelf behind his stool.

'Not now,' he said. 'I am going home.'

The man was near the desk. 'Please, Mr Goulandris, don't touch that bell.'

Goulandris checked himself. He began to rise from his stool, leaning both hands on the desk.

But the stranger, it seemed, didn't want Goulandris to stand up ever again.

Aram Malakian fished out a bunch of keys in his long, slender fingers and fitted one to the lock.

'Patience, patience,' he muttered with a smile. The lock broke and the metal gates of his shop swung back.

'Enter, my friend. You must look and touch – and I have some new treasures I would like to show you. I do not ask you to buy them – today we will not speak of such a thing – but only to look and admire what workmanship existed in the past. Sit down, please. We will have a tea together, Yashim efendi.'

Aram snapped his fingers and a little boy ran up to take his order.

'No, no. Please let us not look there – this is for the people who know nothing at all. Blessed are the ignorant! I have some pieces which are interesting.'

He picked up a linen pouch and slipped several coins onto the low table. 'The English physician, Dr Millingen, is a great collector of coinage. I think he will want these.'

Yashim sighed. 'Incredible. All the collectors come through your shop, don't they?'

The old Armenian wagged his head, neither yes or no.

'Lefèvre, for instance. A Frenchman.'

'Monsieur Lefèvre. I know him, yes. He is an archaeologist of great erudition.'

'What sort of things interest him?'

Malakian picked up a sunflower seed and split it between his teeth. 'Byzantine work. Silverware, mosaic, jewellery. Old icons. Incunabula and illuminated manuscripts.'

'Incunabula?'

'The first printed books. These things are of course very rare – unless one knows where to look. That is the first step.'

33

Yashim waited for him to go on. 'And then?'

'Yashim efendi, what shall I say? I am not a hunter. I sit, and I wait, and if treasure makes its way to me now and then, I am content. Whereas Lefèvre – he is an archaeologist.'

'He digs at sites, yes.'

'I think he digs, but not always with a spade.' Malakian tugged at his earlobe. 'I have a cousin, Yashim efendi. He is a monk, in Erzerum. A Frenchman visited his monastery a few years ago, to study – they have a famous scriptorum. Many, many rare old books – and many ignorant old priests. The Frenchman showed the librarian some books which were badly damaged. Out of gratitude for their help in his work, he offered to have these books repaired.'

'In Istanbul?'

Malakian turned his head this way and that, like an elderly tortoise.

'Tchah! Where is that tea? In Istanbul, yes. But later he wrote to the librarian, explaining that the best bookbinder for the job was in France – in Dijon. That was almost three years ago.'

Yashim arched his eyebrows. Malakian put up a hand.

'In fact, the books came back. This year, I think. It was a long time – but they were well-bound, and the librarian was pleased. I am sorry to say, his pleasure was short-lived. Some of the original illustrated pages were missing. The binder in Dijon – was he careless, or perhaps dishonest? It is hard to say. Lefèvre has stopped answering letters. Do you see?

'I do not think this was an isolated case. Lefèvre seems to be a clever man, well-informed. He is a good judge of quality – better than the poor monks he works on. But he has been lucky, also.'

'Lucky? You mean he sometimes finds what he wants by chance? Surely all antiquarians have that experience.'

'No, efendi. That is not the luck I mean.' He gazed sadly at Yashim. 'Three days ago I sold a counterfeit coin to a dragoman at the Russian embassy. I got a very good price.' He nodded thoughtfully. 'Yes, you are shocked. I see it. Perhaps, you are thinking, I will not buy anything from Aram Malakian again. So, what is lost?'

'My trust, perhaps.'

Malakian smiled and nodded. 'But you see, efendi, both of us knew this coin was a counterfeit. Because it was made in the same era as the real coin, it is a collector's item. Now – like this' – he snapped his tapering fingers – 'your trust is restored, I hope.'

Before Yashim could answer, the tea boy suddenly reappeared, flinging himself against the folded gates.

'The night watch!' He gasped. 'In the book bazaar. They say there's blood everywhere. I'm going to see!'

Malakian turned slowly. 'Blood?'

The boy darted off, his empty tray swinging madly from his fingers.

'Tomfoolery,' Malakian muttered. He looked anxious. He began to shovel the coins back into the linen bag, and Yashim noticed that his hands were trembling. 'I was speaking of trust. A few words and – puff! Trust is gone.' He dropped the bag into a drawer and locked it.

Yashim nodded slowly.

'Sometimes I think Lefèvre must have forgotten that ignorant monks, cloistered from the world, still have powerful friends and protectors. We Armenians are a small people and do not choose to make enemies. But the Greeks? I am surprised that Lefèvre has come back to Istanbul. I think maybe he pushes his luck too far.'

Malakian paused, and looked around his cubicle. 'I'm sorry, efendi, but one can't be too careful. The boy talks of death, and blood. It could be the work of thieves, to make us frightened. We leave our shops to look and – paff, they get in. You understand?'

Yashim was on his feet. 'Stay here,' he said. 'I'll go and see.'

The market was in an uproar: Malakian was not the only trader to be hurriedly securing his goods, ringing down the shutters, while anxious shoppers streamed for the gates. Following on the tea boy's footsteps, Yashim had expected an increasing hubbub as he approached the book bazaar; instead the atmosphere grew tense and frozen, and in the alley itself there was hardly a sound to be heard.

A crowd of silent men blocked his view.

'Palace,' he murmured. The men stood aside automatically, barely sparing him a glance. He stepped forwards, one hand raised, and received a salute from a pale man in the red uniform of a market guard.

'Palace,' Yashim repeated tersely. 'A man dead?'

'That's right, efendi.' The guard swallowed. 'We're still trying to find the kadi.'

'Can you tell me what happened?'

'The door was shut, efendi. That's all. It might have been shut all night, and it looked like it were locked. I mean, the bar was across, and everything.'

'You noticed that on the night watch?'

The guard stirred nervously. 'Well, efendi, not exactly. I – I don't recall. It was just this morning, about half an hour ago, that we sees the bar still up, and the padlock – it was only hanging there. You don't see that much in the dark, efendi.'

'But by daylight – you thought it looked strange?'

'All the traders had come in already. Talak – that's my companion – he says we ought to take a look. I knocked on the door with my stick then. Sounds a bit stupid, doesn't it? What with the door half-locked on the outside.'

'No, but I understand,' Yashim said. He'd seen it before, the way that sudden death made a nonsense of the things people did and said. Murder, above all, overturned the natural order of God's creation: it was only to be expected that unreason and absurdity should crackle in its wake. 'Nobody came – and you opened the door?'

The guard nodded. 'It was dark. We had put out the lanterns, and I didn't see anything to worry about, not at first. I touched something with my foot, and when I bent down I saw it was some scroll. It was stuck to the floor. Then, I felt that my boots were also sticking to the floor. I looked behind the desk, and –' He shuddered. 'Goulandris.'

'The bookseller? Show me.'

The guard looked doubtful. He glanced at the crowd. 'I must stay outside,' he explained. 'When Talak brings the kadi . . .' He trailed off.

'I won't be long,' Yashim said. He stepped past the guard and pushed the green door to Goulandris's cubbyhole. Inside it was stuffy and dark, with a metallic smell. He moved away from the door to give himself light, and glanced quickly around. He knew this room. Goulandris had dealt in many kinds of works in classical and modern Greek, Jewish religious books, imperial scrolls – but the old man could have been selling apples or slippers for all he knew about books: at best, you could say he could read and write in Greek. He priced his stock, as far as Yashim could tell, by reading the expression in his clients' faces: a gruff and shrewd old dealer.

Bending forwards to look behind the Frankish desk, Yashim saw that Goulandris had priced his last book.

He was wedged in between the desk and a stool, pressed up against the wall; his thin arms raised above his head, wrist to wrist, his head jammed against his bended knees. There was an astonishing amount of tacky dark blood staining the floor, as the guard had first noticed, but the nape of his neck gleamed almost

37

white in the dim light. Yashim felt the man's arms: they were quite cold. He took hold of the grey hair on Goulandris's scalp with a tremor of reluctance, and tugged back his head: as it slipped between his arms they shifted stiffly forwards, checked by the rigor of death. Yashim peered down and grunted; then he fastidiously drew out a handkerchief, purled it into a ball and dabbed at the man's throat. He tried not to look into his one glittering eye.

The handkerchief came up clean.

But there was a lot of blood on the floor.

Yashim stood still for a moment. The light failed and there was a man at the door. 'The kadi is on his way, efendi.'

'That's good. This – is his province. He will know what measures need to be taken.'

'But you, efendi –'

'No, my friend. I'm going to the palace. Don't worry,' he added, when he saw the guard step back a pace, 'you have done everything well. And everything you could.'

They saluted each other, one hand to the chest.

⫷ 14 ⫸

Malakian was standing uncertainly in front of his shop, a padlock in his hands.

'Goulandris? Incredible. Who would want to kill him? He was a very old man.'

'He knew very little about books.'

'Very little? You say so, efendi. But yes, stubborn. A stubborn old Greek. It is terrible.'

Yashim shook his head. He was reminded of another stubborn old Greek, his friend George, beaten and left for dead in the

38

street. Like Goulandris he, too, was a trader. 'What do you know about the Hetira, Malakian?'

Malakian rubbed the edge of one of his enormous flat ears between his forefinger and thumb. 'Ask a Greek, efendi. This is something Greek. I would not know.'

'But the word means something to you.'

Malakian frowned. 'This is my shop, Yashim efendi, in the bazaar, like always. It is cheap here, yes. In Pera you will find many new shops – but Pera is expensive.'

Yashim shook his head. 'I don't understand.'

'I am stubborn man, like Goulandris. But I am not Greek. So.'

'Why would the Hetira want to drive out Greeks?'

Malakian said nothing, but he shrugged, slowly.

15

Yashim stopped by the fish market on the Golden Horn. Still smarting from the Frenchman's indifference to the dolma he had so lovingly prepared he chose two lüfer, the bluefish which all Istanbul took as the standard for excellence. He watched the fishmonger slit their bellies and remove the entrails with a twist of his thumb.

Yashim was proud of Istanbul – proud of its markets, the cornucopia of perfect fruits and vegetables that poured into them every day, proud of the fat-tailed sheep from Anatolia which sometimes came skittering and bleating through the narrow streets. What other city in the world could produce fish to match the freshness or the variety offered by the Bosphorus, a finny highway running straight through the heart of Istanbul? Why, at any season of the year you could practically walk to Uskudar on the torrent of fish which passed along the straits –

'Don't wash it,' he said quickly. A fish would begin to deteriorate from the moment it lost its slimy protective coat.

'Bah, we have too little water,' the fishmonger grunted. 'The supply is weak again.'

But it flowed: that was what mattered. Sometimes, standing on Pera hill and looking back across the Golden Horn to the familiar skyline of the city, marked by the great domes of Sinan's mosques; or passing the jumble of buildings – mosques, houses, caravanserai, churches, covered markets, shops – which lined the Stamboul shore of the Horn, it seemed incredible to Yashim that the city should function from one day to the next, and not simply explode, or tear itself apart, or at the very least subside into a confusion of bleating sheep, rotting vegetables, and men gesticulating and thundering in twenty languages, unable to progress or retreat through the overcrowded streets.

Yet whenever Yashim looked more closely, at the level of a particular street, say, he was struck by the air of invisible good order that kept everything and everyone flowing smoothly along, like water in the pipes and aqueducts: so that when a man was murdered, and another attacked – both traders, both Greeks – they seemed inevitably to belong to some hidden economy in the city, a single channel of a commerce freighted with menace and brutality.

Yashim delivered one of the bluefish to the nuns at the hospital.

'Perhaps he can manage a little of this?' he asked tentatively.

The nun smiled. 'It will do him good.'

'And perhaps – then, if he can eat, he can speak – a little?'

She laughed with her eyes. 'Very well, efendi. If he is not asleep, you may have a moment. Not more, please.'

Yashim bowed.

George looked worse than when he had first seen him in the filtered subaqueous light of the reformatory, for the bruising on the side of his head had come up. He was still bandaged, with one eye covered; the other peered with difficulty through swollen, bulging lids. His breathing, however, seemed normal now.

Yashim squatted by the bed. 'They'll be giving you some fish today. Lüfer.'

'Too much soup,' said George finally. His voice was a croak.

'You're a big man, George. Fish is just the start of it. We'll get you onto some proper meat in a few days.'

George made a faint whistling sound between his lips. It appeared to be a laugh. 'Tough to shit,' he croaked.

'Yes, well, perhaps that's right.' Yashim frowned. 'The nuns will know.'

George closed his one eye in agreement. Yashim bent closer. 'What happened, George?'

'I forgets,' he whispered back.

'Try to remember. You were attacked.'

The eye opened a crack. 'I slips, falls over.'

Yashim rocked back on his haunches. 'George. You were badly beaten up. You were almost killed.'

'No beating, efendi. Is accident. I falls on stairs.'

'So you remember that, do you?'

George's eye swivelled towards him.

'Who pushed you, George?'

The eye slid away. Nothing.

'The Hetira?'

But his friend had rung down the shutter on his one good eye. His swollen face was incapable of expression.

George was a proud man. Tough and proud enough to take a beating – and too proud to speak, as well.

Or too afraid.

Yashim had a question for the nun as he left.

'Only his wife, efendi. She's been coming here every day. She always talks. He is a good man. He listens to his wife.'

41

'And does she think – that he had an accident?'

The nun lowered her eyes and answered demurely. 'We do not judge our people, efendi. We try only to heal.'

She glanced at him then, and Yashim turned his head away. Muttering a farewell, he found his own way out into the street, and heard her bolt the door at his back.

16

Widow Matalya's brow furrowed and uncreased as she made her count. She champed her toothless gums together and the hairs trembled on a large black mole on her cheek. Now and again her fingers twitched. Widow Matalya did not mind, because she was asleep.

She dreamed, as usual, about chickens. There were forty of them, leghorns and bantams, scratching about in the dust of the Anatolian village where she had been born more than seventy years ago, and the chickens in her dream were exactly the same as the chickens she had tended as a young woman, when Sipahi Matalya had ridden through her yard and sent them all squawking and flapping onto the roof of their own coop. Sipahi Matalya had taken her to Istanbul, of course, because he was only a summer sipahi, and they had shared a very happy marriage until he died; but now that her children were grown she thought very often of those forty birds. Awake, she wondered who had eaten them. Asleep, she checked that they were all safe. It was good to be young again, with all that ahead of one.

Twenty-nine. Thirty. She scattered a little more grain and watched them pecking in the dirt. Thirty-one. Thirty-two. Or had she gone wrong? The noise of the chicken's beaks hitting the earth was confusing her. Bam! Bam! Thirty-two, thirty-three.

The lips stopped moving. Widow Matalya's eyes opened. With a sigh she levered herself ponderously off the sofa, adjusted her headscarf and went to the door.

'Who is it?'

'It is Yashim, hanum,' a voice called. 'I have no water.'

Widow Matalya opened the door. 'This is because the spigot in the yard is blocked, Yashim efendi. Someone is coming. We must be patient.'

'I have my bowl,' Yashim said, holding it up. 'I'll go and find a su yolcu in the street. Can I get some water for you, hanum?'

Yashim was gone for half an hour, and he came back looking exasperated.

'You needn't worry about the standpipe. It's the whole street,' he said. 'Plenty of water beyond the Kara Davut. Here, I filled your bowl.'

'Thank you, Yashim efendi. I will send the man away if he comes. They will fix the pipes, and tomorrow we shall have water again, inshallah.'

'Inshallah, hanum,' Yashim replied.

He was a good man, Widow Matalya reflected, as she closed the door.

17

He ate the lüfer simply grilled, with a squeeze of lemon and the bread he had picked up from the Libyan baker on his way back from the hammam. Yashim dropped the remains out of the window for the dogs, made a pot of tea and retired to his divan with the oil lamp and a French novel he had been lent by a friend at the palace. He enjoyed Balzac, relishing the light he shone into

43

the secret heart of Paris, a city he had often visited in his imagination, with all its deceit and greed.

He opened the book and smoothed out its pages. As the night air flooded into the city he could hear the building crack as it cooled, easing its wooden joints inch by inch. Down in the street a dog began to bark, with deep, hoarse, repeated barks; then a casement squealed and the dog was quiet. Yashim put out a hand to tug at the shawl that lay beside him on the divan, and heaped it around his shoulders. The lamp threw a steady yellow oval of light around the gleaming pages of his book. He bent his head, and started to read.

He read the first few lines quickly, eagerly: he had already glanced at them earlier, savouring the promise of new faces and unfamiliar names, and the casual-sounding opening phrase on which Balzac had lavished so much consideration in order to create between him and his reader that sense of enjoyable complicity. But when he reached the end of the paragraph, he found he had remembered nothing.

He scratched his thigh and stared absently at the page. Like the old building itself, he seemed to be finding it hard to settle. Odd cracks and reports still sounded through the floorboards; the stairs creaked. He'd been reading too fast.

What did it mean, he wondered, to remember nothing? Like George: thinking of something else, thinking about the Hetira, perhaps. Digesting the blow to his pride, puzzling out his attitude to fear.

Yashim, too, was thinking about the Hetira. Malakian had recognised the name: it was something Greek, he'd said.

Yashim rubbed his eyes with his thumb and forefinger. He was letting this business run away with him. Hadn't he already done his best by George? Bringing him food. Checking on his condition, as a friend should. Goulandris's death was shocking, certainly; but it wasn't his affair.

He pressed his hand down on the Balzac, and stared at the first page, listening to the sound of warm wood cracking as it shrank in the evening air.

He thought of the sultan: fading like the light. It was months since he had been summoned to the sultan's palace. And George, or Goulandris – were they simply victims of the same unease? Like a creak in the rafters, as the sunlight drained away.

Yashim raised his head abruptly and listened. That crack on the stairs outside had sounded unusually loud. But everything was quiet. And then he heard, distinctly, a soft rasping that seemed to come from close to his door.

Yashim slipped the shawl from his shoulders with his left hand and swirled it swiftly around his fist. His other hand closed on a knife that lay on the shelf, a plain straight-shafted blade which he sometimes used to cut tobacco. Slowly he uncoiled himself from the divan and stood up, tensing his legs.

As he did so there came a scratch on the door. Yashim stepped forwards, took the handle in his left hand and wrenched it back, slipping behind the door as it opened wide.

For a few moments, nothing happened. Yashim rubbed his thumb against the knife's hilt and straightened his back to the wall, looking sideways. He heard a moan which sounded almost like a plea, and a man stumbled across the threshold, dragging a leather satchel into the room behind him.

 18

The man took a few steps towards the lamp, and then peered around wildly until he caught sight of Yashim, watching him in astonishment from beside the opened door. For a second he seemed to cringe.

'Monsieur Yashim!' he breathed. 'Shut the door, I beg you.'

As Yashim closed the door, the man clawed at the air and stumbled backwards onto on the divan, where he sat twitching and running his hand through his hair. Had it not been for the hair, Yashim would have found it hard to recognise Lefèvre: he seemed shrunken and incredibly aged, his black eyes darting nervously from side to side, his face the colour of a peeled almond under a new growth of beard.

Yashim laid the dagger aside. Lefèvre trembled on the divan; every now and then he was wracked by a convulsion, his teeth chattering. He hardly seemed to know where he was.

Yashim poured him a glass of cold water as a remedy for shock, and Lefèvre seized it in both hands, hugging it to his chest as if it might stop his trembling. He drank it down, his teeth chattering against the rim.

'*Ils me connaient*,' he muttered. 'They know me. They know me. I have nowhere else to go.'

Yashim glanced at the satchel. It might contain anything – food, clothes, a reliquary, a woven rug. He wondered what books were in it – whether, in fact, it contained nothing but ancient bibles, illuminated tracts, commentaries written on vellum filched from ignorant monks, venal priests, the greedy and the gullible.

'You are quite safe here,' Yashim said quietly. 'Quite safe.'

Lefèvre glanced up and swung his head around the room like a frightened animal.

'Are you ill?'

The word seemed to strike Lefèvre to the quick. He froze, staring into space. Then he was staring at Yashim.

'To get out. Get away. You'll help me? A foreign ship – not Greek.' He shuddered and groaned and pressed his hand to his face. 'No one to trust. I trust you! But they're watching. They know me. It's so dark. And wet. Nobody knows them. Please, you must help me!'

He slid from the divan and stretched out his hands. Yashim raised his chin: it was horrible to see the man grovelling, feverish, prey to his terrors. 'Who are they? Who do you mean?'

Lefèvre squeezed his hands together and his mouth became a rictus of despair.

'What have you done?'

Lefèvre's eyes flickered towards the satchel, then back at Yashim's face. 'You think – ? My God, no. No. No.'

He shuffled on his knees towards the satchel and tore at its straps with shaking hands. Out spilled a collection of old clothes, a leather flask, a few printed books. Lefèvre picked at them, spreading them around. 'No, monsieur. You will trust me. Help me, yes. I have nothing. No one.'

Yashim turned his head away. After what Malakian had told him about Lefèvre's methods, he was not ashamed of his suspicions. But he was ashamed for this man who now knelt muttering among his meagre belongings strewn across the floor.

'Please,' he began, awkwardly. 'Please don't think that I accuse you of anything. I will help you, of course. You are my guest.'

He surprised himself with his own assurance. But as he later reminded himself, there was something rather terrible about being a stranger in a city where even the dead belonged. Perhaps they were not quite so different, he and this Frenchman he didn't like.

Lefèvre clutched at his words with weary gratitude. 'I don't know what to say. They know who I am, you see, but you – you can find me the ship?'

'Of course. You must stay here, and in the morning I shall find you a way out.' There was a bond between them now. It couldn't be helped. He must act with grace. 'You must eat, first, and sleep. Then all things will seem better.'

Yashim turned to his little kitchen and with rice, saffron and butter created a pilaff *in bianco*, as the Italians would say; a soothing pilaff.

47

Later, Lefèvre dropped off to sleep cross-legged. Yashim eased him into a recumbent position and then, for want of anywhere better, lay down on the sofa beside him. Twice in the night, Lefèvre had bad dreams; he twitched and ran his hands excitedly across his face.

Yashim was not superstitious, but the sight made him shudder.

Early the next morning, leaving the Frenchman sleeping on the divan, Yashim walked down to the Horn and took a caique over to Galata, the centre of foreign commerce. In the harbour-master's office he asked for the shipping list and scanned it for a suitable vessel. There was a French 400-tonner, *La Réunion*, leaving for Valetta and Marseilles with a mixed cargo in four days' time; but there was a Neapolitan vessel, too, *Ca d'Oro* out of Palermo, which had already been issued with bills of lading. The Italian ship would certainly be cheaper; if Lefèvre was going back to France, he'd easily pick up another berth in Palermo, so the voyage might not be that much longer – and there was the undeniable advantage that the *Ca d'Oro* might leave the very next day. Yashim had no desire to prolong the Frenchman's agony of mind a moment longer than was necessary.

He found the *Ca d'Oro*'s captain in a little café overlooking the Bosphorus. He had heavy eyebrows which met above his nose and wore a plain summer cutaway coat which looked as if it had been rigged up by the sailmaker. The coat was dirty but the man's fingernails were very clean when he offered Yashim a pipe. Yashim declined the offer but accepted coffee. *Certo*, the *Ca d'Oro* would leave on the morning tide, God willing; *si*, there were berths. The gentleman could come aboard directly; or tonight if he preferred, it was all the same, the ship's boat would be running back and forth from the dockside all day with returning crew and last-minute purchases. Or one of the caiques might bring him out.

He handed Yashim a spy-glass and encouraged him to look out for the ship.

'You'll see her close in to shore, signor. Two-masted brig, high in the poop. Old? *Si*, but she knows her duty, ha ha! She could find her own way to Palermo after all these years, maybe.'

Yashim squinted down the telescope and found the ship, low in the water, with a couple of sailors standing in the waist and the white and gold of Naples hanging limply from her stern. Rather old, for sure, and fairly small – but there, she was the vessel he'd have taken himself, if he was in a hurry. Lefèvre seemed to be in a hurry.

The captain spread out a few papers on the table. 'Half in advance, forty piastres, it's normal.' He made some notes on a worn sheet of paper. 'Your friend's name?'

Yashim's mind went momentarily blank. 'Lefèvre,' he stammered finally.

The captain glanced up. '*Francesi, bene*. He has all his papers, of course – passport, quarantine certificate?'

Yashim said yes, he had all the right documents. He hoped it was true; at least Lefèvre would be on board and underway before anything was known about it. Lefèvre wasn't an innocent: he'd take care of himself.

The captain wrote the name down on his sheet and put the folded papers away in his coat. Yashim dug out the purse from his belt and counted out forty piastres in silver onto the table. The captain picked two coins at random, bit them and returned them to the pile with a grunt. 'It'll pass,' he said.

They shook hands. 'What are you carrying?'

The Italian grimaced. 'You name it. Rice. Egyptian cotton.

49

Pepper. Bees. Eighty pieces of Ottoman silver, I hope, and a Frenchman!'

They both laughed, meaninglessly.

⇜ 20 ⇝

The archaeologist was still sprawled out on the divan when Yashim returned home. He raised his head weakly when the door opened, but he seemed to have lost some of the nervous energy of the night before. Yashim set about making coffee while he explained the arrangements he had made.

'Tonight? That is very soon. *Ca d'Oro* – I don't know her. Does she go to France?'

'Palermo.'

'Palermo?' Lefèvre frowned. 'It's certainly not France.'

'No. There was a French ship, but she wasn't leaving until Monday.'

'Monday. Perhaps the French ship would have been better. I might spend a fortune waiting in Sicily.'

'Well, you owe me forty piastres for the berth. You must pay the same again to the captain.'

'But how much was the berth in the French ship?'

'I didn't ask. More expensive, for sure.'

'You say that,' said Lefèvre, sitting up and picking his teeth with a fingernail. 'There's something wrong with the *Ca d'Oro*?'

'Nothing at all. She's smaller. But she's leaving tomorrow. You wanted to get out, that's what you said.'

'Of course, of course. But *enfin*, Palermo.' Lefèvre sucked the air through his lips. 'You should have woken me.'

Yashim banged the coffee pot on the edge of the table to settle the grounds.

'I'm confused,' he confessed. 'Last night I thought you were afraid of someone. Or something.' He reached for the cups, and found the question that was on his mind. 'Is it the Hetira?'

Lefèvre said nothing. Yashim poured the coffee slowly into two cups. 'But if you like, we will change our plans. You are my guest.'

There was a silence while he handed the cup to Lefèvre. All of a sudden the Frenchman's hands were shaking so much he could hardly hold the cup without spilling the tiny amount of oily liquid it contained. He crammed it to his lips and drank it in little sips.

'Hetira?' His laugh was high-pitched. 'Why Hetira?'

Yashim sipped his coffee. It was good coffee, from Brazil: twice as expensive as the Arabian he drank in the cafés. He bought it in small quantities for the rare occasions that he made coffee at home. Sometimes he took down the jar and simply sniffed the aroma.

'Because I have an eye for Greek antiquities?' Lefèvre's eyes narrowed. 'I ensure their survival. I have sometimes rescued an object from imminent disintegration. You'd be surprised. Unique pieces, which nobody recognises – what happens to them? They may be broken or torn or lost, they get damp, they are nibbled by rats, destroyed by fire. And I cannot look after all these beautiful things myself, can I? Of course not. But I find them – what shall I say – guardians. People who can look after them. And how do I know that they will do so?'

'How?'

Lefèvre smiled. It was not a broad smile. 'Because they pay,' he explained, rubbing his fingertips together. 'I turn valueless clutter into something like money – and people, I find, are careful with money. Don't you agree?'

'I've noticed it,' Yashim said.

'Some people do get the wrong idea. They think of me as a

grave robber. *Quelle bêtise*. I bring lost treasures to light. I bring them back to life. Perhaps, if it is not too much to say so, I can sometimes restore their power to inspire men, and challenge their view of the world.'

Is that right, Yashim wondered? Or could it be that Lefèvre – and men like him – simply chipped away at the foundations of a people's culture, scattering the best of it to the four winds?

'You understand me now a little better, monsieur.' Again that smile. 'But all the same, I will do as you suggest. Tonight, after dark, I shall go aboard the *Ca d'Oro*.'

21

Armed with a black Malacca cane and a pair of Piccadilly boots, Dr Millingen locked his door carefully and went down the few short steps into the street. During his medical studies at Edinburgh he had taken to rambling with other long-haired youths through moorland and mountains. They had declaimed poetry together, admired the awful scenery, and ruminated on Adam Smith, Goethe, the tyranny of princes, and the long-term effects of the French Revolution. These days; in spite of the protests of his Turkish friends and clients, he walked half an hour at most, believing that mild exercise improved his circulation and shook up his liver.

The Turks, as a rule, avoided exercise. One of his clients had gone so far as to observe that he had others to exercise for him: a household of servants to bring the pipes, the coffee or the evening meal. He had even hinted, as delicately as he could, that Dr Millingen was committing an injustice, intruding in another's sphere by attempting any physical effort for himself. As for taking a strenuous walk, it led to the risk of being jostled in the street, or apoplexy; and because an Ottoman gentleman could hardly be expected to appear in the streets without his retinue, the annoyance would be shared by his household. Short of taking a second wife, this gentleman liked to insist, there was no easier way of sowing disharmony and vexation through a man's home than by following the doctor's curious prescription.

The doctor himself did not throw himself into these walks with unalloyed enthusiasm, either. Though often steep and even staired, the streets of Pera were not the Lammermuir Hills; the gloomy alleys of the port could hardly be compared to the dark aisles of his beloved pinewoods; and where the corncrake skimmed across the fields at dusk, or the roe buck barked imperiously across the wild glens, the fauna of Pera, like that of Istanbul itself across the Horn, was lazy, underfoot and had fleas.

Dr Millingen faced the street, flexed his stick, and began to walk.

Nobody ever could say how, or even why, the dogs had come to Istanbul. Some people supposed that they had been there always, even in the time of the Greeks; others, that they invaded the city at the time of the Conquest, dropping down from the Balkans to prowl through the blasted streets and the ruins in the fields, where they formed into packs and carved out territories for themselves which still held good to the present day. But nobody really knew. Nobody, Dr Millingen had realised long ago, much cared.

Not a breed, but all alike, these rough-coated yellow dogs with short legs, large jaws and feathery curving tails spent most of the day slumped in all the alleys, gateways, thoroughfares and backstreets of the ancient city, with one eye closed and the other lazily absorbing the activities of the people around them. It took a visitor to see them properly, and a relatively recent resident like Dr Millingen, trained in habits of scientific observation, to see

53

them with a forensic eye; to everyone else they were so much a part of the fabric of the city, so perfectly integrated into their own mental map of a district, that had all the dogs simply vanished from the streets one night, people would have had only the uneasy impression that something had changed; and nine out of ten Stambouliots would have been hard pressed to say what. The dogs did not impinge. They almost never bit a child, ran amok in the market, or stole the butcher's sausages. You stepped over a dog sleeping in a doorway; you skirted a muddle of dogs sprawled in a patch of sunlight in the middle of the road; you tossed in bed when the howling and barking of the dogs at night grew more than usually intolerable; and you never noticed that they existed at all.

Now and then, perhaps once in a hundred years, the authorities woke up to the omnipresent nuisance of the dogs and attempted to round them up: they were carted off into the country, dumped on islands, driven – surprisingly meek – into the Belgrade woods, or out of the Edirne gate. But either they all came back or they simply grew again, like the lizard's tail or moss in the masonry, the same yellow, rangy, rib-sticking mangy curs, with flea-bites and battle-scars and their own distinct parishes. And nobody minded them, either. Like puddles after rain, or shadow, or the blazing sun at noon, they were simply there; and they scavenged the city streets, and kept them clean.

A soiled crust, a dead bird, a heap of vegetable refuse, old bones, peelings, scraps, rinds, rotten fruit: they missed nothing, and wasted nothing. They could eat anything – even shoes. But they rarely tasted fresh meat.

Dr Millingen had once suggested, in the course of a consultation with the sultan himself, that with five hundred oka of the cheapest horse-flesh and five ounces of arsenic, the sultan could rid his metropolitan subjects of an interminable nuisance, the whole race of mangy dogs – dogs, as he understood it, which Muslims regarded as unclean animals; and the sultan, cocking his head sharply to register his surprise, had replied that he supposed the dogs, too, were a part of God's creation. 'You would think it very barbaric, would you not, if I were to order all the English doctors in Istanbul rounded up and fed with poisoned meat? It is the same with the dogs.'

Dr Millingen could think of several arguments in reply, but he could not argue with the sultan's tone.

Advancing at a brisk pace along the street, he swung his cane from side to side and glared suspiciously at the yellow dogs; while they merely yawned, or scratched their fleas, and pretended not to notice Dr Millingen.

22

Venice and Istanbul: the client and the source. For centuries, the two cities were locked together in trade and war, jockeying for advantage in the eastern Mediterranean. Istanbul had many faces but one, like Venice's, was turned to the sea. Like Venice, too, the greatest thoroughfares of Istanbul were waterways; people were forever passing from the city to Uskudar, from Uskudar to Pera, and from Pera to the city again, across the Golden Horn. The famous gondolas of Venice were no more central to life in the lagoon than caiques to the people of Istanbul, and while the Venetian gondola had its champions, most people would have agreed that the caique was superior in point of elegance and speed. Even after dark, the caiques swarmed around the landing stages like water-beetles.

'Forget the ship's boat,' Lefèvre said quietly. 'It's better that I leave from here, unnoticed. Galata is all eyes.'

They left Yashim's lodging after dark, moving quietly on foot through the deserted streets. Lefèvre shouldered the satchel which apparently contained everything he possessed. The narrow streets of Fener were silent and dark, but Yashim led his companion through them by instinct, now and again pausing to feel for a corner stone, or to put his hand gently on the other man's shoulder. Once, a big dog growled out of the darkness, but it wasn't until they reached the landing stage that they met with any other sign of life: the city could have been uninhabited.

Down by the stage, Pera twinkled out across the black water of the Golden Horn. Lamps bobbed gently on the stems of the caiques drawn up against the quay, where a handful of Greek boatmen sat among the coils of rope, the creels and nets, murmuring together and smoking pipes which glowed red in the dark. Lower down the Horn a few ships rode at anchor, with lanterns at their prows. The water slapped darkly against the pilings where the caiques were moored.

A boatman uncoiled himself with catlike ease and stepped forwards.

'The *Ca d'Oro*? I know the ship. She's moored off the point. Both of you?'

Yashim explained it was just one passenger, and fixed a price. He shook hands with Lefèvre and watched him settle himself into the bottom of the caique, the satchel on his knees. Then the boatman tapped out his pipe, stepped into the caique's stern and pushed off with a practised flick of the wrist which sent the frail craft skimming out into the darkness.

Yashim raised a hand in farewell, certain that the Frenchman would see him framed against the low lights of the landing stage. He thought of his friend Palewski: he'd be pleased by the story. Better pleased by the reflection that neither of them would ever have to see Lefèvre again.

He smiled to himself. The light of the caique had blended into the darkness, so he dropped his hand and turned and went home.

 23

Frozen at an angle just wide enough to admit a visitor on foot, the carriage gates of the Polish ambassador's residency rusted on their hinges, escutcheons peeling on the iron shield. They seemed, like Poland itself, to represent an idea: certainly they had not opened to receive a carriage since the eighteenth century, when Poland succumbed to the territorial ambitions of her greedy and more powerful neighbours. A Janissary guard had once been stationed at the gates, but the Janissaries had been brutally suppressed in 1826, and afterwards nobody thought to replace the sentries. Visitors, in truth, were few and far between.

Turning in at the gate, Yashim was surprised to find himself silently challenged by a sentry, who stood with folded arms, blocking his way. He was small for the job, and had a dirty face; he held a stick across his chest and had a look in his eye that brooked no opposition.

Yashim bowed politely. 'My name is Yashim. Is His Excellency the Ambassador at home?'

The little sentry shouldered his arms, swung abruptly on his bare heel, and walked stiffly towards the front door, where he took up a position at the foot of the steps. Yashim passed him with a nod. At the top of the steps he pushed the door, which opened with a creak.

'Don't bother knocking, confound you,' said a voice from the darkened hall. 'Just push in, do.'

Yashim obeyed. Stanislaw Palewski, Polish ambassador to the

Sublime Porte, was leaning on the banisters, waving an arm in ironic salute.

'Oh – it's you, Yashim! That's all right. Come inside. Ever since I lost the key I keep finding total strangers wandering around the house.'

'I thought you were being rather well guarded.'

'Guarded? I suppose you mean the Xanis. Ye-es. The little boy shows promise. More than I can say for his father. Come upstairs.'

Yashim followed his old friend to the sitting room, where they rang for tea. Yashim tucked his feet up in one of the ambassador's leaky leather armchairs while Palewski fell to pacing between the untidy bookcases and the portrait of King Jan Sobieski. Marta arrived with a tray, and Palewski nodded distractedly. Yashim poured the tea.

When Marta had left, Palewski turned around and said: 'What do you make of Marta, Yashim?'

Yashim raised an eyebrow. 'Marta?'

'My housekeeper.'

'I know who Marta is, Palewski. I've known her for years.'

'Yes. Yes, of course. Well, I'm a bit worried about her.'

'You think she's ill?'

'Ill? No, I don't think so. It's just that there's something – she's started – oh, I don't know, Yashim, but she's gone a bit odd. Dreamy, half the time. I come round a corner and she's there, leaning on a broom, staring into space. And tears.'

'Tears?'

'She bursts into tears. I ask something, and she goes all red and darts away. Fact is, Yash, I'm beginning to think that she's not happy.'

'I see.'

'Do you think that's why she got the Xanis in?'

'The family in the coach-house? Yes, for company. You might be right.'

Palewski looked dubious. 'Can't say they're much by way of company. Mrs Xani seems to spend the day inside sweeping the coach-house, and the children muck about in the courtyard. The boy doesn't talk, for some reason. I don't think he's dumb, just won't talk. It's rather odd. But Marta seems very fond of children, so I don't complain. It was her idea to get them in the first place. Put a roof over their heads. The little girl likes to help her cook.'

'What about the father?'

'Xani? Moved in, all gratitude and smiles. Then he went and joined the watermen's guild. He became a su yolcu. So much for all those little repairs he was going to do.'

'Xani joined the watermen? I thought you had to be born into the job.'

Palewski shook his head. 'As a rule, that's true. But if a waterman dies without a successor, they let someone buy his way in. As long as he's Albanian, that is. I suppose he had a cousin or someone to propose him. But look, enough about Xani,' he added, waving a hand.

He seemed to have forgotten about Marta for the moment, so Yashim told him, instead, about Lefèvre's mysterious arrival – and departure.

'And the forty piastres?' Palewski arched his brows. 'I don't suppose you'll be seeing them again, either. Really, Yashim, you should have made that scoundrel pay up.'

Yashim sighed. 'I did try.'

'But not very hard.'

'No. Not very hard.' How could he explain to his friend how the sight of Lefèvre's pathetic satchel had changed everything between them? 'I'll think of it as a tax. The city is better off without a man like Lefèvre in it.'

Palewski nodded. 'I wonder what he got away with this time,' he said.

Yashim turned his head and stared out of the window. The sky was blue with a touch of heat. Wisteria leaves rustled against the window frame, and a little bird swung on a twig, grooming itself in hurried bursts. 'He didn't have anything, as far as I could tell,' he said quietly.

Palewski snorted. 'That's what you say. I've half a mind to go upstairs and check on the wretched heads. He probably got the caique to drop him off somewhere. I wonder what he came for, anyway.'

'Mmm,' Yashim murmured. 'Books, I suppose. Old manuscripts.'

'Old books? That would hardly explain his funk. I think he must have been angling for something bigger than that, and they set the heavies on him. What's the matter?'

Yashim had looked round suddenly, frowning.

'One odd thing happened while I was coming over this morning. The captain of the *Ca d'Oro*, I saw him outside the fish market. I thought it was him. It was just a glimpse and I lost him in the crowd.'

'Sailing delayed?'

'No, I looked. The *Ca d'Oro* has gone.'

Palewski put his fingertips together. 'Well, you know what Pera's like these days. More Italians than an organ-grinder's funeral. More everyone. Half of them foreign and the other half Greeks pretending to be.'

Yashim smiled. Twenty-five years before, when Palewski first arrived to take up his post, foreigners were rare even in Pera. Nowadays the streets were full of them – sailors, tailors, storekeepers, hatters, forwarding agents, old soldiers and even Protestant priests. Being a foreigner didn't mean much any more.

Many of them were the dregs of every Mediterranean port, too, men whose past didn't bear much scrutiny: they fetched up

60

here to practise their dodges and deceptions without the slightest fear of getting caught. The Mediterranean was like a purse, and Pera the seam at the bottom where the dust and fluff collected.

Centuries ago the Ottomans had allowed foreign ambassadors to judge and sentence their own nationals – an errant sailor, a thieving valet – in the intelligent belief that the foreigners understood one another better than they could hope to do; they didn't want foreign miscreants clogging the wheels of Ottoman justice, either. Now that there were so many foreigners in the city the situation had grown out of hand. Many of the people claiming extraterritorial rights were scarcely foreigners at all – Greek-born Englishmen, for instance, whose papers were in order but who had never been closer to England than the Istanbul docks; Corfiotes who could claim protection from the French ambassador without speaking a word of French; island Greeks who flew the colours of the Netherlands on ships which never sailed beyond the Adriatic. Half the native shipping in Ottoman waters was formally beyond Ottoman jurisdiction. And it was almost pointless to expect the British ambassador to sit in judgement over some Maltese cut-throat who waved his naturalisation papers in the face of the Ottoman police: the British didn't even maintain a jail in their embassy grounds.

'I'm sure you could find a dozen Italians who look like your captain, roaming the streets here at this very minute,' Palewski was saying. 'It's either that, or the ship-owners had to replace him at the last minute.'

'That's unlikely – the ship's registered in Palermo, so the owners –' Yashim paused. He had been going to say that the ship-owners would be far away in Sardinia or Naples or Sicily.

'Probably some local Greek firm,' Palewski observed placidly. 'Neapolitan colours, extraterritorial rights, the whole shebang. Switched the captains over for some reason or another.'

The thread of anxiety which had been running through

Yashim's mind ever since he caught sight of the Italian at the fish-market went taut. He pressed his lips together.

'Cheer up, Yash, it's not your funeral.' Palewski said. 'Anyway, the Greeks are born to the sea. They'll get our unsavoury friend back in one piece.'

'The Greeks – yes,' Yashim said slowly. Lefèvre had wanted any foreign ship, any ship at all – just as long as it wasn't Greek. But that had been in the evening, when he had seemed more dead than alive. The next day he'd been quite snappish about the whole thing. He must have been simply overtired, overwrought.

Pilaff *in bianco*, Yashim mused, had been just the thing. Pilaff, and a good night's sleep.

'A tot of cherry brandy,' Palewski said, rising from his arm-chair. 'Honestly, Yash, we should be celebrating that fellow's departure, not fretting about him. What do you say?'

'You're right,' Yashim replied. 'I'll have just the one.'

Which he did; forcing Palewski, as he said reproachfully, to drink for both of them.

∝≪ 24 ≫∝

Yashim walked slowly across the Hippodrome, towards the obelisk that the emperor Constantine had brought from Egypt fifteen hundred years ago. A gift to his mistress, Byzantium, Lefèvre would have said. He wondered what they meant, those hieroglyphic birds, those unwinking eyes, the hands and feet incised with unearthly precision on the gleaming stone.

He stopped for a moment in the pencil of the obelisk's shade, and touched its base. Trajan's column stood fifty yards beyond, a slender bole of rugged stone, weathered and clamped with great bronze staples, carved with a Roman emperor's Balkan triumphs, helmeted legionaries crammed together with their short swords drawn; the stamp of horses, the abasement of chieftains and kings, the flinging of bridges across rivers, and the lament of women. The scenes were hard to decipher, too; the stone had been softer.

Beneath it, Arab traders had pitched a wide green tent on poles. A string of mules went by, and as Yashim lowered his gaze to watch them pass his eye was caught by the twining stalk of the Serpent Column, hollow and broken like a reed: a twist of ancient verdigris no bigger than a withered palm-tree, set in a triumphal axis between the obelisk and the column.

It had been made over two thousand years before, a miracle of craftsmanship to celebrate the miracle of Greek victory over the Persians at Plataia, with three fearsome snake's heads supporting a great bronze cauldron. It had stood for centuries at the oracle of Delphi, until Constantine seized it and dragged it here to beautify his new capital. The centuries since had been unkind to it. The cauldron was long gone; the heads, more recently, had disappeared.

Yashim had known the Serpent Column for years before he first saw the bronze heads in Palewski's wardrobe. He had imagined them to look like real snakes, with broad jaws and small, reptilian eyes, so he had been shocked by the monsters whose cruel masks he had explored by candlelight that evening. They were creatures of myth and nightmare, fanged, blank-eyed, seeking to terrorise and devour their prey. Malevolence seeped from them like blood.

Yashim leaned over the railing to peer down into the pit from which the Serpent Column sprang. The other columns stood on level ground. Was it because the snakes emerged from somewhere deeper, some dark, submerged region in the mind? He shuddered, with an instinctive horror of everything cultish and pagan. From above, the coiling snakes looked like a drill, a screw digging deeper and deeper into the fabric of the city, penetrating its layers one by one.

If you turned it so that the coils bit deeper into the ground, if you traced the sinuous curves of the serpents' bodies from the tail up, you would bring the fanged monsters closer. And eventually you would find yourself staring into those pitiless hollow eyes and the gaping mouth, into the dark side of myths and dreams: terrorised, and then devoured.

Yashim glanced back at the Egyptian obelisk. It seemed cold and reserved, careless of its fate. The Roman column was nothing but a platitude: empires decay.

But between them, the green-black coils of the brazen serpents referred to a dark enigma, like a blemish in the human soul.

25

Alexander Mavrogordato glanced automatically down the street and then rapped on the door with the knob of his cane. After a while he heard the shuffle of feet inside. He knocked again.

The door opened.

'Yashim efendi,' he said.

The old woman nodded. 'He just came in, I think, efendi. Please, mind your head.'

Alexander Mavrogordato ducked, though not quite deeply enough, and stepped down into the little hall, rubbing his head. 'Where do I find him?'

The old woman pointed up the stairs. Mavrogordato climbed heavily. On the landing he paused, then pushed open the door.

Yashim looked up in surprise.

'You mind if I come in?' The young man's tone was aggrieved, as if he expected a rebuff.

'Not at all,' Yashim replied pleasantly. 'You are almost in already.'

'My mother told me where to find you,' Mavrogordato said, advancing into the room. He looked around and went over without stopping to the stove, putting his hands to the table, fingering the pots. Then he wheeled round and came over to the books, absently running his hands across their spines.

'Mother says your job's done.' He reached into his pocket and drew out a purse. 'Here.'

He threw it across to Yashim, who was sitting on the divan, watching the performance with interest. Yashim put up an arm and closed his fingers on the purse. A Phanariot purse: heavy and musical.

'Your mother is too kind,' he said. 'What exactly is she paying me for?'

The young man whipped round. 'It doesn't matter. She thinks she over-reacted.'

Yashim lobbed the purse back. Mavrogordato was taken by surprise, but he caught it. Then he fumbled the catch and the money fell onto the floor.

'In which case, there's no fee.'

Mavrogordato stirred the purse with his foot. 'I don't think you get it, do you? My mother doesn't want to know about – about anything.'

'I see. We never talked. She never scolded me for being late, or asked why I didn't wear a fez, or told me not to smoke.'

'That's right,' the young man replied guardedly.

'Oddly enough, do you know the only thing she really never did? She never discussed a fee with me. Now take your money, Monsieur Mavrogordato, before I start remembering that you were ever here.'

Yashim didn't move from the divan. The young man kicked viciously at the purse, so that it thudded against the wall.

Then he flung out of the door, slamming it behind him.

The trouble with children who were told exactly what and what not to do, Yashim reflected, is that they grow up unable to think for themselves.

26

The nightwatchman who patrolled the streets of Pera was used to the barking of the dogs. As he approached in the faint gleam of his own swaying lamp, the mangy animals would raise themselves from the shadows, from the doorways and the kerbs, and their ritual protest carried on long after he had passed by. It was a matter of form, without moment: an unthinking ceremony which had long ago ceased to have any meaning for either the dogs, or the watchman.

So it was that as he turned into the road which led past the French embassy he was surprised by silence. For a few moments he stood still, scratching his head, while the lantern bobbed about at the end of a stick and swung a feeble yellow gleam this way and that across the unmade road.

Then, through the silence, he heard a soft sucking and tearing sound. He hoisted his lantern and peered forwards into the dark.

27

Istanbul was not an early-rising city; only the devout, stirred by their muezzins, noticed the dawn as it began to creep from the mountains behind Uskudar. Dr Millingen, who was about to be summoned by the French embassy, was asleep, breathing heavily and dreaming of Athens. Nearby, in the Polish residency, Stanislaw Palewski snored among his pillows, dressed in a voluminous old dressing gown. Along the Bosphorus the sultan slept, his cheek flattened against the breast of a Circassian odalisque; she was stolidly resisting the temptation to fall asleep because, if she had a single fault, it was in snoring with her mouth open. Up the Golden Horn, Mme Mavrogordato was also awake, making an effort to interpret her husband's night-fidgets. Yashim slept silently, half-dressed, covered in an old cloak. Malakian was asleep; George the costermonger was drifting somewhere between the two states.

Auguste Boyer, *chargé d'affaires* at the French embassy, was awake, dressed, and leaning from a ground-floor window into the courtyard, wiping a trail of vomit off his chin with a lace-edged handkerchief. The vomit was thin and smelled of bile and coffee. He retched again; his stomach turned over, and a silver thread of drool sank from his lips onto the dry cobbles below the window.

'Put back the sheet,' he said faintly. There was a sound of the sheet being drawn up, and Boyer turned with the handkerchief to his mouth. 'Send for Dr Millingen. And you may bring – bring the bag to my office.'

Keeping his eyes firmly fixed on the door and the handkerchief in place, he staggered from the room. The middle-aged orderly glanced down once at the bloodstained sheet, watching the stains become shiny again from contact with the dead man's wounds, then bent down stiffly and picked up the leather bag. That Boyer was only a kid, he was thinking. He should have been there with the emperor, at Waterloo. *La Gloire!* Not glory, no. But an acquaintance with the dead.

He closed the door, crossed himself with a reflex movement, and went to find the footman.

28

A pair of white cotton gloves slapped down onto the table, setting the coffee cup ringing. Yashim put out a hand and glanced up to see Palewski standing over him.

'My dear friend! Have a seat.' Yashim beckoned to the café proprietor. 'A coffee. Make it two.' He frowned at Palewski. 'Are you ill?'

'I've felt better,' the ambassador said in a low voice that was almost a whisper. 'Are both these coffees mine? Good.'

It would be an exaggeration to say that the colour returned to Palewski's cheeks as he drank his coffee, for they were bloodless at any time; but when he next spoke his voice was firmer.

'Odd news, Yashim. I've just come from the French embassy. The night watch found a body last night, almost on their doorstep. It's one of theirs.'

'How extraordinary.'

Palewski turned his head and made a signal to the café owner. 'I – I'm afraid you won't like this. It's Lefèvre.'

Yashim stared at him blankly. 'It couldn't be.'

Palewski shrugged. 'I'm afraid so. The embassy need your help in dealing with the Porte,' he said. 'Lefèvre was a French citizen, so he's technically their responsibility. But the authorities have to be informed, and the ambassador's concerned that none of the embassy dragomen know the ropes. He doesn't want too many people involved, either. The body is a mess, apparently.'

'I saw Lefèvre leave,' Yashim insisted.

Palewski ignored him. 'Dr Millingen will be holding an inquest, I expect. Who he saw, where he went, that sort of thing. They'll want you there for that. Maybe you're the last person who saw him alive.'

'He took a caique straight to the ship,' Yashim said.

Palewski shrugged. 'Nothing was very straight about Lefèvre. The French ambassador thinks I know my way about. He called me over at some unearthly hour this morning for advice. I suggested you.'

Yashim said slowly: 'I owe Lefèvre something. He was weak, but –'

Palewski nodded. 'He trusted you. I'm sorry, Yash.'

Auguste Boyer's impression that the Turks were an impassive race was confirmed by Yashim's stony inspection of what remained of Lefèvre's body. The face had been washed, and now presented a more terrible sight than it had at first, covered with blood and gobbets of torn flesh. The Turk, Boyer noticed, studied it with a patience that was almost obscene; at one point he seized the head by the ears and turned it so that the horribly exposed eyeballs fixed on Boyer himself, over a grinning row of bloodstained teeth. When Boyer turned back, Yashim was examining the body's hands and feet, which seemed lifelike compared to the ravaged corpse to which they had been attached. It was the orderly, by a gesture, who suggested that Yashim might like to view the entire corpse. Even then, examining the appalling carnage of the wound, he only pursed his lips.

'The good doctor –' Yashim suggested, straightening.

'Dr Millingen will be here shortly,' Boyer said quickly. And not, he thought, a moment too soon: he wanted urgently to put the horror in the hands of a competent professional.

'Strange, the way the dogs go for the face,' Yashim mused. 'Too well exposed, I imagine. Nose gone, chin torn away, yet they haven't touched the ears at all.'

Boyer felt the nausea returning. Yashim followed him out of the room, standing aside when he realised that Boyer was silently retching into his handkerchief.

'I don't quite understand why the body was brought into the embassy,' Yashim said, after a suitable pause.

Boyer pointed wretchedly to a leather satchel. 'The watchmen found that with – with the body. As I said, the bulk of his remains were underneath some planks and beams, on a building site round the corner from here. The dogs . . .' He trailed off again. 'The stuff in the bag was scattered around. I suppose the murderer was looking for money. Anyway, the watchman recognised the foreign script. He couldn't have known it was in French, of course. I suppose he thinks we're all the same, really, and we were closest.'

'Yes,' Yashim said. 'I suppose. It was a coincidence, all the same.' He voiced the thought which had been nagging him ever since the café. 'You weren't expecting him here, were you?'

'Lefèvre? I wouldn't think so, monsieur.'

'Because it was night?'

'Because –' Boyer hesitated. 'Well, we wouldn't expect to see him. And in the night, of course.'

'But Monsieur Lefèvre was not quite *comme il faut*?'

Boyer took a deep breath through his nose. 'He was a French citizen,' he said.

Yashim looked at the satchel again. He remembered Lefèvre tearing it open three nights ago, scattering its contents across his floor. Once again he felt the unbidden affinity with the dead man, the burden of a special duty. He had not liked him. But Maximilien Lefèvre had feared for his life, and had trusted Yashim to save it. That, in Yashim's mind, had become the obligation of hospitality: a task he'd failed, by a grotesque margin.

The satchel still contained the books Lefèvre had shown him, along with an unbound copy of *Le Père Goriot*, by Balzac; its spine was rough and the stitching was beginning to come apart. There was also the shirt he had worn two nights ago; it was dirty around the cuffs and collar and smelled of the dead man's sweat. Some underwear. Yashim returned the books to the satchel, with the dirty laundry. He wiped his hands on his cloak.

'Nothing else? Just the bag?'

'That was all the watchmen brought in.'

A footman walked downstairs and murmured something into Boyer's ear.

'We can go up to the ambassador now, monsieur.'

❧ 30 ❧

The French ambassador glanced up from his desk. 'I understand you knew this Lefèvre.'

'Only slightly, Your Excellency. Monsieur Palewski brought him to dinner one evening at my home.'

'It's not much of an acquaintance,' the ambassador agreed.

Yashim hesitated. 'Some days later, though, he reappeared at my door. He was frightened and confused, but he asked me to find a ship for Europe, as soon as possible. The next day, when I had done so, his spirits seemed to have improved.'

The ambassador raised a finger. 'Ask Boyer to come in,' he said. 'You were not friends?'

'No. I merely tried to help him,' Yashim explained. 'He seemed anxious. Almost a little crazy. The ship was to have sailed yesterday morning. The Ca d'Oro, of Palermo. How he came to be here, in Pera, I have no idea.'

'And you saw him to the ship?'

'I saw him off on a caique from Fener the night before last. I assumed he had left Istanbul.'

Boyer came in with a secretary. The secretary laid a paper on the desk, and the ambassador framed the paper with his fingers and squared it up with the edge of the desk.

'*Enfin*. As the chief representative of the kingdom of France, it is my duty to see that justice is accorded to French citizens who fall under my jurisdiction in this empire. A man is found where he is not supposed to be, slaughtered in a bizarre and barbaric way. We must make an account of his movements, of course. Dr Millingen has made a preliminary inspection. He says Lefèvre must have been killed the night before last. *En effet*, the night you saw him to the caique.'

'Can he be sure?' Yashim asked.

'Frankly, I do not know. The doctor has his methods, I imagine. Taking the doctor's opinion in the matter, and from what you say, Monsieur Yashim, it could appear that the unfortunate archaeologist spent the last twenty-four hours of his life in your apartment.'

Yashim opened his mouth to speak, but the ambassador pressed on.

'To conclude, monsieur, only three people might have known where Monsieur Lefèvre was likely to be that night. Including, of course, Lefèvre himself,' he added with an ironic drawl. 'And a ship's captain – selected almost at random from the port – who is unlikely to have known Lefèvre.'

The ambassador half-turned in his chair to exchange a glance with Boyer, who coughed slightly. The ambassador flicked the corner of the sheet of paper up and down with his thumb on his desk, not looking up.

'As you say, the *Ca d'Oro* sailed yesterday. This is confirmed. In a month or two, if he returns, we may learn something from its captain.

'In the meantime, Monsieur Yashim, you say you did not know the archaeologist well. You say, euh, he was afraid. But he

72

trusted you, evidently. Why?' The ambassador looked up slowly from his desk.

Yashim had a feeling that he was only an observer, as if he were watching this interview from somewhere else. He heard himself say:

'I don't know.'

The ambassador clicked his tongue. 'I find the situation curious. A report will have to be prepared, naturally. Under the circumstances, however, I do not think that your attendance in this matter will be required. I would prefer to pursue it with the authorities, by other channels.'

Yashim could not remember the last time he had blushed. He stood up and bowed with what dignity he could muster, but once out the courtyard he reeled aside and put a hand to the wall.

So much had been going through his mind that he had simply forgotten the principle rule of his profession, if it was a profession: to try to think like the other man. The ambassador's insinuation was not, he recognised, so very absurd. A curious situation, indeed: in similar circumstances, he would perhaps have made the same inference. Yashim, liaison to the French ambassador! Well, he could forget that possibility now.

He hunched his shoulders and stepped out into the street. A few yards further on, he came across a patch of sand strewn across the cobbles. Yashim stood silently, looking all around, half-hoping to see something that the watchmen had overlooked in the dark.

A report will have to be prepared.

The ambassador's report changed everything for him. His duty to the shade of the dead man had been a private matter – but it was taking on a more terrible, public urgency. He knew what the report would contain: details of a bizarre act of savagery committed on a French national in the streets of Pera;

reference to the mystery of Lefèvre's final days, and to a ship that had already sailed. And at the heart of the whole mystery, of course, something not quite right about Yashim himself. Something uncertain about the role he had played: Yashim and the ship; Yashim and his curious acquaintance with the dead man; Yashim, the last man to see Lefèvre alive. What lay between him and the dead man would become the source of whispers, rumours, innuendo.

The sultan's vast household was riven with cliques and cabals; at the palace your choice of friends decided who your enemies would be, too. Yashim had been the confidential eunuch. The sultan's own discreet problem solver. But the sultan was dying; and not everyone in the palace had reason to appreciate Yashim's efforts.

They wouldn't need to say that he had killed Lefèvre. All that mattered was the cloud of uncertainty – the dust raised by the French ambassador's report. The shake of a head, a fluttering of hands, a frown: those would be enough to damn him.

Powerful friends would drop him in a blink. Not a matter of choice, but of survival. People who had depended on him – just the way Lefèvre had done – would need a new protector.

At the back of Yashim's mind lay the thought that Palewski had run him into a trap. He did not encourage the thought; but he allowed it to relieve him a little of the wretchedness he felt.

Yashim put his hand to his head. He'd been too slow: too slow to save a life, too slow to rescue his own reputation; now Palewski's blundering had cost him his room for manoeuvre.

How long would the ambassador need to make his report? A few days, at most.

A few days, then, was all he had. To find the killers, and to save himself.

The French ambassador didn't care about evidence all that much. A man had been killed, a Frenchman of little account; it was his duty as magistrate to make a report to the proper authorities in Istanbul. Perhaps the Ottoman gentleman, Palewski's friend, knew more than he said; perhaps he was even responsible. Pera was getting more dangerous every day: there it was. One should take more care.

So the ambassador did not pause to reflect, as Yashim did, that his summary had been out of step with the truth. Lefèvre, the captain and Yashim: all three had known, in advance, where Lefèvre was to be found that night. But anyone able to examine the ship's manifest would have known, as well; and the boatmen on the caiques, who saw him leave.

Yashim settled into the bottom of a caique. The boatman shoved off with a flick of his long oar.

'Where to, efendi?'

'Fener Kapi,' Yashim said. The Fener landing stage. The boatman nodded: he was a Greek, and Greeks liked going to Fener.

For hundreds of years Fener had been the seat of the orthodox patriarchate, the soul of Greek Istanbul. In a city where many races and faiths mingled, the Patriarch was a link to the centuries before the Ottoman conquest, when Constantinople stood at the hub of the Christian world. For a thousand years, decked in the insignia of the Church, Byzantine emperors had borne themselves proudly as God's anointed rulers on earth, greater than Popes or Patriarchs, wrapped in an unceasing round of prayer and ostentation – interrupted only by usurpation, betrayal, violent death, palace coups, murders, and the vicious political manoeuvring favoured by tyrants everywhere.

Worn steps led up to a battered door that had seen much since the last Emperor of Byzantium vanished in his purple buskins, as Ottoman troops swarmed across the walls of his desolate city. Behind that door lay the central piece in the elaborate mosaic of the Orthodox faith, which spread from the deserts of Mesopotamia and the roadsteads of the Aegean to the mountains of the Balkans and along the basalt cliffs of the Black Sea; all that was really left of the might and glory of the second Rome, the city of Constantine and Justinian; all that had survived the battle of iconoclasts and iconodules, the treachery of the Latins and the warlike prowess of the Turks.

Yashim gazed at the great door, then stepped along the street to a smaller gateway which for the last seventeen years had served as the main entrance to the Patriarchate. The great gate had been sealed as a mark of respect towards the Patriarch Bartholemew, hanged from its lintel by the sultan's order during the Greek riots of 1821.

At the gate, he asked for the archimandrite.

Grigor was in his private office: a fat man with a big beard in a black surtout.

'Yashim – the angel!' Grigor opened his arms wide across a desk piled with packets and papers done up in purple ribbon.

The angel was Grigor's little joke; not one that Yashim particularly shared. As Grigor had once explained, Byzantine iconography represented angels as eunuchs. Angels stood on the threshold between men and God; eunuchs, between men – and women. Both were intermediaries, dedicated to serve.

'You look well, Grigor,' Yashim said.

'I am fat, and ugly, and you know it, Yashim. But we are, fortunately, all one in the sight of God.'

Many years ago, he and Yashim had worked for the same master, the Phanariot princely family of the Ypsilanti. Grigor, a couple of years older, had made a point of sneering at Yashim's provincialism, sending him on fool's errands and tormenting him with salacious details of his conquests. It was the obscene stories, above all, which had caught Yashim on the raw.

One day Grigor had gone too far. Yashim had folded back his sleeve and they had fought together through kitchen and courtyard. 'About time someone taught that little snot a lesson,' the head-groom had said, as he marched Yashim upstairs to face Ypsilanti.

But after that, they had understood each other. They had even become, in a way, friends. When the Patriarch was hanged and riots exploded in the streets, Yashim had helped Grigor to escape the city.

'You will take a coffee with us?' Grigor rang a bell. 'The school is flourishing,' he added.

'I am glad.' There had been a difficulty, two years before, over plans to expand the Greek boys' school, and Yashim had helped to smooth it over.

They talked for a few minutes, drinking their coffee, skirting around delicate subjects. Eventually the priest returned his empty cup to the saucer.

'It is good to see you. To talk again.'

Yashim took a breath. 'You've heard the rumours about the sultan?'

Grigor leaned his chin into his beard. 'He is very ill.'

'So I understand. It would be an old man who could remember the last time a sultan died this way. Selim was murdered at Topkapi.'

'And Mahmut was just a child. Of course. Now he has reigned for a long time.'

'Reigned, but not ruled. He was under the control of the Janissaries, his own army, for almost twenty years.'

Grigor frowned. 'So he should not be held to account for what happened before he destroyed the Janissaries? The murder of the Patriarch Bartholomew cannot be laid at his door?'

Yashim decided to let this pass. 'There's a mood in the city I've never known before, Grigor. Look at the money. The sultan is slowly dying, and the people are afraid of the money. Its value is sinking every day.'

'I am a priest, not a banker.'

Yashim turned his head and gazed out of the window.

'I meant it as an example,' he said slowly. 'In former times, the death of a sultan stopped the clocks. Only the son who could buy off the Janissaries, take control of the treasury and win the backing of the holy men succeeded to his place.'

'A barbaric arrangement,' Grigor said.

Yashim pressed on. 'When the Janissaries killed Selim, they took power before anyone could react. But Mahmut's illness casts a shadow over Istanbul.'

Grigor sighed. 'All those years ago, when you helped me get away from here, I wandered among the monasteries of Bulgaria. My life changed. And I came back. Do you know why?'

'To join the church,' Yashim said.

'To join the church,' Grigor echoed, with a nod. 'Of course.' He paused. 'I came back, Yashim efendi, because this is my city. We Greeks do not govern it, I admit. But it governs us. For me, this city is not a reminder of what we were. A city of art? Baff! The place where we triumphed for a millennium – over barbarians, over the Pope in Rome, over all our enemies – until the last one?'

He pursed his lips, a thoughtful look on his face. 'We do not seek battles. Our concern is with the spirit, and the mystery of life. Who rules is of no consequence to us. We obeyed an emperor. We obey a sultan. This is the order ordained by God, in the material world, and the Redeemer instructed us to make our peace with that order. Render to Caesar what belongs to Caesar, and to God what belongs to God. This is the Bible.'

Yashim inclined his head politely.

78

'Indeed,' Grigor continued, 'before the Turkish conquest we had a saying: better the sultan's turban than the bishop's mitre. Anything but the Pope in Rome. You Turks are merely the care-takers of our Constantinople.'

He leaned forward, his long beard brushing against the top of his desk. 'It is Greek because its people are Greek. Because it is the scene of our triumphs – and all our trials, too.'

He jabbed the air with a plump finger.

'In this city the Greek faithful have experienced their deepest humiliations. The loss of western Christendom – Rome, Ravenna, all that – ended with the Great Schism with the Pope, right here in the church of the Holy Wisdom, Aya Sofia. Then came the sack of the city by the crusaders, in 1204: for sixty years we endured the rule of heretics. The fall of the city in 1453, and the death of the emperor at its walls. Quite a catalogue. We have suffered the loss of our churches, the rages of the mobs, the death of our Patriarch – ah, yes, we have bought this city with our blood, and we survive. Constantinople is – I say it without blasphemy – our Golgotha.'

He held up his hands, fingers outspread. 'Now, perhaps, you understand what I mean.'

Yashim sat very still. He was impressed.

But he had come for something else.

'Tell me about the Hetira, Grigor.'

A shadow slid across the archimandrite's face. 'I don't know who they are: a many-headed Hydra, possibly. They have noth-ing to do with us here – but yes, their aims have a certain currency in some circles of the church. And beyond that, in the kingdom of Greece.'

A low bell sounded from far away. Grigor got to his feet and opened a cupboard. Inside hung his vestments.

'I officiate at mass,' he explained.

'I think they frighten people, Grigor,' Yashim said.

Grigor put his arms through his robes, one by one, and said nothing. He did not look round.

'I think there is something they kill to possess,' Yashim continued. 'Or to protect. Some – I don't know – some object, or some kind of knowledge. I think that when anyone gets too close, they react.'

'I see.' There was a look of scorn on Grigor's face. 'And you, angel – are you not afraid for yourself?'

'I am afraid only of my ignorance,' Yashim replied carefully. 'I am afraid of the enemy I don't know.'

The priest reached carelessly for a book on the shelf beside him.

'Your enemy is an idea. Greeks call it the Great Idea. For the time it takes to say a mass, you may look at this. After that, the book does not exist.' He laid the cope across his shoulders, and turned to Yashim. 'The church has no part in this affair of yours.'

They stared at one another, the eunuch and the priest. Then Grigor was gone, and Yashim was left alone, clutching the book in both hands.

32

For the time it takes to say a mass. Yashim sat down. The book was written – assembled was a better word – by a Dr Stephanitzes, late physician-in-ordinary to the Greek army of independence. It had been recently published in Athens, the capital of independent Greece. The paper was cheap; the gold-blocked title on the cover was blurred around the edges.

Yashim had never come across such a book before – a wild flinging together of prophecy, prejudice, false premise and circular argument. It preached a story which began with the collapse of Byzantine power in 1453 and wound its way, over hundreds of pages and many false starts and irrelevant asides, to its eventual restoration under its last emperor, miraculously reborn.

Yashim discovered the oracles of an ancient Patriarch, Tarasios, and of Leo the Wise; the prognostications of Methodios of Patara; the curiously prophetic epitaph on the tomb of Constantine the Great, who had founded the city fifteen hundred years before; all of them twisted and sugared up by the visions of one Agathangelos, who foresaw the city liberated by a great phalanx of blond northern giants, while the Turks themselves were to be chased away beyond the Red Apple Tree.

This, then, was the Great Idea. A farrago of blasphemies and wishful thinking – but heady stuff, Yashim had to admit, like sticking your nose through the gateway to the Spice Bazaar. If you were a Greek, and you wanted to believe, then here was the sacred text, without a doubt.

 33

In the church of St George, the archemandrite waved the censer again and filled the air with the grateful fragrance of sandalwood and frankincense. He intoned the words of the creed.

I believe in One God, Father Almighty, Maker of heaven and earth and of everything visible and invisible.

And in One Lord, Jesus Christ, the only-begotten Son of God, begotten of the Father before all ages.

Light of Light, True God of True God, begotten, not made, consubstantial with the Father, through Whom all things were made.

He sang the words; his body trembled to the majestic statement of faith; but his mind was elsewhere. Had he, he wondered, already said too much?

I acknowledge one baptism for the forgiveness of sins.

And then there was the book. The Ottoman authorities probably didn't know that it existed. It was better that way.

I await for the resurrection of the dead
And the life of the ages to come.

That was the way it should be kept.

Amen.

 34

Yashim made his way into the Grand Bazaar. It was two days since Goulandris the bookseller had been killed, and still confidence had not returned: locked doors punctuated the frothy rows of booths, the vendors seemed subdued, the crowd less busy than usual.

Malakian was at his doorway, sitting quietly on a mat with his hands in his lap.

'Do you have news?'

Yashim inclined his head. 'Lefèvre, the Frenchman we talked about? He was killed in Pera.'

Malakian sighed. 'It is like I said. Lefèvre lived a dangerous life.'

'That's not quite what you said, Malakian efendi. You said he did not always dig with a spade.'

'It is the same, my friend. In Istanbul, I think, it is better that the ground is not disturbed.'

'Lefèvre disturbed something.' Yashim squatted down beside the old man. 'Or someone.'

'You will have a coffee with me,' Malakian said.

Yashim could tell he didn't mean it. He declined. 'The Hetira, efendi.'

The old Armenian paused before replying. 'I think a man like Lefèvre would work where money is to be found. But sometimes in these places there are too many secrets, also, and so there is no trust. A negotiation is not easy. I am sorry for his children.'

'His children?' Yashim found it hard to imagine a Lefèvre with children. But then, what would he know? 'Do you have children, Malakian efendi?'

The old man nodded solemnly. 'Five,' he said.

'God's blessing upon them,' Yashim said politely. 'Malakian efendi, do you still have that coin for Dr Millingen? The English collector?'

It was Malakian who looked surprised. 'Of course. He does not come here every day.'

'I will be in Pera this afternoon,' Yashim said. 'I could take him the coin, if you liked.'

Malakian turned his head to look at Yashim. 'You want to meet Dr Millingen?'

'Yes,' Yashim said.

 35

'My French is – indifferent, I'm afraid,' said Millingen. He laughed pleasantly, and held out a hand. Yashim took it: the doctor had a firm grip. Scarcely older than Yashim, he looked in good shape: the grizzled hair, the lean, brown face, the tall, erect posture. He was neatly dressed in a black cutaway coat and a brilliant white shirt; his cravat was loose at the neck.

'Most kind of you to come. Aram's been throwing out hints these past few weeks, and my collector's instinct tells me what you've brought. You aren't an addict, too?'

Yashim smiled. 'I do not collect coins, doctor.'

'Good for you! I caught the bug in Greece – time on my hands. It's nothing much, but I've been making a collection of late Byzantine coinage. All those states and little kingdoms which grew up after the crusaders sacked the city in 1204. Silver obloids minted by the Morean despots, for instance. This, I suspect, may be the one I'm missing.'

Dr Millingen slid the coin from its pouch onto his leather-topped desk, and prodded it with his finger. 'I knew it. An angelus. Damn, but Malakian is clever. I'll wager he had this coin the whole time.' He looked up and pulled a face. 'A collector is a very weak man, wouldn't you say? Six months ago I would not have given five piastres for this coin. Now it arrives to close a gap, and Aram will have me paying through the nose.'

'Well, I suppose if Malakian always supplies you with your coins, he can't help knowing what you are looking for,' Yashim pointed out.

'Ah, no.' Millingen wagged his finger. 'That's part of the game – when I remember to play it properly. I don't rely on Aram, you see. There are other dealers, though I admit he's the best. Sometimes I think they operate a ring, pool their information. So I have to lean on friends outside the bazaar, too. You'd be surprised. There's a monk in Filibe who helps me, and an old friend in Athens. A doctor, like me. But Malakian! He'll ruin me!'

Yashim smiled. 'I'm afraid he only asked me to bring it over. He didn't mention money.'

'Not a word!' Dr Millingen laughed again, and ran his hands through his curls. 'The old fox! He knows I've been sitting here

84

with my tongue hanging out. And in a moment I'll put this angelus with the others, and complete the set. And then how could I ever let it go again? Oh, Signor Yashim, I'm afraid our old friend has quite deceived you. You have just sold your first angelus.'

Yashim smiled. 'I am afraid, Doctor Millingen, that it is I who have perhaps deceived you. I was glad to bring you this coin, but really it is some information that I want.'

Millingen waved his hand. 'Fire away,' he said affably.

Yashim found himself hesitating. 'At the palace, they will speak for me.'

Dr Millingen leaned forwards slightly. 'Yes, Yashim efendi. I believe I know you.'

Yashim felt encouraged. 'I knew the unfortunate Monsieur Lefèvre, as well. The man who was killed.'

'Ah, yes. Bad business, that.'

'He told me you had met once.'

Millingen looked surprised. 'It's quite possible. Who knows? I'm afraid he was rather beyond recognition this morning.'

'You examined the body.'

'An autopsy. It means to have a look for oneself – from the ancient Greek. I never liked the post-mortem stuff, to be honest. I'm a doctor, not a pathologist: it's my job to save lives.'

'Lives may be saved if we can find out who did this.'

Millingen looked dubious. 'A dark alley, in the middle of the night? You can rule out witnesses. Those dogs make enough noise to wake the dead. Anyway, this is Pera, not Stamboul.'

'Efendi?'

'It would take more than murder to get the Perotes out of their own houses on a dark night. Haven't you noticed – the people here are colder than a Scotch welcome?'

'But the cause of death – and the time. You reached a judgement?'

Millingen frowned. 'Yes, I did. It was somewhat spectacular – the trunk was hacked open, from stomach to sternum. But he was actually killed, I suspect, with a blackjack: a powerful blow to the base of the neck. He was almost certainly unconscious when they cut him open. Spatchcocked, you might say, like a widgeon or a teal.'

'But why?'

'Purest speculation: whoever killed him wanted to attract the dogs. Quite decent plan – although it's the dogs, ironically, which help me suggest a time of death.'

'How's that, Dr Millingen?'

'The teeth marks. Some are older, which caused a loss of blood when the body was still fresh. Then an overlapping set of marks, sometimes a parallel set. The dogs tend to feed by night, as I'm sure you've noticed. Last night the body was pulled apart. And of course there are other indications, like the state of decomposition, desiccation of the eyeballs and such. He couldn't have been killed much later than the night before last; possibly, I suppose, a little earlier. I'll be suggesting a time of death between noon Monday and, say, six o'clock on the Tuesday morning.'

Not good, Yashim thought: that put him and Lefèvre together, alone, at a time when he could have been killed.

'How soon can you make your report, Dr Millingen?' He hoped it sounded casual.

Millingen smiled. 'Between you and me, it could be tomorrow. But the ambassador's given me a week.' He glanced down at the coin on his desk. 'I wish you luck, Yashim efendi. These sort of crimes are the hardest to resolve.'

Yashim nodded. He liked Millingen's air of detachment: it was a professional air. The manner of a man trained to notice things. 'Dr Millingen, you've been among the Greeks. You have some experience of their – ambitions.'

86

Millingen frowned. 'I know many Greeks, of course. But their ambitions? I'm afraid I don't quite –'

'No, forgive me,' Yashim said. 'There's a society, a secret society, I've learned a bit about recently. The Hetira. I wondered if you'd heard of it?'

'Umm.' Millingen reached forward and picked up the Morean coin. 'Secret societies.' He shook his head and chuckled. 'The Greeks are a very charming people. But. I got to know many of them years ago, in the Morea. They were all involved in the struggle for Greek independence, of course – I went to Missolonghi with Lord Byron.

'What was it that Lord Byron used to say? The Greeks don't know a problem from a poker. The truth is, they'd intrigue over a potato – and when I say they were involved in the struggle, I don't mean they went out to win it. Most of the time they fought each other. Very disappointing. Byron wanted them to be like classical Greeks, full of the Platonic virtues; and they aren't. Nobody is. They're a good people, but they're like children. A Greek can laugh, cry, forget, and want to kill his best friend all in the space of an afternoon!' He leaned back and smiled. 'When I was a boy, we used to make ourselves dens in the bushes. We'd have Bonaparte marching through the garden, and we'd be ready to take him on – and his army. That's the Greeks all through. They make themselves secret worlds. It's politics, if you like – but it's play, too.'

He held the coin between finger and thumb and flicked it, so that it spun round.

'A Greek's a brave fighter on the battlefield – the battlefield that exists in his own head. He slaughters Albanians, routs the Turks, and battles Mehmed Ali to the very gates of Cairo! He'll take on the world, like Alexander the Great – except that afterwards he smokes his pipe, drinks a coffee, forgets and sits like an old Turk. It's what you call kif, isn't it? A state of contented contemplation. The Greeks pretend they don't have it, and to look at them sometimes you'd believe it – but they've got the kif habit worse than anyone.' He closed his eyes and let his head drift slowly; then he snapped awake, and chuckled again. 'But do you know why he doesn't fight? I'll tell you this for nothing. A Greek can never obey another Greek. They're all in factions, and every faction has a single member.'

Yashim laughed. What Dr Millingen said was unanswerable: the Greeks were quixotic. No one could deny that the little Kingdom of Greece had been founded largely in spite of the Greeks' own efforts. Eleven years ago, in 1828, an Anglo-French fleet had destroyed the Ottomans at Navarino, and dictated the terms of Greek independence to end a civil war that had been dragging on for years.

'A secret society, doctor?'

Dr Millingen had begun to let the coin run across the back of his hand, weaving it in and out between his fingers.

'In my experience, there are many Greek secret societies. It's in the blood. Some are for trade. Some for family. In the Kingdom of Greece, so I've heard, some agitate for a republic, or socialism.'

'Yes, I see. And Hetira?'

'I've heard of them. You are a friend of Malakian's, so I'll tell you what I know: it's not to be repeated, if you understand me. The Hetira are anti-Ottoman, in a fairly subdued way. Most secret societies are, or they wouldn't exist. But the Hetira really despise the Kingdom of Greece. They believe that the kingdom was constructed by secret negotiation between the Ottoman Empire and the European powers, to keep Greeks in the Ottoman lands quiet.'

'A conspiracy?'

'Between a cunning sultan and compliant foreign ambassadors. For the likes of the Hetira, Greece is nothing more than a sop to European opinion. In the meantime, they indulge a dream. They want a new empire. Greeks don't live in Greece alone. Trabzon, Izmir, Constantinople: they're full of Greeks, aren't they?'

Yashim watched in fascination as the angelus rippled between Millingen's knuckles. 'But also Turks. And Armenians, Jews. What of them?'

The doctor turned his wrist, and his fingers closed around the coin. When he opened his hand, it had gone.

Yashim smiled, and stood up. 'That's a pretty trick,' he said.

'Missolonghi was a very long drawn-out affair,' Dr Millingen laughed. 'As I say, we had time on our hands. But interesting company.'

He flexed his fingers.

The ancient coin winked in his palm.

36

'Who is it now? Any more builders, and I swear I'll scream. You're quite fat enough, Anuk, put that pastry away. Read this, Mina sweetie. Tell me if it's spelled properly. If it's not a builder we'll see him.' She opened her arms. 'Yashim!'

Preen went into a mock swoon. Nobody in the room paid the slightest attention except Mina, who looked up and smiled. Preen snapped out of her swoon and threw her arms around Yashim's neck. 'I thought you were a builder! I might not have recognised you anyway. It's been months.'

Yashim grinned. Preen's sense of time had always been elastic, stretching or shrinking according to her mood; but she lived in a world that was more vivid and extravagant than his, where the boundaries between reality and make-believe were fluid. Long ago, as a boy, Preen had been trained as a köçek dancer, as sultry and provocative as any of the köçek 'girls' who danced at weddings and parties and reunions in the great city of Istanbul. No one knew exactly how or when the köçek traditions had evolved: perhaps they had danced for the emperors of Byzantium, perhaps they had come with the Turks from the steppe; but they were, like the dogs, or the gypsies, as much a part of the city as the sunshine, or the damp.

Preen had not lost her energy for life, nor her sense of humour, when she set aside her wigs and bustiers in favour of a bristled scalp and loose pyjamas. There was grey in the bristle now, and her face bore no trace of make-up beyond a little rouge, some antimony, and a touch of the eyebrow-pencil and the kohl. She was wearing an embroidered scarlet waistcoat. Two of the fingers of her right hand were permanently crooked, the result of an accident involving an assassin and a tricky flight of stairs.

'Months, Preen? More like a week.'

'A week for me – it's a month! I don't have time to sleep, Yashim, honestly.' Her fingers fluttered to her eyes. 'Do I look tired?' She sounded chirpy, but Yashim was familiar with Preen's methods, her underlying anxieties.

'Tired? You're crackling with energy, I can feel it. You look like a new –'

'I am a new woman, Yashim.'

They both laughed.

'It's true – that accident was the best thing that could have happened to me. It made me think. Face it, Yashim, I was getting too old to dance every night.'

'You were dancing as well as ever.'

Preen smiled. 'I've seen too many dancers grow old, Yashim. The theatre will be something different.' She pronounced it *tay-art-re*, the French way Yashim had used when he first explained the idea. 'I've got jobs for three of the older girls when we open, selling tickets and sherbet and coffee.'

Yashim had been astonished by Preen's talent for organisation. Gone was the dancer who worked for tips from clients, who fretted about her vanishing good looks, who slept and danced and whiled away whole days in the hammam. As soon as she had grasped the idea of a theatre she had set about it with enthusiasm. She tracked down good premises in Pera, found a team of builders and bent them to her will, planned the bill and organised the décor – all in the space of a few months. Preen had an unexpected streak of steel. She took no nonsense, brooked no contradictions. But she lavished praise where it was due.

She lavished it on him, of course. Yashim only hoped that he was right: that Pera could support a theatre. It would be something between an English music hall and a Parisian revue; he had read about such places. Many people would disapprove. Yashim, if he were honest, disapproved slightly himself. But for Preen's sake – and the sake of all her tribe – he hoped it would work.

'I came into a little extra money,' he said, holding out Mavrogordato's purse. 'Can you use it?'

Preen turned her head away. 'We despise it, Yashim. You know that.' Her arm snaked out and he dropped the purse into her hand.

'Thanks. Do you want a coffee?'

'No. But I've got a favour to ask.'

'You surprise me. Shall we not despise the money, after all?'

'Better not. A wealthy boy, Preen. Greek, rather good looking.'

'Mmmm.' Preen arched a delicate eyebrow. 'Sash, skirts and hairy legs too?'

'More like lace-ups and a stambouline, I'm afraid. And whisky-breath.'

Preen turned her head and traced a pattern idly on her scalp. 'Academy boy?'

'That's my guess.' Since Greek independence ten years before, many rich Greeks had been sending their sons to be educated in Athens. 'Alexander Mavrogordato. The bankers.'

'Ah, *those* Mavrogordatos,' Preen said roguishly, as if there were any others. Then her expression changed. 'We might need the purse, at that.'

37

Yashim laid the basket on the floor and fished out three onions and a handful of courgettes. He pulled down the chopping board and set it on the little high table where he kept his salt, rice and dried spices. He took a sharp knife from the box beside him and honed it on an English steel which Palewski had given him once, as a surprise. Cookery wasn't about fire: it was about a sharp blade.

He ripped the outer skin from the onion using the blunt edge of the knife. He halved it and laid the halved pairs face down, curves touching. The knife rose and fell on its point. The board gave a momentary lurch and rocked to one side; Yashim continued chopping. He swept the slices to the edge of the board. The board rocked back again. Yashim raised one edge and swept his hand beneath it, dislodging a grain of rice.

For a few moments he stared at the tiny grain, frowning slightly. Then he glanced up and poked his finger into the spaces between the rice crock and the salt cellar and the spice jars at the back of the table. A few grains of rice stuck to his fingers. He moved the crocks and jars to one side, and found several more.

Yashim rubbed the tips of his fingers together, opened the lid of the rice crock and looked inside. It was almost full, the little scoop buried in the grain to its hilt.

He looked around the room. Everything was in order, everything left as the widow would have left it after she'd been in to clean, the shawls folded, the clothes bags dangling on a row of hooks, the jug of water standing in the bowl.

But someone else had been in here.

Searching. Looking for something small enough to be hidden in a crock of rice.

Yashim picked up a folded shawl and spread it out across the divan beneath the window. He picked up the rice jar and tipped it forwards, spilling the grain onto the shawl. Nothing but a mound of rice. He looked inside the jar. It was empty.

He put the rice back into the crock with his two hands at first, and then the little scoop. He brushed a few grains of rice off the rim and replaced the lid.

The Frenchman. Lefèvre. How long had he left him on his own? Two hours, three. So he'd woken up and wanted to make something to eat.

Lefèvre didn't cook. Didn't know olives from sheep droppings.

I believe everything I read in books.

Yashim frowned.

He went to his bookcase and looked along the shelves. The books were in no particular order, which told him nothing. Perhaps they had been disarranged, perhaps not. He tried one or two at random, and they slid out easily.

He pushed the jars back to the wall and carried on chopping the onions.

He sluiced olive oil across the base of an earthenware dish.

He halved a lemon and squeezed its juice into the oil. He dried his hands on a cloth.

He went to the bookcase and ran his finger along the middle shelf until he found the book.

It had been a gift from the sultan's mother, the validé. She'd received it unbound, no doubt, in a thick manilla wrapper.

Before she passed it on she'd had it bound in imperial green leather, with the colophon of the House of Osman, an egret's feather, worked onto the spine in gold leaf. Title and author, stamped on the spine in gold.

GORIOT – BALZAC. It was a rare gift.

At the embassy, Lefèvre's satchel had contained half a dozen books. They were the very books the terrified man had spilled out apologetically across the floor, before he died. Except for one, Yashim remembered. There had been a paper-bound copy of *Goriot*, slightly tatty around the spine, which he hadn't seen before.

He pulled the Balzac from the shelf and opened the leather cover.

Lefèvre, at least, had found a hiding place.

You hide jewels on a woman's neck. A man can lose himself in a crowd.

Yashim sighed: the validé's gift was ruined beyond repair.

It takes a book to hide a book.

❧ 38 ❧

Enver Xani fitted his key into the lock and pressed the door gently. Beyond the door lay a cool, dim chamber which echoed to the sound of running water. He stepped inside, grateful to escape the heat and dust of the city, and bent down to unstrap his shoes. He laid them carefully on a stone, pushed the door shut behind him, and stood waiting for his eyes to adjust to the gloom.

The coldness of the water still surprised him. In winter, the brothers said, it seeped into your very marrow; you spent the day wet, frozen, moving between the siphons and the cisterns of the city in fur-lined boots, your hands and hair permanently clammy, the joints of your fingers and toes swollen with the cold. It wasn't work for old men. Which was why most of the water-men took an apprentice with them on their rounds; invariably one of their own sons.

In summer one could be grateful for the chill and the darkness, for the quiet and refreshing sound of flowing water. Outside the dust was baked in the hot streets, stirred up by the passage of many feet, untouched by the slightest breath of wind. In here, in any one of the dozen or so siphons and cisterns dotted around the city, one could step into the cool stillness of the forests, fif-teen miles off, from where the water began its long, slow descent towards a thirsty capital. It was a privilege. Enver had paid well for it.

He hung the key on a hook, the way he had been shown: it certainly would not do to drop a key into the maze of channels that swirled and eddied at his feet. In three months, he had been taught everything that an apprentice could be expected to know after years of following his father on the job: only by following the rules could he perhaps make up for the experience he lacked. For the brothers, the rules were like a religious ritual; just as this siphon-room was, in its way, like a church or mosque, cool and quiet amid the heat and bustle of the city.

Enver took a stick from its place on the wall and dipped it into the broad receiving tank, measuring its depth. The water from the incoming pipe flowed gently into it at one end; on the far side, in the shadow, the water brimmed against the rim of the tank, sliding noiselessly over seven shallow scoops into the dis-tribution basins. At the appointed hour he would stop up the outlets to basins three, five and six, open the pipe to release the flow from basin two, and pass the signal down the main bore to the next man.

Enver felt a squeeze of anxiety in his chest as he ran over the mnemonic verses he had learned. 3, 5, 6. Then 2. They belonged to the rules, as did the tarnished hollow ball of tin which would shortly shoot from the delivery pipe and set his work in motion. His job now was to watch for the ball.

Enver squatted at the edge of the receiving tank, frowning as he focused on the spout. The water purled over the lip of the spout and tumbled in a thick coil into the tank, on and on, without stopping. From time to time he saw the coil flicker; sometimes he felt sure that the water was arriving not in a ceaseless stream but by a series of almost imperceptible pulses, like blood through the veins of a man's wrist, *gluck-gluck-gluck*, and he had to close his eyes and breathe deeply to dispel the illusion. But was it an illusion? Many of the brothers were able to tell precisely when the ball was set to arrive by the most minute change in the volume of delivery, the smallest shift in the music of the waterfall. 'Steady, now. Stand by,' they'd say, ever alert to the subtle change, breaking off a conversation. And a few moments later the tin ball would drop into the tank, sink a few inches and then bob up to the surface and glide softly to the edge.

'Not yet,' Enver thought; but he had misjudged, for at that moment a tiny scraping noise announced the ball's arrival at the near edge of the tank. He hadn't even seen it come: it must have dropped from the spout when he closed his eyes, trying to decipher the rhythm of the water.

Disappointed, he stared down into the tank. He should pick up the ball, block the necessary distribution pipes with the rags, and then drop the ball into the exit pipe, to float away on its long journey through Istanbul. 3, 5, 6. Then 2. Light from a spangling of small holes in the roof of the chamber danced and dissolved on the surface of the water, as black and depthless as a pool of oil. With a sigh he bent forwards and retrieved the tin ball. For a moment the light seemed to bounce from the surface around the chamber, a sudden brightening which Enver caught in the corner of his eye; then it settled once more, and he shivered. He had heard the brothers' stories of ifrits and demons who haunted the darker corners of the cisterns; but it was growing cold now, too.

He gripped the ball in his fist and stared down at his own reflection in the black water.

For a fraction of a second, he caught sight of a second face, staring up out of the dark tank.

Enver had no time to wonder. He gasped, and something took him by the back of his head, so that the last thing Enver Xani saw in this world was the sight of his own face rushing towards him, its mouth open in a silent scream.

❄ 39 ❧

It was late in the evening when Yashim arrived at the gate of Topkapi Palace. Two halberdiers scrambled to their feet as he entered, and one of them placed his foot carelessly over a pair of dice on the stones.

'Quiet times,' Yashim murmured.

The halberdiers grinned foolishly. Yashim went past them and into the first, more public court of the palace. He crossed the cobbles in the shade of the planes, remembering when the great court had been full of people – soldiers respectfully dismounting, the standing grooms, the pashas coming to and fro, surrounded by their retinues, cooks bawling out orders, flunkeys darting everywhere on errands, cartloads of provisions rolling slowly towards the imperial kitchens, turbaned kadis gravely discussing the judgements of the day, oblivious to the noise, harem carriages rattling off towards some sheltered picnic spot by the Sweet Waters, black eunuchs trotting home with their shopping in a string bag, a swaggering group of Albanian irregulars, trying not to look awed, with pistols in their sashes, little boys staring up at the collection of severed heads displayed on the column, and around them, between them, the ordinary people of Istanbul, whose conversation was an underlying murmur like the sea.

The court was silent; only the gardeners squatted at their quiet tasks, beneath the swaying branches of the planes.

Where, Yashim wondered, had it all gone? Not to Beşiktaş, certainly – the sultan's new Frankish palace on the Bosphorus, where sentries in kepis stood to attention outside little boxes, close to the railings. At Beşiktaş, carriages turned in smartly across the raked gravel, wheels crackling on the stones, and people in stamboulines got out, went up the steps and disappeared.

Across the First Court stood the Gate of Felicity, whose conical towers could be seen from the Bosphorus and the Golden Horn. He wondered if it was still the Gate of Felicity, now that it no longer opened into the dwelling place of God's Shadow on Earth. Could one still count oneself happy to pass through that gate, yet no longer able to share the same ground as the sultan himself?

As soon as he had phrased the question in his mind, Yashim knew it wasn't the ground that he was thinking of, but the shadow of protection under which he had always operated. The sultan trusted him. A word would save him – but the word would not come from a sick man, far away in his palace on the Bosphorus. The French ambassador's report would pass into other hands. Yashim's involvement with the archaeologist would seem, at best, foolish. The slur would mark him like a stain on his character, a faint question mark over his good judgement.

He knocked, and waited. After a while the wicket gate opened, and an old Halberdier of the Tresses, a man he knew, welcomed him in without ceremony.

'The validé, it will be, efendi. She's expecting you?'

Yashim nodded. Only a few years ago – it seemed a lifetime – he would have been challenged instantly, and whisked through with the certainty that a hundred pairs of eyes were watching him enviously from behind! The old man fished up a bunch of keys, and led Yashim across the Second Court, fiddling with them in his hand.

'I have 'em all now, efendi,' he said cheerfully. He paid them out as they walked: the key to the kitchens, the key to the stable block. 'This one,' he said, holding a huge iron key up to the light, 'you'd never guess.'

'The grain bins,' Yashim said.

'That's right, efendi. That's the one. The grain bins. Heavier than the grain, now, I expect. This little one?'

'I've no idea,' Yashim admitted.

The old man chuckled. 'I'll show you something, efendi. Just you watch.'

They stopped at a small door set into the further wall of the second court. To their left stood the divan room, with its vast jutting eaves, where the great pashas had discussed the business of an empire which stretched from the gates of Vienna to the Pyramids. Kingdoms had been broken in that hall; armies raised for glory, and defeat; the fate of whole races settled; men had been honoured or destroyed by a word, a sign, a stroke of the pen. Now it was empty.

The halberdier fitted the key into a tiny lock. With a single twist the door swung open.

'Surprised, efendi? That's right, that little key.'

There was no need to say any more.

Yashim went inside. The entrance to the harem was like a street in miniature, open to the sky for the next few yards, with the windows of the black eunuchs' apartments projecting over the paving stones. Only it was a street of perfectly polished marble, with fountains that flowed from niches in the walls; and it was utterly silent.

The door closed behind him. He heard the slap-slap of slippers on the flags, and an old black man in a beautifully embroidered kaftan and a vast white turban came round a corner, fanning himself with a fan made of reeds.

'Hello, Hyacinth.'

'Oy, oy, Yashim. It's getting late.'

'I'm sorry.' Only two or three years earlier, this would have been the most important time in the life of the harem: the hour of gossip and intimacy over food, when thousands of succulent dishes would stream from the palace kitchens to the sultan's apartments; the hour, above all, of the gözde's final preparations, bedecking, perfuming, calming the nerves of the girl fortunate enough to have been selected to share the sultan's bed that night. The whole harem would have fluttered and twittered like a forest of little birds.

The stillness was audible now.

'Ask the validé, Hyacinth, if she will receive me.'

❦ 40 ❦

'*C'est bizarre*, Yashim. As he gets older, my son grows more and more infatuated by the European style – yet I, who was born to it, find that I prefer the comforts of oriental tradition. He hardly comes here any more, only to see me. His new palace delights him. I find it looks like a manufactory.'

Yashim inclined his head. The Queen Mother was propped up on her sofa against a cloud of cushions, with the light as ever artfully arranged behind her head, a blind drawn across the little side-window, and one knee elegantly raised. She walked rarely now, if at all; yet her figure was still graceful and the shadows on her face revealed the beauty she had once been and still, in a sense, remained. Beneath a kaftan of silk velvet she wore a fine chiffon robe whose collar and sleeves were embellished with the most delicate Transylvanian lace; the lace, Yashim recalled, was made by nuns. The swirl of her turban was fixed in place by a diamond and emerald aigrette. Her hands were white and delicate. Did the validé not know that her son was dying at Beşiktaş?

'I am very old, Yashim, as you well know. Topkapi has been my home – some would say, my prison – for sixty years. It, too, is old. Well, the world has moved on from us both. By now, I like to think, we understand each other. We share memories. I intend to die here, Yashim, fully dressed. At the sultan's palace at Beşiktaş I'd be popped into a nightgown and tucked up in a French bed, and that would be an end of it.'

Yashim nodded. She was perfectly right. So many years had passed since a young woman, the captive of Algerian corsairs, had been delivered here, to the harem quarters of the aged sultan Abdül Hamit, that it was easy to forget how well the validé knew the European style. Aimée Dubucq du Riviery, a planter's daughter on the French island of Martinique: she was a Frenchwoman. The same inscrutable law of destiny that had taken her to the sultan's seraglio, where she had finally emerged as validé, had led her childhood friend, little Rose, to the throne of France, as Josephine, Napoleon's own Empress.

A nightgown. A tight French bed. Yashim knew how the Europeans lived, with their mania for divisions. They parcelled up their homes the way they segregated their actions. The Franks had special rooms for sleeping in, with fussy contraptions created for performing the act itself, and all day long these bedrooms sat vacant and desolate, consoled by the dust rising in the sunlight – unless they belonged to an invalid. In which case the invalid herself shared the loneliness and desolation, far away from the household activity.

The Franks had dining rooms for dining in, and sitting rooms for sitting in, and drawing rooms for withdrawing into – as if their whole lives were not a series of withdrawals anyway, tiptoe-ing from one room and one function to the next, changing and dressing all over again, forever on the run from engagement with real life. Whereas in an Ottoman home – even here, in the harem – everyone was allowed to float on the currents of life as they sped by. People divided their lives between what was public, and what was reserved for the family, between selamlik and haremlik: in the poorest homes, they were divided only by a curtain. If you were hungry, food was brought in. If you wished to sleep, you unfolded your legs, reclined, and twitched a shawl over yourself. If you were moody, someone was sure to drop in to cheer you up; ill, and someone noticed; tired, and nobody minded if you dozed.

The validé took the book and raised an eyebrow.

'I may seem terribly old to you, Yashim, but I do hope you aren't wondering whether I knew the author.'

Yashim giggled. The validé reached for a pair of spectacles and put them on. She glanced warningly at Yashim over the rims. 'I have my vanities, *quand même*,' she said.

Yet Yashim was too delighted in the novelty of seeing a woman in spectacles to consider their effect on the validé's beauty. He knew her for a reader, of course; but the spectacles made her seem, well, magnificently wise.

She examined the brown leather cover of the little book at some length, turning it this way and that. She ran a slim finger behind the boards and opened the first page. She tilted her head.

'I do not think,' she said, 'it is the sort of book which would interest us. For a start, it's not in French. *De Aedificio et Antiquitae Constantinopolii*,' she read, slowly. The hand hold-ing the book sank to the cushions. 'Dancing. Deportment. The interminable tragedies of Monsieur Racine.' She paused. 'It was a long time ago, Yashim, and we were educated – to adorn, not to be scholars. I think it's Latin,' she added, with a little shiver.

Yashim, who had already guessed as much, tried to conceal his disappointment. 'I thought – perhaps – you would be familiar with it.'

'Latin, Yashim?' The validé gave a bright little laugh. 'But no, you are right. I'm sorry, it is so long ago.' She ran a finger beneath an eyelid, to wipe away a tear. 'How silly of me. I was thinking of my mother. A very clever woman. Not in my way, of course. She was a dreamer, *idéaliste*. Father wanted us to be pretty. But my mother – she did try to teach us something, beyond dancing and the use of our fans. Even Latin.' She smiled sadly. 'I think it was always too hot.'

She looked up almost shyly. 'I have not spoken of them for many years,' she said.

The validé removed her glasses and set them down on the carpet beside her. 'The edifices and antiquities of Constantinople,' she said, handing the book back. 'I'm not much help. You probably already know when it was published.'

'1560, in Rome.'

The validé gave Yashim a long look. 'There is something going on between you and your friend Palewski, *n'est-ce pas*?'

'Validé?'

She tut-tutted, and wagged a finger. 'Tsk-tsk-tsk-tsk. Palewski is a well-educated man, and he was brought up in a Catholic country. A cold country, where it is easy to learn Latin, among other things. I think his Latin would be better than mine. Why do you not consult him? He is your friend.'

Yashim looked away. 'Monsieur Palewski has put me in an awkward situation,' he said stiffly.

'I see. It was his intention to do so?'

Yashim shook his head. 'No.'

The validé cocked her head to one side. 'Friendship is an opportunity, Yashim, and our lives are short. Have you spoken to him?'

'I have not.'

'*Flûte!* Don't be such a fool, young man. Take this book to your friend.' She smoothed the shawl around her shoulders. 'Now, I am tired.'

She closed her eyes and let out a great sigh.

'Latin!'

❧ 41 ❧

Yashim left the palace gate and crossed to the fountain of Sultan Ahmed. In spite of himself he veered left, passing the domed baths which the great architect Sinan had built for Roxelana, the wife of Suleyman the Magnificent. One of the baths was being used as a store. Weeds, even a little crooked tree, sprouted from the cracked lead roofs.

He went out into the Hippodrome.

There was nothing overbearing in the serpent column's height, nothing to draw the eye: but once your eye was drawn, Yashim had found, it was always hard to look away again. Its very little-ness mocked the pretensions of the greater monuments. Denuded of their plaques, speaking a lost language, they only gestured helplessly at vanished glory.

Three snakes, symmetrically entwined, raised themselves high above the ground. Simple yet intricate. Yashim wondered what Lefèvre's little book had to say about it: *The Edifices and Antiquities of Constantinople*. It would say, presumably, that it had come from the Temple of Apollo at Delphi, the seat of oracular wisdom in the ancient world. But what of the author himself? Would the author have been frightened by those glaring heads?

He would have stood where Yashim was standing now: a scholar, no doubt, learned and dispassionate. He would have gazed on that column, as a marvel from the ancient world; the same way that Yashim looked back across the years to the age of Suleyman – where among the Janissaries and tents, the standards of defeated armies and the milling crowds, he saw the author carefully taking notes.

He shrugged, and turned away. He walked back to the Fener, and took a seat outside the café he liked on the Kara Davut, where he slowly turned the pages of Lefèvre's book, looking for pictures.

When he next glanced up, Preen was coming down the street; he recognised her walk, although her head, he noticed with amusement, was covered by a modest charshaf.

She caught sight of him and waggled her fingers; then she strode up, sat down and flung back her scarf. A number of old men nearby creaked on their chairs, and stared. Yashim smiled. He signalled to the proprietor, who nodded and shrugged.

'The Academy boy,' Yashim prompted.

'Alexander. The picnic set, of course. Caiques up the Golden Horn to the Sweet Waters. Music, wine, and an interest in the Ypsilanti girl, I gather.'

'Decorous,' Yashim murmured.

'So far,' Preen nodded. 'But he enjoys a night life, too.'

'Not so decorous?'

'It's hard for me to say. He's known at various taverns on the waterfront. Kumkapi, a bit, but mostly on the Pera side. Tophane, for instance. Some of those places are pretty low, Yashim.'

Yashim nodded. Tophane, the cannon foundry, had a rough reputation.

'He hasn't been seen much recently, apparently. Someone said he might be smoking.'

'You mean opium?'

'It could happen.'

'It was liquor I smelled on his breath the other day.'

105

'Opium would explain why he hasn't been seen around too much, though. The dens of Tophane.'

'Do you know them?'

Preen arched an eyebrow. 'What do you take me for, Yashim?'

'I'd like to go down to Tophane. There's a piece of information I'd like to have.'

'People go to Tophane to forget, Yashim. They don't like questions.'

But Yashim wasn't listening.

'We can go tonight,' he said.

42

For centuries, Ottoman navies had been refitted and supplied by the arsenal, close to Tophane, which exceeded in size and scope any naval yard east of Venice's own forbidden Arsenale. By day, the district was an inferno of blazing kilns and molten metals, of sailors struggling to unload the ships that came down from the Black Sea with their cargoes of timber and hemp, the mastic boats from Chios, Egyptian flax, Anatolian copper, iron ore from the Adriatic ports: the raw materials of the Empire which served to keep its navy afloat – if no longer formidable.

By night Tophane drew in upon itself. The foundry fell silent; the views across the Bosphorus to the hills of Asia bled into darkness; the cargo ships creaked wearily at their moorings. No lamps were lit in the twisting alleyways, where sailors and brothel-keepers, loafers and thieves jostled and cursed one another in the darkness; only flickering lanterns were hung in small windows, or at the low lintels of a doorway, guiding men to their taverns and drinking holes, to rum and raki and tired couplings on straw pallets and the sweet, cloying smell of the pipe.

Yashim let Preen lead the way.

It was in the third tavern they tried that a Maltese sailor, reddened with drink, abruptly explained to Preen his plans for the evening. Those plans included her. When Preen demurred the Maltese smashed a bottle on the floor and went for her face with the jagged edge.

Yashim blocked the blow with his forearm, which earned him the attention of a party of Maltese sailors who were still apparently upset by the massacre of innocent men, women and children on the island of Chios by Ottoman irregular troops sixteen years before.

'He hit me! The bastard!'

'Baby killer! You murderer!'

Yashim didn't know what they were talking about.

They backed out of the door together.

Preen began to walk very fast downhill. The lane led away from the city and towards the waterfront. Before Yashim could call her back the tavern door flew open and the Maltese party spilled out onto the lane.

They decided they would cut Yashim up for his part in a massacre at which none of them had been present. Some of them flicked knives open. They began to run downhill.

Yashim heard them coming.

He needed to get Preen ahead of the Maltese by one corner, a few seconds to hide.

He grabbed her arm.

At the first turning he glanced at the walls: in the dark they seemed smooth, not even offering a doorway. There was an alley running downhill again, a few yards further on: they had to make that corner before the Maltese saw them. He spun Preen to the right.

'Baby killer! We'll cut you!'

The alley dropped away: there were steps, of a kind. Preen and

Yashim took them three at a time. They were close to the shore.

At the bottom of the steps Yashim bore round to the right: he had a vague idea that they could follow the shoreline and cut back up later.

'There he is! Get him!'

The Maltese were on the steps.

Preen stumbled and screamed.

Yashim caught her by the arm again and wrenched her around the corner.

The wall on their left dropped away: they were on the quay. Ahead he could see the upright poles of the landing-stage, with a single caique resting between them.

If they could just make it to the boat –

A man came out from an alley to the right and walked towards the caique.

'Wait!' Yashim bellowed.

The man did not look round. He stepped into the caique. The rower put his hand to the oar.

Yashim and Preen were twenty yards off. The caique started forwards with a lurch.

'Wait! Help!' Yashim shouted. 'Help me!' He shouted in Greek.

He flung an arm around the mooring pole. The caique was ten feet out. The rower looked at Yashim, then back along the quay to where the Maltese had just appeared.

The man in the caique glanced round. He nodded to the rower and the caique slid back. Preen and Yashim rolled aboard.

As the caique shot forwards again, the Maltese slowed. They jogged along the waterfront, shaking their fists.

'Baby killer!'

Yashim looked up to thank the man, and to apologise.

'We need to get a watchman here,' he said.

The man shrugged.

It was Alexander Mavrogordato.

43

'Thank you for stopping.'

'What are you doing here?'

'I was looking for some people,' Yashim said.

Mavrogordato glanced back, at the quay. 'You found them, it would seem.'

'They were the wrong people.' Yashim rubbed his forehead and took a breath. 'You took me off the case.'

The young man shrugged. 'Mother did.'

In the dark it was hard to tell if he was lying.

'Lefèvre was already dead,' Yashim said. 'You couldn't have known that, could you?'

'Why should I care? A man like Lefèvre.'

Yashim heard water dripping from the scull. 'It was a coincidence, then?'

'You are in my caique,' the young man pointed out. 'That looks like a coincidence, doesn't it?'

'Perhaps. But then – I was looking for you, too.'

'You – you followed me?'

'No. But I heard that you came down here, sometimes.'

'That's not true. Who said so?'

'It's true tonight, isn't it?'

Alexander Mavrogordato did not reply. If he'd been smoking, Yashim thought, he sounded calm.

'Who owns the *Ca d'Oro*?'

The caique rocked as it crossed the wake of a fisherman's boat.

'What's that got to do with it?'

' Is it one of your father's boats?'

'Listen, friend.' Alexander leaned forwards. 'I don't know the old man's business. In six months I will be out of here, God willing.'

'Out of here? Why?'

'That's my business,' Alexander retorted. 'You wouldn't understand. The Fener. The Bosphorus. The Bazaar – you think it's the world, don't you? You all do. And just because the sultan makes a few changes here and there, you think you're living in the most modern place on earth. Rubbish. Constantinople's a backwater. You'd be surprised, efendi. The rest of the world – they laugh at us. Paris. St Petersburg. Why, in Athens they even have gas lighting in the streets! A lot of the streets. They have – politics, philosophy, everything. Concert halls. Newspapers. You can buy a newspaper and sit and read it in a café, and nobody looks twice. Just like the rest of Europe. People have opinions there.'

'And they read newspapers which have the same opinions?'

'Amazing, isn't it? I'm going there, friend. I'll be married, and – I'll go.'

'Your wife – are you sure she'll want to go?'

'My wife? She'll do what I want, of course. I'll give her fashionable clothes, and we'll have dinners and go to the opera, and such like. We'll be completely free. You wouldn't understand.'

Yashim shook his head. The boy was right: if freedom meant taking your opinions out of newspapers and dressing up like everyone else then it was certainly something he would never understand. A pleasure, perhaps, he would never be entitled to enjoy.

'Thank you for stopping,' he said. 'You can drop us wherever you like.'

Alexander growled something that Yashim didn't catch. Probably, he thought, it was better that way.

⫷ 44 ⫸

By day, from the water, Pera resembled a huge crustacean drawn from the sea. On the Stamboul side there were minarets and trees; but over the Golden Horn Galata Hill was grey and dry, encrusted with roofs, the windows of buildings overlapping as they dropped to the water's edge. Patches of greenery still lingered, where weeds and creepers had reclaimed areas cleared out by the fire which had swept through the town four years before; but they would not linger long. Rents were on the rise; fortunes had to be made; new buildings were going up every day, and the Perotes had no use, it seemed, for trees or gardens.

Yashim walked slowly up the Grande Rue. If Pera was a sea creature, the Grande Rue was its spiny ridge, all the way from the top of the steps that led up from the waterfront to the great water tank which gave its name, Taksim, to the district beyond. It was the thoroughfare on which the foreign embassies were built; in the past decade it had become as cosmopolitan as Paris or Trieste. Yashim saw classical stone facades, and big glass windows; shops here sold hats and gloves, liquor, patisseries, umbrellas, English boots. Everywhere he looked, new buildings were plundering the styles of vanished empires and lost civilisations – Egyptian motifs and Roman caryatids. It was rootless – for money has no roots – and it was profuse, eye-watering, ugly and exciting, too, by turns.

The giddy mix of styles was echoed in the street below. In the crowd that swirled up and down the Grande Rue were men and women of every nationality, and none: all the races of the Mediterranean, Arabs and Frenchmen, men in burnouses, men in hats, ladies in heels, broad-shouldered Slavs, punctilious Englishmen, Genoese sailors, Belgian tailors, black Nubians, olive-skinned Druzes from the heights of Lebanon, pale Russians with fair beards, hawkers, loafers, actors, vagabonds, pimps, water-carriers. Two dozen wandering street-sellers cried their wares. A monkey jumped on a barrel-organ. Even a bear shuffled its feet, and looked round at the company with a pleasant grin.

Yesterday he had wondered where the great parade had gone, when it vanished from the court at Topkapi. Not to Beşiktaş, where a sultan lay dying in his European bed.

He pulled the bell of a large, grey stone building set back slightly from the street, and a grey-faced flunkey in immaculate tails answered the door.

'Mr Mavrogordato is at his correspondence. He won't be seeing anyone before eleven.'

'Would you inform your master that I am a friend of the Frenchman, Lefèvre? I want to see him very urgently, on private business.'

The clerk pursed his lips and frowned. The Turk at the door was dressed in the old style, but he was dressed well. Had he been wearing the fez, like any man of business, he would have been easier to dismiss; but his turban lent him a sense of mystery, combined with that air of confidence that clerks were quick to detect. The combination might mean money. Private business, now. Certainly, his master liked to deal with his correspondence undisturbed. But he was not a man to relish missing an opportunity. Private business. Well, private business could mean many things.

'A few moments, efendi,' he said, with a greater show of politeness. 'If you will step inside, I will carry your message in to Mr Mavrogordato.'

The hall was narrow and dark; there was nowhere to sit. Yashim stared out at the street through the glass panes of the door. The sunlit crowd flowed by at a steady rate; someone might stop or dawdle for a few moments, but the movement was strong and eventually picked them up again, to vanish in the stream.

Yashim thought of the book that Grigor had shown him, with its sleeping emperors and ancient prophesies. How futile it seemed, this Great Idea! How shallow, against the deep drift of time and events. Byzantium was long gone. He remembered the old lines the Conqueror had murmured, as he surveyed the ruins of the imperial palace. 'The spider weaves a curtain in the Caesar's palace: the owl hoots in the towers of Afrasiab . . .'

'Mr Mavrogordato will see you, efendi.'

Mavrogordato was small and square with dark hair and a carefully trimmed moustache. He sat with his jacket on the back of his chair, sleeves rolled, his thin, white, hairy forearms resting on a desk covered in papers, like a shipwrecked sailor clinging to a raft. It was hard to guess his age: fifty, maybe. Older than his wife. And Yashim had been right: the boy, Alexander, took after her.

'How do you do? Coffee? Stefan, coffee.' His voice had a rasp to it, and an accent which Yashim could not quite place. When Stefan had left the room he leaned forwards, blinking.

'You have some business interest, ah –' He glanced down at a card on his desk. 'Yashim efendi.'

'The name means something to you?' Yashim asked; but the banker looked apologetic. 'I thought – perhaps your wife . . .'

Mavrogordato startled. 'My wife?'

There was a moment's pause. Yashim fluttered his hands. 'Forgive me. I should explain – Maximilien Lefèvre, the archaeologist.'

Mavrogordato frowned. 'Lefèvre,' he repeated. In a sombre tone he added: 'You haven't heard?'

'I knew him slightly,' Yashim said slowly.

Mavrogordato grunted. 'Hmm. Knew him.' He began to tap his fingers absently on the table.

'I'm investigating his death. Trying to establish some facts.'

'I know nothing about that,' the banker said.

113

'I didn't mean to suggest –' Yashim raised his hands. Even in this office he could still hear the murmur of the crowd outside, the faint ringing of little bells, the rattling of carriages on the cobbles. 'You had met him?'

'I – he came here once. He wished to borrow some money.'

He paused. Yashim said nothing.

'I lent him the money,' the banker continued. 'A small amount.' Mavrogordato paused, as if remembering, then levered himself briskly away from the desk. 'Very unfortunate. But business must go on.'

'Of course, efendi. If I might just ask – did you talk together? He was an interesting man.'

Mavrogordato looked surprised. 'I'm afraid I have no interest in archaeology. Dull of me, I am sure, but I am a man of business. You understand.'

Yashim cocked his head. 'How much did he borrow?'

The banker blew out his cheeks. 'If you ask me, I believe it was two hundred francs.'

'Ah. French money.'

'You know, these days . . . One can't lend piastres.'

'Because . . .?'

'The value, it's too unsettled.' Mavrogordato waved a podgy hand. 'These are financial things, efendi.'

'About which I know so little,' Yashim agreed. 'Is that why he came to you, do you think?'

Mavrogordato gave a deprecating shrug, and picked up a paper on his desk. 'I couldn't say, efendi. I wish you luck.'

'Thank you so much for your time.' Yashim paused, with his hand on the doorknob. 'One final thing I forgot to ask – what kind of security did Lefèvre give you?'

For a moment Mavrogordato's eyes searched the room. He gestured with the paper in his hand. 'He was a Frenchman. It was only a small loan.'

'Yes, of course. He gave you nothing.'

As he closed the door, he saw that Mavrogordato was still watching him, blinking.

45

'Poor bastard,' Palewski said. He glanced through the window, where the bees were dozily buffeting the wisteria. 'Don't you find these summer evenings unbearably sad? It must be my age.'

Outside, a stork clattered its bill; a pair had lately taken up residence on the new pinnacle of the Galata Tower a few hundred yards away.

Palewski bent forwards and retrieved the book from the table. 'Lefèvre must have been very frightened to leave this in your flat.'

'I suppose he thought of it when I went to get him a berth on the boat,' Yashim said. 'It cheered him up, somehow.'

'Thinking it was safe, yes.' Palewski could not quite rid his voice of its contempt.

He stuck his nose in the book and began to murmur to himself. Yashim helped himself to the ambassador's tea and leaned back in his chair, trying to recall Lefèvre's mood, trying to remember their last words. He had got into that caique – how? He could remember that he, Yashim, had been slightly impatient with the whole affair – the money, and Lefèvre's petulance about the boat. After that, he hadn't paid Lefèvre too much attention. He thought he would never see him again.

But Lefèvre must have pondered the possibility. Hence the hidden book. And he had stepped into the bobbing caique and pushed off without a word.

There were many things you could find to dislike about Lefèvre, but you couldn't fault his bravery.

Meanwhile, everyone was shortly going to be invited to think that Yashim had killed him. It didn't matter whether they believed it, or not: just airing the possibility would be enough. Slander was only raised against the weak: nobody flung accusations at people whose power was secure. To be placed under suspicion showed a want of luck on Yashim's part; and nobody in Istanbul, least of all in the palace, liked an unlucky man.

Yashim raised his cup and squinted at his friend through the steam, with a sudden upsurge of affection. Palewski seemed to feel his regard, because he looked up from the book and smiled.

'I can't think what all the fuss is about,' he said. 'I know this book. Petrus Gyllius,' Palewski explained, 'was an antiquarian. Like your unfortunate friend, I suppose. Like him he was a Frenchman. Pierre Gilles. But in those days educated men wrote in Latin, so it's Gyllius to you and me. He came out here in the reign of Suleyman the Magnificent. Mid-1500s, your days of glory.'

Palewski had risen from his seat and was bending down by his bookshelves. He pulled out a couple of tomes, flicked through them one after another, and finally ran his finger down a page.

'Here we are. Gyllius. That's right. Comes out here in 1550 with the French ambassador. Stays on a few years, then all of a sudden he joins Suleyman on a campaign against the Persians. It's an odd interlude, but he gets back the following year and then goes on to Rome. Writes his book, *De Aedificio*.'

'This book,' said Yashim morosely.

'Hmmm. I suppose you wouldn't come by a copy all that easily. 1560 – that's the first edition.'

'There were others?'

'Oh, it's been translated. I've got a French edition, though I can't see it for the moment.'

'No,' Yashim said decisively. 'There has to be something about this copy of the book that's unique. If only I could read it.'

'Leave it with me, Yash. I'll investigate. Quite enjoy it, actually.'

'Watch out for the little notes inside – don't let them fall out.'

The book seemed to have functioned as a hold-all, its pages stuffed with notes and folded papers.

'Why was he murdered so brutally? They hacked his sternum in two, and split his ribs apart.'

Palewski winced. 'God! Like a Viking sacrifice.'

'A what?'

'Viking, Yashim. You've heard of the Vikings, surely? The beserkers? Like your old regiment of the deli – people who turned mad when they went to war. These were the northern variety – red hair, beefy joints, terrific sailors. Exploded out of their fjords about twelve centuries ago. Ships carved like dragons. Primitive range of gods. Blood and thunder all summer: rape, murder and pillage. Long poems about it to keep them happy all winter. Tough wasn't the word. They scuffed Europe into what we call the Dark Ages. Most notable product, after widows: Russia.'

Yashim was leaning forwards, listening intently. Now he shook his head. 'What do you mean, Russia? Or is it a Polish joke?'

Palewski looked pained. 'Not at all. The Vikings didn't just sail across oceans. They used the Baltic rivers, too. Built ships which could sail on a heavy dew. But when they reached the Volga, they didn't have to make their own water. Up the Volga, down the Dnieper. The Black Sea. Constantinople. Easy. They attacked a few times, too. Set up shop in Kiev – a good safe base for their raids down here, and it's been the tradition ever since. In the end, of course, the Byzantines found it cheaper and easier to convert them to orthodox Christianity – their leader took the name Yaroslav and thought he was the emperor's little brother. But he was a Viking all the same.'

'And that's the origin of Russia?'

'Broadly speaking, yes. The origins of Russian orthodoxy. Once they'd got them friendly and half-civilised, the Byzantines used them as an imperial guard, the Varangian guard. All six foot ten and Viking to their hairy toes. Just about the only thing that kept the Greeks safe in Constantinople.'

Yashim started. 'The Varangian guard protected the Greeks? And used this barbaric style of execution?'

Palewski pulled a dubious face. 'Well, I don't know that they still used it then. Perhaps they'd dropped it, along with all their pagan gods. I don't know. But here's a curiosity for you, if you like. The spread-eagle was the symbol of the Byzantine emperors. And after their fall, the Russians began to use it themselves. To demonstrate their kinship. You know, claims to the throne of Byzantium, protectors of the orthodox, all that.'

He paused, and rubbed his hands.

'History lesson over. I don't know that it's been any good. Sun's gone. Let's have a drink.'

He picked his way past the table and opened the door.

'Marta!' He bellowed. 'Vodka, glasses, and ice!'

Yashim smiled.

'I always shout these days,' Palewski remarked affably, from the door. 'Saves me having to say please. Marta's become rather a stickler for the niceties, I can't think why. Anyway, the bell's broken.'

46

It was already dark when Yashim reached the landing stage at Karaköy. Istanbul across the Golden Horn looked strangely unfamiliar, the outline of its hills concealed in the darkness, false heights picked out by the lamps that burned on minarets and domes. For a moment it was possible to believe that the city had been replaced by mountains, their peaks and slopes dotted here and there by charcoal-burners' huts.

He closed his eyes, swaying slightly, and when he opened them again he had the impression of looking across a vast expanse of black water, towards the lamps of distant ships riding an invisible horizon that seemed high up, and far away.

He took the first boat that offered itself, aware that a caique was not a craft for a man who had drunk too much. Its thin, light hull was at best a flimsy wrapper to protect two men from the water which lapped up almost to the vessel's rim. He reclined automatically on the red cushion, shifting his weight to his left elbow to help trim the elegant dark hull. Now he could see the bulk of the city as he usually did, and the warm, low lamplight of the landing stage where the caiques were moored.

The rower fixed a weak lantern to the prow and took up the sculls, pushing the caique away from the landing stage with a practised sweep of his arm. Like an arrow, the lacquered vessel hissed through the water. Yashim let his eyelids sink shut.

The air was warm. Across the water, murmurs and snatches of conversation drifted lazily from the landing stage. The dogs barking on Galata Point sounded close by. Yashim felt the rhythmic tug of the sculls; the water trickled on the hull beneath his head. The rower spoke, but not to him, and there was a faint lurch, a stillness, an absence of the familiar sound. A ripple caught the caique and rolled it minutely. Yashim opened his eyes.

The caique had stopped moving. Very dimly against the lantern light the rower could be seen, his shoulders still: he seemed to be resting on his sculls. The lights of the city travelled slowly round behind his head, like the lights of a fairy carousel. Yashim liked that explanation. For the moment, he could not think of another.

He blinked a few times. The silent boatman, he reasoned, was waiting for him to speak.

A light on the shore snuffed out. When it reappeared on the other side of the boatman's black silhouette, it dawned on Yashim that Istanbul was not spinning; rather the caique itself was turning gradually with the current.

'What's the matter?' he finally said.

The rower didn't move. Instead another voice close by replied:

'Nothing is the matter, efendi. In a moment, if you likes, you continues with your journey. You are good man, I am sure.'

Yashim felt the hairs on his neck prickle. 'What do you want?'

'Yes, yes. A good man.' The caique trembled slightly. In the dark, Yashim realised, another caique had pulled alongside. 'You do not like to have some things what belongs to other mans, no?'

The voice was coming from somewhere behind his head. Yashim was awake now, his mind working fast to construct a picture of his situation. He saw it, as it were, from above: if his rower was leaning on the oars, still spread above the water, the other caique must have come in beside him, unless its oars were shipped. He had a feeling that the anonymous voice in the dark was too close for that. Which made it likely that the two boats were stern-to-stern: he had only to reach out and he would encounter – what? The speaker's hand on the rim of his caique. The knuckles bent over the gunwale.

'Whassat? What'ya talking about?' He hoped he sounded drunk.

'I talks about a book, mister. Is little. Black. Is not belong to you, you understand? But we make it all right. Give me the book, and go your ways.'

Yashim's hand went to his chest. Lefèvre's book was not there.

'Who are you?' he said thickly.

'Please. The book, only.'

The caique gave a little lurch, and there was a metallic click. Something winked momentarily in the darkness.

'What worth your life, efendi?'

It would be very soon. There was little time.

Yashim sat up. He put his hand out for support and brushed against the man's fingers where they clutched the rim of his caique.

On getting into a caique firmly held against a fixed landing-stage or piling by the oarsman, it is possible to stand up for a few seconds.

In open water, when there is nothing to steady the boat and the oarsman is unprepared, you do not have seconds. You have maybe one.

Yashim stood up.

He stepped forward and stamped down, hard.

There was a crack, and the caiques dipped together. As the hull of his caique flipped upwards, Yashim took a step back and kicked himself off into the water.

He flicked the water out of his eyes and released his cloak, letting it float. He brushed the white turban from his head: it could catch the faint light, and he let it go. With his head above the water, he concentrated on staying afloat as silently as possible while three men floundered, cursing, close at hand. Yashim took the hem of his cloak in his teeth and paddled gently backwards; the cloak would protect him, and give him warning if someone tried to grab him in the dark.

He could hear the men more clearly now. One of them was cursing: perhaps the man whose hand he had trodden on. Another was lamenting the loss of his oars. Someone eventually told him to shut up.

With their caiques gone, the men would have to strike out for the shore. The Pera side was slightly closer; they would probably swim that way. Yashim went on quietly paddling until he heard them splashing, and then he released the cloak and turned onto his front. He swam breast-stroke, not trying to fight the current that was bearing him slowly down towards the Bosphorus.

About twenty minutes later, a pair of barefooted chair-men enjoying a quiet smoke outside the New Mosque were surprised to be hailed by a man who squelched towards them out of the darkness. It was a shame the man was so wet, but he doubled their usual fare to the Fener baths. Business had been pretty quiet all evening.

 47

The curtains of muslin and silk brushed together, stirred like a breath by the night air. Sometimes he could see a tiny diadem of stars through a chink close up by the rail, and it came and went, came and went, the way people did when you were dying, looking in to observe the progress of death, to render a report on the invisible struggle; all that was left.

The sultan wondered if this was the way all men died, alone, in doubt, troubled by memories.

He listened to the breath in the room, the woman's breathing, the shush of the muslin against the silk. This would, of course, go on: the world would breathe, without him. His own breath was less; it made no sound; he barely moved. Now that a great sleep was drawing close, he no longer needed sleep. The rehearsals were over.

Out on the water, something splashed. The Bosphorus was full of fish. He imagined himself gliding with them, their cool, metallic bodies holding level, the moonlight refracted through the surface of the water, cold and silvery, and the fish glinting like the stars.

He swam with them easily, borne along by the current and an effort that was minute, imperceptible. Hadn't they always been there, too? Waiting for him – or perhaps not him, especially: for anyone who was ready to come, that night, any night.

He looked ahead; it seemed that his eye skimmed like a shear-water across the dark ripples, zigzagging between the headlands where the hill ridges dropped to the water's edge.

On to where the straits opened out into the restless sea.

 48

Marta half-turned with the tray in her hands and nudged the door open with a sway of her hip. Inside the room was almost dark, and only a thin crack of light between the shutters showed that the morning was well advanced. Palewski's room smelled strongly of candlewax and brandy, a smell that Marta associated with her employer and which she had never learned to properly dislike. The table, she knew, would be piled with books and glasses, so she set the tray down on the floorboards and went to open the shutters she had closed on Palewski and his studies the night before.

Daylight poured into the room, and the bedclothes stirred and groaned.

Marta tugged at the window frame and succeeded in opening it about two inches at the top. For a few moments she stood looking out into the yard. Suela, the Xanis' daughter, was sweeping the ground with a little besom broom; Shpëtin, her brother, played silently in the dirt, rolling a ball to and fro. Marta sighed.

She cleared a space on the chair by the bed, moved the tray to it, and set about collecting the bottles and glasses, returning the candlesticks to the mantelpiece. She was very careful not to disturb any of the books scattered around the bed. The ambassador was a magnificent scholar, after all. Night after night he wearied himself looking into those books of his, and she knew better than to let her carelessness spoil his work. What made his work all the harder was that he possessed so many books, more than anyone had ever seen in their life, so that finding the thing he needed was a real chore.

'A Greek came round earlier,' she said, passing a cup of tea to the hand which had emerged from beneath the bedclothes. Marta, who was Greek herself, invested the word with powerful contempt. 'I told him that you did not admit callers, but he could write and make an appointment.'

Palewski swam up from the duvet and sipped weakly on his tea. 'Very good,' he mumbled. 'Probably some sort of swindle.'

Marta nodded. That was it, exactly. The man had looked like a swindler.

'The water is weak again today,' she said.

'Tea's all right, though.' Palewski put out his cup and she filled it from the pot. 'Thank you, Marta. I can manage now.'

Marta curtsied. Inwardly, she could not resist a smile. The ambassador was a clever man, to be sure; but to manage – no. Beyond his books he was simply a big child.

'Thank you, sir,' she said.

'Thank you, Marta.'

When Marta had gone, Palewski leaned from the bed and groped around on the floor. One of Lefèvre's hand-written notes had fluttered out of the book as he lay reading the night before. He had read it twice before he understood what it was; then he had very quickly snuffed out the candles and rolled up in bed.

Now he opened the book again, and in the cooler light of day he re-read the paper.

Serp. Column. Mehmet II hurled mace – broke off one jaw.
Patriarch of H.S. aghast. 'This ancient and illustrious talis-
man was erected here for the purpose of driving serpents
from Constantinople and, in the event of its destruction, it is
most probable that the city will be destroyed by an invasion
of serpents.' Sultan desists. Heads broken off c. 1700; Polish
noble. ???query.

The word serpent was underlined.
Palewski's legs stirred uneasily beneath the featherbed.

❦ 49 ❦

'Permission to enter?' Yashim stood at the gates, peering round
at the children in the yard. The little girl – what was her name?
– looked up and gave him a brief smile; but Shpëtin tucked his
chin into his chest and stared sullenly at the ground.

'Don't shoot – it's only me,' Yashim said brightly, as he
crossed the yard.

He found Palewski in bed, balancing a cup of tea on his knees.

'I see your sentry's been withdrawn,' he said.

'What? You mean the little boy. Well, I don't know. His
father's gone off somewhere without telling and everyone's feeling the pinch. Mrs Xani is gloomy enough at the best of times,
but it's Marta I worry about. Again. She's quite upset for the little boy.'

Yashim nodded. 'Children like a routine,' he said.

'Hmmm. They'd been going out together recently, Xani and
the boy. A sort of apprenticeship. Then the boy came back rather
late one evening, on his own.'

Yashim nodded. Marta, the little boy: it was obviously a diffi-

125

cult morning for Palewski. He wanted to talk about Lefèvre's book.

'I was attacked last night,' he said.

'My dear fellow!' The ambassador looked shocked. 'The whole place is going to the dogs.'

Yashim told him about the caiques and his unexpected dip. 'They wanted that book.'

'My God! You were lucky. Have a look at this.'

He passed across the copy of Gyllius. On the back page, stamped in green ink, was an oval containing the words in Greek: Dimitri Goulandris, Bookseller.

Yashim gave a dismal snort. 'But Goulandris could barely read himself. He wouldn't have understood anything in the book.'

'Not many people would. But perhaps the killer didn't know that. Didn't know Goulandris, except that he sold books. Including this one.'

Yashim stared at the book in his hands. 'You told me it's not even all that rare.'

'Hmmm.' Palewski was enjoying himself. 'An original copy of Gyllius? I've never come across one. But you're right. Nonetheless,' he added, pointing, 'that copy is quite unique. It's a matter of provenance.'

Palewski put his hands behind his head and lay back against the cushions. 'Take an old book or an old painting. In fact, let's take one of Lefèvre's favourites, say a Bible. Illuminated. Thirteenth century. It's Byzantine. Probably done in Georgia. All well and good – but what would its story be? How would it come to be sitting in the window of a shop in St Germain six hundred years later?'

'Lefèvre would have stolen it, I suppose.'

'Of course he'd have stolen it, but that's immaterial,' Palewski said. 'What matters to him – and his clients – is that this book has spent the last six hundred years, let's say, in a scriptorium in Georgia. Better still: it formed part of the last Byzantine emperor's own personal collection in Istanbul, and then was rescued by the Georgians after the Ottoman conquest in 1453.'

'Giving it a history.'

'It is called provenance. Tells people it's the genuine article. I mean, if the monks liked it and hung on to it, it must be the real stuff. But also, of course, it's the story of the piece. I wager that Lefèvre knew how to tell a story.'

'It is the same with the House of Osman. Anyone could rule the empire – even I. But only the sultan has – this provenance.'

'In a manner of speaking, yes, you're right.' Palewski frowned. 'I suppose when we – the Poles – began to elect our kings, we lost track of the story. Then we lost our country, too,' he added, dejectedly.

'You said this book was unique,' Yashim said quickly.

Palewski rallied himself. 'From what I've seen, I would say that it belonged to Delmonico.'

Yashim shook his head.

'About forty years after Gyllius came to Istanbul,' the ambassador explained, 'an Italian called Delmonico wrote an account of the city himself. He'd been a page in the household of the sultan – the Grand Signor. Knew what he was talking about. But forty years later, Yashim. He was interested by Gyllius, because Gyllius saw the city as it had been.'

'And what was that?'

'Byzantine Constantinople.' Palewski frowned. 'No, that's not quite right. Gyllius is really writing about three cities, one above the other. The first – it's classical Constantinople. Fifth century. Gyllius has got an old book, a description of the city as it stood in Justinian's day. With this in his hand, he goes about trying to identify the old monuments, the old palaces – ruins, most of them. Interesting stuff.

'But there's another Constantinople he's describing, too – the one he's walking around. It's the city that rose up in the intervening centuries – during a thousand years of Greek religion, Roman law, Greek language. Of course, it's changing again, in front of his very eyes. The Ottomans have taken charge. So Gyllius collars old Greeks who can still remember how it was before the Conquest – the name of an old church, for instance, which has been demolished, or turned into a mosque. He's not so interested in all that himself – but we are.'

'I see what you mean,' Yashim agreed. 'And the third city?'

Palewski clasped his hands together. 'The third city, Yashim, is being built around him. Ottoman Istanbul.'

Yashim took the book from the bed and turned it over in his hands.

'It was a time of change, Yashim. Like today, I suppose. You and I watch Istanbul being made more Western, every day. Gyllius recorded the opposite: the remaking of Istanbul along Muslim lines. By the time Delmonico, the Italian, arrived, the process was to all intents complete. The city we have today.'

'And this man – Delmonico – examined Gyllius's book.'

'Of course. To learn what had changed.'

'How do you know?'

'I didn't notice it, until I started reading – he writes in the margin of the text. He used brown ink. I've got Delmonico's own book, and there are pieces I recognise. General observations. No one else was so close to Istanbul, writing in Italian, at the right period. It has to be Delmonico. And that, Yashim, is provenance.'

'You think Lefèvre would have spotted it?' But Yashim knew the answer already. Lefèvre would have known immediately, the moment he found the book in Goulandris's little store. Goulandris would have had no idea.

'I expect he bought it cheap,' Palewski said.

Yashim nodded slowly. 'Somebody writes a book – Gyllius. Another man comes along and scribbles a few thoughts in the margin. Delmonico. Why does Lefèvre think it's so important?'

Palewski threw up his hands. 'As to that, Yashim, I've no idea. He could have sold it for a little more, I suppose, by playing up the Delmonico angle. But it wasn't going to make him rich.'

Yashim thought of the Frenchman, with his neat hands and veiled threats. 'I'm quite sure that Lefèvre smelled money in that book. Did you say you had a French translation?'

'I found it last night.'

Yashim stared down at the book in his hands. 'Lefèvre died because he acted on something he believed in,' he said. 'You reminded me that he believed everything he read in books.'

He stood up. 'Whatever it was, maybe Gyllius believed it, too.' Yashim scratched his head. 'Didn't you say that there was something odd about Gyllius? His going to war?'

'He went east with Suleyman, to fight the Persians. It does seem an odd thing to do, for an antiquarian.'

'Why would Suleyman want him along, anyway?'

'Oh, as to that, I think Suleyman had no objection to foreigners witnessing his triumphs. Let me fetch you the French edition.'

 50

'Yashim efendi. Excuse me, please.'

Yashim looked round. Marta was standing in the shadows below the stairs, knotting her apron between her fingers.

'Marta!' He took a step closer.

'Enver Xani, efendi. He is disappeared!'

129

'I heard, Marta. But you mustn't worry. There are any number of reasons why he might have had to stay out.'

He tried to think of one. A catastrophic leak, perhaps? A crumbling reservoir? He wondered how far the watermen's guild communicated with the families involved: if Xani was being kept on overnight, someone should have sent a message. So perhaps it was really a night out with the lads instead, in the taverns of the port.

Marta put a knuckle to her lips.

'I do not want to trouble the lord ambassador,' she said. 'But perhaps you will help? You are his friend, and a good man.'

Yashim inclined his head. Marta had done him kindnesses in the past: he would not refuse her.

'Mrs Xani says they must pay the moneylender tomorrow. Forty piastres. She has very little money.' She lifted a small red leather purse that hung from the belt slung around her hips. 'I have twenty-seven piastres. It is my money. If they do not pay, the debt will grow worse.'

Yashim frowned. He tried to remember Mrs Xani, but his impression was indistinct: a woman in red skirts, a broom in her hand. Was Marta right to give her savings to this woman? Forty piastres: it was quite a lot of money.

'Can't Mrs Xani ask for time, until her husband gets back? Maybe he can pay off the debt.'

Marta shook her head. 'You don't understand, efendi. Forty piastres is the interest. Every month they pay.'

Yashim pursed his lips together and blew out. 'Forty a month! I don't believe it. How much does Xani owe?'

'Six hundred,' said Marta, lowering her voice. 'Mrs Xani, she is afraid for the children, if they cannot pay the money.'

Yashim knew nothing of the Xanis, but any fool could recognise Marta's gullible good-nature. Marta was fond of the children, Palewski had said. He wondered if it had all been planned: an estimate of Marta's resources, Xani staying away to provide a pretext for this approach. My children, Marta! Oh, I am so afraid! Just forty piastres . . .

'Marta,' Yashim said firmly. 'Xani is a poor man. Where would he borrow six hundred piastres? Why would he ever need so much money?'

Marta almost jumped in surprise. 'Oh no, efendi! Xani is a good man. And a waterman, too. But he needed this money to pay the guild. An entrance fee, you understand, to buy the position.'

Yashim scratched his head. That, he admitted, made more sense. The guild would expect a payment – Xani was a kind of apprentice.

'But now he's not here to pay? It's convenient, Marta.'

'His wife is afraid, when he does not return. Maybe –'

She made a frightened little gesture, sketching a possibility she didn't want to shape aloud.

Yashim tapped his foot angrily on the ground. He folded his arms and looked away.

'And Mrs Xani has no money?'

'No, efendi. She does not. And the lord ambassador is very kind, but – Mrs Xani does not want him to know. You understand, Yashim efendi?'

'Tchah!' Yashim exclaimed. 'Very well. Who is this money-lender?'

'A Jew. He is called Baradossa. He lives in Balat, but Mrs Xani does not know where.'

'Then how does she plan to get the money to him?'

Marta looked down, and stirred the ground with her foot. 'Yashim efendi, I thought – maybe, as a favour – maybe you could take him the money. You could find out where he lives. Please?'

Yashim stamped his foot and said, angrily: 'Baradossa. Balat,

131

forty piastres. Very well, Marta – no, you can keep your money. I'll show you I can be a bigger fool than you or your master. And when Xani gets back, he can deal with me.'

Marta began to protest, holding out her little purse, but he waved her away.

Going out, he almost slammed the door: but not quite. Just in time he had remembered that he should have left ten minutes before.

'Bloody Albanians!' he said under his breath. 'Balat!'

51

Before heading across the Golden Horn to Balat, Yashim made a stop at the kebab shop at Şişhane. At times when he didn't feel the need or urge to cook he often searched out something simple: a bean stew, perhaps, or a tripe soup recommended by his old acquaintance the Soup Master, whose strictures on simplicity were, if anything, more fierce than his own. Yashim was suspicious of elaboration in a public restaurant: like his sauces, the best results were achieved by cleaving to tradition, and using nothing but good judgement and the best ingredients. So many lifetimes had been devoted to the perfection of bean piyaz, or tarator: Yashim had only one. It was a shame to waste an opportunity.

Poor Lefèvre: it had been a mistake to expect the man to know anything. The Turks had been testing and refining dishes when the Franks chewed meat off bones held in their two hands!

The kebab shop was open to the street, where sliced hearts of lettuces were set out on a marble slab beside sheep heads and feet, bowls of yoghurt and clotted cream, some toorshan, or pickles, and a small array of simple meze. A waiter was flicking away the flies with a clean cloth; he nodded at Yashim. Inside, china pots, plates and glasses sparkled on the shelves; a small fountain played in a corner. There was a glazed screen where a man with long moustaches ruled over a small empire of vases containing syrups and preserved fruits; on the other side the grills smoked against the wall, a half-tunnel of brick and clay lined with small coals. Various cuts of meat were on a spit; little skewers sizzled and popped above the flames; now and then the bare-armed cook slapped another pide on the hot bricks, and peeled it away as it began to crisp at the edges.

Yashim was led to a seat in the gallery, from where he could look down on the cooks. He saw the cook swing a spicy köfte kebab from the coals and wipe the meat from the skewer onto a fresh pide. Yashim felt hungry: he and the waiter put their heads together and decided what Yashim would eat. As he sipped his turnip juice, Yashim looked about him. It was a working crowd, he noticed: people who came to eat, not to loaf about with a pipe and a coffee. The sight of a small, stocky man with a shaved head across the restaurant reminded Yashim of an old friend, Murad Eslek. He was a supplier for markets across Istanbul, a cheerful, honest young man who had helped Yashim in a week when it sometimes looked as if the whole city was about to explode with fear, anger – and a sense of loss. Help was hardly the word: Eslek had once saved his life.

It wasn't Murad Eslek, of course, who touched his kebab to the red pepper flakes on his plate and bent forwards to eat; just someone who looked a bit like him. But from now on Yashim looked up when anyone walked in. These images didn't arise by accident, Yashim was sure of that. Eslek the marketeer: he'd be a good man to talk to right now.

Yashim could smell the lamb on the coals, and the clean, singeing smell of the coals themselves. He had nothing against Xani. He would be like the quiet, hard-working men eating around him; a man with a wife, two children, the usual ambitions. Given a chance to escape the grind of poverty he had seized it with both hands. A man to be congratulated, perhaps.

Debt, it was true, was dangerous ground. Yashim's own were debts of honour: to those like Eslek, who had saved his life; to friends who helped him live it; and to others, innumerable, who gave him what he needed because they were good people. But at least Xani's had not been the wasting indebtedness of the poor, the shabby contrivance that leads to penury and the betrayal of one's loves and beliefs. A chance had come. The calculation was sound: with a proper job, the capital could be repaid. It was a shame that Xani had been driven to borrow from a stranger. Perhaps there hadn't been time to make the necessary tour of his homeland somewhere in the Albanian hills.

Yashim's kebab arrived. He took a piece of smoking lamb between the fingers, and recognised its texture: this was good. He put it into his mouth, and with the same hand he broke off a piece of pide. He wondered that he had never eaten here before: he would like to come again.

He glanced down into the restaurant. There was the kebab cook, riddling a grill; another man ladling sweet syrup from a jar for a cooling khoshab: guild members, every one. The waiter had said the water came from the Khorosan spring, and Yashim had a comfortable sense of everything being done well, unhurriedly, according to the proper formula. Xani had taken that step himself, hadn't he? From a common porter, to membership of a noble guild!

Istanbul was a city of water, of course: but salt. Salt on three sides – and half a million people who needed to wash and drink fresh water every day. Paris had the Seine; London the Thames; half the cities of the Ottoman empire were watered by the mighty Danube; but Istanbul – however perfect its setting – had only the Sweet Waters. A pretty name for the measly springs that bubbled up at the head of the Golden Horn. Water for a village.

Pipes and channels, siphons and aqueducts: for fifteen hundred years the city had leeched its water from the eastern hills, where streams ran through the stands of oak and beech. Istanbul itself was a city of trees, of course: the old Janissary Tree which stood at its centre, on the Hippodrome, was like a sturdy root from which the others sprang – the cypresses and the planes, even the great gnarled oak which sprawled out over the water at Galata; but the Belgrade Forest was a wilderness.

It was twenty years since Yashim had gone up there – he was surprised it had been so long. In the time of Grigor and his barbs, when he struggled to stay sane because he was not whole, he would sometimes take a cart-ride to the hills, and walk all day under the shade of the trees. Odd people there, he remembered: the scent in the kebab shop reminded him of the charcoal-burners with their conical huts, and of gypsies with sunburned faces, men who talked cheerfully in impenetrable languages. There were descendants of the Serbs who Mehmed the Conqueror had settled in the hills, and who gave the woods a name. The watermen would have been there, too, though he had never seen them: only the lovely reservoirs they tended, where the water slid out in thin sheets across marble slabs, and frogs had mocked him, coupling incessantly among the reeds.

Yashim knew that Istanbul drew its water from the forest, but he had only a vague idea how the water arrived at his standpipe in the yard, or at the city fountains. Heirs to the traditions of the Roman Empire, whose aqueducts they copied and repaired, the Albanian watermen practised an art so vital and arcane that its secrets were handed down from father to son. And the thousands who drank and washed and cooked and refreshed their tired eyes and ears in the music of the fountains thought no more about it than of the dogs, or the gulls, or the paving underfoot.

That, then, was the secret that Xani had offered to learn. Six hundred piastres, Yashim thought: it was not, after all, so very much.

He rubbed his hands with a wedge of lemon and dipped his fingers in the bowl.

Murad Eslek had not yet appeared. It was a just matter of time, Yashim decided happily, as he dabbled with a napkin, and touched the cloth to his lips.

Just yards from the Balat landing stage the alleyways closed in. He was funnelled between old houses rotten at their base, green with mildew, stepping past mounds of rubbish that spilled out into the passageway, negotiating stones and holes and ducking the laundry strung at head-height. The lanes of Balat were all but impassable in winter; at the height of summer some were wet and squelchy underfoot, the mud green with algae, the stench of rot sweet and pervasive. A few children, whose shaven heads exposed the red sores of ringworm, tagged him up the alleyways. Women in loose turbans which covered their hair and their ears watched him from the doorways of their houses; the alleys were so narrow he felt his cloak brush against them as he passed. From time to time he stopped to ask the way: a rabbi in a long robe, a clean-shaven young man with a yarmulka, an olive-skinned dandy in tight European trousers who lounged by a recess in the wall.

An elderly man with a thin white beard came carefully down the lane towards Yashim, prodding the ground ahead of him with a stick, and now and then touching the wall for support.

'Excuse me, efendi,' Yashim said. 'I am looking for Baradossa.'

The old man touched the wall with his knuckles.

'You need money?'

'I'm paying a debt.'

The old man turned his head away, spat, and put out his stick.

'Do you know where I can find him?'

The old man mumbled a few words, and began to walk away. Yashim felt his fingers tense, and flex.

When the old man had gone, Yashim retraced his steps. Balat was still a maze to him, who had walked over most of Istanbul in his time, but once he found his way to wider streets he remembered how to find Rebecca's store.

Rebecca gave him an ironical smile when he stamped into her shop, setting the bell ringing.

'Yashim efendi!'

She was in her early fifties, taller than Yashim, with a heap of red hair, dark freckles, elegantly plucked eyebrows and astonishingly fine lips.

'I'm lost,' said Yashim brusquely. 'Lost and unwanted. Help me, Rebecca.'

Rebecca laughed. She had three gold teeth. 'You look hot and cross. Let's have some ayran.'

She brushed past him in two strides and stuck her head out of the door. Yashim heard her give a piercing whistle.

Rebecca put her hands on her hips. 'So, you've come to our part of the city. You think it's dirty and the people are unhelpful.'

'I didn't say –' Yashim began to protest.

'No, but I see it. And it's good. If you go into a house here, it is spotless. So clean you could eat off the floor.'

'I know that.' Yashim put up a hand. Rebecca folded her arms. A little boy with a shaved head came in with a silver tray.

'We are the same. Not much to look at, eh? If we are rude, it is like the dirt in the street. Your people do not look for gold in dross. Do you understand what I'm saying?'

Yashim nodded, and took the glass of ayran.

'That is why we are able to live in peace. Not like those Greeks.' She snorted. 'Whatever they have, they like to show it off. If it is jewels, or happiness, they wear jewels or go around smiling. If it is sores and afflictions, the long face and the crazy grief. Today they are your best friend, and tomorrow they want to kill you in the street. A Greek, he is like a child. Every day he forgets. A Jew is a man. He is a man who remembers, every day.'

'Remembers what?'

Rebecca gazed at him and shook her head. A lock of her hair swung across her face, and she slipped it back. 'Ah,' she said, 'that you would never understand.'

Yashim smiled: he knew she was right. Was it Spain, he wondered, whose language they still spoke? That al-Andalus which the Jews – like the Moors – mourned as the Paradise they had lost, treasuring the keys to a vault in Granada, as some old Jewish families did; recalling the pattern of streets and synagogues in Seville? Or was it a promise? Spain was a long time ago. And it must have been many centuries since the Jews had received a sign.

He drained his glass, and placed it carefully on the counter. 'If your memory is so good,' he said drily, 'perhaps you can tell me where a moneylender called Baradossa lives.'

Rebecca pursed her lips. 'You're a glutton for punishment,' she said.

53

Yashim picked his way through the rubbish that had gathered in the courtyard; three tiers of wooden galleries sagged overhead, blocking out the light. The chill air smelled fetid. Yashim knocked several times before a cracked voice demanded his business. He put his lips close to the door.

'I want to talk about a debt.'

'Talk, talk. What is talk?' There was a long silence, then a click. A small hatch in the door opened, and an eye appeared. 'Do I know you?'

'I'm here for Xani. The Albanian. Six hundred piastres.'

'When?'

'About six months ago.'

The hatch slid shut again. Inside, he could hear Baradossa muttering to himself.

The eye reappeared. 'Who's that with you?'

Yashim glanced round. The courtyard was empty.

'I'm alone,' Yashim said.

'Will you step back, and show me your hands?'

Yashim stepped into a windowless room. Baradossa slid the bolts home and hobbled to the far end of a table, carrying a candle. The cold air reeked of cabbages and sweat. So clean, Rebecca had said, you could eat off the floor. He'd have liked to fetch her in.

Baradossa set the candle on the table and rubbed his hands. 'Cold?'

He was a small man, slightly bent, with a grey, bushy beard and small white hands which he held up in front of his chest, like a squirrel. He might have been forty-five, or seventy-five, except that he wore, Yashim noticed with surprise, artificial teeth: they clicked in his mouth when he talked. He was dressed in a dark woollen coat, with a patterned shawl across his shoulders. His stillness was expectant.

'Xani,' Yashim said. 'I've come to pay.'

'Oh yes?' The old man sniffed. 'It's you now, is it?'

'I come as a friend.'

'A friend, is it?' Baradossa rubbed his chin. 'Would that be capital or interest, efendi?'

Yashim reached into his cloak and drew out a purse. Baradossa's eyes flickered towards it. Yashim held the purse softly in his hand. 'Interest. Forty piastres.'

'Forty piastres?' Baradossa sounded surprised.

'Xani couldn't come,' Yashim said.

Baradossa glanced from the purse to Yashim's face. He moved his head slightly.

'Do you know Xani, efendi?'

Yashim shook his head reluctantly. He felt confused. The old man didn't move.

'They asked me to come. The interest is due.'

Baradossa slowly raised his shoulders until they almost reached his ears. Then they dropped.

Yashim counted out the money onto the table. 'Forty piastres.' He looked up. Baradossa was watching him. Then his upper lip peeled back into a grin, exposing a row of little yellow teeth.

'Forty piastres, efendi? What makes you think I want your money?'

He came around the table and put his hands to the bolts, sliding them back.

'He owes you six hundred piastres!'

'Is that what they told you, efendi?' Baradossa swung the door wide open, and peered out.

Yashim felt the surge of goodwill that had followed him from the kebab shop evaporate. His fingers clenched around the French translation. At least he'd saved Marta's little hoard.

'There never was a debt, was there?' It was a statement, not a question. 'Forgive me, efendi.'

He took a last look around the room. At the doorway Baradossa's eye wandered to the table, then back to Yashim's face. Yashim glanced down. It had been there all the time. A sheet of paper, on which was written in a neat Arabic hand the name Xani, and the sum of 600 piastres. Below the rubric, in red ink, a date in the Jewish calendar and the words: *Paid in Full*.

'The month of Tammuz,' Yashim said dully. 'It's just begun.'

Baradossa merely raised an eyebrow.

'So Xani came and paid it off?'

'Who else?'

It was Yashim's turn to shrug. 'Yes,' he echoed. 'Who else?'

The courtyard seemed bright after the dimness of Baradossa's cell. He picked his way downhill through the crooked streets, towards the Golden Horn.

'Who else?' he muttered to himself. A little breeze touched his cheeks; it came off the water. He didn't feel it.

Xani had paid off his debt, out of the blue. And then, almost immediately, he disappeared.

It didn't make sense: the waterman should be enjoying his new-found freedom.

Yashim stopped in the street. Enver Xani, he thought, had disappeared for good.

⊰ 54 ⊱

'I don't know who they were, Yashim efendi. I wouldn't have let them go up if I'd known. There's never been anything like this here, and I've been here for fifty years next April.'

Widow Matalya closed her eyes and shook her head. She was not a woman to give way to hysterics. Yashim stood patiently in the dark hallway, where she had been waiting for him, his head bowed.

'I'm sure you're right, Matalya hatun. Can you tell me what exactly has happened?'

'Two men, my efendi. I heard the door go while I was cleaning. I always do my cleaning in the afternoons. You know that, don't you, my kindly efendi? In the afternoons.'

Yes, and in the mornings, too, Yashim thought. He resisted the urge to hurry. Widow Matalya had had a shock, and she was getting round it in her own way.

'There was a lot that needed dusting, too. Not that I neglect my dusting, efendi, I wouldn't have you think that. But the carpets pick it up, have you noticed? I was thinking it was a good day for beating the carpets, with the sun shining in the yard, and the carpets getting a bit dusty – it must've been ages since they were taken out, I thought, at least not this year. How could I, with all that rain we had in the spring?'

'Much too wet, yes,' Yashim murmured. 'And these two men?'

'I was coming to that, my all-forgiving efendi. It's like I said, I wouldn't have let them in if I'd known. I saw you go out earlier, and that's what I told them. They said they'd wait. Friends of yours, they said.' She clamped her gums together. 'I wouldn't go up there now, efendi. I'll try to make a bit of sense first, that's best. Now that you know, that is.'

'Thank you. You've done everything right,' Yashim reassured her. 'But there's really no need to worry. Please. You just go and sit down, and have a glass of tea.'

He kept talking until he had steered the old lady back into her apartment. He put the kettle on the stove and saw her to the sofa. 'The men – were they Greek?'

'Greek? Maybe, I don't know. They could not have been Muslims, my only efendi. Like animals,' she added, as he closed the door.

Yashim took the stairs two by two. The door at the top of the stairs was closed. He pushed it back with his fingertips, and watched as it swung slowly open onto a scene of desecration.

'Suela, will you tell your mother something? Tell her that my name is Yashim. I am a lala.'

A guardian: he hoped that Mrs Xani would understand. The ordinary eunuchs of Istanbul, the lala, served in families: they acted as chaperones, protectors, messengers and mediators.

The girl nodded as if she understood, but when she spoke in Albanian her mother shook her head hopelessly.

'Tell her that I want to find your father.'

Suela's eyes widened for a moment. She looked as if she were about to cry, but instead she bowed her head and murmured something in Albanian. Her mother raised her red-rimmed eyes and looked sadly at Yashim.

Xani received a salary of forty piastres a month, far more than he had earned as a porter. He had come to Istanbul fourteen years before: he had sold his land in Albania to his brother because it was not enough to keep a family. No, there was no bad blood between them; the brother had supported their marriage, twelve years ago. Both parents were dead. She had a mother living, who had been pleased with the match.

'So the family have no enemies in their village?' Yashim asked. 'No feud?'

The woman spoke. Suela said: 'When Shpëtin was a baby we went to the village. We went in a boat. It was very far.'

'Where did you stay?'

'At my uncle's house. I have four cousins, two boys and two girls. I like the girls very much. We played every day.'

'And here you have Shpëtin to play with.'

Suela nodded doubtfully. Shpëtin was six; Suela was growing too old for little boy's games, perhaps. Yashim pressed on. 'Do you have family in Istanbul?'

'My father's uncle was here, but he was old and he died. My father was – he – was very sad.'

Yashim sat back, keeping his eyes on the ground. Instinct told him that Xani's disappearance had nothing to do with the family: it was entangled, somehow, in events in the city, in the debt. 'I want to ask your mother, has anyone been to see you in the last few days? Anyone asking for money?'

But nobody had.

'And in his work – your father is happy?'

'My mother says he is happy. He is proud to be a waterman. I think – I think he works very hard.'

'I am sure. Your mother – she doesn't know where he might have gone?'

Suela gave her mother a frightened glance. 'No.'

'Friends?'

The girl looked uncertain. She repeated the question to her mother, who merely shook her head and looked sadly again at Yashim. 'Istanbul,' she whispered.

'My father and mother do not have friends in Istanbul,' Suela explained quietly.

Yashim pulled at his lip. 'You say he liked his job, and he worked hard. Did he work the same hours every day?'

Suela screwed up her face, to remember. 'In the beginning, he was always at home for supper. But he stayed at work very late, before he – he . . .' Her lip trembled.

'I understand,' Yashim said quickly. 'Every evening, or just sometimes?'

'Just sometimes.' Suela turned to her mother. The two spoke together for several minutes. When Suela turned to Yashim her chin was tilted.

'My mother says that he stayed out quite late three times last week.'

'Do you know why?'

Mrs Xani cast vaguely around the room. 'My mother,' Suela translated eventually, 'says that they had problems with the water.'

'Yes,' said Yashim slowly. 'Yes, I think there have been some difficulties.'

He got up. He wanted to add, your debt is paid. But the words stuck in his throat, as if they carried a meaning that no one wanted to hear.

Yashim descended the hill by the Sublime Porte and crossed in front of the New Mosque, where he had found the litter-bearers the night before. Passing the entrance to the Egyptian bazaar he hesitated, then plunged in. The rich aromas of cinnamon and cloves, of cumin, coriander and pounded ginger made his head whirl. Mountains of vividly coloured powder rose on every stall, pungent spices gathered from all across the world, from the coasts of India and the mountains of China, from Persia and Arabia and the islands of the South Seas, brought here to this great entrepôt of the world's trade by dhow, by carrack, by camel train and mule train, over deserts, through wild seas, crossing the passes of legendary mountain ranges, bartered and bought, fought for and pilfered, growing ever more valuable and rare until, at last, they reached this market on the edge of Europe, and vanished into a soup, or a dish of rice.

Yashim paused, dizzied by the reflection. What a world men had made! What adventures they undertook, simply to give colour and pungency to their diet! The bazaar was a treasure-house – yet nothing would be changed if a wind scattered the powders to the skies; no one would starve; empires would not fall. The very stones of the bazaar would reek of spices a thousand years from now: what of it?

For something as trivial and evanescent, men could be killed. For an idea as immaterial as the scents which rose from the multi-coloured hillocks of ground seeds, people were prepared to die. An immigrant in the city, struggling to better himself and provide for his children, disappeared: for what? Nothing stolen, as it seemed. No one ate better. But perhaps an idea had been realised, a dream had been served. Lefèvre: dead in the street. No money on him, nothing taken. Killed for a book, perhaps: a few scraps of observation about a city that no longer existed, the thoughts and memories of men long since dead and gone. The city still lived and breathed and ate and slept. A pilaff could be eaten without saffron.

He left the spice bazaar by the northern gate, to wind his way through the alleys and arcades of the Grand Bazaar. He bought a new shawl and examined some old Korassian carpets; he dithered over a selection of English padlocks, before deciding that he didn't need one, bought some plain china plates, and finally walked home through the book bazaar. Goulandris's shop was shuttered up.

Widow Matalya and her ladies had done a thorough job. The floors were scrubbed. The walls had been whitewashed again, and they glowed in the golden afternoon light. His landlady had found a carpet for the sofa, and replaced some of the cushions, but the empty bookshelves looked skeletal. Of his kitchen and its stores, only the metalware remained, iron pots and knives. The room smelled of soap.

Yashim sat down on the edge of the sofa and unwrapped a tiny parcel from the Egyptian market. The folded paper contained a single yellow block of ambergris, the strangest substance in the pharmacopoeia of spices, and so rare that one sultan had been censured for using it on his beard. Ambergris was gathered from the Atlantic ocean, hundreds of miles away: taken, so Yashim had heard, from the belly of the whale.

Its odour was sweet, yet not cloying; it was also irresistible, all-pervasive, the strongest, most penetrating scent in the whole world. Yashim lay back on the divan, with the tiny lump of ambergris resting on his own belly.

Slowly its scent stole out across his bare room, possessing it invisibly, permeating the air.

57

Stanislaw Palewski had tucked himself up in the window seat of his sitting room with a glass at his elbow, Gyllius in his hand, and a bottle not far away, before he became aware that there was something unusual about his room.

He looked round, mystified. He glanced out of the open window. The girl, Suela, was sitting under the tree, watching her brother playing in the dirt with a stick and a concentrated look on his face. Palewski sniffed the air, then his glass. His gaze fell on the sideboard, beneath the oil portrait of Jan Sobieski, the victor of Vienna. He looked at the sideboard for quite a while, and then, with a puzzled grunt, he got up and went over to look at the flowers.

Marta had made a very beautiful vase of late-flowering tulips, the Turkish sort, with frilly petals. It seemed to Palewski, as he ran his finger over the surface of the sideboard, that she had polished that, as well.

He went back to his seat, wedged himself into it with his knees up and his feet against the shutter board, and took a drink.

It was all very extraordinary, he thought to himself. Poor

Marta! This business with Xani must be upsetting her more than he'd thought.

Where the devil, he wondered, had the wretched man got to?

58

Yashim riddled the stove, threw on some coals, and blew on them until they caught. While the charcoal heated, he unpacked his basket. Flour, rice, oil: he had bought replacements, but he would have to look for some new containers. A pat of butter, wrapped in paper. He frowned, thinking ahead: he had forgotten pepper.

He went to the window and looked down into the alley. It was empty. He leaned further out and shouted: 'Elvan!'

He went back to the fire, took out three ripe aubergines and wiped them with a damp cloth. He laid them on the coals, then took a knob of butter and dropped it into a small pan. On an impulse he lifted the pan to his nose and sniffed: it smelled perfectly clean, however, so he put it down guiltily on the side of the brazier, where the butter would melt.

He turned the aubergines, and went back to the window. 'Elvan!'

The butter was sliding off across the pan, so he stirred it with a wooden spoon, watching it begin to bubble. He took a big pinch of white flour in his left hand and began to sift it slowly over the butter, still stirring; as he watched it began to form soft crumbs, and then a yellow ball.

He took the pan off the heat, turned the aubergines again, and went to the window.

A small boy was standing in the alley with his hands on his hips.

148

'Elvan! It's me, Yashim!'

The boy looked up.

'Some milk, please. And white pepper, if you can get it,' Yashim shouted. Elvan held up a hand, Yashim flipped a coin, and the boy dived and caught it, as he always did.

When the skins were charred Yashim swaddled the aubergines in a cloth. He sharpened a knife. After a minute or two he began to scrape the skins with the edge of the blade. Underneath the blackened skin the flesh was white; he remembered Mavrogordato's arms on the desk, and pulled a face.

Elvan came in with a jug of milk and a screw of pepper.

'You remembered, white?'

'Of course, efendi.' The little face took on an expression of injured innocence, and Yashim laughed.

'You may keep the change,' he said.

He wiped the aubergines with a soft cloth, then pounded them in the mortar. He warmed up the pan again, and slowly began adding the milk, drop by drop.

In the French embassy in Pera the ambassador would be penning his report. Word by word the case against Yashim would form, and swell, in the smoothest diplomatic style: accusing no one, implying much.

There was a tap on the door. Yashim frowned. 'Elvan?' He called, not taking his eyes off the pan.

He heard the click of the latch, and felt a prickling at the back of his neck.

Very carefully he set the pan aside. He glanced at the door, slowly swinging inwards, then at the knife on the block.

'Who's that?' he called. 'Who's there?'

59

Madame Mavrogordato's face was set. At the opposite end of the long table, Monsieur Mavrogordato cast her a furtive glance, and helped himself to a dish of lamb.

Madame Mavrogordato watched the footman place the dish on the side-table.

'You may remove Alexander's setting, Dmitri. When he comes in, he can eat in the kitchen. And tell him that his father wants to see him.'

'Yes, madame.'

Dmitri withdrew. Monsieur Mavrogordato picked up his knife and fork.

'So!' Her voice was like a milled edge.

His hands froze in mid-air.

'So! You can eat!'

'We have to eat, Christina, or we'll die,' said Monsieur Mavrogordato unhappily. His knife wavered uncertainly over the lamb.

Madame Mavrogordato stared him down. 'Sometimes, Monsieur Mavrogordato, one must choose between disgrace and death.'

'Now, Christina, please . . .' He put the knife and fork down gently by his plate.

'Disgrace, Monsieur Mavrogordato,' she intoned. 'This time I want you to speak to Alexander. If he carries on in this way, he will earn a reputation for himself.'

Mavrogordato nodded.

'A reputation, Mavrogordato. And the Ypsilanti girl is almost seventeen.'

Mavrogordato nodded.

'We cannot allow the match to fail. The Ypsilanti may not be so rich, but they have –' Her head quivered gently. She could not quite bring herself to say the word.

Mavrogordato nodded. He blinked. After a pause he picked up his knife and fork. 'A strange fellow came to see me today,' he said casually.

Madame Mavrogordato did not reply.

'He was – ah – called Yashim. I believe he was a eunuch.'

Five minutes later, when Mavrogordato's lamb had congealed on the plate, he wished he hadn't changed the subject, after all.

⊰⊱ 60 ⊰⊱

Yashim picked up the knife and took a few steps towards the swinging door.

A woman was standing in the doorway. She wore a blue travelling cloak edged with satin, its hood drawn up to hide her face. A foreigner. Her hands were loosely clasped in front of her. A small carpet bag, with a leather handle, lay on the floor beside her.

Yashim's fingers relaxed. He took a step back.

The woman reached up with both hands and pulled back the hood. Brown curls tumbled around her shoulders, and a pair of steady brown eyes met his.

'You are Yashim efendi, *n'est-ce pas?*'

Her voice was soft and light. Yashim nodded, unable to speak.

'*Très bien.* I am Madame Lefèvre. Where is my husband?'

Yashim felt the blood pounding in his ears. He heard himself say, '*Entrez, madame, je vous en prie,*' and he bent down to take her bag. She moved at the same moment, and their shoulders brushed together.

Yashim gestured to the sofa.

Madame Lefèvre glanced around his apartment and Yashim

noticed how tall she was, almost his own height. She crossed the room with long-legged grace, smoothed her cloak behind her and sat down on the edge of the divan. With a shake of her head she ran a hand under her curls to free them from the collar of her cloak. Beneath it she wore a dress of sprigged cotton; the toes of her black pumps could be seen peeping out from below the hem. The evening sunlight reddened her curls and caught the curve of her cheek. Her eyes, Yashim noticed, were huge.

She gave him a tired smile. 'Please,' she said, reaching for the bag. It was in Yashim's hands. He had forgotten it.

He laid it on the floor, close to her feet.

'I was cooking,' he said, shyly. 'When you arrived.' He didn't know what else to say. He looked down and saw the knife in his hands. He turned away to put it down. 'Madame Lefèvre. I had no idea.'

She pulled a face, which meant 'What can I say?'

Yashim passed his hand over his brow. 'And you, madame – you have just arrived in Istanbul?'

'From Samnos, only. I was cataloguing some of my husband's finds.' She laid her finger on the tip of her nose, and closed her eyes. 'Imam bayildi! I smell the aubergines.'

Yashim blinked in astonishment. I must tell her, he thought to himself. I must tell her now, before it's too late.

'Not imam bayildi,' he said, raising a finger. 'Hünkar beyendi.'

"Hünkar beyendi,' she repeated. 'Tell me again, what does it mean?'

'It means – the sultan approved.'

'And imam bayildi? The imam fainted?'

Yashim smiled. 'Yes. He was so happy.'

'Ah, yes. And when you cook – hünkar beyendi? – are you not happy too? Or do you merely approve?' She pulled a frown, like a sultan, then undid the clasp on her cloak and jumped lightly to her feet.

Yashim laughed. 'No. I am – I am happy then.'

'Forgive me,' Madame Lefèvre said. She glanced around his little kitchen. 'I have interrupted your happiness.' She saw the milk jug, and peered into the pan. 'You are making – it's a roux, *n'est-ce pas?*'

'We call it miyane.'

'If we're quick, it will not be too late!' Madame Lefèvre swept her hair off one shoulder and seized the pan. 'You stir, monsieur – and I'll add the milk.'

Stop her, Yashim thought. Tell her what she has to know.

He took the pan and laid it back onto the coals, stabbing the ball of flour and butter and milk with a spoon. It was still warm: Madame Lefèvre was right, he needed to carry on or it would spoil. Madame Lefèvre took up the jug and carefully allowed a drop into the pan, and then another, and another. They faced each other across the handle of the pan. Madame Lefèvre looked up, and her eyes were smiling.

'Look, it's working!'

The miyane began to spread across the bottom of the pan. A little milk slipped down the outside of the jug and dripped onto the table.

'There,' he said. 'Stop.'

He reached for the pepper. 'We always use white pepper,' he explained, 'for the beauty of the dish. It should be very pale.'

He felt awkward as he said it: he was aware of her own pale skin.

'*En effet*, it's a béchamel,' she said.

'It's a very old recipe, in this part of the world. Butter, flour.'

Madame Lefèvre looked interested. 'A nomadic dish? Why not? Perhaps we learned it from you?'

'Well,' Yashim hesitated. 'I think so, yes. Maybe not directly.' This was one of his pet theories – how had they got onto that so soon? 'The Italians were in Pera. Perhaps they brought the idea to France.'

153

'Catherine de'Medici,' Madame Lefèvre said.

'I think so!' Yashim grinned with delight. 'I read it in Carême – listen!' Then he remembered. 'At least – I had it before.' He went to the shelves. 'Carême, here we are!' He flicked the pages. 'I was just reading this. *"The cooks of the second half of the 1700s came to know the taste of Italian cooking that Catherine de'Medici introduced to the French court."* Perhaps you are right, Madame.'

It was her turn to laugh. '*Mon dieu!* Carême !'

'It's lucky I still have it,' Yashim admitted. 'I lost a lot of my books recently. Yesterday.'

'You were robbed?'

Yashim smiled. 'It doesn't matter. Nothing important lost. But I'm afraid the apartment is a little bare.'

'I didn't think such things would happen, in Istanbul,' Madame Lefèvre said. 'Max always tells me how safe it is.'

Max? Yashim frowned: she must mean her husband.

'Madame Lefèvre,' he said, 'Istanbul is not safe. Not safe at all.' He balled his fists. 'I have some terrible news.'

Her eyes widened. 'What are you saying, m'sieur? Not safe? But what do you mean?' Her voice rose. 'Where is Max? Where is my husband?'

'He's dead,' Yashim said.

 61

Widow Matalya went out into the yard with the big fan she used for beating her carpets, to shepherd her chickens into their run.

'Come along, pretty one,' she crooned. She put out a leathery hand. The hen crouched close to the ground, its feathered shoulders raised. The widow took it gently in two hands, lifted it under her arm and snapped its neck.

'You were too old anyway,' she said, admonishingly.

She carried the hen through the house, picking up a basket from behind the door, and sat down on a small stool in the alley. The sun had gone, but the wall was still warm against her back. She began to pluck the hen, dropping the feathers into the basket.

'Soup's best,' she muttered to the hen. 'And this one makes a good stock. A bit of rice. Nice, after a shock.'

She turned the bird on her lap and began to snatch the under-feathers from its breast.

'Not but what I'm in shock, too,' she went on. The hen's head dangled over her knee. 'It's a disturbance, and not at all what I expect at my age. A foreign woman, too. An unbeliever – in my house!'

She gave an angry little twitch and tore the bird's skin.

'Now look what I've gone and done.' She paused and made a shape with her fingers, against the Evil Eye. 'She ought to go to her own people, poor thing. No husband now, and such a way from her own mother!'

She worked over the legs, and then the wings. She wondered how many chickens she'd plucked in her life. It must be hundreds. Not that she was greedy. She fed them and they fed her, and that was the way it was.

How she'd howled when Matalya died! A full day, a real clamour. She was that upset! Not the way it took those Frankish women, perhaps. Thin blood, it might be.

Widow Matalya made a mighty effort of imagination: perhaps you needed to be around your own people to properly let go, she concluded.

And there was no denying, it was good to have a bit of soup, for when you got a shock.

62

Yashim dabbed vaguely at the skin that had formed on the miyane. The fire was almost cold: he felt no urge to start again. He wasn't really very hungry.

He looked around for a bit of bread, or a biscuit, but of course the place was bare.

He climbed onto the sofa and sat with his knees drawn up, looking out of the window across the rooftops.

Miyane! It was what you made when a guest showed up unexpectedly: a thicker mix, of course. You turned some pasta into it and ate it cut up into chunks.

Madame Lefèvre had been, of all things, wholly unexpected.

Lefèvre had not been the man he would have imagined for her; he had seemed too cagey and underhand in his manner. Whereas his wife – but there, he hardly knew what to think. She had struck him as beautiful: he who walked permitted and unaffected through the sultan's harem, among dozens of women selected from every corner of the empire for their loveliness alone.

More than her beauty had affected him, of course. She had talked to him like a friend. They had even laughed together, as if they had known each other already a long time.

She had made him laugh.

And he had been too intoxicated to say what he knew had to be said. Too cowardly to break the spell.

The widow had a kind heart. She would answer for the moment, but tomorrow he would have to see Madame Lefèvre to her own people – the embassy again. He winced at the idea.

Mavrogordato. What had he learned from Mavrogordato?

Only that a Frenchman, in a European suit, could raise the kind of loan from a respectable banker that an Albanian in the same city struggled to raise from a loanshark. Two hundred francs!

Yashim stopped dragging at his hair.

Two hundred francs: as far as Yashim knew, that was about six hundred piastres.

63

It was not yet completely dark when Yashim reached Balat. Dim figures brushed past him in the alleys; doors banged; a little boy carrying what Yashim recognised to be a box of paper leaned his burden wearily against a wall, then hoisted it up again and pressed on. The Jews, he thought, are coming home.

The idea caught him by surprise. From all over the city, the Jewish poor were streaming home with the fading light. The boy with the paper would be at his post tomorrow, soon after sunrise, crying 'Carta! Carta!' all day long the way the paper-sellers did on the Grande Rue. There were, now he considered it, so many little trades in the city from which the Jews could draw a precarious living. They shone shoes, they sold flowers, they collected scrap paper and metal; they went out young – and they came home late, plodding through their broken alley-ways and dirty streets with a few piastres for the family purse. The Jews were city-dwellers: they worked the streets like furrows on the earth, stumbling back to Balat as if it were their village. Yashim had seen villages more filthy and decrepit than Balat, too.

He paused to remember the way, then set off down a dispiritingly narrow, twisted alleyway as fast as he dared: he wanted to reach the moneylender's courtyard before it was dark.

The courtyard was silent. Overhead, he could make out the

dark tiers of balconies, and here and there a stray line of light to indicate a drawn shutter. He knocked softly on the door of Baradossa's cell, and then, after a minute's silence, he knocked more loudly.

He took a few steps back, and almost tumbled on a broken tile. A shutter banged open above, and a woman's head appeared silhouetted against the dim light.

'*Que es?*'

'I'm looking for Baradossa,' Yashim called back. He had no Ladino. The head disappeared and an arm reached out to pull the shutter to.

Yashim scuffed the tile with his slipper. Nobody came. Another fragment of tile lay on the ground at the side of the door: it must have slipped from the roof of Baradossa's lean-to porch. Yashim gave up waiting for the woman to reappear and bent down to look at the tile. He wondered why it had fallen.

He went back to the opening of the courtyard and looked up the wooden staircase leading to the balconies. The stairs creaked as he climbed. He followed the balcony to the corner, passing a couple of doors, and found himself looking down onto the little pantiled roof.

He could just make out where the broken tile had come from, about halfway up the roof where there was a gap like a wound between the tiles.

There was no light showing from the room beneath.

Yashim snaked over the balustrade, which rocked dangerously, and placed his feet on the pantiled roof.

He descended the slope cautiously, keeping his feet on the ridges. Then he squatted over the gap and quietly lifted the overlying tile. He raised the next one a little, to let it slide out, and set it down gingerly beside him. He slid his fingers into the gap and the underlying tile came away with a dry rasp. The battens were about eighteen inches apart.

High overhead a door opened and he heard a woman's voice; it was suppressed but full of anger. A man answered brusquely, from along the balcony; the door slammed shut and the man came heavily down the staircase. On the first-floor landing he turned unsteadily. Yashim saw him put his hand on the balustrade and lean forwards, as if he were peering into the dark; then he took a step backwards, straightened up, and sighed. Yashim relaxed; after a few moments the man adjusted himself and lurched back to the staircase. He went down into the courtyard and out into the alley beyond.

Yashim put his weight on the battens and eased himself into the hole in the roof. At the last moment, as he was trying to hold his position, he lost his grip and slithered roughly between the battens, falling several feet onto the floor below.

He stood up, rubbing his knee. He nudged a table, and his fingers crawled over it until they encountered an oil lamp. Yashim picked it up, and shook it gently. On a ledge by the door he found a box of matches, but the hiss of the match igniting frightened him, as though it identified his position: he swung round with the match above his head until it burned his fingers. He put the lamp on the table, removed the mantle, and struck another match to the wick. When the blue flame began to spread he dropped the mantle back and trimmed the wick. A dim glow illuminated the room.

He expected to see a couch at the back of the room: on his first visit, in the candlelight, it had been impossible to see the farther wall. Now he could see that another room, maybe a set of rooms, lay beyond a door in the far corner. It occurred to him that Baradossa might still be there asleep, in spite of his knocking; in spite of the noise he had made coming through the roof.

The book was lying on the table, exactly where it had been before. Yashim opened it with his free hand and flicked the pages until he found what he was looking for.

Xani. 600 piastres. There were five entries below, with dates, recording the monthly receipt of forty piastres. At the bottom, in red ink: 200 French francs: Paid In Full.

Yashim raised his head and listened. He heard voices overhead, and then – incongruously – the tramp of feet on stone, as sounds from the courtyard were filtered through the hole in the roof. A man spoke, close by. Someone knocked on the door; it sounded as if they were using the head of a stick.

Yashim listened intently. There were several voices outside, in the courtyard: anyone roused to look down over the balconies from one of the overhead apartments would see the light shining through the hole he'd made in the roof. Yet he felt a great reluctance to put out the lamp.

There was another possibility. He went over to the inner door and put his ear to it. There was no sound. He turned the handle slowly, pushed back the door, and stepped inside.

Baradossa was at home.

He was sitting bolt upright on the floor, arms raised in front of him, staring at Yashim. What had been his chest was nothing but a bloody mess. Yashim had seen many corpses in his time: but what unnerved him were the teeth. They seemed to be starting from his face, as if they had grown.

The lamp slipped through Yashim's fingers. He clutched at it: the burning mantle scorched his hand and separated from the lamp, which shattered on the ground. With a sullen whump the oil on the floor ignited. Yashim jumped back. The old moneylender leered at him from the floor.

Yashim raced to the front door and flung the bolts.

'Yangin-var!' he roared. Stamboulists knew to dread that cry. 'Fire! Fire!'

Yashim's natural instincts were to help douse a fire, but not this time. A group of men outside started back in astonishment as Yashim barrelled past. One, more quick-witted than the rest, made a lunge for his cloak; Yashim twitched it away and pelted for the street, not attempting to look round.

He ran, without stopping, until he reached the Fener, his own district. His heart was pounding.

The Jew had been killed that afternoon; no later. In rigor, Baradossa's mutilated body had slowly stiffened, raising itself from the floor on which it lay; the tendons in the arms had pulled tight. And Baradossa wore artificial teeth – they had sprung open and slipped forwards in the dead man's mouth, a horrifying chaplet of wire and bone: the grin hadn't been meant for him.

Whoever killed him had escaped the way Yashim had gone in: through the roof, leaving the door locked from the inside.

And a book on the table.

A book which demonstrated, beyond all doubt, that Xani had had a friend. Someone who had discharged his debt in good French silver. Two hundred francs.

Yashim's thoughts turned to a Frenchman, now dead, whose wife was asleep in Widow Matalya's apartment.

He went in quietly through the front door, into the silent house.

❧ 64 ❧

Yashim slept badly. In his dreams he saw Baradossa's livid face, and the teeth protruding; then the dead man's eyes turned dark and as the flames rose he saw it wasn't Baradossa but the brazen serpent that was staring at him in all the terror of victory. And Lefèvre was there, cramming his money into the serpent's maw.

When he woke up, it was with a nagging doubt in his mind.

He lit a lamp and took out Gyllius's book in French translation.

All other cities have their periods of government, and are subject to the decays of time, he read. *Constantinople alone seems to claim a kind of immortality and will be a city as long as humanity shall live either to inhabit or rebuild it.*

He turned the page. Gyllius described the layout of the city and its walls, discussing Aya Sofya in detail, with reference to ancient sources. There were a few remarks about the Hippodrome, and the Serpent Column: Yashim made a pencilled note beside them, intending to check against Lefèvre's copy.

He could feel his concentration slipping. First someone had surreptitiously searched his flat, leaving nothing more than a few scattered grains of rice; next time they had smashed it apart. He thought of some of his books with a pang of anxiety. For Yashim, regret was an emotion which held nothing but danger, and he had long ago succeeded in achieving a distance from it. But books were the glory of Ottoman art, and he had some he treasured. He flicked through Gyllius's book and opened it at random.

The Cistern remains. Through the inhabitants' carelessness and contempt for everything that is curious it was never discovered, except by me, who was a stranger among them, after a long and diligent search for it. The whole area was built over, which made it less suspected that there was a cistern there. By chance I went into a house where there was a way down to it and went aboard a little skiff. I discovered it after the master of the house lit some torches and rowed me here and there across through the pillars . . .

He read the passage again, wondering what it could mean. *Never discovered, except by me.* Typical scholars. What of the man whose house stood over the cistern – had he not discovered it? With a skiff, no less! Yashim smiled to himself: scholars were all the same, at all times, in all lands.

He was very intent upon catching his fish, with which the Cistern abounds, and speared some of them by the light of the torches.

Yashim blinked. An underground lake, full of fish? He wondered how the fish would taste: pale, perhaps blind, their flesh would be insipid. More likely, Gyllius had simply made the whole thing up.

But the image stuck with him as he lay there in the dark, trying to sleep: of a man rowing under Istanbul in a little boat, spearing fish by torchlight.

⪻ 65 ⪼

Widow Matalya bobbed from foot to foot. She didn't know what to suggest: the Frankish lady had woken up hours before, but whenever she looked in she said nothing, simply stared at her with sad eyes. Eventually Widow Matalya brought her something to eat, and a glass of tea.

The woman sat up in bed. 'Chai,' she said, shyly.

Widow Matalya nodded, encouragingly. She pointed to the plates one by one. 'Bread. Cheese. Olives. Eat up,' she added. 'It's good.' She patted her stomach. Then, quite unconsciously, she stroked the girl's cheek. 'I know how it is.'

The Frankish woman gave her a small smile. Widow Matalya sat down on the bed, encouraged.

'Even for me, it was a shock. We have them and then we lose them. Why should we be surprised? The men, always racing to and fro – one day they're just little boys, and the next – well, they're gone. But at least –' She checked herself, for once. At least they leave something behind, she had been going to say. But she couldn't presume. She took the little white hand in hers, and patted it. Then she picked up an olive and popped it into the girl's mouth.

The woman said something. Widow Matalya smiled and nodded. 'That's right. There'll be a lot of crying to be done, and you could do with building up your strength.' She carefully broke a bit of bread and dipped it in the olive oil. Frank she might be, but she was like everyone else, like a little bird. A pretty little bird.

'This is good bread. The olives are good,' she said kindly. 'Learn to smile again! You're barely twenty-five, I'd say, and who knows what Frankish gentleman wouldn't jump to that smile?' She put out a hand and stroked the girl's hair. 'And you've got lovely hair, I'll say that for you. You're a real peach.'

The girl put her hand over the old woman's and held it there, pressed against her hair, with her eyes shut.

'She'll live,' Widow Matalya later told Yashim. 'But it's a cruel shame, efendi. She is very far away from her own people. The only word she knows is chai. Not that she asks, she's very sweet. But can you – can you talk to her?'

He met her in the yard at the back of the house: Widow Matalya had thought it somehow more proper. Madame Lefèvre was sitting on the stump of an old column, under the shade of a fig tree, wearing a new blouse and the skirt she had worn the day before. Her thick curls were held up in a ribbon, and her neck was bare. Even though her eyes were red, Yashim thought she looked very lovely.

'Madame Lefèvre,' he began. 'I am – I am so sorry.'

She cast her eyes to the ground. 'I had not expected . . .' She trailed off. Then she looked up, tilting her chin. 'You have been very kind, monsieur.'

Yashim looked away. He rubbed a fig leaf between his fingers. 'I meant to tell you straight away. And did not know how.'

He heard her breathe. 'Please tell me – how it happened.'

He told her. He spoke about his Thursday dinner, the first time they had met, making it sound as if they had become friends. He told her about the way Lefèvre had reappeared, afraid, and the way he had sought his help, with the story of the ship, and the caique, leaving out little.

'You sent him to his death,' she said, trembling.

Yashim inclined his head. 'I had no idea,' he said. 'It seems to me now – I think he went to meet someone. Before he left.'

Her eyes searched his face. 'It would be like him,' she said. 'Forgive me, efendi. You did your best.'

Yashim thought that nothing she could have said would have made him feel so small.

'I shall take you to the embassy,' he said.

'The embassy,' she repeated dully.

'Your people, madame,' he said. 'They can take care of you.'

She bent down to slide her finger between the leather and her stockinged foot as if there were something there. She straightened up. She let slip the ribbon from her hair and with a shake of her head let it fall in a cascade over her shoulders.

'I am sorry, Monsieur Yashim. I am Amélie Lefèvre. Nobody – least of all an embassy – takes care of me.'

 66

The man with a knife moved easily through the city. Its blade was very bright and very sharp, and it hung openly from his belt without a scabbard.

Sultanahmet. Bayezit. It was the hour of prayer: from the

minarets overhead the muezzins were calling the faithful to their devotions. The man didn't hear them. He didn't notice the crowds, streaming towards the mosques. He skipped the turning towards Bayezit and carried on at a loping run towards the third hill. The crowds meant nothing to him: they could not impede him as he moved across the city, always at the same pace, making the familiar turns.

Now Bayezit was behind him.

He knew this, although his eye was fixed on darkness. This, he thought, would be his single contact today with the people who sifted and surged through the city streets.

He would fulfil his errand, and the crowd would still move in its appointed rhythm. The city's appetite would remain unchanged.

It would pray, and wash, and drink and eat: because it was bigger than a single man. Like a scoop of water taken from a tank, the fate of one man would make no difference to the people of Istanbul: they would close over his head like water.

And the secrets would be preserved.

Fener. At Fener he moved from the darkness into the light.

Still the people would not bother him. He had an errand to fulfil.

He followed the instructions. He located the door, which was unlocked. He did not think the door would be locked.

He went in quietly: so quietly he could easily hear the murmur of an old woman talking to herself.

He found the stairs, and they were dark and enclosed. They suited him.

At the top of the stairs there would be another door.

And the weight of the dagger which he drew from his belt felt comfortable in his hand.

67

Yashim flopped down into the old armchair in Palewski's draw-ing room. The ambassador sat on a stool, cradling his violin. Now and then he plucked one of the strings and fiddled with the pegs.

'Doesn't like the heat,' he explained. 'Or neglect, for that mat-ter. Gone very dry.' He picked at the four strings.

Yashim grunted. 'Lefèvre was paying Xani off.'

'Very decent of him.'

'I imagine he had an ulterior motive.'

Palewski bent over his fiddle and started turning a peg.

'The thought occurred to me. Lefèvre could have sidled up to Xani and promised him a fortune to find out if the serpent's heads were really here. But Xani hasn't been in the house for weeks.'

'And the fortune, as you call it, was already paid. Lefèvre wouldn't have necessarily known that Xani wasn't around here much. But now Lefèvre's dead – and Xani has disappeared.'

'Do you think he got scared?'

Yashim ignored the question. 'Have you checked the serpent's heads are still here?'

Palewski looked up at the ceiling. 'Do you know, Yashim, the one treasure I possess outright? That's actually mine?' He picked up his bow, leaned forwards on his stool, and tapped the door of the sideboard. The door swung open without a sound. Behind it stood a bottle. It was squat and green and had a heavy cap. 'My father bought a whole case the year I was born,' Palewski said. 'Martell, through Berry's in London. The last bottle.'

Yashim sighed. 'The heads, Palewski.'

'Funny you mention it. I moved them from the armoire just yesterday. Terribly heavy. Put them under my bed.'

'Good idea,' Yashim said.

'I thought so. On the other hand,' Palewski added cheerfully, 'I seem to have acquired a guardian angel. Someone who doesn't want me to lose them. Kills Lefèvre. Kills a mouldy old bookseller he dealt with. Kills the Jew, who could connect Lefèvre with Xani. Xani disappears. Maybe he's dead, too. And so the trail goes cold. I keep the heads.'

He closed the sideboard with the tip of his bow.

Yashim rolled his eyes. 'Maybe you're the killer, Palewski. You have the most obvious motive.'

'Motive, yes.' Palewski smiled and laid the violin down. 'But you, Yashim, had the better opportunity.'

'We're in danger, Palewski. Perhaps Marta, too.'

His friend looked up. 'Marta? She doesn't know about the serpent's heads.'

'So you say. But they don't know that, do they? I think you should send her away for a while.'

'I will,' Palewski said doubtfully. Both of them knew instinctively that Marta would refuse. 'And your Madame Lefèvre?'

'My Madame Lefèvre, as you call her, was never involved. Anyway,' he added, glancing at Palewski's violin, 'she's staying with Widow Matalya. Not with me.'

He reached forwards and picked up the violin to miss the expression on the ambassador's face.

'I should talk to Xani's people, I suppose. Maybe they know where he is, or where he's likely to have gone.'

'The watermen's guild?' Palewski looked doubtful. 'They're very close, from what I gather. Oldest guild in the city, all that. I don't suppose you can just drop by for a chat.'

'I wasn't intending to. I do have a few contacts, you know,' Yashim said stiffly.

68

Yashim found Amélie Lefèvre on his divan with a book in her hands.

She jumped up when he came in.

'Monsieur Yashim!'

'Madame!'

They both stared at one another. Then both began at once:

'I was curious –'

'I didn't expect –'

Amélie was the first to recover.

'I felt lonely, Yashim efendi. The door was unlocked, and I found some books. French books.'

She held up a slim volume. He took it, and read the title on the spine. De Laclos: *Les Liaisons Dangereuses*.

'I've never read it,' she said.

'It's unlucky,' Yashim replied.

'You believe that?'

Yashim slipped the book back into the shelves. 'I read it once. I liked it, very much.' He pushed against the spine with his thumb. 'Six, seven people died.'

'And now?'

'Three men have died,' he said. 'One was a bookseller. One was a moneylender. Your husband was the third.'

Amélie flinched. 'My husband,' she echoed. She drew her arms over her knees and rocked back and forth on the divan. 'Tell me. Tell me who the others are.'

Yashim sat down beside her, trailing his arms between his knees.

'There was a bookseller,' he began. He told her about Goulandris.

'So who killed him?'

He let his head hang.

'I thought – for a moment – it might have been your husband.'

Amélie stood up. 'Max?'

'Please. Monsieur Lefèvre paid for information. The man he paid has disappeared: I think he's dead. He owed money to a moneylender. Your husband paid him off: two hundred francs.'

'You know so much,' Amélie said. She sounded bitter.

'The moneylender I found last night,' Yashim pressed on. 'After you came.'

'So Max paid for information. What of that?'

'The moneylender was dead.'

Amélie went to the stove and leaned over it. She turned. 'I don't understand. Max – this bookseller, the moneylender. You didn't like him? My husband.'

Yashim blinked in surprise.

'He wrote to me about you,' she said. 'He thought that you were his friend.'

'I thought – I thought that we were alike. In certain ways.'

'You!' She snorted. 'Max was many things, yes. But he was a man.'

Yashim thought: she is alone, her husband dead. He gestured to the divan and she sat down where she had sat that first night, when they were friends.

'I am sorry, monsieur. Please forgive me.'

'I am making coffee,' Yashim said. 'Will you have some?'

She nodded, and Yashim turned gratefully to the stove.

'A man came here,' she said. 'He opened the door.'

'Yes? Who?' Yashim measured the coffee into the copper pot.

Amélie bit her lip. 'I don't know. He just sort of – stared.'

'Did he say anything?'

'I tried French – then a little Greek. But he just backed away.'

'How was he dressed?'

Amélie pursed her lips. 'He looked like a bandit, really. He opened the door with a knife.'

Yashim felt the hairs prickle on the back of his neck.

'A knife?'

Amélie laced her hands under her chin. 'Forgive me. You and Max – you are alike, I think. He likes to find things out.' She paused, then corrected herself. 'He liked to, I mean.'

'Yes.' He dug the pot into the coals. 'I only wish I knew what he'd been looking for.'

He turned and looked at her. It was a question. Their eyes met: she shook her head and shrugged.

They must have been a strange couple, Yashim thought. She seemed so – fresh, with a face that told him everything he wanted to know. How had Lefèvre found her? In their country, Yashim knew, people took their pick. What made her choose Lefèvre, then, with all his secrets? The assignations. The hints. And the hidden life, too: this Amélie. She was the most surprising secret of them all.

'Your husband didn't tell you why he had come?'

'To meet some people he knew.' She looked uncomfortable.

'People?' He had been under an impression that Lefèvre worked alone.

'Some Greeks, I think. We were working on Samnos.' She hesitated. 'You see, we had the money my father left me when he died. At least, I thought it was so – but Max, he was unlucky on the Bourse, and of course, even a small archaeological dig can be expensive. So there was a problem for us. Max hoped he could find some people here, in Istanbul. To help.'

The coffee bubbled. Yashim lifted the pot by its long handle and let the grounds subside. He poured two cups.

'He saw Mavrogordato, the banker,' he said. Amélie said nothing. Yashim brought the coffee to the divan, passed her the cup and took a seat. Lefèvre had raised some money; he just hadn't taken it back to Samnos. Then something frightened him, and he tried to reach France.

171

It would seem he'd been prepared to abandon his wife.

Yashim frowned. Was it possible to believe that of Lefèvre? But if not, what else did he have planned when he stepped into the caique, in the dark?

That was always the starting place to which Yashim returned again and again: the walk through the deserted streets, the lights of the caiques glimmering on the Golden Horn, and the upraised hand: Lefèvre's farewell. A brave departure: so he had come to believe. But with Lefèvre nothing was truly certain.

'How long were you married, madame?'

'Five years.' She pushed back her curls; her ear looked small and delicate, like a tender white fern. 'I wanted to be an archaeologist, too.'

Yashim saw it clearly: a clever young woman, a reader, a scholar – why not? Men of her own age would shrink from her: she wouldn't encourage them. And then Lefèvre arrived: older, established, and talking of archaeology and Troy and the things she read; believing them, too. Believing what he read in books.

For her – the life she wanted. For him, a loyal *assistante*. With an inheritance, even.

Perhaps, Yashim thought, Amélie knew how to read a book better than a man's character.

'I'd always been fascinated by the ancient world. Max brought the Greeks back to life.'

'The ancient Greeks, yes.' He thought of the Serpent Column, the three snakes intertwined in what – victory? 'And he was interested in the later Greeks, too – the Byzantine Greeks.'

Amélie pulled a face. 'We used to argue about that. He said the Byzantines were degenerates. He called them – Asiatics.'

Yashim smiled. 'A word can't hurt. What did you think?'

'I said they were a spiritual people. You only have to study their mosaics, their icons, to appreciate that. Max wouldn't agree, though. He said he'd had too many Greek friends to have

172

any illusions about the Byzantines. The same people, he said. It made him sick to hear them talk, sometimes.'

'He understood Greek, did he? Modern Greek?'

'Oh yes. He spent years in Greece, in the twenties. That's what turned him into an archaeologist.'

Greece in the twenties: the revolutionary years. It was extraordinary, Yashim reflected, how many Franks had been drawn to that country. Millingen – and that English poet Palewski had mentioned, and now Lefèvre. Dreaming of the ancient Greeks, Millingen had said. Were all of them disillusioned, then? Discovering instead a race of – what, childish Asiatics?

What did these people expect? A race of Socratics? The ancient Greeks had killed Socrates themselves, hadn't they? Why should the modern Greeks be any better, or any worse? Or better or worse than other men? Everyone was new: every man, every woman, came innocent into this world.

Yashim was an Ottoman. The Ottomans had always understood that men acted for good or ill not because they were Greek, or Serb, or peasants from Anatolia: but because they chose a path for themselves, selected the tools they wanted on their journey through life. Sometimes the choice was limited. But many a great pasha – many a Grand Vizier – stroking his beard in the Divan as he formulated some great policy of the state, had sprung from the humblest origins. Greeks, Bulgars, Serbs – you gave the right man good tools, and he would make them work for him.

To love Greece – and hate the Greeks: only a Frank, Yashim thought, could make such a ridiculous blunder.

He thought of the man with the knife.

'What will you do now?' He had to ask.

'I will help you find the men who killed my husband,' she said. Exactly as he had expected.

Just as he'd feared.

'I have to go to the palace,' he explained. 'Don't go out.'

173

69

A girl came in, bearing mint tea and baklava on a tray. 'It's these girls I am sorry for,' the validé remarked. 'They have so little to do with everyone gone to Beşiktaş. But they know that I can't go on for ever, so. Eat these pastries, and tell me about the big city.'

Yashim told her, sparing none of the details he knew she would enjoy. He told her about the gruesome murder near the Grande Rue, about Goulandris and his adventure in the caique and the two men who had come to destroy his flat. The killing, and the attempted assassination, interested her; but she was transfixed by the details of the men's bestial behaviour in his apartment.

'*Quelle sacrilège!*' she murmured, quite horrified. 'To think that there are men capable of such acts! It must make you proud.'

'Proud, validé?'

'*Mais, bien sûr.* Only a milksop has no enemies. To be hated – that is a mark of character. Hold by your friends, take risks, and – *écraser les autres à la merde!*' She raised a delicate eyebrow. 'I did not become validé as a reward for *politesse*, Yashim. But these days people are far too timid and polite. It's good to hear you talk, even if the details are inappropriate for an old lady's ears. Go on, have another pastry. I have no appetite.'

'I hope I haven't spoiled it,' Yashim said.

The validé cast him a mischievous look. 'Not at all. Perhaps you have restored it. What are you reading? But of course, your collection is destroyed, and you have come to me for a book.'

'No. It's something else I want, validé.' He saw the corners of her mouth harden. 'For the sake of the archaeologist, your compatriot,' he began, sweetening the story with a little lie, 'I'd like to consult with the master of the watermen's guild.'

That 'consult', he thought, was a good touch.

174

'*Et alors?*' The validé gave a little shrug. 'I am so out of touch, my friend.'

It was Yashim's turn to use the mischievous look. 'I don't think so,' he said.

The validé suppressed the beginning of a smile. '*Enfin*, I may be able to write a note. The sultan's bostanci, I suppose, could help – he deals with the watermen all the time. He's an old friend, though he goes by some other title these days. Commissioner of works, or nonsense of that sort.'

She knows his new title perfectly well, Yashim thought. She sits here, in a palace half-deserted, and not a thing that goes on here or in Beşiktaş escapes her notice.

The validé rang a little silver bell. 'Notepaper, and a pen,' she told the girl who answered. 'In the meantime, Yashim, you may read to me a little from this book. I don't understand it, and I don't think I like it. But it also makes me laugh. So don't be afraid – I shan't be laughing at your accent.'

And with this whisper of a challenge, the faintest tinkling of her spurs beneath the raillery, she held out a copy of Stendhal's *Le Rouge et le Noir*.

70

'Tell me,' Yashim said. 'Tell me about the ancient Greeks.'

Amélie was lying face down on the divan, her head in the sunlight, resting her chin on her hands. Yashim heard her giggle.

'I could talk for days,' she said. She moved her head so that her cheek was resting on her fingers, and looked at him. 'Let's do a swap,' she suggested. 'I'll tell you about the finest hour of ancient Greece, and you tell me about your people. The Ottomans. Their greatest moment.'

Yashim cocked his head. 'Agreed,' he said. He crossed his legs and sat by her in the window. 'A time of war? Or a time of peace?'

Amélie smiled. 'War first,' she said.

'Ah, war.' Yashim straightened his back. 'The sultan Suleyman, then. Suleyman, the Giver of Laws. In French – the Magnificent. He is twenty-two when he leads our armies to Belgrade. The White City – impregnable, lying between two rivers, the Sava and the Danube, defended by the hosts of Christendom. It is a long and a weary march . . .'

He told of Suleyman's victory at Belgrade and his conquest of Rhodes two years later, of his prowling the borders of Austria, and humbling Buda.

'You look different when you talk like that.'

'Different?'

'Fierce. Like Suleyman.' She nestled her cheek against her palm, and her hips moved against the carpeted divan. 'Tell me about peace.'

'I'll tell you about a poet,' Yashim said. 'In a time of poetry – with a sultan who surrounds himself with poets. Every night they hold a divan of poetry, each man trying to outdo the other with the beauty of his words. Rhyme, metre, the highest expressions of love and sadness and remorse. But the sultan is better than them all.'

He heard Amélie give a little snort. He glanced down. Her eyes were closed, and a light skein of her brown hair had fallen across her cheek. She was smiling.

'Ah, but he was,' Yashim insisted. 'He was a poet of love – because of all our sultans, he was the one who loved one woman most. He had hundreds of women – the most beautiful girls from Circassia and the Balkans – but one he loved beyond all the rest. She had red hair, and pale white skin, and dark, dark soulful eyes. She was – they say she was a Russian. Roxelana. He married her.'

176

He bent forwards and softly recited the lines he knew by heart.

Amélie lay still for a few moments. 'What was his name? The poet-sultan?'

'Suleyman. Suleyman the Magnificent.'

She opened her eyes and sought him out. He was very close.

'The same sultan,' she murmured. She arched her back and raised her head, until she was looking at Yashim.

Slowly, hesitantly, she moved closer to him. Her eyes flickered from his eyes to his lips.

Yashim felt himself weightless, like a feather in the wind.

Their lips touched.

Her arm slipped around his neck. He put out a hand and touched the curve of her hip.

It was a long time before either of them could speak.

'You were going to tell me about the Greeks,' Yashim said.

Amélie smiled and touched a finger to the tip of his nose.

'Right now,' she said, 'I'm more interested in Ottomans.'

≪ 71 ≫

Sunlight slid across the divan as the afternoon wore on.

He broke away from her once: from her interest. She had understood. She soothed him back to her with little cries, like a bird. She had put her fingers to his lips.

'Max never kissed me like that,' she said, finally.

He left her reading the Gyllius: it was the least he could do.

'Remember, Gyllius is writing about a vanished world. Perhaps something in this will spark a memory.'

He caught a last glimpse of her on the divan: her hair in the sun, a finger on her chin, and the curve of her hip like a wave that could drown him.

Palewski was not at home; Marta said he'd gone for a walk, and invited Yashim inside to wait.

'I'll sit out here,' Yashim said.

He wanted the light – he needed air. He had walked all the way, hoping to drive the agonising tedium from his limbs, breath into his constricted lungs. It was no good: Amélie that afternoon had invaded him, opening the space in his mind which he kept always closed.

He sat at the top of the steps with his back to the wall, in the sun, watching the little boy playing in the yard. He was kneeling by the front wall and digging in the earth with a stick.

The little boy didn't look up when Yashim came and squatted down beside him.

He carved the stick into the dirt again, then laid it flat and began to polish the sides of the trench he had dug, a short, shallow trench which sloped gently from one end to the other.

At the lower end the boy had dug a small hole in the ground. He laid the stick aside and began to smooth the sides of the hole.

When it was done to his satisfaction he sat back on his heels and surveyed his work. Yashim gave him a smile but he did not receive it.

The little boy stood up and walked away.

Yashim stared at the figure on the ground, puzzled.

The boy was gone a few minutes. He came back carrying a jar and a ball. The ball was made of tin and had a big dent in it. The boy placed the ball in the trench, with the dent uppermost. Very carefully he stood the jar on its base and began to tip water from the jar into the trench. The ball floated a short way then it rolled over slowly and came to rest on its dented side.

The boy sighed. He looked up at Yashim for the first time and there were tears in his eyes.

'It's only because the ball's got a dent in it,' Yashim said quietly.

The boy looked down, but made no effort to touch the ball.

'I can get you another one, just like it,' Yashim said.

The boy didn't move.

'Where did you get this one? From your daddy?'

The boy looked up, and his head seemed to shrink into his shoulders. He doesn't speak, Yashim thought: his words are soundless shapes inside his head.

Yashim stood up, and held out his hand.

'Show me,' he said.

⋘ 73 ⋙

Amélie lay on the divan, fiddling with a lock of her hair, her attention focused on the old book her husband had left behind in Yashim's flat.

She read quickly, sometimes skipping whole pages, sometimes turning the book in her hands the better to read the tiny brown scrawls which decorated the lines and margins of the text. Yashim was right: hers was an expressive face, and so as she read her expression changed. She frowned and bit her lip; she smiled; and once, holding the book with one finger between the pages to mark her place, she got up and walked around the little apartment with an anxious glance at the window.

When she had finished examining the book, she sat up, quite still, with her hands in her lap and a deep, faraway expression in her clear brown eyes.

The boy walked fast, without turning his head. When they struck the crowds Yashim stumbled against a porter too tired and over-burdened to complain, as the boy darted through a cloud of women in charshafs ambling, ample-hipped, along the water-front.

Yashim dodged round them instead, craning his neck to keep his eyes on the boy's shaved head. A willowy girl with a shawl across her head and face stepped between them and for a moment he lost sight of him – but no, there he was again, his shoulders stooped against the sea of people coming down the Horn, stubbornly making his way through without a backward glance as if he were afraid a spell would break.

Yashim wondered if the boy remembered he was following. They crossed the bazaar quarter. In front of the Patriarchate at Fener the crowd thinned. The little boy flung himself uphill, following a maze of alleys where Fener gave way to the Jewish settlement at Balat to reach the summit. There, not half a mile from Yashim's home, and about fifty yards shy of the hilltop on the farther side, he stopped and looked round for the first time.

Yashim caught up with him, panting from the effort.

'You move fast,' he said. 'I had no idea we were going so far.'

The little boy's eyes slid from Yashim's face to a low, white-washed building across the street, and back again. Yashim turned his head to look. There were no windows, only an out-side staircase made of stone, with a rendered balustrade, climbing from the street to a small wooden door.

The boy heaved himself up onto a low wall and sat kicking his legs, with his chin in his hands, looking at the door. Something easy and practised about the movement made Yashim think he had done it many times before. Finding a place to sit, swinging his legs, watching. Waiting.

Yashim glanced back at the little door, high up in the blank wall across the street.

'It's through there, is it?'

The taut little face didn't move.

'Stay here, then. I'll be back in a minute.'

The boy's glance dropped to the ground. *Stay here.* Is that what Xani used to say? Were those the words his father used?

Yashim glanced about. The street was empty. He crossed to the stairs and climbed up. At the top he looked round. The boy was gone.

Beyond, over the roofs, he could see where the hillside dropped to the ancient walls of the city, those great brick-banded walls which had been built by the emperors a thousand years before; and beyond them the hills of the Belgrade Forest.

The door was bolted, the hasp secured by an iron padlock.

Yashim hesitated. He glanced back to the wall where the boy had sat, and reached into his shirt.

Long ago, in another life, Grigor the archimandrite had shown him how to pick a lock.

Yashim slid the bolts and the door swung open without a sound.

75

The crowd absorbed her, as Amélie had known it would. She stayed close to a group of women in charshafs, holding the shawl up close to her face, her hand touching her nose, as they walked lumpily down the Golden Horn. Porters came past, bowed beneath terrific parcels, sacks of grain, chests.

In front of the Spice Bazaar she changed direction and began to make her way up the street that led from the New Mosque to the ancient Han of Rüstem Pasha. The crowds were thinning now; around the han, where merchants sat cross-legged in front of their shops, she attracted the odd glance. It was hard for her to walk like a Stambouliot woman, and now she was walking on her own.

At the han she turned into the cobbled lane which ran beneath the walls of the Topkapi Palace. Glancing up, she recognised the enclosed balcony from which the sultan had always inspected marches and processions; ahead, she could make out the swooping eaves of the fountain of Ahmed III, its marble panelling chased with Koranic verses.

The sight made her feel thirsty.

 76

It took Yashim a moment to focus his senses as he stepped through the doorway. Outside he had been hot, breathless, caught in the dust and the heat of sloping alleyways where the ground balled in broken rubble beneath your feet and the sounds of the city were never far away.

But as his eyes adjusted to the faint light from overhead, his ears were tuned to a new and gentler sound, the bubbling of water and its liquid echo from the walls and roof. The sweat cooled on his skin, and he raised his arms to embrace the air. When he breathed, deeply, it felt as if the air was cleansing him from the inside. He felt an urge to laugh, to step forwards through the dim light and plunge himself into the glistening black pool that was spread out at his feet.

Yashim brought his arms across his chest, rubbing his hands up and down.

The big tank was fed, as far as he could see, by a spigot set in the wall, and at various points around its edge the water shimmered over into smaller tanks, like basins. In the great tank the water seemed black until it spilled across the lip: this is how the water is divided, he thought, observing the way the basins were set against the walls, each basin higher than the next, each one letting the water gurgle across its lip to the basin below.

Yashim went forwards cautiously, balancing on the broad rim of the great tank.

He glanced back at the spigot. Water was pouring from it in a steady stream: it seemed impossible that a single spout like this could serve so many people across the huge city – the standpipes and the fountains. Unfaltering, never-ending, the stream twisted and flexed as if it were alive. Looking round, Yashim could see the small openings set in the walls where the flow was channelled out across Istanbul: a series of little black mouths, like snake-holes. Some of them were stopped with rags. Some were open.

Yashim shuddered involuntarily. It was cold in the siphon.

On the lowest basin of them all, about six feet beneath the tank where Yashim was standing, lay the mouth of a low tunnel, far larger than all the rest, into which the water skimmed so broad and shallow that its motion was imperceptible.

Yashim descended from basin to basin, treading on the rims, feeling the air grow colder with every step.

The tunnel puzzled him. Even if all the outflows, the little pipes, were blocked by rags, the tunnel would never come close to overflowing: the largest amount of water that could flow down it came from the spigot above. He glanced up. Its discharge was no thicker than a man's arm.

As he watched, a silver ball dropped from the spigot and floated gently across the great tank.

And at the same moment a great shaft of light illuminated the

183

tank, the basins of water, and sent huge ripples of their reflection across the walls and roof.

The door swung open.

And in the eruption of the glare, Yashim did the only thing he could. He ducked down and made a dive for the tunnel.

Far away, at the other end of the city, Amélie stood back and shielded her eyes with her free hand, like a woman trying to see far off on a sunlit day.

Very slowly she turned her hand to let her eyes travel upwards, every moment revealing more details of the celestial form of the greatest building ever raised on earth.

She saw the great, bronze doors that were cast two thousand years before in the sands of Antioch. The pilasters, sculpted from marble, gleaming white in the sun. The windows of the tympanum, black and small and crisp, their decorative ironwork all but invisible in the glare, and the great arch curving above them, slender as a bird's wing, strong enough to assume the weight of the great dome.

She saw, and did not see, the graceful minarets that fluted upwards from the squinches of the dome.

She saw the red ochre of the great drum overhead, pierced with windows to admit the light. She saw the lead cappings of the dome.

And at the top, high above, she saw a silver crescent on its slender rod: a crescent that stood where the cross stood for a thousand years, before the last days of May 1453.

In the last days, the cross had glowed with an eerie light. It had been concealed by fog. It saw the sky turn red and the crescent moon glow like a sliver in the dark, with the Ottomans readying themselves outside the walls, preparing for a final assault.

Slowly, Amélie lowered her hand.

She had seen the Pantheon, in Rome: a tribute to Roman strength and the Romans' faith in concrete. She had seen the shattered remnant of the Parthenon. She had lain awake at night, willing herself to dream of the Pyramids, whose massive and enigmatic bulk she had met with in the great work of the Napoleonic savants.

But Aya Sofya was a case apart: the last and grandest gesture of the ancient world.

And the world had been trying to measure up to it ever since.

She raised her arms, to frame the vision between her two hands. There was, she thought fiercely, only one more thing that remained to be done.

She began to walk forwards, towards the Great Church.

⊸≪ 78 ≫⊶

Yashim pulled himself into the tunnel like a snake disappearing into its hole. Light from the doorway danced and sparkled on the walls: ahead lay only darkness.

Two steps. Five steps. He was deep inside now, crouched in the dark. He turned around, with difficulty, resisting the urge to press his back in panic against the low roof of the tunnel. Breathing hard, he looked back at the mouth of the tunnel, towards the light.

He saw a pair of sandalled feet approach the rim of the great tank. The man knelt down: Yashim could see his knees, and the arm reaching into the tank. The man stood up. He began to move along the rim of the tank as Yashim had done moments before. He took a step down, and stopped. After a moment he moved on, disappearing from view.

The man was coming down the basins like a semi-circular flight of stairs, stopping and opening the little pipes as he came.

Yashim took several steps backwards, shrinking further into the darkness of the tunnel.

As he watched, an orange light began to flicker against the side wall, close to the opening. He had not realised that the man was carrying a torch.

Yashim's mind raced, riffling through a pack of images. He saw the boy waiting for his father on the low, stone wall.

He saw the sun setting. The boy at the door of the siphon, calling his father's name.

A little hand closing around a silver ball. A dented little hollow ball like the one that had fallen from the spigot just minutes before. It seemed an age.

Yashim worked himself round, facing the darkness. Feeling the horror of a light at his back. Feeling the weight of the tunnel on his bent neck.

He put out his hands, touched the rough masonry on either side, and began to creep forwards into the dark.

 79

Faisal al-Mehmed nodded his head gently at the faithful as they slipped off their shoes and proceeded, in chattering groups, into the Great Mosque for prayer. For himself, he wished that they did not chat so much; he wished, above all, that they had washed themselves in the fountain before they took the step of entering the holy precinct – but there it was, he was an old man and people had changed. Maybe, he told himself, every old man believes that the people have changed; but maybe every old man is right. For every generation from the Prophet (peace be on him) did seem to be doomed to be less reverent than the next. After the Prophet (peace be on him) came four men who were good men, and great warriors, men who had expanded the Domain of Peace beyond all limits – and yet they were men, and had died at the hands of men, and at the end of the four there had come confusion, and divisions within their house.

A Turk with a black moustache and a fez and a heavy belly kicked off his slippers and bent, awkwardly, to pick them up and hand them to Faisal al-Mehmed.

Faisal tucked them away. The fat man went into the mosque.

Faisal al-Mehmed hoped the man would remove his fez. He himself wore a green turban, signal of his descent from the Prophet (peace be on him). When men saw the green turban, wherever it was, even far from the mosque, they would be reminded of the Prophet (peace be on him) and so they would adjust their behaviour accordingly. A man could not be near a mosque every moment of his life, and Faisal was well aware that very few men could be close to his mosque, the greatest mosque in all Islam; some had travelled many miles, even across whole lands and peoples, to visit this place. But those who were descended from the line, wearing the green turban – they were legion. Their turban was a precept. And that was good, a blessing upon the faithful.

Faisal al-Mehmed turned his attention to the courtyard. Even he would have to admit that the courtyard of Aya Sofia was not perfect, as the courtyard of the Suleymaniye was sublime. It had its fountain, where men were sitting in silence, washing their hands and feet; but it was a truncated court, without a colonnade to provide the faithful with shade, and the white marble threw off a fierce glare in the morning sun.

He squinted into the bright light. It seemed to Faisal al-

Mehmed that a woman was coming across the court, a tall woman who walked with immodest ease, unveiled. His eyebrows met in a black frown. He looked again, shielding the side of his face. It was unthinkable – but there she was, a woman, a very beautiful woman, making her way past the knots of men standing in the courtyard, waiting for the hour of prayer, towards the fountain. He scanned the courtyard, looking for the man who was with her. How could he allow such a thing! Already, some of the men had stopped talking, and were staring after her. And now, Faisal al-Mehmed saw, she was unlatching her shoes, as if she were a man, preparing to wash.

It was too much. Sometimes madmen did appear at Aya Sofia – ranting dervishes, perhaps, from the hills, strange, bearded fanatics from the deserts, once even a naked man who had come rushing into the precincts of the holy place, laughing and clapping his hands. It was not the gatekeeper's place to judge them, for they were all of God's creation: who was to say that the mad were not greater men, who had looked on the face of God and found rapture? So said the wise. God, they said, took care of his people: but a mad woman? A man should be taking care of her. It was very shocking.

He began to hobble forwards. He raised a trembling hand. Already, the men were standing around the woman, watching her dumbfounded. Somebody spoke to her: she looked up and smiled and shook her head. Her scarf slipped back an inch.

The gatekeeper began to run. He waved his arms. 'No! No! Haram! Haram! It is forbidden!'

One of the men pointed to the woman's hair. The others looked round at the running gatekeeper, then back at the woman.

'See!' a voice cried out. 'She is an unbeliever.'

The woman had put up her hands. She was backing away. A ring of men gathered behind her. She turned. They began to shout.

The gatekeeper took her by the arm. 'What is this, you foolish daughter?'

A stone landed at their feet. The gatekeeper looked down at the stone, then swung around. There was quite a crowd now. Some of them were shaking their fists. Somebody stooped down and another stone whizzed through the air. Faisal al-Mehmed tugged at the woman's arm.

He saw the fear on her face. A look of surprise.

'This is forbidden, don't you understand. You must go!' He shook her roughly. He was pulling her away: the crowd parted, but only just. People were shouting. The muezzin began to cry from the minaret, and to the men below it seemed as if some hideous miracle were being enacted, some challenge had been issued. The shouting grew in intensity. Faisal al-Mehmed was afraid now.

A hand reached out and plucked away the woman's scarf. Somebody spat. The woman shrank closer to the gatekeeper, who waved his hand ahead of them, trying to clear a path.

'She is a mad Giaour! Only mad! Please, good people, let us pass. She is going!'

The crowd surged round them, angry, yelling faces, men jostling for a better view: Faisal al-Mehmed's voice was lost in the hubbub.

The crowd surged round them as he took the woman to the narrow gate. Faisal al-Mehmed began to pray, his voice echoing the voice of the imam overhead. 'There is no god but the One God!'

The gate was thronged with worshippers arriving for prayers. It seemed to Faisal al-Mehmed that they would be cut down before they ever got through.

80

Yashim slid his feet through the water, one hand trailing against the wall of the tunnel, the other outstretched in front of his face.

He tried not to think. All his life he had had a horror of confinement: even as a little boy he had fought like a wolf if his playmates tried to pin him down. He never followed them, either, into the caves they used to explore around his home on the Black Sea coast: there were rockfalls sometimes; tales of miners trapped underground used to visit him at night. Once he had been trapped himself. Confined, unable to move, staring wild-eyed at the men, and the knife. The horror had risen in his gorge – and his life was changed.

He tried not to splash; it seemed to him that the level of the water had risen, that it was by his ankles: but the cold was so intense that he could not be sure. All that mattered was to get deep into the tunnel, away from the torchlight.

If only the pipe would curve.

A few steps further on his hand came up against a curved edge. He stopped and groped around. As far as he could tell in the dark, the channel forked; he was between two openings, both the same size, both carrying the current. He squatted down, and glanced back.

For a dizzying moment he felt that he was staring at a solid wall, as if the tunnel had sealed itself behind him, and he reached out in a panic. The movement of his hand revealed to him the existence of a faint glow which seemed to hang in the air in front of him: as he watched it grew brighter, an aureole of faint light surrounding a pinprick of flame in the darkness.

The waterman was coming down the tunnel.

Yashim felt sick. He squeezed his eyes shut, and fought the

panic, fought the thought that he was being pressed deeper and deeper into the ground.

It's a maze, he murmured to himself. Only a maze. In a maze, you must follow a rule.

Two tunnels. One bore to the left: it might descend the hill towards the Fener. The other, tending to the right, presumably took a line to the south. Yashim tried to picture the shape of his city, the rise and fall of its hills. One or both of these pipes might lead to another siphon, where the water pooled at a lower level than the tank it came from. Sooner or later, if that were the case, the pipe would start to grow full of water, like a curving reservoir, and he would have to stop moving.

Left or right?

Which way would the waterman come?

Yashim was right-handed.

The rule, in a maze, was to keep turning the same way at every bend. Trail his left hand on the wall, and reach forwards with his right.

That was the way.

Yashim put out his hand, and groped for the opening on his left.

He started down. He felt the floor of the tunnel sloping. His hand trailed along the wall. It was no longer rough to the touch, but slimy and knobbled: he imagined it caked in calcareous lumps, dripping with shiny algae.

He advanced several yards. He almost missed the first turn, because he was swaying as he scuttled forwards and his hand missed the wall for a foot or two. When he reached out again he felt a hard corner; groping back, he discovered the opening he'd missed, and turned into it. He thought of the horror of losing his way back.

Now he leaned his shoulder against the wall on his left: like that he was in less danger of missing a turn, and from time to time he could pause and rest.

He wondered how much further he needed to go. Three turns already: the chances of discovery were increasingly remote.

He decided to make one last turn, and then he would wait.

He shoved himself along, spreading the weight between his legs and his left shoulder, and that is when he found the turn.

He swivelled into it.

Something hard caught his foot as he slid around the corner.

He put out his hands, and fell into the void.

81

Amélie felt the crowd around her, dense and hostile, and the old man's grip on her arm. He had been angry, but now he seemed only afraid. She bowed her head and tried to avoid the blows she could almost sense were about to rain down on her head.

She had no time to think that she had been a fool.

Someone touched her shoulder, and she wriggled forwards, propelled by the weight of the crowd at her back and the old man's insistent tugs. There was the gate, crammed with men; the sound of voices she couldn't understand filled her ears. She lowered her head, and saw blood on her bare foot. She didn't remember cutting herself. She had left her shoes at the fountain.

They neared the gate. Whether the angry crowd behind her couldn't make itself understood over the muezzin's chant, or whether people were simply too astonished by the spectacle of the gatekeeper half-dragging a foreign woman from the precincts of the mosque, the churning flow through the gate seemed to stop, and for a moment there was a way through. The old man plunged in.

They surged through the gate: the men coming in met the following crowd like two waves, and for a moment each checked the force of the other. It was just enough time.

The gatekeeper dragged her forwards.

A carriage was rattling down the slope from Topkapi Palace, pulled by two greys; the coachman stood on the box and someone was leaning from the window.

Amélie made a sudden wrench and the gatekeeper's hold on her arm was lost. Without a thought she flung herself towards the horses.

The nearest horse flung back its head. The driver lunged on the reins.

Amélie closed her eyes, and turned her head away.

From far away she heard a voice saying, in French:

'*Vite, madame, vite!* Jump in.'

Another hand was beneath her elbow, tugging her upwards.

She half-fell, half-leaped through the carriage door.

'Quick, Hasan! Drive on!'

The jolt threw her back into a seat. She opened her eyes.

There was a man in front of her, kneeling up on the opposite seat and giving orders to the driver through the hatch.

He turned to her with a worried expression.

'I have no idea, madame, what brings you here, but I believe we have been of some service.'

He glanced through the window.

'We'll beat them yet,' he said darkly. 'Allow me to introduce myself. I am Dr Millingen, the sultan's physician.'

 82

Yashim shot to his feet. The water reached to his knees. He was aware of a searing pain in his left arm.

A kind of sob escaped him, like a cough. The pain made him wince, but he could move his fingers and he did not think he had broken a bone. He sloshed forwards through the icy water, sliding his feet over the ground, and touched the wall.

Like the tunnel itself, it was slimy. He reached up with his good arm and tried to find the top, and when that failed he began to follow the wall with his hand, looking for an opening. He counted four corners, and didn't find one. Once he stumbled against something soft and large, which seemed to be rolling on the floor under the surface. He drove it away with his foot, and tried not to think about it again.

He put a hand to the wall and leaned his forehead against it. It seemed that he was in a small chamber, some seven feet across, without exits. There was about two feet of water at the bottom. He had dropped through an opening in the channel or pipe above: it could not, he thought, be more than twelve feet above, or he would have got more badly hurt.

However high it was, it was still beyond his reach.

A thin trickle of water slid over his fingers and onto his forehead.

He wondered if, by a miracle, the waterman would come this way.

Then something touched his leg again, and he reached down into the water and knew immediately that no one was ever going to help him out.

83

The little boy slipped through the gates and went slowly up to his trench in the dirt.

A window flew open with a squeal. The boy did not look up.

Marta put her head out. 'Shpëtin! Did you see where the efendi went?'

The little boy picked up his stick. He pushed the dented ball along the trench.

At the window, Marta gave an exasperated sigh and shrugged. She turned to the ambassador.

'No, lord. I don't know. They went together, I think, but I don't know.'

Palewski frowned. 'I'm not easy about this, Marta. If Yashim went with the boy, he must have had a reason.'

'Yes, lord.' Marta nodded her head slowly.

And this, Palewski thought, is the second time the boy comes home alone. 'You talk to him, Marta. He thinks I'm some sort of ogre. See if he'll show us where they went.'

Marta gave a doubtful shrug. 'The boy – he's a little strange, lord.'

'He's a boy, isn't he? Boys are all – well, like boys.' Palewski felt himself at a loss. 'Just ask him for me. Please.'

⚜ 84 ⚜

Yashim put his hand on a human face.

He sprang away from the corpse, flailing through the water. He was backed into a corner before he remembered that here, in the dark, he could soon lose all sense of direction.

All sense of proportion.

There was no need to guess whose body it was that rolled through the water. The missing man had been found.

Yashim tried not to think about what would happen next. He would grow cold, and weak. In the end, he would drown in two feet of water, sharing the Albanian's liquid grave.

He needed a way out.

Carefully now he felt his way around the pit, searching for anything that could help him climb the slippery walls. The floor was covered in loose stones and fallen bricks: the ceiling, he supposed, was slowly falling in. Once again he brushed against Xani's corpse. Fighting a wave of nausea, he rolled the body over, feeling for anything the man had carried – a knife, a coil of rope. Something bubbled on the surface of the water and Yashim gagged at the stench.

He groped at the man's chest, feeling something hard there, like a chain. On the chain was a crucifix. He pulled hard and the body lurched upwards, then the chain broke and he heard the corpse sink back into the water.

He went back to the wall, hoping it was the right one, and scratched at the wall with the end of the cross. It didn't get him far.

He ran his fingers over the wall, looking for a crack, a projection, anything. The wall was smooth as butter.

He unfastened his cloak and wrung out the water. Holding one end with his back to the wall, he flicked the cloak up and over his head. The end he was holding went limp for a few seconds, then the cloak tumbled down over his head. The end he had thrown was sopping wet.

He thought for a few moments with his eyes shut. Then he shook the cloak out flat on the water's surface. He started groping on the floor for bricks, lobbing them as best as he could judge towards the centre of the cloak. After a minute he gathered the cloak together by its edges and hefted the weight. It was as much as he could do to drag it through the water.

He set the bundle against the wall and tried climbing on it. The stones slithered down under his weight. He stepped off and tried to tie the ends of the cloak together, to make a tighter bundle. After three or four attempts he gave up. He couldn't get the wet, slopping half-knots of the cloak to hold together.

He wasted half an hour using the crucifix and the chain to sew the cloak tight. He floated Xani's corpse over the bundle of stones, and tried to get a footing. The corpse was soft underfoot, and would not keep still. He could not reach the opening.

He felt very tired.

He shook the cloak to dislodge some of the stones, tucked in the corners, and dragged the bundle up to the level of his chest. Water poured from the cloak. He squeezed it, and it grew lighter.

He summoned his strength and tossed the bundle high up against the wall. It dropped back, into his arms. He tried again, taking a step back. When he had thrown it he reached forwards to catch it, if it fell. This time he heard a muffled splash. The cloak did not fall back.

Yashim found stones on the floor and began to lob them upwards.

The work kept him from feeling the cold.

When he had lobbed a dozen stones into the dark, he stopped and listened. There was a new sound, of gurgling water. He stepped forwards and touched the wall. He couldn't feel anything. He put his lips to the wall and felt the water trickling down.

It was cold as ice.

He went back to lobbing stones in the dark.

It was only another way to die.

 85

'You're quite sure?'

'Quite sure, Dr Millingen. Thank you.'

'At least you have some fine Turkish slippers now,' he said, smiling.

'Yes. You have been kind.' She turned to the little sunken door and knocked.

Widow Matalya answered the door. She did not know what to think, finding the Frankish woman on her doorstep with a strange man. Dr Millingen tipped his hat politely, and the old woman sniffed, transferring her distaste onto a solid target: hats, she thought, were very nasty things.

'Please, madame – do keep in touch.'

Amélie gave him a curious smile. 'I shall have to, I suppose,' she said.

She went in. The old woman closed the door, and turned with a very set expression on her face, her lips compressed.

'Monsieur Yashim – Yashim efendi – he's upstairs?' Amélie pointed a finger.

The widow's eyes bored into her.

'I think I'll just go up and see,' Amélie said gaily. '*Ciao!*'

86

Palewski put his hand on the boy's shoulder. 'Look here,' he said, breathing hard. 'Are we going far? A long way?'

The boy looked up and nodded.

'In that case,' the ambassador said firmly, 'we'll take a chair.'

He snapped his fingers at a couple of men squatting against a wall.

'My treat,' he said, smiling. 'Just point these fellows in the right direction, there's a good boy.'

Down on the shore they swapped the chair for a caique. The little boy pointed up the Golden Horn.

'Fener? Balat? Fener stage, boatman, please.' Perhaps Yashim had simply gone off home, he thought. But once they reached

Fener, the little boy made some complicated signs and shook his head vigorously.

'All right,' Palewski said. 'We'll walk, I see. Not too far now, eh?'

He regretted taking the boy's advice as he toiled up the hills, but they were in a shabby neighbourhood which Palewski did not know, and there were no lounging chair-men here.

Finally the boy jumped up onto a low wall and sat there, kicking his heels and looking intently at a doorway across the street.

'He went in there?'

Palewski climbed the steps. There was a padlock on the door, so Palewski turned round and caught the boy's eye. He pointed at the door. The little boy nodded.

Palewski glanced up and down the street. Apart from the little boy on the wall, it seemed perfectly empty.

Stanislaw Palewski, unlike Dr Millingen, was not a man who placed much faith in the benefits of regular exercise. His arms were thin; his legs were long. But he was still capable of sudden, violent physical effort.

He stood back, leaned against the parapet, and doubled those long legs by bringing his knees up close to his chin.

Then with a splintering crash he brought both feet down hard on the door, and burst it open.

The ambassador turned to the little boy who was watching him in astonishment from across the street, and gave him a most un-ambassadorial wink.

Then he went into the icy gloom, to find his friend.

87

Yashim was singing an old song from the Balkans, about a man who went down to the river and caught the soul of his dead lover in his nets.

He spun slowly in the darkness, sometimes kicking his legs, sometimes reaching for a better grip on the man who had become his new friend. They'd only just met, too, he thought. Dear Xani! Stinking, buoyant and obliging. What very good luck it was they'd met, at last.

If only Xani were still warm, Yashim thought dreamily. The pit was slowly filling, deeper and deeper as the flow backed up against the cloak and stones overhead. He heard a tapping, unlike the sound of water gushing into the pit from the blocked conduit above. For some minutes he tried to imagine what it could be, before he discovered that it was the sound of his own chattering teeth.

He found that his whole body was shaking, convulsing in sudden spasms that shook his grip on the dead man and sometimes sent him spluttering and flailing beneath the surface of the ice-cold water. Sometimes he had a sense of being underwater altogether; sometimes he closed his eyes and felt a wave of great lassitude and peace wash through him, so that he wanted to let go and sink, gently and dreamily, into the depths. He had not touched the bottom of the pit in hours, it seemed. Now and again he found himself beneath the spout of water dropping from the blocked conduit.

He heard someone singing an old Turkish marching song in a small, tired voice. He thought it must be Xani. Then he supposed it was himself. Either way it no longer mattered. He could not feel his legs.

But he must have drifted off into another pit, because the

spout had stopped dropping on him: he could no longer hear it splashing on the surface. He saw himself floating endlessly from pit to pit; but he was too tired to be anxious about that. Xani's corpse began one of its gaseous rolls beneath him, and he felt himself sliding off again, back down into the deep murk, into the comfort of the cold and the dark. He'd fought it so hard before, but he could no longer remember why. He knew that this time he would let himself go.

It was then, and only slowly, that he began to sense that he was not floating any more. He lay face up, with a pain in his back, breathing air. His elbow stirred. It made a rough, rasping sound – the first noise that was not gaseous or liquid he had heard in hours. He turned himself over with difficulty, and stretched out his hands. The movement seemed to take minutes, as if he were rolling a huge stone uphill. He could no longer feel his hands, and to make them obey him he tried hard to imagine them there, at the end of his unfolding arms, groping weakly on the bricks.

With a slowness that was immeasurable, in the dark, he began to squirm up the conduit. It was hours before he remembered that he had to keep to the right: it was the first moment of real terror he had experienced since his ordeal began. Perhaps he had already missed a turn? He might have gone a hundred yards already; he might have gone five. He could no longer judge.

He saw Xani crawling up the pipe beside him, with his guts trailing in the water.

A blaze of magnificent fireworks went off inside his head.

He heard his old friend Palewski calling his name.

He crawled for a minute, then for a year, and after a night and a day Palewski was there, but very, very small, like a mouse in his little hole.

Palewski was shouting, and then Yashim was in a litter and

was jouncing, jouncing over the cobblestones, retching and trembling and wishing he could simply die.

Like happy Xani. Big and fat and soft, twirling forever and forever in a little eddy underground.

 88

Bundled into shawls, Yashim slept for sixteen hours. He woke to find Amélie beside him, reading a book.

'What you need,' she said, 'is the old lady's soup. I'll fetch you some.'

When she had gone, Yashim tested his limbs: his joints were sore, he had some chafing on his chin and chest, and all his muscles ached, as if he had run a long way. He sat up, feeling weary. The thought of soup made him feel sick; but strangely, when Amélie presented him with the bowl, he found that he was starving.

'There's no bread,' she said apologetically.

'It can be arranged,' Yashim said. 'I'll call the boy. You'll find some money in that purse.'

He stuck his head out of the window. 'Elvan!'

'Is this enough?' Amélie held up a coin.

Yashim nodded. 'That will be enough.' He set the soup aside and closed his eyes.

Darkness. He was in the pit, again. His limbs twitched. He opened his eyes and there was Amélie, the steaming bowl, his own room.

'The Gyllius. You read it?'

'Yes.'

'And it suggested – some idea?'

'Yes. I think so.'

Yashim closed his eyes again. He was very tired, but he was not afraid of the dark. He, above all people, could not be afraid of the dark.

Long ago, reaching manhood, he had stepped into a region that was darker than any tunnel underneath the city: an unrelieved blackness that ran through his veins and turned his eyes backwards in their sockets. His despair had been a cell from which there was no escape at all: the prison of his own ruined body.

But in the end he had found a way. Not a way out, exactly; but a way, perhaps, of seeing in the dark. It made him useful. Yashim the eunuch: a guide, when others fell into the darkness, too.

Until sometimes a woman came, beautiful, shedding her own light: a woman, perhaps, with brown eyes and a cloud of brown hair, who watched him as he slept. And fetched him soup. And who shed so much light that as she passed he was dazzled, blinded – and would stay blind, long after she had gone away. Groping in the dark, again.

It was not her fault.

Yashim opened his eyes. Amélie had her arm stretched out, and she was looking at her hand with a concentrated expression on her face, wiggling her fingers.

Then the coin fell to the floor. She bent to pick it up.

'The Great Church,' Amélie said, turning the coin around her thumb. 'Aya Sofia.'

Elvan knocked on the door. Yashim sent him to the Libyan baker for a round of bread. He took the coin with a curious glance at Amélie, and sped off on his errand.

'The Byzantine Greeks believed in an old legend about Aya Sofia,' Amélie explained. 'The legend was that one day an enemy would succeed in breaking into the city. Everything would appear lost – except that the enemy would never reach the Great Church. Before that happened, the archangel Gabriel would appear with a flaming sword, and drive the invaders out.'

'Hmmm,' Yashim looked doubtful. 'It didn't happen.'

'No. But Max always said that every myth contains a kernel of truth. So when the Turks broke into the city there was, in fact, a miracle at Aya Sofia. Just not the miracle everyone hoped for.'

'No archangel.'

'No. But a priest, saying Mass. When the Turks arrived, he vanished.'

'Vanished?'

'Stepped into one of the great pillars, apparently, carrying the host. The legend goes that he'll reappear on the day the cross is raised over the dome again.'

Yashim frowned. He tried to picture the scene: Ottoman troops crashing against the great doors of the church, the terrified people huddled inside for protection, and a priest at the altar with a cup and plate. Something about the picture in his mind was vaguely familiar: he couldn't remember. Something he'd seen, perhaps? Something Lefèvre had said. But at that moment Elvan re-appeared with the bread, and the memory was lost. Yashim gave him a few piastres and he bowed out with unusual solemnity.

Instead, Yashim recalled a legend in Grigor's book, about the emperor being turned to stone.

'Max thought those stories carried a message,' Amélie explained. 'Perhaps the tale of the priest means that the Greeks had time to hide their treasure before the Turks came in. Aya Sofia is one of the biggest buildings on earth. The most ambitious building project in world history, after the Pyramids.'

She took a lock of hair and twisted it with a finger.

'But there's no crypt in Aya Sofia. Most churches have crypts, to represent the world of the dead. At Aya Sofia they raised the largest dome in the world, like a microcosm of the universe – the whole of God's creation. It's odd if they didn't build a crypt in there, as well.'

Yashim broke the bread and dipped it into his soup. 'It's said that Mehmed came into the Great Church the morning after the assault, and found a soldier hacking at the marble floor. He was angry. He said: you soldiers can take whatever you can carry, but the building belongs to God – and me. Aya Sofia was preserved.'

'Perhaps he knew there was something under there. But they never got an opportunity to look, did they? As far as I know, Aya Sofia hasn't been touched now for four hundred years.'

'They added minarets,' Yashim pointed out.

'On the outside.'

They looked at each other.

'That trick,' Yashim said. 'The trick you were doing with the coin. Where did you learn that?'

Amélie laughed. 'I still haven't. Max used to teach me, but I haven't got the fingers for it, I suppose. He could make the coin run through his fingers and then – pouf! It vanished. Just like that priest.'

Yashim drank his soup. He put down the empty bowl. 'Your husband – Max. Dr Lefèvre. He was a doctor of archaeology, wasn't he?'

Amélie looked surprised. 'Of archaeology? He was an archaeologist, yes. But he started out in medicine. He was a doctor of medicine.'

'A doctor of medicine,' Yashim repeated slowly. 'I had no idea.'

There was a knock on the door, and Palewski came in, fishing a green bottle out of his coat pocket.

He bowed to Amélie and then peered closely at Yashim.

'He seems to have been eating soup,' he said. He patted the bottle. 'Brandy. Excellent with soup. Good for invalids. I thought he might be dead.'

'He'll live,' Amélie said.

Palewski looked disappointed. 'Brandy's good for a wake. I

thought we might sit around his corpse, remembering, madame.'

'I think I'm recovering,' Yashim said in a small voice.

Amélie laughed. She glanced from Yashim to Palewski, and flexed her back. 'Madame Matalya will want her bowl back, Yashim. I'll take it down – and I'm a little tired.'

When she had gone, the ambassador uncorked the brandy and poured two glasses.

'It's not the first time that you've saved my life,' Yashim said.

Palewski dismissed him with a wave. 'I'm not too busy at the moment.'

Yashim smiled. With the sultan dying, most ambassadors would be filing their reports and trying to sound out the crown prince. The Polish ambassador could afford to wait on events.

'I don't quite understand why I found you crawling out of a tunnel, Yashim.'

Yashim told him. He told him about Shpëtin's little tin ball, and the siphon. He told him how he had got lost in the maze, and about Xani's body floating in the pool. He told him, too, how he had escaped.

'So Xani's dead. They followed him into the siphon, killed him and threw him down the pipe?'

'What else would they do? The little boy was watching the door from the other side of the road.'

'He saw them go in – and come out. He knows who they are.'

'But he can't speak, Palewski.'

The ambassador cracked his knuckles.

Yashim levered himself up on one elbow. 'There's another thing. Amélie – Madame Lefèvre – read the Gyllius book. It gave her an idea.'

'The serpent's heads?'

'Aya Sofia.'

Palewski shook his head. 'I don't understand.'

'Gyllius mentions the serpent's heads – but they were still in their place on the column when he was here. And in Delmonico's time, too. That little book doesn't tell us anything important about the serpent's heads, Palewski. So why was it so important to Lefèvre?'

'I don't know. But if it wasn't the serpent's heads, why would he have needed Xani? And then, why was Xani murdered too?'

Yashim ran his hands through his hair. 'Xani. Amélie. Gyllius's book. I feel as though I'm trying to recreate a rare and astonishing dish from a memory of how it tasted, Palewski. We have all these ingredients in the dish – but the flavour's wrong, somehow.' He looked up. 'Amélie told me something just now. Lefèvre was a real doctor. Not a doctor of archaeology.'

'A doctor. So what?'

'I'm not sure. He spoke Greek fluently, too. Modern Greek. He learned it in the twenties, in the Greek provinces.'

'Are you sure? There was a war going on at the time.'

'Missolonghi, yes. That's what interests me. Your poet – Byron. Millingen, his doctor.'

'Byron,' Palewski echoed. 'It's Thursday, Yashim. I've got an idea.'

'Thursday?' Yashim frowned. It was a ritual, their Thursday dinner; but time was short. 'I'm sorry, but I haven't –'

'No, no, Yash. It's quite all right. Tonight, for once, you'll dine with me.'

⋘ 89 ⋙

Yashim was relieved that he didn't have to shop or cook. It was already past noon. He dressed with care, and an hour later he presented himself at the door of the sultan's harem, in Topkapi Palace.

Hyacinth emerged from his little cubicle in the corridor and grinned, showing a row of reddish teeth. 'I knew it would be you,' he said softly.

'The validé?'

The elderly eunuch wagged his head, and looked serious. 'Not receiving today. A little shock. She is resting.'

'Come on, Hyacinth,' Yashim said testily. 'Everyone here is resting.'

Hyacinth giggled uncertainly, and tapped Yashim on the chest with his fan.

'It seems it's all your fault, Yashim,' he said. 'You and your little favours.'

Yashim blinked. Years ago, when three hundred women or more were cooped up in the harem apartments, attended by a cohort of black eunuchs, it was only to be expected that everyone would know everyone else's business. Now there was only one, the validé, with a handful of girls and a few attendants. But some things never changed.

'The bostanci refused her?'

Hyacinth's hands fluttered. 'I never said a word,' he insisted, raising his eyebrows. 'Her Highness is not receiving – anyone.'

Yashim bowed: he admired the glint of steel beneath the black man's gentle manner. But he wondered what would happen if he brushed him aside and pressed on: Hyacinth, he guessed, was stronger than he looked. A sort of giddiness swept over him. There would be no men at arms springing forwards to enforce compliance: there never had been. It would never have been necessary.

'Is that you, Yashim?'

The voice from along the passage was unmistakable. Yashim looked up; Hyacinth whirled round.

The Validé Sultan was advancing very slowly along the passageway, one hand gripping the knob of a stick, the other raised to the shoulder of a girl whose arm was passed around the validé's waist. What struck Yashim was not that the validé herself was bent, or very frail, or that her knuckles looked huge beneath the thin skin of her hands, but that she was wearing jewels: a welter of diamonds at her ears, around her neck, pearls gleaming from her diadem, and at her breast a lapis brooch with the figure N picked out in ivory. As she stepped forwards into the sunlight it seemed to Yashim that she sparkled like a leaf after a storm.

Yashim bowed.

'The bostanci!' The validé stopped, and worked her hand on the cane. '*Il m'a refusé!*'

Hyacinth lowered his eyes. His hands were draped around his enormous belly. The girl cast a frightened glance at Yashim.

The validé set both hands on the head of her cane. Very slowly she drew herself upright.

'Pssht!' She raised her chin. Hyacinth and the girl withdrew, bowing.

'Refused, Yashim,' the validé repeated quietly. 'Why not? I am an old woman, far from the seat of power. The bostanci no longer fears me.'

Yashim stepped closer.

'The sultan should have stayed in Topkapi. My son.'

They looked at one another.

'How long, Yashim?'

'A few months,' he said. 'Weeks.'

The validé's hands rubbed together on the head of her stick.

'So little time,' she whispered at last. And then her lip trembled, and to Yashim's astonishment the corner of her mouth lifted into a regretful smile.

'Men,' she said. '*Ils font ce qu'ils veulent.*'

They do what they want. Yashim bent his head.

'*Mais les femmes*, Yashim. They do what they must.' She turned around. 'And you, Yashim, I wonder? Perhaps you do what we need. Give me an arm.'

Slowly, without talking, they made their way back up the corridor to the validé's courtyard.

❦ 90 ❧

The validé lay back on the divan, against a spray of cushions.

'The bostanci makes me tired, Yashim. No, don't go. I have something to tell you. A coffee?'

Yashim declined. The validé settled the shawl around her legs.

'I thought I would die of loneliness when the sultan moved first to Beşiktaş. I have not been alone for sixty years, and I had grown so used to people around me, everywhere, at all times. For the first few weeks, I was in mourning, I admit. And you were very charming, to visit me – even if it was only my novels you wanted! No, no. I am teasing.

'But then I discovered something, Yashim. How to explain? Look: there is a little bird which comes to my window every day, to get food. The gardeners showed him to me – I had never noticed him before. Just a little bird! You may laugh, *mon ami* – but I scattered crumbs.'

Cross-legged on the divan, Yashim hunched forwards and stared at his hands. He had a peculiar sense that he knew what the validé was about to describe. Years ago, as a very young man, almost a boy, he had constructed hope.

'Believe me, Yashim, the place was quiet. One little bird – *c'est rien*. But little by little I began to see that it was not a matter of one bird at all. There were many. And more than birds. The gardener told me there were djinns. He said, "Now they have room to breathe, at last!"' The validé paused. 'I come from a superstitious island, Yashim.

'Remember the great women who have passed through these

apartments, Yashim. People remember them. Kosem Sultan. Turhan Sultan. These are the rooms they kept, the corridors they used. I think of them, and I feel that I am still validé Sultan – for them. For all the women who have lived here, within these walls. So many, Yashim.'

He bowed his head. He wanted to say that when one is spent and useless in the world's eyes, it is still possible to live for others. For the living, or the dead.

'Yes, validé,' he murmured. 'I understand.'

She regarded him narrowly.

'I think you do, Yashim. Djinns, ghosts: these are the privileges of age. But like the little birds, there are men of flesh and blood who inhabit this place. One sees them more clearly.'

Her world is shrinking, Yashim thought: the girls, the eunuchs, nothing more. Every day, the circle will grow smaller.

'Don't suppose I am thinking of Hyacinth, or my slaves,' the validé said. 'The sultan – and his pashas – may have thought that everything in this palace depended on them, but they were wrong.'

'Validé?'

'Each year, on the same day, someone puts flowers on the column where they displayed the heads of rebels.'

'I see.'

'It's only an example. But when things are calm and clear, and you watch, you find that many things haven't changed. I have not changed because I am used to these walls, these courtyards and apartments. Just as the watermen are used to meeting in the arsenal.'

Yashim blinked. 'The watermen?'

'They are, as I understand it, the oldest guild in the city. They would not go to Beşiktaş.'

Yashim pictured the arsenal, an ancient basilica which formed the lower corner of the first, most public court of the old palace.

It had been used as a store-house and a treasury; the last time he had seen inside, its walls were hung with flags and standards, and patterned with an arrangement of pikes and halberds from another age.

'But I don't understand. Why would they meet there?'

The validé gave a pretty shrug. 'Not why, Yashim, but when.' She raised a finger. 'Tomorrow morning. They have a ceremony to introduce a new member to the guild.'

She watched Yashim's astonishment with satisfaction. 'I may attend,' she added. 'As the oldest representative of our House, it is my right. But I am not so strong as before. I shall need – assistants. Perhaps, Yashim –'

'I am at your service, validé,' Yashim said humbly.

Yashim walked slowly out from the palace. Time was short, he'd told Palewski; but so far he hadn't made much headway. He wondered what he should do next.

He thought of visiting the hammam, but instead of returning to Fener he found himself in the Hippodrome again, considering the broken column.

The serpents of the column emerged from a bronze ring, where you could read the names of thirty-one Greek cities – Athens, Sparta, Patras, Mycenae, and the rest of those jealous, warring city-states which combined in 479 BC against the Persian invader. At the battle of Plataia, the Persians were defeated by an army of Greeks, united for the very first time.

To commemorate that victory, the bronze weaponry and armour of the defeated Persians was melted down and recast to make the Serpent Column. It was set up at Delphi, a neutral place, the seat of the oracle respected by all Greeks alike. Entwined one upon the other, the three serpents soared into the air: unity was strength.

Yashim supposed that had the battle gone the other way, there would have been no Greece. No philosophy; no academy; no Alexander – and no Greeks.

Solemnly, he leaned against the rail. Twelve years ago, the Greeks had attempted to unite again. What was it that Dr Millingen had said? That the Greeks were incapable of working together. Missolonghi was scarcely a battle. It was a siege, and the Greeks had lost it. No serpent column could be cast to commemorate those years.

But Lefèvre had been there, hadn't he? A doctor, like Millingen. Working together – for a cause.

Yashim pressed his forehead against the railings, and closed his eyes. He tried to think: he had a sense that time was running out.

'Efendi.'

He turned, recognising the voice.

'I saw you cross the Hippodrome, efendi.'

Yashim smiled at his friend. He had known, in the kebab house a few days earlier, that they would soon meet.

'I am glad to see you,' he said, and it was perfectly true. Seeing Murad Eslek standing in front of him, short, sturdy and grinning from ear to ear, Yashim realised exactly why they were supposed to meet. Murad Eslek was a man who took each day as it came. He thought on his feet. He was efficient, reliable: a friend. He had once saved Yashim's life.

But above all, Murad Eslek was an early riser. Every day, long before dawn, he would be at one of the market gardens beyond the city walls, overseeing the delivery of vegetables and fruit to half a dozen street markets around Istanbul. Carts and mules, donkeys with panniers: Murad Eslek and his men saw them into the city and arranged their distribution, so that when Istanbul woke up the stalls were piled high, as if by magic, with all the produce of the season.

'There's something I wanted to ask you,' Yashim said. 'Shall we have a coffee together?'

⋞ 92 ⋟

Dr Millingen closed his bag and snapped the catch shut.

He glanced up the bed, to where the sultan lay drowsing against the pillows. Ten grains: enough, and not too much. Laudanum helped ease the pain.

The doctor frowned. When he told the eunuch that his business was with the living, not the dead, he was telling a half-truth. Sometimes people who were well came to him, he bled and dosed them, and they lived. Sometimes he protected people who would otherwise have died. But his business was neither with the living, or the dead: it was with the dying.

His job was to give them courage, or grant them oblivion; for it was seldom death itself that people feared. For most of them, it was the realisation of its approach; as if death was easy, but dying came hard.

The sultan was sunk back against the pillows, and his skin was sunk back against the bones: he looked papery. His mouth was open, at a slight angle; his eyelids were almost purple. His breathing was so faint as to be almost imperceptible.

Millingen bent forwards to put his hand close to the sultan's mouth.

The sultan opened his eyes. They were lifeless and yellowed around the dark core of the iris.

'*S'agit-il des mois, des jours ou des heures?*' His lips barely moved. Hours or days? Millingen had heard that weariness before. The sultan did not lack courage.

'*On ne sait rien*,' he said quietly. '*On va de jour en jour.*'

The sultan did not drop his gaze. Only his hand moved slowly over the counterpane, as if there were some effort he wished to make.

'Sultan?'

'The crown prince. Summon him now.'

'Yes, sultan. I will send for him.'

Millingen turned and went to the door, instinctively aware that he was being watched. At the door he looked back. The sultan moved a finger: go.

He opened the door and stepped out into the corridor. Two footmen snapped to attention on either hand, and a small, thin man in a fez sprang up from the sofa.

'He asks to see the crown prince,' Millingen said. He knew it was probably futile: the prince had a morbid horror of the disease.

The little man bowed. Millingen wondered if he knew it was futile, too, as he scurried off down the corridor.

Millingen folded his arms and let his chin sink towards his chest.

A week, he thought. If only he could have another week.

A memory of something he had once read came into his mind: Suleyman the Magnificent, dead in his screened litter, rushed from the battlefield as if he were still alive. The Grand Vizier having discussions with his corpse, in order not to alarm the troops.

He pushed the thought aside.

This is not the age of Suleyman now, he told himself. This is the nineteenth century.

93

George was sitting out in the little courtyard behind the hospice, his big face tilted to the sun, his eyes closed, with a skein of wool looped around his hands.

He opened his eyes and saw two men standing in front of him.

'Ha!' George boomed, lifting the wool from his lap. 'You finds me like old womans now!'

He slipped his huge hands out of the wool and set it gently on the bench beside him.

'I sleeps like an old Greek lady,' he grumbled. He squinted up at his visitors. 'What for you bring this rogue here, Yashim efendi? You wants I have bad dreams?'

Yashim smiled. 'Murad Eslek, this is George.'

Murad Eslek shook his head. 'I know George, efendi. Old bloke. Sells veg at that excuse for a market up the way from here. This ain't George. Why, this man's half his age, and twice his size.'

George closed his eyes again and laughed weakly.

'Murad has been telling me about the Constantinedes brothers,' Yashim said.

George's laugh turned into a cough. His eyes bulged, and he thumped his chest.

'What for you cares about such shits?' He spat on the cobbles. 'Even Murad Eslek knows. They is bad mens, efendi.'

Eslek cut the air with his hand. 'Too true, George. And I get the word that you was fitted up,' he added. 'Valuable pitch, right? They made an offer.'

George rubbed his chest. 'Those bastards,' he said quietly. 'I works that market before they is born.'

'It was your father's pitch,' Eslek pointed out.

'My grandfather had the farm,' George said. 'Old Constantinedes lived nearby. He drink too much, beat his wife. So – my father helps his boys, brings them to the market. But they is bad boys who cheats peoples. My father says – we finds you new pitch. You cheats too many peoples, the peoples don't come.'

George wiped his eyes with his massive thumb, and spat.

'When my father dies they says: George, it is finish for you now at market. Stay on farm, sell us your vegetables, and we sell to the peoples. But I think, no. These boys cheats the peoples. If I stops the market, why you not think they try to cheat me, too? Of course!'

'No one else asked you for money, then?'

'Money?' George looked surprised. 'You asks rich man for money. Not the vegetable man.'

'And the men who attacked you. Did you recognise them?'

'No, efendi. I never see them before in my whole life.'

Yashim and Eslek exchanged glances. 'Leave it to me,' Eslek said. 'And don't worry. When you feel all right you can go back to your pitch. The Constantinedes brothers won't be bothering you again.'

94

Yashim paid a hurried visit to the hammam before crossing the Horn by caique. It was still light when he arrived at the Polish Residency. Palewski greeted him at the door.

'Come upstairs,' he said. 'I thought of opening up the dining room, in your honour – but I'm afraid it's a bit too far gone. The sitting room will be cosier.'

Yashim tried to imagine Palewski's dining room. Holes in the plaster? Cobwebs? The windows obscured by creepers, perhaps, growing unchecked for years.

One of the little jobs that Xani had been going to undertake, no doubt.

He stopped on the stairs, one hand on the rail. 'I think I've got Xani wrong,' he said.

Palewski turned.

'Wrong?'

Yashim nodded. 'Just like the Hetira. I thought it was a protection racket, something like that. I thought it could have people murdered.'

They began to climb the stairs again.

'Why not? Look what happened to George. Look at the way they jumped you on the caique that night.'

'George wasn't done over by the Hetira. It was a turf war between him and another stallholder. Very vicious, and very unexpected. But not Hetira. I learned that this afternoon.'

'But the caique? And your apartment – remember that?'

'What do those events really amount to? Threats, yes. Unpleasant, certainly. But I'm still alive. So, for that matter, are you.'

Palewski pushed the door and they went into his sitting room. 'The Hetira came after you for the book, but they didn't kill Lefèvre. Is that what you're saying?'

Yashim looked round. There was a small folding table set up in front of the empty grate. 'They came after me – but I'm alive. Lefèvre was disembowelled. Just like Goulandris, and the Jew.'

Palewski's hands were on a yellow bottle.

'Tokay, Yashim. Wonderfully cold.'

He took a heavy crystal wine glass from the table, and filled it. Yashim noticed the table was laid for three.

'Who else are you expecting?'

'An old friend of yours, Yash. Third permanent undersecretary to the secretary to the ambassador at the British embassy – something like that.'

'The British embassy?' Yashim frowned. 'I don't have any old friends there. The only person I know is that ridiculous boy Compston.'

Palewski grinned. 'George Compston. Highly ridiculous, as you say. But he happens to be a Byron fanatic. And if I'm not mistaken, that's him arriving now.'

A few moments later they heard a heavy tread on the stairs, and Marta ushered in a stout young man, with a shock of yellow hair and an open, cheery red face.

Compston's infatuation with the life and legend of Lord Byron had begun on the ship which carried him to his first diplomatic posting in Istanbul. It was a six-week voyage, and Compston had kept close to his berth throughout; by the time the ship reeled into the Sea of Marmora he had not only read the epic poem *The Giaor* but was able to pronounce its title, too; an indulgent relative had kept him supplied with *Don Juan* and *Childe Harold's Pilgrimage*, and his adulation had advanced and ripened over the past two years. Nowadays he wore a cummerbund without reflection, and a pencil moustache, and tilted at the knee when talking to European ladies, to 'make a leg'.

It was his friend and mentor at the embassy, Ben Fizerley, who first noticed his limp, and later remarked, a little crushingly, that it seemed to travel uneasily from foot to foot; but few people meeting Compston for the first time, cummerbund or no cummerbund, would have readily associated the boy with the open red face and big soft hands with the saturnine poet whose untimely death all Europe had mourned.

Compston did not mind: he had reached that stage in a young man's passion for an idea when all that he looked on conformed to it, and confirmed it in his mind. A set of chestnut ringlets recalled Byronic locks; a sigh, Byronic looks; a friendly wave, a Byronic gesture. His letters home to his sister had become so full

of Byronic paradox and risqué skits that she could hardly understand them any more; and his speech was truffled with
quotations from *Childe Harold*. Even Fizerley had declared that
Compston was becoming quite a bore.

Over dinner – boiled beef, with a sorrel sauce – Yashim more
than once found himself unwittingly echoing Fizerly's opinion. It
was not until Marta had cleared away the plates, and set a
decanter of port on the table, that Palewski coughed, and
brought the Englishman to the theme in hand.

Compston put his fingers to his chin, and talked in profile.

'Missolonghi, excellency? The pride – and the shame of
Greece.' He sighed. 'The sultan had brought the armies of Egypt
into Greece, as you'll remember. They linked up with the
Albanians, and Ibrahim Pasha drove the Greeks back into this
forlorn spot, nothing but a marsh, really, running along the
shore, and there, for a year, the banner of freedom fluttered
above the wretched town, shattered by the Egyptian artillery,
and cut off from all hope of aid.'

He poured himself a glass of port.

'I often try to imagine it. There's a bit of coast where I'm from,
Burnham Overy, with simply miles of dunes. Just imagine Burnham Overy with palm trees, and that's Missolonghi. Hotter than
Burnham Overy, of course. Otherwise the palms trees wouldn't
grow!'

'Quite so,' Palewski murmured.

'Of course we don't get any Greeks in Norfolk, either. One or
two in Norwich. I think you get a few Jews. A parcel of Greek
fugitives – they'd cause quite a stir! Without doubt.'

He downed his glass and stared hard at the decanter.

Yashim coughed gently. 'But Missolonghi, Mr Compston.'

'Yes, of course. Missolonghi – there were thousands of Greek
rebels there, men with their women and their children. Bit of a
town. Too many tents. All protected by an earth bank. And

every day they died, like Lord Byron himself. Cholera, hunger, Egyptian gunnery.' He squinted at his glass. 'Not much like Burnham Overy at all, really,' he added.

'They couldn't break out?'

'It's like this, monsieur. In the first place, Ibrahim had them surrounded. In the second – well, the Greeks were divided among themselves, in spite of Lord Byron's noble efforts to bring about a reconciliation. I happen to believe that's what killed him – he was too generous with his energy and time, not to mention his money. Bringing the Suliotes up to scratch, as soldiers. Trying to appease the rivalries between the factions.' Compston rubbed his eye with a finger. 'The patience of that man! He knew what fools the Greeks were, but he never complained. Not to their very faces, at least. He died of a noble heart.'

Yashim cocked his head. 'I heard he died of fever, and bad doctors.'

Compston looked aggrieved. 'Well, that of course. We shouldn't blame the doctors. Not really. I suppose they did their best,' he added bitterly.

Palewski harrumphed quietly. 'More port, Mr Compston.'

'Dr Millingen attends the sultan now,' Yashim pointed out.

'Yes. But there were others.'

'I'd heard – Stephanitzes, perhaps? Dr Lefèvre?'

'Lefèvre?' Compston frowned and shook his head. 'Stephan-itzes was the only Greek among 'em. Jenkins, Bruno.' Compston had forgotten his Byronic poses and was now leaning forwards, frowning, like a small boy trying to remember his lesson. 'And poor Meyer, too.'

'Poor Meyer?'

'Well, unfortunate. A Swiss. Byron said he had no manners. Banned him from coming to his house. Meyer edited a sort of journal. *Chronica Hellenica*, I think. He and Byron had differences about the paper.'

'And what happened to them all – after Byron's death, I mean? At the end?'

'I'm sure you know, monsieur, how Missolonghi ended. They were down to gnawing hooves and bones, and they decided to break out. Two thousand rebels succeeded in pushing through the Turkish lines, and escaping to the hills. The others – I'm afraid they lost their nerve. Turned and fled back into Missolonghi. Ibrahim saw his chance. Unleashed his army. Albanians and Egyptians. Terrible, terrible times,' Compston murmured vaguely.

'But the doctors like Millingen, they got away?'

'Mostly. Millingen was captured a year later, by your lot. Spent a while in prison, then came on out here. Stephanitzes – I don't know. Oh, Meyer didn't make it, of course.'

'The unpopular Swiss?'

'That's right. Not altogether unpopular, I should say,' Compston added, with a huge wink at the port. 'According to Lord Byron's letters, Meyer seduced a girl at Missolonghi.' He struck his knee. 'Come to think of it, we had a case like that in Burnham Overy a few years ago. Caused a lot of bad blood, actually. Father fixed it up, in the end. Same way Byron did, once he'd got wind of the affair – I mean the one in Missolonghi; Byron never came to Burnham Overy. Meyer wanted to bluff it out, but Byron set the Suliotes on him. Blacked his eye, knocked out two of his teeth, and pretty much dragged him up the aisle. Quite right, too – Byron saw it as a question of morale.'

'So what happened to him?' Yashim asked.

'The chap in Burnham Overy?'

'Meyer.'

'Married the girl.'

'I mean afterwards,' Yashim said, with infinite patience.

'Oh, I see what you're after. No, he didn't get out. Must have been included in the general massacre which followed the fall of the town.' Compston frowned, and sat a little straighter. 'A rather inglorious moment in your history, I'd say.'

'I don't know that war ever reflects well on anyone. Except your friend Byron, of course.'

'Byron's a special case, monsieur.' Compston took out a big lace handkerchief and blew his nose. 'S'what genius means, I suppose.'

He sat, broad and glum, staring at the polished table. His eyelids fluttered, and closed; and then, very slowly, he keeled forwards, resting his forehead on the table, and began to snore.

Palewski and Yashim regarded him in silence.

'I was about to offer coffee. Yashim?'

They took their coffee to the window seat, having turned Compston's head so that his nose was not pressed flat against the mahogany. Outside it was dark, the distant sound of barking dogs mingling with the slow rumble of the English boy's snores.

'Poor Byron!' the ambassador exclaimed. 'One minute the chap had a headache – who wouldn't, with all those Greeks dunning him right left and centre? – and the next, dead. Bled and physicked by a pack of quacks: he didn't stand a chance.'

'No. Perhaps it was deliberate?'

'Deliberate? No, no. Doctors spend their professional lives killing people. It's what they do.'

'Even so,' Yashim said, 'Millingen was at Missolonghi for the Greek cause. Byron's death led on to Greek independence. It rallied the Europeans.'

'Deep, Yashim. I like it. Deep, improbable, but worth contemplating. You're beginning to think like a Pole.'

Yashim gave a wan smile. 'You think it's ridiculous.'

'Not altogether. A fashionable Scottish doctor who accidentally let the greatest living English poet die on him. Not a calling card in Mayfair, is it? Millingen must have come here because there wasn't a patient in Europe who'd have him. Byron was *huge*. But Millingen feels safe out here. You Ottomans – it's what makes you so lovable – wouldn't know Byron from a syringe. You told me that yourself.'

Yashim nodded. 'I've been thinking about that,' he said. He took a sip of coffee. 'We wouldn't know Dr Meyer either, for that matter, if he suddenly showed up in Istanbul.'

'Meyer?'

'The doctor Byron couldn't abide. The man who didn't get away.'

Palewski half-turned his head. 'As Compston says, Yashim, it was a massacre.'

'A massacre. Sometimes – in the confusion – people have a chance to escape.'

Palewski nodded. 'True. They lie doggo in the water, breathing through a reed. Or play dead. Tumbled into a common grave, sneaking out when the devils are gone. That sort of thing.'

Yashim shrugged. 'Meyer survives. Twelve years later, he comes to Istanbul.'

'Very well.'

'He has headaches. He consults a doctor – Millingen. Dr Millingen would remember him.'

Palewski slowly closed his eyes. He shook his head. 'Why consult a doctor if you are one?'

'I don't know. But that's exactly what Lefèvre did – he told us so.'

A look of pain slid across the ambassador's face. He sank back against the shutter-case. 'Yashim.'

'Dr Meyer was the one with the interest in Greek archaeology. The one Byron disliked on sight.'

Palewski considered the ceiling.

'You disliked Lefèvre on sight yourself,' Yashim insisted. 'And then there's a coin trick they all learned from one another. Lefèvre did it. Millingen does it.'

Palewski whistled. 'You think Meyer and Lefèvre were the same man?'

'One or two things I still don't understand – but yes. It makes sense.'

'You can't fault Lord Byron's judgement, if that's the case. But why? Why change his name, and all that?'

'I don't know yet,' Yashim confessed. 'If I did, I'd have the answer to how he died.'

'Why show himself to Millingen?' Palewski asked. 'The man who could still prove who he was?'

Yashim clasped his hands together. 'Look at it this way. What was Lefèvre doing, in the days before he was killed?'

'Reading old books. Getting scared. What else?'

'Negotiating, that's what Malakian thought. Lefèvre had something he could sell.'

'Or buy?'

Yashim shook his head. 'Not so likely. After all, he had no money left.'

Palewski took a deep breath. 'But he had nothing of value on him, either, except the little book. And it's not worth all that much.'

'He didn't necessarily possess what he was selling. Or not yet.'

'Very well. But why break his cover and go to see Millingen?' Palewski unfolded himself from the chair and went to the door.

'Marta! Brandy!'

He stood by the door, listening. Then he came back and flopped back into his chair.

'I said you were thinking like a Pole, Yashim, but don't overdo it. Have one of these,' he added, as Marta brought the tray into the room. 'Thank you, Marta.'

Marta smiled and poured two glasses of brandy. When the door closed Yashim said:

'The Hetira is a society devoted to the restoration of the Greek

225

empire – that's the Great Idea. But restoration means healing too. Restoring to health.'

Palewski pulled a face. 'A society of doctors?'

'Millingen was at Missolonghi for the cause, wasn't he? We know Stephanitzes was, and he was the only Greek among them. Bruno worked for Byron: he followed the poet. Meyer edited the *Chronica Hellenica*. Perhaps he believed in the Great Idea, or perhaps he simply hoped for reward when the kingdom established itself. '

'That fits,' Palewski said. 'Damn it, Yashim. English doctors don't go around murdering people like that.'

'I couldn't say,' Yashim remarked. 'But Lefèvre also visited another man before he was killed. Mavrogordato.'

'That's it!' Palewski slapped his thigh. 'The Greek banker, ship-owner, whatever. He knew where to find Lefèvre that night – you'd booked him a passage on one of his ships. These bankers are doing quite all right, don't want to rock the boat. Lefèvre comes in, babbling about the relics, and Mavrogordato panics. He uses his wealth and influence to have the whole thing discreetly taken care of.'

Yashim sighed. 'I wouldn't call any of those murders discreet. If Mavrogordato wanted Lefèvre killed, why did his wife call me in to dig around? Mavrogordato doesn't sneeze without his wife's permission. He wouldn't organise a string of murders on his own. She might. But then she wouldn't have called me in.'

'Confound it, Yash. Why in the name of God *did* she call you in?'

'Exactly. Why was she so interested in Lefèvre?' Yashim put his fingertips together. 'Something about him confused her.'

'Confused her?'

'I don't think that Lefèvre came babbling to her husband about relics. Mavrogordato could have told her if he had. There was something about Lefèvre that she wanted to know – some-

thing Mavrogordato couldn't tell her. Not because he wouldn't –
he'd tell her everything he knew. No secrets.'

'Out with it, Yashim.'

Yashim smiled. 'I don't have the answer, my friend. At least,
not yet.'

'But you have an idea?'

Yashim nodded thoughtfully. 'Yes. Yes, I do have an idea.'

Compston gave a huge snort and rolled sideways off his chair,
onto the floor.

He sat up blearily, rubbing his head.

'I – I wasn't asleep,' he mumbled automatically.

 95

The validé leans forwards. Some things, she says to herself, do
not change: they must not. I did not believe it, when I was
young. I fought the old women, I scandalised them. But I see it
clearly now: this is my role.

She watches for a deviation. She can remember her last visit:
she compares it with this.

Now he drinks the pure water from the cup, and now he dips
his bread in a plate of salt, to show his brotherhood.

The watermen cross their arms flat against their chests.

They bow to the new recruit. There are spots of colour on his
cheeks.

The sou naziry, the chief of the watermen's guild, raises his
hands. 'Water is life.'

'Water is life,' the new recruit answers, in a firm voice.

'It is the blessing of the spirit.'

'And the spirit is with God,' he answers.

'Be He blessed, the Merciful, the Creator.'

'And may his blessings fall upon us, as the rain.'

The sou naziry steps forward and places his hands on the other man's shoulders. He kisses him three times.

The validé almost smiles: it reminds her of gentlemen on Martinique.

She glances round, to share her smile with Yashim.

But Yashim isn't there.

96

The validé frowned. Minutes had gone by. Prayers concluded, the watermen were beginning to file out into the courtyard through the great doors, under the watchful eye of the sou naziry. In a few moments he would come and present his salaams to the purdah screen. It was really too much! Where was Yashim?

She looked round, just in time to see him emerge from a tiny doorway between two of the great pilasters of the old church. The screen, she observed with relief, concealed him from the watermen: he was brushing his knees which were covered in old lime and the hem of his cloak seemed to be wet.

He gave her the blandest of smiles, and bowed.

The validé frowned. 'Where have you been, *scélérat*?' She hissed.

Yashim put out his hands. 'I saw a door, I went through . . . I have never been here before.'

The shadow of the sou naziry fell across the screen.

'Validé! Your fragrant presence here this day brings much honour upon us. It shall be known that the company of the sou yolci was not forgotten, by your grace.'

The validé's face softened at a stroke. 'You are most kind,

naziry. I do not forget that of all the treasures of Istanbul, that which you guard is the most precious to the people.'

'Validé, you speak the truth. Is it not written that of all living things water is the vital principle?'

'It is written,' the validé replied. 'I have a servant, naziry.'

'Yes, validé?' The sou naziry sounded faintly puzzled.

'Yashim, he is called. A lala. He is an honest man, and desires to talk with you.' She waved Yashim forwards, and her bangles clinked.

Yashim stepped out from behind the screen, and bowed. The naziry gave a curt nod, and then raised his hands.

'You will forgive me, validé. I have no time for the lala now,' he said. 'For two days, I must inspect the bents. On my return . . .'

He bowed before the screen. The validé made no sound.

97

Yashim placed the vegetables in his basket, and took the money from his purse.

'Yeh, yeh, yeh – and no offence, efendi! But this coin's light – look, five piastres more, and there's the deal.' The brother hopped from foot to foot, one hand outstretched, glancing up and down the road. 'I'm coming, hanum! Five piastres, efendi.'

Yashim felt a surge of irritation as he counted out the tiny coins.

When he got back to the apartment he was not surprised to find Amélie on the divan, reading a book.

'I hoped you'd come back,' she said.

'You prepared the stove.'

'If you needed it . . .'

'Yes. I'll make pilaff,' he said. 'Don't move. Just read your book.'

He stripped two onions from their hulls, chopped them fine and dropped them with a handful of pine nuts into a pan of olive oil which he set on the coals. He crushed two cloves of garlic and brushed off their skins with the knife, then chopped them roughly and added them to the onion with the flat of the blade. He drizzled two handfuls of rice from the crock into the pan and stirred it when the rice began to stick. After a few minutes the rice was becoming clear, so he pulled the pan from the coals and looked into the stock-pot, which was starting to steam. He let it rise to the boil.

Amélie had been watching him.

'Max never liked to cook,' she said. 'He didn't have a sense of taste. Perhaps, you know, that's why he never liked to kiss.'

Yashim put the rice back on the heat and ladled out some stock.

'It certainly explains something,' he muttered. When she asked what he meant, he told her about the dolma he'd given her husband.

Amélie laughed. 'You chose the wrong Frenchman.'

The rice was drying out: Yashim put a few more ladlefuls of stock into the pan and stirred it in.

'I think he was a Swiss,' he said carefully.

Amélie was silent for a while. Yashim added salt, pepper and a pinch of cinnamon to the rice, and covered it with a domed lid. 'Did he tell you about his time in Greece?'

'Oh yes. He saw the Parthenon, and Epidaurus in the Peloponnese. He said there was so much more, waiting to be unearthed – and thank God Napoleon had invaded Egypt, not Greece!'

'But he had a war there, all the same,' Yashim said. 'If he went in the twenties.'

'He never told me much about that,' Amélie said.

'What about Byron? Did he mention Missolonghi?'

'Was that where Byron died? No. Max never said anything about that.'

'So he never said anything about Dr Millingen – or Dr Meyer?' Yashim trimmed the stems of four baby artichokes, and set them to steam over the stock. He glanced round.

Amélie was holding her head in her hand, as if deep in thought.

'Millingen?' She looked up quickly, in time for Yashim to notice a pink flush fading from her cheeks. 'The sultan's physician?'

Yashim stood with the knife in one hand, the disc of the choke in the other.

'I –' She gave a little laugh. 'I met him, just yesterday. Isn't that a coincidence?'

'Extraordinary,' Yashim agreed mildly, turning to the chopping block again.

'I didn't want to tell you – I thought you'd be angry with me.'

Yashim began to slice the choke carefully.

'I was stuck here with nothing to do, so I decided to go and have a look at Aya Sofia. I'm afraid I got a little carried away, and I forgot that Christians are not welcome in a mosque.'

'That depends on the mosque,' Yashim said. 'But Aya Sofia – no. An unbeliever – and a woman, alone. At least – you *were* alone?'

'It was thoughtless of me. I'm sorry. I hope I haven't offended you.'

Yashim looked down at the chopping board. 'No,' he said. 'What happened?'

'They chased me out. It was frightening – I wasn't sure what they would do to me. Then a carriage pulled up and I tumbled in.'

'I see. And Dr Millingen?'

'It was his carriage. He brought me back here.'

Yashim pursed his lips gently, sunk in thought.

'You came straight on here, from Aya Sofia?'

'Yes. He was perfectly gentlemanly, very stiff and English. He was in a hurry. I thought you would be angry – and then you weren't here. And when you did come back, you were half-dead, and, well, you know the rest. I forgot the whole thing until now.'

Yashim picked up the board and swept the slices of artichoke into the pan with his fingers. He had a prickling sensation in the back of his head.

He stirred the rice slowly.

Something here, he knew, was wrong – and it wasn't his pilaff. There was something about Amélie that was odd, as well, beyond her hesitation, or her blushes.

She was wearing a pair of little pointed slippers.

98

Palewski reached out from under the bedclothes to take the tea. 'Thank you, Marta.'

'Wrong,' Yashim said, settling himself at the foot of the bed. Palewski opened his eyes.

'Good God, it's you! Really, Yashim, you may as well have a bed here until the wretched Lefèvre woman's gone.'

'Too late.' Yashim pulled a folded paper from his cloak. 'I found this note under my door this morning.'

Palewski opened it.

Mon cher Monsieur Yashim – Few words can express my gratitude to you. To lose a beloved husband, to find oneself cast adrift in a foreign land, to realise that all one's highest hopes and fondest dreams are gone irretrievably: these are blows that strike to the depths of a woman's soul.

Without you, cher monsieur, I should have sunk beneath them before now. Your kindness and hospitality gave me the energy to meet such adversity – perhaps, even a sense of

*hope. But now, I feel, that energy is spent; I feel weary and,
but for you, alone. I intend to present myself without further
delay to the French ambassador – who will, if he is kind as
I believe him to be, ensure my safe return to France.*

*I shall remember you with affection, and wish that you
will sometimes think of me, your very humble and obedient
friend,*

Amélie Lefèvre

'A very proper expression of sentiment, Yashim,' Palewski
said warmly. '"Blows that strike to the depths of a woman's
soul." Dear me. You're probably sorry she's gone. I think I am.'

Yashim wrung his hands. His lips still burned where she had
kissed him.

'The embassy was my first suggestion. I must have made her
feel unwelcome. She was my guest.'

Palewski looked at him intently. 'My dear fellow, this won't
do. Is Marta awake?'

'She made the tea.'

'I was afraid it might be too early.' Palewski flung back the
feather bed and went to the door. 'Marta!'

Yashim heard the swish of Marta's skirts on stairs.

'Marta, my dear. Our friend Yashim is feeling a little out of sorts
and wants a capital breakfast to set him up. Coffee, eggs, bread.
Can we manage? There's a blueberry jam that's just arrived from
the village, we'll have some of that. Cheese, olives. What else?
Perhaps some of the – ah – diplomatic sausage, too. Lay it out in
the salon, will you – looks like a lovely day, we can eat at the window. Bit of fruit? Thank you, Marta, you're splendid.'

He turned to his friend and rubbed his hands vigorously. 'No
more misery, Yashim. The girl's gone – Lefèvre's girl, I mean –
and she's done the best thing. Can't have her moping around in
a foreign city with no one to talk to but you. France, that's the

place for her. Just let me pull on a few things, and I'll be down in a moment.'

Yashim was having coffee in the sitting room when Palewski rejoined him.

'She doesn't know that her husband was Meyer,' Yashim said. 'But yesterday she met Millingen.'

He told Palewski what Amélie had said.

'And she was holding something back?' Palewski frowned. 'I don't get it, Yash.'

Yashim sighed. 'Neither do I,' he admitted.

99

Supported by a sturdy slave-girl on either arm, the validé descended from the litter in the great hall of the sultan's palace at Beşiktaş. At the foot of the steps she graciously inclined her head to acknowledge the attendance of the sultan's highest household officer, the chief black eunuch.

He stood at the head of a party of ladies, all dressed in the latest French fashion, ranged with their parasols for a stroll through the palace gardens; many of them craned their heads to see the validé better. She smiled at them, nodding.

'Ibrahim Aga,' she said. 'Mesdames.'

The sultan's concubines returned a murmured greeting. The chief black eunuch bowed deeply. 'Validé.'

'I see you are filling out, Ibrahim. It's most becoming.'

Ibrahim Aga smiled uncertainly. 'Thank you, validé. May I present the ladies?'

He escorted her down the line. The girls curtseyed, modestly lowering their eyes until the validé had passed. Now and then she put up a pale hand to straighten a lace jabot, or to pinch a cheek, and for every girl she had a flattering word or two. 'What lovely hair! Very pretty. A little less rouge, mademoiselle, perhaps. Your smile is charming,' and so on. The ladies blushed and smiled.

At the end she turned to the Kislar Aga. 'They are a credit to you, Ibrahim. They dress well, and seem altogether charming. I am delighted to see them taking advantage of the garden. We did not always have such a luxury in my day.'

'Yes, validé. We walk out every morning.'

The validé nodded, and sighed.

'They need exercise, Ibrahim. Take me to the sultan.'

The ladies bobbed politely as she began climbing the stairs. How very trivial they looked, the validé reflected, in their French gowns and corsets, their shawls and silk pumps: no more consequential than a tray of Belgian chocolates. A manufactory: yes. In her day, at Topkapi, how she and the others had prided themselves on their style – the way they wore colour, the arrangement of their hair, the artful collage of shawls and pelisses, silks and furs. Then they had paraded like a pride of she-tigers, jewels ablaze, loose-limbed and glorying in their fine skin and perfect teeth! Not like these girls, these fashion-plates, these trained canaries in their cage.

It was such a shame!

She paused at the top of the wide stairs, leaning on the rail. How very dead this palace was, how still. The French paintings hung unexamined on the stairs, like the epitaphs of soldiers who had died and were not remembered. Empty, straight-backed English chairs were ranged against the walls.

At the top of the stairs the chief governess was waiting to make her obeisance. Tall and plump, wearing traditional harem dress, she carried a long staff tipped in silver; a bunch of keys at her belt clanked softly as she bowed. At her signal, several girls stepped forward to help the validé out of her satin coat and conducted her to a sunlit room overlooking the sparkling water of the Bosphorus. She felt the breeze on her face. Sinking into a gilded sofa, she let the girls gently arrange her hair and smooth the creases in the folds of her robes. One girl plumped the pillows at he validé's back; another fetched a stool for her feet.

'May we humbly offer a cooling sherbet, Validé Sultan?' The governess indicated a tray.

The validé settled back against the cushions and sighed. Always the same tender rituals, the same half-concealed glances of affection and respect: she should have made her visit sooner.

She took a sip of sherbet, and returned the glass. Then she glanced at the governess, and gave an almost imperceptible nod.

The imperial governess stepped up and took her place at the validé's side, standing motionless with folded arms and lowered eyes. The sultan's first wife, mother of the crown prince and future Validé Sultan, glided into the room like a swan. With an elegant bow, she approached her imperial mother-in-law and took the hem of her robe in one hand. In a signal of respect and obedience, she made a motion of touching the hem with her lips and putting it to her forehead.

'How is Mecid, our imperial grandson, daughter?'

'He is praying for your good health, validé.'

The remaining three Kadınefendis entered softly to greet their mother-in-law, one by one bowing and bringing her hem to their lips. They moved with graceful calm, silent and unhurried, and stood back to attention. The validé spoke to them kindly, and they blushed and smiled. Looking at their beautiful faces, their pretty smiles, she felt a lump rising to her throat.

Two girls helped her to her feet. The Kadınefendis bowed demurely, and the validé put her hand on the aga's arm.

'*Allons*,' she said. She felt her heart fluttering in her breast.

Doors opened silently at the approach of the odd couple, the black eunuch with the tiny white woman on his arm, taking slow, careful steps across the polished parquet. At monotonous intervals the validé looked down through thickly curtained windows onto the Bosphorus below – a scene of activity that was at once vigorous, silenced, and remote. At last, the validé entered the sultan's bedroom.

The shutters were half-drawn against the glare of the sun, and for a few moments the validé paused on the threshold, peering round. She moved slowly across to the bed. The aga fetched a chair, and as she sat down she groped on the counterpane for her son's hand.

She found it, bony and cold: for a moment her heart skipped a beat, but then she felt the faint returning squeeze of his fingers, and saw the pillows twitch as he turned his head.

For a long time neither of them said a word.

'My little lion,' the validé said softly at long last, and with her other hand she bent forwards and traced her fingers across his brow, to brush aside a lock of hair.

'Mother.'

She squeezed his hand. 'Courage, always,' she whispered. It should never be like this, she thought: the old bring no comfort to the dying.

A mother cannot bury her own son.

The sultan's eyes slid away from hers. 'He does not come.'

The validé said nothing. The crown prince was young, and yet afraid of death.

The sultan shifted slightly under the bedclothes. 'There is much that he cannot understand, validé.'

He breathed with difficulty, and speaking was a struggle: but he spoke for several minutes, still holding his mother's hand, unburdening his mind.

The validé heard him out in silence.

'With God's help,' she said at last. 'The people will stay quiet.'

She felt the pressure of his fingers as they clenched around her own.

100

George Compston picked up the note and turned it over in his hands. He walked through the embassy tapping it against his teeth, looking for Fizerley.

He found him with his feet up on a desk, rubbing olive oil onto his moustache. He started when he saw Compston.

'Got a note,' Compston said carelessly.

Fizerley swung his legs to the ground. 'Is she pretty?'

Compston opened the note, read it quickly, and blushed.

'I'm afraid that's between me and these four walls, old man,' he said, rather thickly.

Fizerley shrugged. It was so infernally hot.

Compston read the note again. He'd lit a spark there! A Turkish Byron enthusiast – whatever next?

It was from that eunuch, Yashim.

101

The sou naziry slid from his horse and passed the reins to an apprentice. He knelt on the rim of the tank, and plunged his hands into the cold water: it had been a hot ride, even beneath the trees. He wiped the dust of the road from his face and the back of his neck. Leka presented him with a towel.

'I don't see anything wrong with the levels,' the sou naziry said.

He patted the towel into a ball and tossed it at Leka. The reservoirs had been exactly as he had imagined: a drop of about six inches. Normal for the time of year.

'It is the old women who like to spread this kind of talk,' he added. 'A sultan is about to die, and they think the sky is falling on their heads.'

The shade was black under the trees. There was no wind, but the forests exhaled a refreshing coolness, and the monthly ride had given the sou naziry an appetite. It would be good to sit by the edge of the woods, and eat.

The foresters had prepared the usual refreshments. A black tent was set up on the grass, with carpets and silver trays, and jugs of sherbet made of sour cherries and oranges covered with a little square of gauze, the edges weighted with dangling beads. To one side a fire was crackling under a tripod, where a cook was preparing a bulgur pilaff; two foresters were squatting by the tandir. Long before dawn they had begun to make and tend the fire, fetching brushwood and logs, reducing the wood to a pile of glowing coals. The pit they had dug was invisible, beneath a covering of baked mud and sticks.

The cook had selected a lamb from the flock the day before. He had skinned and gutted the animal, studding its flesh with garlic spikes before he rubbed it with a mixture of yoghurt and sieved tomatoes, crushed onion and garlic, coriander and cumin. At dawn, when the fire began to sink, they trussed the lamb to a stake by its feet, and lowered it over the pit, setting the meat deeper and deeper as the morning progressed. Now the meat was cooking underground, sealed by a makeshift lid.

One of the foresters looked up. Recognising the naziry, he motioned to his companion, and the two men carefully raised the lid. The naziry saw the slightest trickle of smoke emerge from the pit. Overthrowing the lid, the forester bent forwards, and with a flash of his knife removed one of the kidneys, which he presented to the naziry on the point. The naziry took the smoking morsel in his fingers and ate with relish, standing by the pit, gazing down into the glowing fire.

Men, like animals, were afraid of fire, the naziry thought.

But fire itself feared the naziry. Fire was afraid of water.

One of the foresters yawned. He was holding a green branch, which he waved gently over the roasting meat to chase the flies away.

The naziry settled himself on the carpet, crossing his legs beneath him, and watched the men draw the lamb out of the tandir. Beyond, the sunlight glittered on the surface of the bent; frogs croaked in the reeds; swallows skimmed the water and rose twittering and whistling into the air. A servant picked up a copper tray and polished it carefully with a cloth. The cook nodded.

He arranged a mound of pilaff on the tray, then took the long knife hanging at his belt and began to carve the meat.

A horseman rode up the track and out of the trees. At the sight of the tent, and the smoking meat, he reined in and bowed from the saddle.

The sou naziry raised a hand, in greeting.

'May you eat well, efendi,' the stranger said, politely.

The naziry hesitated. There was something familiar about the rider: he had an impression that they had met, but he could not remember where.

'Thank you,' he said.

The stranger slipped from the saddle. Holding the reins in his hand he said: 'Forgive me, naziry. I did not recognise you, in the shade. I am Yashim. Yesterday I attended the validé, at the induction ceremony.'

The naziry had already realised who he was. 'Yashim efendi, of course.' He glanced at the lamb. 'You will join us, please.'

It was Yashim's turn to hesitate. 'You are most generous, naziry; but I do not mean to intrude,' he said.

'There is meat,' the naziry said, with a gesture towards the lamb. 'And you have ridden far.'

He motioned to the syce to take Yashim's horse.

Yashim sat down, and the tray of pilaff and lamb was brought to the tent. Afterwards there was a blood-red watermelon, refreshingly sweet. The two men ate quickly, in silence. Once or twice, Yashim caught the naziry looking curiously at him out of the corner of his eye.

A servant poured water, and they washed their hands.

The coffee was served on a salver, with a tchibouk.

'I have not been here for many years,' Yashim confessed, at last. 'This is the bent built by Sinan, isn't it?'

The naziry grunted. 'It is a bent, like another. Sinan repaired it, at our direction.'

At our direction! It was a magnificent phrase, Yashim thought, for Sinan's career as an architect had begun almost three hundred years ago.

'It existed already, then?'

The naziry nodded. 'It was smaller, I believe, in the Greek time.'

Yashim smiled. 'I did not realise, naziry, that the guild had such a long memory.'

The naziry looked surprised. 'How should it be otherwise?' He took a whiff of his pipe. 'Greek or Turk, a man needs water to live.'

'Of course.'

'For a village, it is enough to make a well. But for a city? The people must wash, and drink, and cook food, Yashim efendi.'

Yashim nodded.

'How do men make a city? You think a sultan claps his hands, and it appears like the palace of a djinn? No, not even a sultan can do this. Water. Water to build a city. And water to defend it, also.'

'Defend it?'

'Of course. Great walls, brave soldiers, even a wise sultan in command – these can delay a city's fall. But water decides the battle.'

Yashim considered the naziry's remark. 'Istanbul is vulnerable, then,' he said.

The naziry raised an eyebrow. 'It is not as vulnerable as you might guess, Yashim efendi. That is our responsibility. But without us, the city is dust. It cannot eat. It cannot live. This,' he added, pointing the stem of his pipe towards the glittering bent, 'is the blood of Istanbul.'

Yashim looked at the shimmering water. The foresters and the naziry's men were squatting in a circle, sharing out the rest of the pilaff and meat.

'The men of the guild,' Yashim began. 'They are all Albanians, aren't they?'

The naziry made a motion of dismissal. 'They are men who understand one another, that is all.' He was silent for a moment. 'But yes, also we have a gift. Is it because we come from the mountains, that we understand the fall of water, and the measure of distances? I do not know how it is, but God gives every race some special task. A Bulgar knows his sheep. A Serb can always fight. A Greek knows how to talk and a Turk how to be silent. But we Albanians – we can read water.'

And keep secrets, Yashim thought. Sustain memories.

'You have great experience,' he said.

The naziry shrugged. 'Even with a gift, a man must learn. Do you see the blood of a man – his liver – his lungs? A doctor sees a man this way, after many years' experience. You see a city: you see its streets, its hills, its houses, its people. But you do not see as deeply as we can. We, who are members of a guild two hundred strong.'

'And what do you see, naziry?'

'Another city, Yashim efendi; like a maze. In parts it is older than memory.' He puffed thoughtfully on his pipe. 'A dangerous place, for a man without experience.'

Yashim leaned forwards. 'There was a man, called Xani –'

'It is a maze,' the naziry repeated.

He raised his hand, and the servant stepped forwards.

'I wish to sleep,' the naziry said. 'Take these away.'

He put his hand to his chest, and inclined his head, very slightly, towards Yashim. 'As I say, a most dangerous place.'

He lay back on the carpet and closed his eyes.

Yashim sat watching him for several minutes, not moving.

The naziry began to snore.

 102

Dr Millingen came down the steps of his house and climbed into the sedan chair waiting for him in the road. The chair-men shouldered their burden and began to lope placidly through the crowd streaming downhill towards the Pera landing stage.

Dr Millingen settled his hands on the clasp of his leather bag. Edinburgh, he thought, had prepared him for much: but nothing could ever quite reconcile him to a sedan chair. The sultan had ordered it, of course, so there was little point in refusing the apparent honour – and as a mode of transport it was certainly well-suited to the steep and convoluted streets of modern Pera, where a horse might struggle through the crowd, or slip on the cobblestones going downhill. But Millingen always felt ridiculous, and exposed: like a cherry on an iced cake.

He breathed heavily, and patted his bag. It was all in the mind. The thing to remember was that no one cared, but him. He caught sight of his own reflection in the wide glass window of the Parisian patisserie, in his swaying litter, and smiled to himself. The cherry on the cake, indeed.

Nobody in Istanbul would give him so much as a second glance.

103

Palewski bit down on the éclair and wiped a squirt of crème anglaise from his cheek with his thumb. 'Pera, these days. It's not the patisseries I object to,' he mumbled. 'Only the people.'

Yashim nodded and took a sip of his tisane, watching the English doctor disappear, swaying, through the Pera crowds.

He reached into his coat for an envelope, which he smoothed flat on the little marble table. 'The people,' Yashim echoed finally. 'And when, do you think, they began to change?'

There was no mistaking the chair-men's livery. Even without the gold edging, the waistcoats they were wearing were far too new and clean to rank them with the ordinary chair-men of the city. It was Beşiktaş, then, for the doctor. He could be gone for hours.

Palewski raised an eyebrow, and sucked the end of his thumb. 'For hundreds of years,' he said, 'Istanbul's people lived in peace together. That started to change after '21,' he said thoughtfully.

'The rioting against the Greeks.'

'Riot. Massacre. Whatever, Yashim. Hanging the Patriarch.'

'Driving out the old Phanariot dynasties.'

Palewski frowned. 'More than that, Yashim. Fear and mistrust. They hanged the Patriarch from the gate of his own church, then they got the Jews to cut his body down. They say the Jews cut it up to feed to the dogs. I doubt it, frankly. But that isn't what matters. The Turks were afraid. They turned on the Greeks. The Greeks were afraid. Now they hate the Jews. Everything changed.'

Yashim nodded.

'Then the Janissary business five years afterwards,' Palewski added. 'End of a tradition.'

'It didn't take long for the new men to appear, did it?' Yashim leaned forwards. 'Mavrogordato. Did he arrive here before, or after, the Janissary affair?'

Palewski picked up a napkin. 'Before, I'd swear. He was in Istanbul by '24, at the latest.'

'Mavrogordato couldn't have known Meyer, then?'

Palewski considered the question. 'Meyer was at Missolonghi in 1826, but Mavrogordato was here in Istanbul, getting rich and keeping his head down.'

'Hmmm. When Lefèvre – Meyer – visited Mavrogordato the other day, he got an unsecured loan. Why not? French, archaeologist, very respectable. But whatever Lefèvre told the banker, it upset Madame. It made her – curious. She called me in, remember?'

'You said she was confused.'

Yashim nodded. 'Mavrogordato had never seen Meyer. Madame hadn't seen Lefèvre. She only had her husband's account of their meeting – and his description of the man who came asking for money.'

'And?'

Yashim glanced out of the window. 'She began to suspect.'

Palewski had picked up his éclair, but he set it down again. 'Suspect? That Lefèvre was a phoney?'

'Lefèvre said something that made Mavrogordato give him money. And Madame to wonder who Lefèvre really was.'

'Go on.'

'She wondered if he might be Dr Meyer.'

Palewski blew out his cheeks. 'Madame Mavrogordato? She knew Meyer?'

'Mavrogordato, you see, wasn't at Missolonghi.' Yashim drained his cup. 'She was.'

'And met Meyer?'

The door to the street opened with a jangle of bells, and a man with shiny whiskers and a black cane came in: it was just like Paris.

'Better than that,' Yashim said. 'She married him.'

Palewski groaned and buried his face in his hands.

Yashim looked through the big glass window. Further up the street, the door of Millingen's house opened and closed again and a man in the livery of a servant ran lightly down the steps with a basket in his hand. The crowd was very dense, and the servant lifted the basket and set it on his shoulder.

'Compston told us that Meyer seduced a Greek woman at Missolonghi,' Yashim explained. 'Lord Byron made him marry her.'

Yashim followed the bobbing basket through the crowd: the man was going to the market.

Palewski shook his head. 'What Compston said doesn't mean that she was Madame Mavrogordato.' He frowned. 'She couldn't be – her son, Alexander, must be at least twenty years old.'

'If he is her son.'

'No – but! Yashim, you told me yourself, Alexander's the spitting image of her.'

'She's his aunt. Mr Mavrogordato is her brother.'

'Brother?'

Yashim stirred the envelope with a finger. 'I got Compston to do a little research for me. He dug up the name of Meyer's wife, and guess what?'

'It was Mavrogordato?'

'Christina Mavrogordato. She's living with her brother, and his son.'

Palewski sat hunched over his éclair. After a few moments he raised his head.

'But why?'

Yashim framed the envelope with his hands. 'I think what happened was this. Meyer escaped Missolonghi – and abandoned his wife. Somehow she survived the massacre and made her way to Istanbul, where her brother was already doing very well. He was a widower – he had a child, Alexander, living in Chios. Alexander needed a mother.'

'But she could still have declared that she was his sister,' Palewski objected. 'No impropriety there.'

Yashim shook his head. 'She knew what Meyer was like: he'd abandoned her to save his own skin, but there was no knowing whether he might try coming back. Her brother was a very rich man. And legally, she was Meyer's wife.'

'She was afraid he'd claim her – and touch Mavrogordato for money, into the bargain?'

Yashim leaned forwards. 'She's lived with that fear for the past thirteen years. The Orthodox Church teaches that a woman belongs to her husband. Christina Mavrogordato was Meyer's property. And she had had her fill of Meyer. Meyer seduced her. He abandoned her. But he liked money.'

Palewski put his fingers flat on the table. 'An interesting side-light on this situation,' he said slowly, 'is that it proves Lefèvre to have been not only a bounder, a coward, a bolter, a traitor and a thoroughgoing shit, but a bigamist, as well. Unless –' A look of comical horror crossed his face. 'You don't think he had become a Muslim, too?'

Yashim flashed him a look of mild rebuke.

'A joke, Yashim. Sorry.' He folded his arms. 'So Madame Mavrogordato had Lefèvre killed, then.'

'I thought so, once.' Yashim got to his feet. 'I haven't got much time, and there's something I still need to find out.'

'From who?'

'Dr Millingen – indirectly. I'm going into his house. Do you want to come?'

'No doctors for me, Yashim.'

'But he won't be there.'

Palewski narrowed his eyes. 'I'm not sure that makes it any better. I'm still the ambassador, you know. And I am planning on enjoying this éclair.'

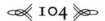

104

Yashim crossed the street, mounted the steps, and rapped smartly on the knocker to Dr Millingen's house. When nobody answered, he launched himself into the crowd. Twenty yards down the street he entered a bakery. He walked past the counter with a nod to the baker, past the loaves, through the kitchens and out of the shop at the back, into a small yard surrounded by a low wall. Yashim heaved himself up onto it and jumped lightly down the other side, just managing to avoid crushing a clump of horseradish growing in Dr Millingen's tiny physic garden.

From a door in the far wall a cinder path led directly through the garden to the back door. Yashim moved closer to the house. The windows on the ground floor were barred, the back door locked with a patent American mechanism, but there was a coal-hopper at the end of the house which suggested possibilities. Yashim went to work on the padlock, and after a few minutes he saw it click open. He lifted the doors and lowered himself into the chute.

There was a little coal pressed up against a sliding panel at the bottom of the chute. Yashim lifted the larger lumps aside, working his fingers into the coal to find the lower edge of the panel. It slid upwards with a sound of falling coal.

Yashim paused, listening; then squeezed feet first through the opening. Once through he stood brushing the dust from his cloak while his eyes adjusted to the darkness. There were some steps, and a door on a catch; but the door was not close-fitting.

In a moment Yashim had slipped his knife between the door and the jamb and was stealing out into the corridor.

Millingen's study lay just across the hall. Yashim whipped in, leaving the door open, and looked around. The green and gold striped wallpaper hung with sporting prints, the mantelpiece with an ornamented clock over an English grate, the big walnut desk with its black leather top, and a set of shelves set into an alcove, full of books: neat, methodical and prosperous.

He tried the drawers of the desk. Notepaper, sealing wax, a box of steel nibs. In a lower drawer, some papers. Yashim riffled through them. They were written in English, in a barely legible scrawl. He closed the drawer and went over to the bookshelves.

The lower shelves contained a series of leather-bound boxes which at first glance resembled books. Yashim squatted down. For the most part the boxes contained more papers: accounts, copies of the doctor's bills, notes about patients written in English, and in the same difficult hand. But one also contained a series of letters, written in Greek, between Millingen and a certain Dr Stephanitzes in Athens.

Yashim was about to lift the box to the desk when a sound from the corridor – light footsteps, perhaps, and a peculiar swishing noise – made him freeze. He was about to turn around when he heard the door click, and the sound of a key turning in the lock.

He sprang for the handle. At the last moment he decided against rattling the handle and knocked on the wooden panel, instead: if the servant had returned, he might think the doctor had absent-mindedly left the door ajar. But no one came. Yashim knocked again, much louder.

There were no sounds of retreating footsteps; he had certainly not heard the front door open or close. He pressed his ear to the panel. For a moment he had a sense that somebody was standing on the other side of the door.

He looked around the room. The window was hung with

muslin curtains against the street, and was barred like the windows at the back of the house. He looked at the empty grate, and sighed. Everything that made this room in Pera solid and English made it also a perfect prison.

He crouched down, with a faint hope that he might be able to retrieve the key from the keyhole on the other side. But the key was no longer in the lock.

Whoever had locked the door had done so deliberately, knowing that Yashim was inside.

The idea made Yashim frown. He went back and squatted down by the bookshelves, from where Millingen's desk almost hid him from the door. To see him, someone would have had to lean in at the door. They would have had to approach along the corridor very quietly – as if they already knew he was there.

In which case, someone must have seen him going in. Not Millingen: he had gone out. But the servant – could he have doubled back, while Yashim was coming through the coal chute?

But then – why wait so long to lock the door?

Yashim bit his lip. He lifted the box of papers onto the desk, and bent over it.

He'd come to do a job, and now, it seemed, he was being afforded the leisure to complete it.

 105

Several hours passed before Yashim, sitting in the doctor's chair, heard the sound of the doctor coming back.

The manservant had returned long before, making his way noisily down the passage to the back of the house. He had let the servant go by: he wanted to see Millingen, after all. He closed his eyes and set about concocting an imaginary supper.

In his mind's eye he had already set the meze down, when he heard the sound of the key grating in the lock and Dr Millingen came in, holding his hat like a tray. He was followed by the manservant, scowling fiercely.

'You!'

Yashim slid out of the chair and bowed.

Millingen glared at the box on the table. 'This is an outrage!' He said. 'I am a doctor. My practice depends on the bond of confidentiality. This study is where I keep my patients' notes.'

'But I'm not interested in your medical records, Dr Millingen,' Yashim said.

'I suppose I must take your word for that! The assurances of a mere house breaker.' Dr Millingen sneered. 'Perhaps you would be so kind as to explain what does interest you, before I turn you over to the watch.'

'Of course, forgive me. I came here on account of your coin collection.'

'My coins? The devil you did.'

Yashim spread his hands in a calming gesture. 'I admit that I have no particular interest in coins. But I am intrigued by the collecting process, Dr Millingen. Your method of acquiring specimens. Malakian, for instance – you described him as an excellent source.'

Millingen put his hat on the desk and picked up the box. 'What of it?'

'Malakian is here in Istanbul. Athens might be a better place to look, if your speciality is the coinage of the Morean despots. I imagine that hoards of these coins are discovered there, buried in the ground or hidden in old buildings, or whatever. Is that so?'

'It happens,' Millingen said. He glanced at the label on the box, and set it down slowly. 'Mostly in my dreams.'

'I wondered – your Athenian friend, who sends you coins?

251

You said he was a doctor. Perhaps you were at Missolonghi together?'

'I have made no secret of my presence at Missolonghi, Yashim efendi. Dr Stephanitzes was a colleague.'

'Of course. Now he writes books. He's a firm advocate of what the Greeks call the Great Idea, isn't he? I was curious about your correspondence.'

'Well, well. I wasn't aware that even in Turkey curiosity was a warrant for entering a man's house and rifling his private papers.' Dr Millingen's expression hardened. 'I suppose you will tell me what conclusions you were able to draw?'

'Very few – I merely confirmed some ideas of mine. That, for example, the traffic between you and Dr Stephanitzes was not all one way. In return for his coins, you were able to put him in the way of expanding his own collection.'

'I see. Well, go on.'

Yashim reached forwards and opened the lid of the box of papers.

'Here, in his most recent letter, Dr Stephanitzes refers to a former member of the collectors' club. You've mentioned him surfacing in Istanbul with a potentially devastating offer. Stephanitzes remembers him leaving the club without paying his dues.'

'That's correct,' Millingen said. 'Ours is a very small world.'

'Yes, isn't it?' Yashim said pleasantly. 'Dr Stephanitzes confesses to being highly interested in the former club-member's offer. A late Byzantine hoard – no, forgive me: the very last Byzantine hoard. But I expect you remember all that.

'He urges you to inspect the hoard personally. I'd say your Dr Stephanitzes is a sceptic: he doesn't seem to trust the ex-member very far. But if the hoard proves to be genuine, he thinks that it could be exchanged for a considerable collection of valuable Greek coinage.'

'But what of that, Yashim efendi?' Dr Millingen took a pipe

from the rack on his desk. He opened a drawer and scrabbled with his fingers for the tobacco. 'It strikes me that you have had a very dull afternoon here. You, after all, are not a collector. What would you know of our curious passions? You'd be surprised by the jealousies and satisfactions we experience in our little world. The intensity of our feelings. Even the level of our mutual mistrust.'

He sat down and tamped the tobacco into the bowl of his pipe. 'Malakian – through your good offices – completed the set for me. I was elated for a day or two. But now? Rather depressed. I think I shall donate the collection to the British Museum.'

Yashim cocked his head. 'I'd rather you explained about Lefèvre's hoard,' he said.

Dr Millingen leaned back in his chair and gave a chuckle. 'Well, well.' He sucked on his unlit pipe. 'You've guessed, then. I did see the unfortunate Dr Lefèvre. And yes, we discussed a hoard. Unfortunately I was never able to inspect it, as my friend advised, so I don't suppose we will ever really know what it was he was offering to exchange. Poor fellow. He had so many irons in the fire.'

'Another buyer, maybe?'

'Yes, that too.'

Yashim frowned. 'But you and Stephanitzes: you could trump all buyers, couldn't you? If you wanted what he offered badly enough.'

Millingen hesitated. 'You are forgetting, Yashim efendi, that Lefèvre was only offering an idea. A promise, if you will. Why would I trust him?'

'Because he'd been your friend.'

'Lefèvre my friend? I never knew Lefèvre.'

Yashim shrugged. 'Strictly speaking, no. But you did know Meyer. The Swiss doctor at Missolonghi. You shared a cause.'

He expected Millingen to jump, but the Englishman merely reached for a match, and frowned. 'Meyer?' He struck the match and it flared between his fingers. 'He was a Savoyard, in fact.'

'A Savoyard?'

'French Swiss. Swiss when it suits, and French when it doesn't.' He paused to light his pipe. 'We shared a cause, as you say. It seemed a cause to fight for, when I was young.'

'And now?'

Millingen tossed the match into the grate and put his hand around the bowl of his pipe. 'I don't know if you heard what happened at Missolonghi, Yashim efendi. The daily bombardments. The daily toll of disease. All the world knows Byron came to Missolonghi and died, and half of them think he was leading a cavalry charge at the time, with Suliotes in scarves and fustanellas brandishing pistols at his side. They think he was glorious because he was a poet, and that his death was glorious. But it wasn't so. Missolonghi was just a trap, and Byron died just like most of them died, of fever, or cramp, or dysentery, or cholera. Sometimes people died when a shell landed on them in the street, out of the blue. Good for a doctor, eh? Plenty of cases to puzzle over. Plenty of widows and orphaned children to doctor and send to their graves. And that, my friend, was our revolutionary war.'

Millingen clamped the pipe between his teeth and stood up.

'I told you before, I don't like post-mortems. And I said why, too. I doctor to the living, not the dead. It's my job to preserve life.'

Yashim nodded. What Millingen said sounded true. It also sounded like a speech.

'I was wondering about Meyer.'

Millingen scowled. 'I see. What about him?'

'Well, if Byron disliked him, I suppose he didn't attend the poet – as a doctor, I mean.'

'No.'

'So he was lucky, in that sense.' Yashim sounded embarrassed. Millingen's scowl darkened. 'What are you saying?'

'Nothing, I mean – but after all, the poet died. In spite of – everything. Everything you could do.'

'For God's sake!' Millingen swore, in English. 'You think we killed Byron? Rubbish! Cuppings. Purges. We took out pints of blood – all by the book. Don't think Meyer could have done any better!' Millingen's tone was incredulous; spots of colour had appeared on his cheeks.

'No, forgive me.' Yashim put out his hands in a soothing gesture. 'I only meant – I'd heard – how Meyer was lost, when the rest of you got away. You joined the break-out, and it worked. The lucky two thousand. It must have been a scene of dreadful confusion. A crowd of terrified people, groping their way through the Turkish lines in the dark. Losing each other. Unable to raise their voices. People taking different routes into the hills. Is that how it was?'

Millingen's lips were tight. 'Something like that.'

'Yet Meyer stayed behind. Trying – and failing – to protect his wife, perhaps.'

Millingen flexed his fingers. He was breathing hard.

'He had a wife to think of, didn't he?' Yashim said.

Millingen rubbed his eyes with his thumb and forefinger and when he opened them again they looked pink and tired. 'Maybe Missolonghi ended just as you say. Meyer wasn't in the break-out – that much is true. But he didn't stay behind, either.'

Yashim looked puzzled. 'But then –'

'He'd already gone.' Millingen tinkled the fire irons with the toe of his boot. 'The break-out was our only hope, but everyone knew how risky it was. Ten thousand people, trying to escape through the enemy lines. In a body, all together, some of us stood a chance.'

'But Meyer?'

255

'Didn't wait to find out. He cleared off the night before we'd planned to escape. I don't know that I blame him all that much: he stood a far better chance of getting out alone. But he didn't say a word to anyone – least of all his wife.'

'I see. He abandoned her?'

'He abandoned all of us. You might say, monsieur, that he jeopardised the whole plan. If the Egyptians had caught him – well, you can imagine. I suppose he did what he felt he had to do to save his own neck. We had an uncomfortable day of it, once we'd found him gone. We couldn't be sure the Egyptians didn't know we were coming.' He straightened up, and took a breath.

'But Meyer wasn't caught by the Egyptians.'

'No,' Millingen said, slowly. 'He wasn't caught.'

Yashim stood very still. His eyes travelled slowly over the figure of the man in a frock coat leaning against the fireplace, over the two chairs, then over the ornate rug on the wooden floor.

'And *Chronica Hellenica*? Do you still subscribe?'

'*Chronica*?' Dr Millingen frowned. 'No one subscribes to the *Chronica* these days. It folded years ago.'

Yashim tilted his head back. 'I've been wondering if he taught you that trick with the coin? Was that how Dr Meyer whiled away his time? Or was he too busy, with the Hetira? Was that formed at Missolonghi, too?'

The question hung in the air.

'I thought – at first – that the Hetira was like a secret army,' Yashim continued, when Millingen did not reply. 'Taking control of the Greeks in the city – raising money from them, terrorising them, punishing them for stepping out of line. Preparing, perhaps, for an uprising. These are delicate times. I thought that the Hetira were killers.'

Millingen sighed. 'I told you once, what the Hetira was. A boys' club. A learned society. *Chronica Hellenica* – edited by Meyer – was our society journal. Our aim has always been to preserve Greek culture. We raise money for the maintenance of churches, here and throughout the Ottoman empire. We sponsor schools. It's nothing so very sinister.'

'Then why the secrecy?'

'Partly for amusement. Partly because, when we founded the society, we thought of ourselves as rebels. And partly for the sake of prudence. You might call it a matter of tact. Not everyone in the Ottoman Empire takes kindly to the idea of Greek cultural unity. But perhaps we have pushed the secrecy too far.'

Yashim looked doubtful. 'But Dr Stephanitzes's book is inflammatory, isn't it?'

'Dr Stephanitzes has a mystical turn of mind, Yashim efendi. And he is something of a scholar. You might take that book as a statement of intent, I don't know. For Stephanitzes, it is simply an exercise in tracing the development of the restoration legend over the centuries. He's a Greek, of course: he wants to show that the Greeks are different. It really matters to him that the Greeks developed a cultural resistance to Ottoman rule – otherwise, they would simply be Ottomans in Greek costume. And then what do you have left? Only politics. And politics, as I have no doubt said before, is the Greeks' national vice.'

Millingen paused to relight his pipe. 'That,' he said, puffing, 'is what Missolonghi taught us. And it's why we established the Hetira. Secret, cultural – and essentially un-political.'

'If that's true,' Yashim said dejectedly, 'you have wasted a great deal of my time.'

A skein of blue smoke edged upwards from Millingen's pipe.

'When you saw Lefèvre,' Yashim said slowly, 'did he mention the possibility of other buyers?'

Millingen shrugged. 'A man like Lefèvre,' he began. 'If you were trying to sell something, wouldn't you try to create an auction?'

'But no one could trust him.'

'No. But don't forget, I was instructed to buy on sight. We

wanted Lefèvre to find his –' He paused, looking for the right words. 'His Byzantine relics. But other people might have wanted them – not to be found. It's only an idea.'

Yashim was silent for a moment.

'Do you think the Mavrogordatos had him killed?' he asked at length.

'Why? What makes you say that?'

'You know the answer to that, doctor. Madame Mavrogordato.'

'What rubbish,' Millingen retorted, rising to his feet.

'Lefèvre was married to Madame Mavrogordato. At Missolonghi – until he ran away.'

'I don't know what you're talking about,' Millingen said furiously. 'Petros!' He got up quickly and bellowed at the door. 'Petros!'

There was a sound of rushing feet outside. To Yashim, it sounded as if someone were going up the stairs – and again, that curious swishing noise he'd heard before. But then Petros appeared, looking alarmed.

'This gentleman is leaving,' Millingen said crisply. 'Show him the door, Petros.'

◈ 106 ◈

The Suleymaniye Mosque stands on the third hill of Istanbul, overlooking the Golden Horn. Built by Sinan, the master architect, for his patron, Suleyman the Magnificent, in 1557, it reflects all the piety and grandeur of its age. Some of the foremost scholars of Islam toiled in its medrese, or consulted its well-stocked library; its kitchens fed over a thousand mouths a day, in charity; and its central fountain, in the great court, gladdened the hearts of the faithful and cooled the hands and faces of shoppers emerging from the Grand Bazaar nearby.

When, in the course of the morning, the spurting jets of the fountain declined to a mere dribble, it aroused irritation – and some anxiety. Some of the faithful objected that the water could not be very fresh; some of the more superstitious wondered if the unspoken crisis was approaching, and asked for news of the sultan's health.

Fifty feet or so beneath the ground, in a spur off the main pipe which Sinan had himself constructed, water was backing up against an obstruction, formed at a point where two pipes of a different gauge met. The obstruction, at first, was a tangled mass of wool and loose stones, but it became a nuisance when it was compounded by the drifting corpse of a former waterman called Enver Xani. Xani filled the hole quite neatly; and as the water level rose, so the blockage of bloated flesh and wool and stones was jammed ever more firmly against the narrow lip of the smaller pipe. It became the perfect seal.

The dribble of water from the fountain of the Suleymaniye eventually stopped flowing altogether; but the sultan, according to reports, was still alive.

⚮ 107 ⚮

Yashim sat in the sunshine, nursing his coffee. He ordered some baklava: the hours in Millingen's sunless study had drained him of energy.

An elderly Greek, bent at the waist, hands clasped behind his back, was coming down the side of the road. He wore a red fez, a long jacket and white pantaloons. Every so often he stopped to look in a shop window, or craned his neck to inspect some new building work; once he turned round completely to follow the swaying hips of a pretty Armenian woman with a basket and her hair in a plait. His blue eyes sparkled under a pair of bushy white eyebrows. When he caught sight of Yashim he stopped again, smiled and raised those eyebrows slightly, as if they had shared a joke together, or a regret, before resuming his stately progress down the Grande Rue de Pera.

A group of Franks, led by a man with a huge belly who mopped his brow repeatedly with a handkerchief, sauntered along the road. The men wore black coats and striped waist-coats; the ladies wore bonnets and turned their heads about, like blinkered horses. Yashim couldn't catch what they were saying but guessed they were Italians, probably staying at one of the new lodging-houses higher up the street: their dragoman carried a fly-whisk and wore moustaches. Yashim wondered if he was Greek, but thought not: more likely an Italian-speaking native of Pera, descended from the city's original Genoese inhabitants.

It seemed to Yashim that he had once been able to glance at people's feet to tell who they were, and where they belonged. In Fener, or Sultanahmet, perhaps; but in Pera, no longer. The distinctions blurred; the categories no longer held. That lanky figure in a Frankish suit – was he Russian? Belgian? Or an Ottoman, indeed – a Bosnian schoolmaster, perhaps, or a Russified Moldavian shipping agent?

The baklava was hard and sticky: he suspected it was made with sugar syrup as well as honey.

And where did he stand, among these people whose origins were so clouded and confused?

Years ago, Yashim supposed, the distinctions had been simple. You were born to a faith, and there you lived and died. It was given to very few – Yashim among them – to change their state in life. But now people cast their skins, like snakes. Lefèvre was Meyer. Istanbul was Constantinople. A lecherous bully became a priest, and Millingen was Hetira – a revolutionary organisation that on close inspection turned out to be an antiquarian club. Sometimes the only evidence of their presence was the outer layer of their skin, shed as they moved from one incarnation to another. Perhaps the old prophecy was true: with the Serpent Column destroyed, Istanbul had become overrun.

He thought again about Lefèvre. He had spoken of his passion for Istanbul, for the layers of history that had built up on the shores of the Bosphorus, at the point where Asia and Europe met, and the Black Sea defiled into the Mediterranean. A man and a city whose identities had been reshaped. Constantinople, or Istanbul. Meyer, or Lefèvre.

Yashim sighed, drawn in spite of himself to acknowledge an affinity with the dead man. Yashim the boy, expecting to become a man – the man he did not, in the end, quite become – was the memory of a self that clung to him the way the serpents coiled together on the Hippodrome. The snakes had had their three heads and their three coils, but they occupied the same space, in a single column.

Meyer. Lefèvre. Could it be that there was, perhaps, a third aspect to the man? He had a fleeting vision of the dreadful corpse, as fanged and terrible as the serpent's head itself.

What was it that Grigor had said? That a city doesn't change because you change its name. A city is not a name: it's a sequence of lives, gestures, memories, all entwined. Lefèvre found stories in its rubble: for Yashim, these stories were found in the voices you heard on the street, in the murmur that surrounded mosques and markets, in a tired boy leaning his burden against a dirty wall, a cat jumping after bats in the dark, the curve of a caique-rower's back.

A city endures which also grows, forever adding new identities to the old. To a Parisian, Istanbul was the east. To an Indian, it was the west. What of the Jews, clustered in Balat – did they live in a Jewish city? Did Preen see a city of entertainers? Or the validé a city of palaces and concubines?

One day, if men like Dr Stephanitzes had their way, Istanbul could revert to being the capital of Greece. They could tear down the minarets, exchange the crescent for the cross: but Suleyman's Muslim city would still survive, nestled into the very fabric of the place, submerged like the cisterns of Byzantine Istanbul.

This city, Yashim reflected, was very resilient. A survivor.

Like Lefèvre himself.

◅ 108 ▻

'I didn't think we'd see each other again,' Grigor said.

'We still share this city.'

Grigor sighed. 'In space, Yashim, and time. But here?' He jabbed his thumb to his chest. 'Or here?' And he placed his index finger to his temple.

Yashim bowed his head. 'We share – certain responsibilities, at least.'

'To whom?'

Yashim heard the sneer in Grigor's voice.

'To the dead, Grigor.'

Grigor put up a hand and ran his fingers through his beard.

'Experience has taught me that we should keep to our own spheres. Our own circuits. There are boundaries in Constantinople: beyond them we trespass at our peril.'

'You told me before that the Church is concerned with the things of the spirit,' Yashim answered carefully. 'Caesar wants obedience. But God wants Truth, isn't that so?'

Grigor made a dismissive motion with his hand. 'I don't think

God is very interested in your sort of truth, Yashim. It's very small. Who did what to whom – who talked, who was silent, the year 1839. God is the Eternal.'

'We have long memories, though. Ideas outlive us.'

'What are you saying?' Grigor growled.

'Byzantine treasure, Grigor. The relics. I know where they are.'

The archimandrite glanced out of the window. 'You, too?'

'Would you pay me for them?'

Grigor was silent for a while. 'What I would or would not pay is beyond discussion,' he said at last. 'It would be for the Patriarch to decide.'

'What did the Patriarch decide – the last time?'

'The last time?'

'Lefèvre.'

'Ah. Monsieur Lefèvre,' Grigor echoed, placing his hands flat on the table. 'Doesn't that answer your question?'

'What is that supposed to mean?'

'I think,' Grigor said, rising, 'that I will forget we ever spoke. Do you really know where the relics are?'

'I'm not even sure that they exist.'

'Believe it or not, I'm glad you said that, Yashim. For old times' sake.'

Yashim walked slowly back to his apartment, mulling over Grigor's words. If Grigor believed the relics did exist himself . . . But that was not what Grigor had said.

He turned at the market, to start uphill.

'Yashim efendi!'

Yashim stooped to the gradient.

'Yashim efendi! I knows what they takes from you – and this is not ears! What for you's deaf today?'

He raised his head and turned around. George was standing in front of his stall, hands on his hips.

'So! You eats in lokanta this days? You forgets what is food? Little kebab, little dolma makes like shit!'

George had made a remarkable recovery, Yashim noticed.

'You sees a ghost, Yashim efendi?' George bellowed, thumping his chest. 'Yes, I am a thin man now. But this stall – she is like womans! Happy womans, to see George again. So she – she is veeerrrry fat!'

Yashim strode up to George's stall. 'What happened?' He asked, gesturing to the great piles of aubergines, the cucumbers and tomatoes spilling out of baskets, a pyramid of lemons.

'Eh,' George sighed, absently scratching an armpit as he surveyed his stock. 'Is mostly shit, efendi. My garden,' he added apologetically, cocking his head at a basket of outsize cucumbers curved like thin green sickles. 'Today, I gives away everything for nothing.'

Yashim nodded. In the week George had been in hospital the vegetables on his plot would have run riot.

'But' – and George's voice became hoarse with conspiracy – 'I finds one beautiful thing.'

He dug around in the back of his stall and came out bearing two small white aubergines in the palm of one massive hand, a thread of miniature tomatoes in the other.

'Is very little, you see? No water.'

Yashim nodded. 'These are so pretty I could eat them raw.'

George looked at him with a flash of concern. 'You eats these raw,' he said, jiggling the aubergines in his hand, 'you is sick at the stomach.' He shoved the vegetables into Yashim's hands. 'No lokanta, efendi. Slowly, slowly, we gets better again. You. My garden. And me, too.'

264

Yashim took the gift. On his way up the hill he thought: George left his garden for a week, and now he is back.

The sound of the muezzins caught him halfway up the hill. The sun was fading in the west behind him: ahead, darkness had already fallen. Across the Horn, Yashim considered, the French ambassador would soon be writing his report.

At his door, at the top of the stairs, he paused and listened.

There was no sound: no rustle of pages being turned, no sigh. No Amélie.

Yashim pushed the door cautiously, gently, and peered into the gloom. Everything was in its place.

He went in slowly and fumbled for the lamp; and when it was lit he sat for a long time on the edge of the sofa with only his shadow for company.

Amélie had gone, leaving nothing behind. Only a sense of her absence.

After a while Yashim leaned forwards, his eye drawn to his shelves.

Something else, he noticed, had changed. The Gyllius, too, was gone.

❦ 110 ❦

Auguste Boyer, *chargé d'affaires* to the ambassador, had not been sleeping well. Drifting off to sleep, he remembered with a start of shame his own appearance at the courtyard window, drooling onto the cobbles. Asleep, he dreamed of faceless men and wild dogs. He woke up with a comfortlessly forensic vision of Lefèvre's mutilated body on the table, a vision which again and again in the early hours of the morning he would be miserably and unwillingly forced to explore.

Yashim's arrival shortly after Boyer had dressed, and before he had drunk his bowl of coffee, collided unhappily in the attaché's mind with the memory of the bloodless corpse.

'This is not an hour at which the ambassador can possibly be disturbed,' he said, vehemently.

'He's asleep?'

'Certainly not,' Boyer retorted. 'Already he is settling various affairs, in discussion with embassy staff.' The chef, for one, he thought: there was a luncheon planned. Provided, of course, the ambassador was awake. Boyer's tummy began to rumble; he pulled out a small handkerchief and coughed.

'Do you happen to know if the ambassador has completed his report into the death of the unfortunate Monsieur Lefèvre?'

Boyer regarded the eunuch with some distaste. 'I have no idea,' he said.

Yashim still entertained a small hope of delay. 'And the testimony of Madame Lefèvre? Did that prove useful?'

Boyer looked at him blankly. 'Madame Lefèvre?'

'Amélie Lefèvre. His wife,' Yashim explained. 'She came here the evening before last.'

Auguste Boyer thought of his bowl of coffee, growing cold.

'Of Monsieur Lefèvre,' he said, drawing himself up, 'the embassy is aware. But as for Madame – no, monsieur. I am afraid that you are utterly mistaken.'

Yashim rocked slowly on his heels.

'Madame Lefèvre came here to the embassy. She had been in Samnos, and she needed help to get home. To France.'

Boyer seized on Yashim's change of tack. The ambassador's report was beyond his jurisdiction, but this was easy.

'You are quite mistaken. This Madame Lefèvre, whoever she may be, has not been seen at the embassy,' he said crisply, mentally connecting himself with his coffee and a warm croissant. 'Good day, monsieur.'

He turned on his heel and strode off across the hall, leaving Yashim staring after him, a puzzled frown on his face.

Either the little diplomat was lying – or Amélie had gone somewhere else, after all. She had disappeared into the great city as suddenly as she had come, taking her little bag and a head full of dangerous new ideas. Determined, she had said, to find out who had killed her husband.

Yashim's frown deepened. Ideas were dangerous, certainly; but men could be deadly.

❯❮ I I I ❯❮

Amélie Lefèvre shivered as the door swung shut behind her.

She set her lantern on a low shelf, opened the glass pane and lit the wick with a trembling hand. The air was very cold.

She held the lantern over her head, gathered up the hem of her skirts with her free hand, and began to slowly descend the spiral of water basins leading down to the mouth of the tunnel.

At the bottom she stepped into the shallow water. Drops of condensation on the lantern threw whirling freckles of light deep into the tunnel, skimming across the rough brick walls to vanish suddenly in the black wings of her own shadow on the roof.

She reached into her pocket and took out a small ball of white wax and a reel of black cotton thread. She softened the wax against the lantern and used it to fasten an end of thread to the opening of the tunnel, an inch or so above the waterline. She stood up and tucked up her skirts. Loosely holding the cotton-reel in the crook of her fingers she entered the tunnel, paying out the thread behind her.

At the first fork she veered to the right, without hesitation, but about five yards in she stopped to listen. The water sluiced softly around her feet. Instinctively she glanced back: the pressing darkness took her by surprise, and she swung the lantern nervously over her shoulder. A drip from the roof landed on the tip of her nose and she jerked back.

Calm yourself, she murmured, wading on. Concentrate on the detail. Roman bricks. A later repair, using cruder materials: perhaps builders had crashed through the roof in some remote age. The Turks seemed to have rediscovered the secret of Roman cement, she thought. The walls were bare; nothing could grow down here.

Amélie Lefèvre. An archaeologist. Like my husband.

She began to count her steps.

She counted a hundred, two hundred. At five hundred paces she began to feel the weight of the city pressing down on her, slowly sealing off the distant mouth of the tunnel. She stopped counting.

This is the Snake, she told herself. It has stood firm for a thousand years, a lost feat of Byzantine engineering.

I'm in good hands: Byzantine workmen, a Renaissance scholar – and Maximilien Lefèvre.

She had read it all in Yashim's book: the book her husband had hidden in his apartment. The book that Max had always meant her to find.

The reel snagged in her hand. She looked down and took another out of her pocket. She tied the ends of the thread together, curved her fingers over the new reel, and went on.

⤜ 112 ⤛

A thought, a memory, was stirring in Yashim's mind. He leaned against the wall and closed his eyes, oblivious to the people passing in the street.

Amélie had vanished into thin air. The only clue to her plans lay in the book she had taken with her. Gyllius must have identified to Amélie – and perhaps, before that, Lefèvre – the location of the Byzantine relics.

Amélie believed in their existence. They lay, she had said, in a hollow space beneath the former Church of Aya Sofia. A crypt.

The way to the crypt lay through a network of tunnels that ran beneath the city. Most of them were no bigger than rabbit burrows but some were big enough to admit the passage of a man. One, at least, seemed to run from the siphon in Balat to church of St Irene in the grounds of the Topkapi Palace, where Yashim had seen its mouth.

Close to where Gyllius claimed to have gone down beneath a man's house, and flitted through a cavernous cistern in the dark. A hollow hippodrome, as Delmonico had said: the Atmeidan, where the Serpent Column had stood for fifteen hundred years.

Between Topkapi Palace, Gyllius's cistern, and the Suleymaniye Mosque stood another ancient building even more famous. Aya Sofia, the Great Church of the Byzantines.

Yashim held his eyes shut tight.

The water-pipe must lead to the Hippodrome.

Gyllius would have realised that, three hundred years ago: he must have guessed where the relics were to be found.

And then he had left the city to go with the Ottoman armies to Persia. As if someone, or something, had frightened him away. Just as Lefèvre had been frightened, three centuries later.

Men do not live for three hundred years: but ideas do. Memories do. Traditions do.

The sou naziry had made the point himself.

Yashim flung himself from the wall, and began to run.

113

Amélie stood at the lip of the tunnel with her lantern raised. Her eyes were shining.

Gyllius had been telling the truth.

She was standing a few feet above a vast underground lake. From its glittering black surface huge columns of weeping porphyry reared upwards from their massive plinths, glinting in the lamplight until they were lost in the darkness overhead.

Slowly she descended the steps until she reached the level of the water.

She shivered involuntarily in the silent forest: columns as far as she could see, beautifully made, the pride of pagan temples from all across the Roman world. The Byzantine emperors had plundered them for this, the greatest cistern ever built, lost to the world and buried beneath the ground.

She took another step, and the icy water closed around her ankles. She felt for the next step with her foot; the water reached her knees. There were no more steps. She let out a gasp of relief.

She set the cotton reel on the step behind her. Gritting her teeth, she began to wade through the inky water.

The relics were here, she knew it.

Somewhere here, among the frozen columns of antiquity, she would find the sign.

114

One hand outstretched, the other coiled loosely around the thread in which he had placed his faith, Yashim scuttled forwards in the dark.

Somewhere up ahead, linked to him by the slenderest filament of cotton, a woman was advancing to her death. Whether she was brave, or ignorant, Yashim could not judge: but the penalty would be the same.

Grigor had talked about the city's boundaries. Between faith and faith; between one district and the next; between the present and the past.

But the watermen patrolled another boundary few people in Istanbul were even aware of: the frontier between light and dark. Beneath the streets, hidden from view, the pulsing arteries of Istanbul.

The dead, cold, dark world which gave the city life.

And the watermen were prepared to kill to preserve their unique knowledge of that world.

Yashim's turban brushed against the low roof, dislodging a shower of mortar. Amélie had a lamp, he was sure of that: any moment he would see it.

He glanced over his shoulder. For a moment he was confused, disoriented: had he somehow doubled back – moving away from her lamp? For there it was: a dim brightening that came and went behind him.

He shook his head: his eyes, in that darkness, were playing tricks.

He kept going.

115

The sou naziry blinked. He stooped and touched the ball of wax with his finger.

The wax broke away easily from the stone. The sou naziry picked it up, and felt the tug of the thread between his fingers.

He put out his tongue and moistened his lips.

He had thought, until this moment, that the job was done.

The sou naziry picked up his lantern and loosened the dagger in his belt. The dagger had a jewelled hilt and its blade was curved.

The sou naziry picked up the line of thread and entered the tunnel.

⇜ 116 ⇝

Amélie fought the weight of her skirts trailing in the water as she zigzagged to and from between the great columns, tracing their cold outlines with her fingers, searching for the sign she knew would be there.

Not five hundred yards away Yashim felt a change in the atmosphere of the tunnel, the dampness lifting as he blindly approached the cistern. He looked back: there was no doubt that someone was coming down the tunnel behind him now. He felt the faintest tugging of the thread in his hand and saw the lamp swaying as it grew closer. Whoever it was could move faster through the cramped tunnel than he could. Someone practised. Someone prepared.

Yashim hesitated. Sooner or later, the man would track him down – unless he found some side-passage where he could hide. But in the dark his chance of finding one were slim. And what if he did? What if he saved his skin – and the waterman went on to discover Amélie?

He let the thread drop from his fingers. Without it he could move faster, trusting to luck that the tunnel would not fork again, or that when it did he would be able to retrieve the thread and find out which branch the Frenchwoman had taken.

His fingers trailed against the walls. For several yards he felt the rough serrated brick beneath his fingertips and then, quite suddenly on the left side, his hand trailed through the thin air. Gingerly he traced the opening with his fingers. He slid one foot, and then another, into the gap. There was a step up.

Yashim wasted no more time. He scrambled into the opening and up several steps, then flattened himself against the wall, and waited.

He saw the darkness gradually dissolve.

He heard the splash of the waterman's feet as he ran through the shallow stream.

Then the light was blinding and Yashim could see nothing at all, only the light and the sparkle of the light as it bounced from the curving surface of a steel blade.

And somewhere hundreds of yards away, up a bad-smelling side-tunnel that had been blocked now for almost a day, a thin trickle of water began to seep through a bloated lump of meat and bone, and stones, and sodden wool.

⊰⊱ 117 ⊰⊱

Yashim flung himself back against the steps and kicked up at the waterman's lantern with both feet. It exploded as it smashed against the roof of the tunnel and the light went out, but he and the sou naziry had recognised each other. As Yashim's feet hit the ground he twisted and struck out with his right hand, knuckles bent.

He hit something, he couldn't tell what, and whirled around. He slipped his cloak from his shoulders and held it out like a screen in the tunnel.

He felt the drag on his fingers as the naziry's knife sliced into the cloth; then he brought both hands down as hard as he could,

273

trying to bundle the man by his wrists and pin them to the ground.

But the naziry was quick: the bundle was empty. Yashim fell sideways on his knees, onto the steps, and felt the pressure of the naziry's foot against the torn cloak.

He sprang for the steps again on one leg, the other kicking out into the darkness. It touched something, but without force. As he tried to pull it away the naziry seized hold. Yashim kicked down with his free leg, but his strength collapsed as a searing pain tore through his calf.

He bent forwards, his outstretched hands colliding with the second blow aimed at his body. Yashim felt the blade slice through the joint of his thumb: he grabbed in the dark and found a wrist. For a second his grip held: he pulled up his right leg and slammed it down as hard as he could along the line of the naziry's knife arm, catching him on the side of his head.

The wrist slid violently from his grasp. Yashim scrambled backwards, up the steps, and listened with one leg raised. In the other he could feel the blood pulsing through a wound in his calf.

He heard nothing: no breath, no splash. Nothing but a sound like a gentle smack that seemed to come from far away. A sound that meant nothing to him, couldn't help him win.

And then silence.

A faint breeze hit his face.

Yashim kicked out with all his strength, into the darkness.

He realised that the naziry had been closer than he'd thought when he caught him on the shoulder before his knees unbent. He followed through with a mighty heave, and had the satisfaction of hearing the naziry fall back with a grunt.

Which was the last thing Yashim heard before the tunnel erupted with a roar that seemed to fill the darkness, echoing from wall to wall like a cannon shot. A foam-flecked wind rushed over him, dragging at his legs. Something struck at his foot. He heard a screech like metal.

Then nothing. Only a rumble, far away, and a soft gurgling in the tunnel below.

Yashim lay perfectly still. The event had been so sudden that he could not understand it.

But two hundred feet away Amélie turned in terror as a vast jet of water surged from the mouth of the tunnel, shattering against the nearest column in an explosion of spray and flying debris with a noise like thunder.

Bits of rubbish slapped into the water all around her, and then the water stopped. Something that could almost have been a human figure slid from the column, crashed onto the plinth, and toppled with a splash into the dark lake.

As Amélie reached up to brush a streak of slime from her cheek, she noticed something very pale and tentacled bobbing beside her in the water. She lowered her lamp for a better look.

Motionless on the hard steps, Yashim heard her scream.

◅ 118 ▻

He saw Amélie first, bathed in a halo of light from the lamp she had set beside her on the plinth. She had a hand to her mouth.

He called out. 'Amélie! *C'est moi.* Yashim!'

Amélie moved back against the plinth. Her skirts spread around her like a lily pad.

Yashim started down the steps. He barely noticed the water, until he stumbled over the naziry, floating face down.

He waded past the corpse.

Amélie was crying as he approached, her hands at her neck not trying to stop the tears.

Yashim took her silently into his arms. She seemed to be rattling against him: he squeezed her tight, absorbing the convulsions that had gripped her.

Very slowly, holding her against his chest, he turned around. Her head moved as if she were staring at something, then it relaxed and fell against his shoulder. Yashim looked down, through her hair, at the hem of her skirt in the water. In the dim light he could make out a human hand.

He shivered, and squeezed the girl hard. How it had happened he did not properly know: but Enver Xani, long since dead, had saved his life a second time.

Amélie calmed down gradually. First she stopped shaking, then she lifted her head.

'We're very close,' she said, and she pulled away.

'Close? To each other?' Yashim said stupidly. He was aware of a throbbing in his leg, and when he lifted his hand to the light he saw it was black with running blood.

'To the relics,' Amélie said. Her eyes shone in the lamplight.

Yashim felt dizzy. He heaved his way through the water and found the steps. He unwound his turban and began to tear it into strips, binding them around his calf. Amélie waded up to him. She helped him to tie the bandage, and wrap another around his hand.

'I – I didn't mean you to come.'

'No.' He felt terribly tired. 'Except for you I would have stayed behind.'

Her hands were shaking. He watched her try to tie the knot with fingers which were stiff with cold.

'I've found the relics now,' she said.

He knew it wasn't true. Not yet.

'The naziry was coming to kill you,' he said.

He watched her straighten up, the bandage done. She put up a hand and pushed a lock of hair from her forehead.

'You can still help,' she said.

She waded away, with the lamp in her hand. Wearily Yashim stumbled to his feet.

'He would have killed you!' His shout sounded very faint, there in that eerie dark forest. 'The way he killed the others. The way he killed your husband. The watermen –'

She didn't stop, just turned her head over her shoulder and said: 'I'm doing this for Max. It's what he'd want.'

Yashim shrugged, from the cold.

'You went to Millingen, didn't you?' he called. 'That's where you were. You locked me in.'

Amélie didn't answer. Her skirts trailed behind her like a train.

'Look,' she said, at last. She lifted the lamp and its glow fell on a plinth, supporting a column that vanished into the darkness overhead. The joint was concealed by a band of greenish copper, dappled with moisture, and on the plinth itself, partly submerged in the black water, Yashmin recognised a chiselled head.

Even though it was upside down, the brow lost underwater, Yashmin found himself transfixed. Majestic in their classical symmetry were the great blind eyes, the flaring nostrils, the full curving lips – but demonic, too, was the expression of agony and command. It was the face of a woman. Her hair was thick and knotted.

Yashim moved closer, forgetting the cold, while the lamplight trembled in Amélie's hand and cast shadows which flickered and ran across deep incisions in the stone. Then he pulled back with a gasp: for a moment the strands of those loose knotted locks had seemed to twist and writhe like living things.

'The Medusa,' he murmured, with a shiver.

'Don't you see?' Amélie gave a sudden peal of shaky laughter. 'Max guessed – the myths! The Medusa turns men into stone. Her gaze is a lock. It confers a kind of immortality.'

277

'The emperor,' Yashim stammered. 'Turned to stone.'

The snakes reared again as Amélie wheeled on him. 'Yes, the emperor dies, and the emperor will awake. Something hidden will one day reappear and shake the world.' She set the lamp on the plinth. 'The emperor was just a poor, brave man who could do nothing to stop the Turks. But in myth – he's an idea! God's agent on this earth. The idea of sacred power.'

She ran her hands over the sculpted marble. 'It's about suspending time. Freezing it.'

She put her hands on the top of the plinth and began stirring the water with her feet. 'They're here. I know it. The relics are here.'

'I don't think so, Amélie.'

She didn't answer, but moved slowly round the plinth, feeling the ground with her feet.

'It's too cold! I can't feel anything. Yashim, for God's sake, help me.'

Yashim didn't move.

'We can do this for Max. We must do it, can't you see? After this there'll never be another chance.'

He thought she was going to wring her hands. Instead, she waded through the water and put her arms around his neck.

She drew him down and kissed him with her cold lips.

'Not for Max, Yashim. Do it for me.'

He felt her thigh pressing against his. She kissed him again.

She broke away slowly and sank down into the water, kneeling. Her skirts billowed around her like the scalloped edge of a fountain.

She gathered them towards her, then plunged her hands into the water, groping around the base of the plinth.

Yashim closed his eyes. For a moment he saw Maximilien Lefèvre on his knees, that night in the apartment, tipping the contents of his bag onto the floor.

He stepped up to the plinth and began to circle its base, scudding his icy feet across the floor of the underground lake. They met on the far side, in the shadow, and when Yashim raised her up she came up dripping and shaking.

'It's enough,' he said. *Ça suffit.* 'We have to think now, how to get out of here.'

Her teeth were chattering now too hard for her to speak. She tried to pull away, but Yashim had her by the waist and she was shaking. He picked up the lamp.

Halfway across the lake, Amélie fainted in his arms.

Her head dropped back and her weight fell on his arm. His other arm shot up to keep his balance, and the lamp flew from his hand. For a moment it blazed in an arc above the sunken cistern, throwing its light across the hall of columns, across the black water, before it cracked audibly against a plinth, and vanished.

Yashim watched it go.

He stood for a few moments in the dark.

And a sound he had not heard for what seemed like a very long time broke the impenetrable silence of the cistern.

It was weak, and shaky, but it was, after all, his own.

Yashim's laugh.

119

There was nothing for it, Yashim thought, as he ran his hands around the tunnel's mouth.

He turned and groped for Amélie's arms. He put his hands under her armpits and began to drag her back, into the tunnel. The angle was awkward, his back bent and protesting. Every few yards he stopped to catch his breath, the sweat now rolling down his face. To make things worse, the cut on his hand had begun to run again, where the bandage had slid off.

He had no real idea of what to do next. Even if he could drag Amélie a hundred, five hundreds yards along the tunnel, his chances of finding the right way out in the dark were slim. Amélie's thread had disappeared – probably the naziry had gathered it up as he followed.

He gritted his teeth and pulled his burden for another few yards. He felt dizzy and sick, weak with the cold and the loss of blood. He put out a hand to steady himself, and almost toppled sideways.

He felt a step beneath his fingers. Presumably, he thought, the steps where the naziry had found him. It seemed long ago.

He wondered if he should leave Amélie here, on the steps, while he groped for a way out. But even if he did get out, what then? How would he get back? What help could he possibly call on out there – he could hardly expect the watermen to come running. And in the meantime Amélie might wake up, and find herself in the dark, alone. Buried alive.

He dragged her onto the lower step and laid her head down gently on the stone. Stepping over her with exaggerated care, he began to mount the steps.

The stairs took several right-angled turns before Yashim found himself in what felt like a narrow corridor, in which he could stand upright. The walls were straight, and he ran his fingers along them until he reached another set of steps at the far end. The entrance to these steps was festooned with hangings that crumbled at his touch and stuck to his fingers.

The second flight of steps was spiral, and they went on turning and turning until Yashim felt bewildered. He seemed to have been climbing for hours. Several times he slipped and fell: climbing stairs hurt his calf. Then, in the dark, he walked straight into a wall.

He recoiled, tasting blood. The wall was built across the stairs. Yashim ran his hands over it, and over the surrounding walls, uncertain what he was looking for but deeply unwilling to admit that the whole exercise had been futile. But so it was: if there had once been an entrance to the tunnels from this spot, it was blocked now. If Amélie's cistern was the same one Gyllius had seen, it lay beneath the Hippodrome; except for the open space, much had changed in that district since olden times. Ibrahim's palace. Ahmed I's Blue Mosque. The lovely baths which Sinan built for Hürrem Sultan, Suleyman's Russian wife, close by the entrance to Topkapi Palace and Aya Sofia. Monumental buildings.

He laid his head against the wall and screwed his eyes tight. He felt sick and dizzy: everything he touched felt as though it were toppling, sliding, moving about. He wondered how long he had been away from Amélie: perhaps even now she was awake, blundering about and crying in the dark . . .

He raised his head and turned, eyes closed, feeling for the outside wall of the stairs, where the steps were widest. He set his back against the curve and began to descend. A festoon of cobwebs brushed his hair, so old and dusty that they hung in strands, like the matted hair of a dervish. He jerked his head away.

For a few moments he stared back, incapable of believing what he was seeing. Understanding that he could see.

He glanced up the steps. At the top, where the wall ran across the stairs, a thin vertical bar of light had opened in the angle of the two walls.

Yashim scrambled back down the spiral stairs. Amélie was still lying where he had left her. Her breathing was shallow and her skin felt like ice. He took her in his arms and sat her upright, then slapped her cheeks.

After a while she began to moan.

He dragged her to her feet, holding her arm around his shoulders, his other hand encircling her waist, and began to half-drag, half-carry her up the steps. The movement seemed to bring her round. He felt her stumbling on the last few steps, and when they entered the corridor he was able to take the lead, holding her firmly by the arm and murmuring encouragement.

'We're almost there, a few more steps. There's a way out, you'll see the light soon.'

He got behind her as they reached the spiral staircase, and helped her climb. Her movements were slow and heavy, and he remembered how hard it had been for him to move when he crawled out of Xani's pit, when every muscle had weighed a ton and all he had wanted to do was fall asleep. Sometimes Amélie did seem to drift away, and he had to brace himself and catch her as she slid back on top of him. But at last he saw the darkness starting to dissolve.

She sat quiet while he put his shoulder to the stone. A little grunting noise gradually changed into a low growl as the stone began to move and the bar of light widened inch by inch.

Before it was six inches wide, Yashim paused and put his eye to the crack.

The light hurt his eyes, but he was looking across an expanse of cracked and polished marble towards a vast barred window, about fifteen yards away. Looking up, he saw a domed ceiling. Something about the scale of the building, and the dusty blackness of its walls, reminded him of somewhere, but for a moment he could not imagine where he was.

He pushed again: the wall, he saw, was mounted on a pivot so that as one end swung out the other swung inwards. Soon he was able to squeeze himself into the gap and use his back against the stone, and it was then that it rushed in upon him.

They had found a way into Aya Sofia.

Not on the ground floor, and nowhere near the old high altar.

The spiral stairs had been built inside one of the vast pillars that supported the great dome, and they were emerging much higher up, in the deserted gallery that stretched out beneath the quarter domes of the greatest building of the ancient world.

120

Faisal al-Mehmed ran his eyes along the low shelves which surrounded him in his booth outside the Great Mosque, and shook his head. So many shoes! In weather like this, everyone wanted to go into the Mosque; nobody wanted to come out. But as soon as the rain stopped they would rush upon him, demanding to have their shoes again, causing confusion.

Faisal al-Mehmed abhorred confusion, in a holy precinct above all.

A movement in the crowd made him look round. A couple he could not remember having seen before were coming out of the doorway. The rain had come suddenly, out of a blue sky: they must have been caught in it properly, to have got so *very* wet. The woman, he noticed, could barely walk: the man had one arm around her, and the other held her hand.

Faisal ran a hand down his beard, and nodded. So many people came to this mosque without a pious thought – merely, even, to shelter from the rain. Where was the piety, in using a mosque as shelter? True piety was oblivious to rain.

Faisal smiled a benediction on the couple, for in his heart he understood that they possessed Enthusiasm.

121

When Yashim woke it was late. The thunderstorms had cleared
away as if they had never been, and a hot afternoon sun was
already tracing a pattern of slanting shadows across the room.

He got up slowly, feeling light and hungry. There was a loaf of
bread which was no longer fresh; he broke off a piece and
chewed at it, and then in self-disgust he put the bread down and
riddled the stove. He blew on the embers and fed their glow with
trickles of charcoal from his fingers, listening to its dry rustle,
feeling its insubstantial weight, wondering as he watched the
glow spread how something so light could generate so much
heat. He placed his hand flat above the stove and savoured the
burning heat on his palm.

He looked into his vegetable basket. In an earthenware dish,
under a domed lid, lay a slab of crumbly white cheese, beyaz
peynir.

He skinned two onions and chopped them roughly, then sprinkled them with salt. He sliced the tops off two tomatoes and
chopped them, with peppers, garlic, and a bunch of wilted parsley. He mashed the cheese with a fork.

He split the stale loaf lengthways, and rubbed the insides with
a cut tomato and a garlic clove. He drizzled them with oil and set
them at an angle over the heat.

He dipped the onions into a bowl of water to remove the salt,
and tossed them into a bowl along with the peppers, the tomatoes and the parsley. A drop of oil fell onto the coals with a hiss.
He sprinkled the salad with the crumbled cheese and a big pinch
of kirmizi biber, which he had bought after the desecration of the
apartment – usually he made it himself, with a big bunch of
dried chilli peppers crushed in a mortar, rubbed with oil and
roasted black in a heavy pan on the coals.

284

He poured a generous lick of olive oil over the salad, added salt and pounded peppercorns in the mortar. *Clink clink clink.*

He stirred the salad with a spoon.

He took the toasted bread from the fire and set it on a plate. He washed his hands and mouth.

He ate cross-legged on the sofa, the sun on his left hand, thinking about the dark burrows under the city, the huge cistern like a temple, and the wavering light that had pursued him through his dreams. The light he'd seen in Amélie's eyes.

I am doing this for Max, she'd said. Fulfilling his desires. Following his instructions as if he were still alive; as if, like Byzantium itself, he still had the power to direct and to control the actions of people in the living world.

Yashim spooned up some of the vegetables with a chunk of toasted bread.

I am doing this for Max.

For Max: for the man whose grossly mutilated corpse both he and Dr Millingen had examined days ago. A body without a face, but good teeth.

❊ 122 ❊

'It's you.' Dr Millingen leaned forwards and turned up the wick; a warm, soft light spilled across the room.

Yashim placed a bag on the floor beside him. 'Madame Lefèvre?'

'Very weak, after her ordeal. But she is a fighter, Yashim efendi. I am sure you know that.'

He leaned forwards and picked up a coin that lay dully on the leather desktop.

'A survivor? Yes. Like her husband. Your old friend Meyer.'

285

Dr Millingen frowned and glanced at the door. 'I have already arranged for Madame Lefèvre to be repatriated,' he said, holding the coin to the light. 'She leaves tomorrow, for France.'

'A French ship?'

'*L'Ulysse*. She's berthed at Tophane, on the quay.' He leaned back, bringing the coin with him. 'My man will be seeing her aboard. No more accidents, Yashim efendi.'

Yashim said coldly: 'It wasn't my idea to send her into the cisterns, Dr Millingen.'

The coin began to run through Dr Millingen's fingers.

'I suppose you know she found nothing,' Yashim said.

'So she told me.'

Yashim stepped forwards and spread his hands. 'The clues added up. You would have had your relics, had they been there. But they weren't. I don't believe they exist,' he added, shaking his head. 'Lefèvre was a salesman.'

Dr Millingen considered Yashim thoughtfully.

'I agree with you,' he said at last. 'And yet, as you say, the clues added up.'

'The trouble with clues – you can make them point wherever you like. A few old legends, a rare book – Lefèvre only had to choose a theme, *et voilà*! A story he knew how to sell.'

Millingen frowned. 'But I told you – he got nothing from us until the relics were found.'

Yashim smiled. 'On the contrary. From you he got everything he needed. Authenticity, Dr Millingen. I believe it is called provenance. Your interest alone raised the price – for others.'

'But Madame Lefèvre – she believed the story, too.'

'Did she?' Yashim thought of Amélie in the lamplight, sinking to her knees in the dark water. 'I think, Dr Millingen, that the only person who may have believed in the whole charade was you. It was you who once told me that a collector is a weak man. Do you remember? You with that coin of Malakian's I brought

– the missing coin in your collection – eager to own it, at almost any price. Maybe you couldn't be sure of Lefèvre. Why should you trust him? But in the back of your mind you hoped he might be right.'

The doctor pursed his lips, making no effort to deny it.

'So you persuaded Madame Lefèvre to pick up the trail.' Yashim clasped his hands together across his chest. 'I don't know if that meant you were weak. But it made you unscrupulous.'

'Steady on,' Millingen growled.

'You could have offered her money for the relics. She needs money, I'm sure.' Yashim remembered Amélie in the water, wading from him, turning her lovely head to say that she was doing this for Max. For a dead man. 'But I think you offered her something else. Something that mattered more to her even than money.'

The fingers turning the coin fell still. 'I wonder what you're going to tell me, Yashim efendi. I'm very interested to know.'

'I don't think Amélie ever really believed in the relics herself. And I don't think you did, either. But you wanted to be sure, Dr Millingen, didn't you? So you devised a trade, risking one life for another. That's your business, isn't it? Life.'

Millingen didn't move. Yashim cocked his head, and said: 'You promised her Maximilien Lefèvre.'

❧ 123 ❧

Millingen placed the coin on the desk with a loud click.

Their eyes met.

'Lefèvre is dead,' Millingen said. He was watching Yashim now, trying to gauge the effect of his words.

Yashim nodded slowly. 'It wouldn't be the first time, would it? Lefèvre, dead.'

'I don't know what you mean.'

'Come on, Dr Millingen.' Yashim frowned impatiently. 'It's a question of identity, that's all. He told me that, himself.'

'He told you – what?' Millingen's tone was scornful.

'Byzantium. Constantinople. Istanbul. They're all real names. All real places. Lefèvre was fascinated by them, too: three identities, woven into one – just like the snakes in the column, on the Hippodrome. They are all the same place, of course. Just as Meyer and Lefèvre are the same man.'

Millingen made a gesture of impatience. 'I don't go in for metaphysics, efendi. I'm a doctor – and I know a dead man when I see one, too.'

'That body, in the embassy,' Yashim said mildly, 'was certainly dead. It just wasn't who we thought. It wasn't Lefèvre at all.' He cocked his head. 'Who was it, Dr Millingen? I'm very curious. Was it a corpse you procured for the occasion? Or just a hapless bag-carrier, in the wrong place at the wrong time?'

Millingen began to tap his finger on the coin.

'Well, it's not the most important thing now,' Yashim said peaceably. 'You were happy to let the world believe that Lefèvre was dead.' He looked up and smiled. 'You thought the Mavrogordatos would be satisfied, I suppose. Is that what he hoped, too?'

Millingen bent his head and frowned at a corner of his desk; but he did not open his mouth.

'But he couldn't count on your help, could he? Not after Missolonghi. So he did the trade: his life, for the relics. The last, lost treasure of Byzantium, spirited away by a priest at the altar as the Ottomans invaded the Great Church. A chalice and plate – if they still existed. And the collector in you couldn't turn him down.'

Dr Millingen leaned his elbow on the desk and shaded his eyes.

'Some people think' – he spoke slowly, and there was a tremble in his voice – 'that it was the Holy Grail.'

Yashim looked at him in silence. 'You've kept him hidden,' he said at last. 'In the port, perhaps.'

Millingen heaved his shoulders, shrugging.

Yashim frowned. 'He hid the book at my apartment. There's not much trust between you, is there?'

Millingen gave a scornful bark. 'Only a fool would trust a man like Meyer,' he said.

'Amélie did.' Even as he spoke, Yashim remembered the three snakes. The three cities. Meyer: Lefèvre: and a dead man.

But Lefèvre was not dead. He was still alive. He had one identity which was not fulfilled.

One skin he hadn't cast.

'You both needed someone to carry out the plan.'

'That was his idea,' Millingen said, dragging his palms down the side of his face. 'He wouldn't trust me. And I couldn't let him go. He left the book with you, and sent for his wife.'

Yashim bent forwards and leaned his palms on the edge of Millingen's desk.

'What was your deal, Dr Millingen? Why is Amélie going home alone?' His legs felt weak. 'Because she failed?'

Millingen nodded gently. 'I'm afraid, Yashim efendi, that Dr Lefèvre has died, after all.' His voice sounded ragged and old.

Yashim flushed with sudden anger. 'I don't think so, Dr Millingen. This time he can't run away from who he is. Madame Lefèvre has something else to sell.'

He knelt on the ground, and unlaced the bag.

Millingen leaned forwards. Yashim brought up something wrapped in a cloth, and laid it on the far side of the desk. It was about two feet long, and it sounded heavy.

Yashim put a hand on top of the object. 'I hope you understand me, Dr Millingen. Madame Lefèvre risked her life. She risked her life – for Max. I don't think she should have to go away alone.'

Millingen's eyes were like gimlets.

Yashim flicked the cloth open.

Millingen started back. He glanced up into Yashim's face, then back into the deep-set eyes and the cold frown.

'The Serpent of Delphi,' he said. 'I don't – where did you get this?'

'I won't say where,' Yashim said. 'But I'll tell you why. Madame Mavrogordato never tried to kill Lefèvre.'

'But that's not true! Her people simply got the wrong man, as you say, and –'

'No, Dr Millingen,' Yashim said softly. 'That's your mistake. Madame Mavrogordato never quite found out who, exactly, Lefèvre was. She suspected, but she wasn't sure.'

Millingen frowned. 'Then who was trying to kill him?'

'Let's just say he trod on a serpent's tail,' Yashim said, 'and it bit back.'

Millingen threw up his hands.

Yashim looked at the snake's head.

'I am giving you this for two passages on the *Ulysse*, to France.' He blinked. 'Dr Lefèvre goes home, with his wife.'

❊ 124 ❊

It took Yashim less than ten minutes to reach the theatre; but he was aware as he arrived that he had travelled further than he knew. A crowd had gathered on the street outside – the same crowd, he noticed with amusement, that turned out for street brawls, house fires or public executions: the usual Greeks craning their necks for a better view, and the customary Turks in fezzes standing gravely with their hands by their sides; foreign loafers in tall black hats, who ran their fingers hopefully through their pockets, exchanged glances with busy-looking madrasa students in turbans who had come to protest, and had been intimidated by the nature and variety of the crowd. Much of the movement in the crowd was supplied by foreign crews, who seemed to haul themselves in towards the main gate by invisible warps. One knot of sailors Yashim recognised by their curious brimless caps, embroidered in gold with the word *Ulysse*.

Yashim worked his way slowly and unobtrusively forwards in their wake until he reached the gate itself, where tickets were being sold in an atmosphere of ribald misunderstanding. A small, preternaturally wizened old man in a small turban was carefully examining the money people thrust towards him, with the help of Mina, who Yashim recognised leaning over the old man, volubly judging the quality of the coin by her interest in the faces of the men who tendered it. It looked like a full house.

Yashim found Preen backstage. She had beads of sweat on her forehead and was pounding the air, talking very fast to a small, fat man wearing the biggest turban Yashim had ever seen. She caught sight of Yashim and stayed him with a gesture, still talking anxiously to the fat man, whose eyes appeared to be closed. At last the fat man nodded solemnly, his whole turban tilting to and fro like a shipwreck, and withdrew.

'Chaos!' Preen muttered. 'Pandemonium!' She smiled suddenly. 'Always a good sign, Yashim. Where have you been?'

Yashim murmured a reply, then stepped back to allow a woman in European dress with a monkey on her shoulder to address Preen in a low, urgent voice. Preen gave her some brisk assurance, then wheeled to face a deputation of musicians, who were complaining that they didn't have space to perform. Mina came in, looking flushed and triumphant, and whispered something in Preen's ear. Preen nodded absently. Mina waved at Yashim.

Yashim took a seat at a café table to watch the performance. It was vulgar, loud, and a great success. The lady ventriloquist and her monkey; a snake charmer; an extravagantly pretty girl dressed as an odalisque, who sang and danced and, later, reappeared to be sawn in half by a Russian magician; interspersed with several interesting tableaux vivants – a Frankish home, a wolf hunt in the Carpathians, and an assignation in a Persian garden, in which scene the lady seemed to be represented by a small jewelled slipper. In the meantime the audience were served with coffee, tea, sherbet and chibouques by slim, pantalooned dancers, and everyone talked non-stop, between applause.

Halfway through the second act, Preen slid gracefully into the seat beside Yashim. She put an elbow on the café table and spoke into her hand.

'Small world,' she said. 'Your friend Alex Mavrogordato just arrived.'

Yashim suppressed the urge to turn around. 'Alone?'

'He's with a man. A Frank. Older, short. Smoking a little cigar.'

Yashim exhaled slowly through his teeth. Onstage, a drowsy cobra was rising slowly from a basket while an Indian blew at it through a little pipe. The snake turned its head to follow the music. The Indian danced gravely round the basket. Yashim turned in his chair and saw Alex Mavrogordato and Maximilien Lefèvre, né Meyer, watching the performance without speaking.

Lefèvre's eyes slid towards him.

The cobra's head was now lifted high out of the basket, swaying on its thick, undulating body. Behind its head, the hood flattened and widened.

Lefèvre and Yashim looked at one another. Without smiling, the Frenchman nodded and made a slight gesture of salute with his cigar.

Yashim shook his head. Then he blinked and turned his attention to the stage.

The charmer and the snake were now moving together: as the Indian swayed backwards the cobra leaned out towards him, its little tongue flicking in and out. The Indian slowly put out his hand, palm down, until the tips of his fingers were just below the cobra's throat. Very gradually, to the soft notes of the pipe, the cobra laid his head on the man's fingers.

Yashim watched in disgust as the man's hand turned slowly black: the cobra was rippling forwards onto the man's wrist, its hood over his hand, slowly advancing out of its basket and up the extended arm, oozing upwards from the basket to the charmer's shoulder. The Indian continued to play his pipe with one hand, keeping his arm very still until the entire snake had ranged itself along the thickness of his arm. He turned, and faced the crowd. There was a gasp as the snake's head appeared over the charmer's head and reared up, spreading its hood like a pagan crown.

The man and his snake did a little tour of the stage, bowing together; then the man reached up and took hold of the cobra by its head and slipped it back into the basket, clapping on the lid. The audience broke into applause.

'Come on, Yashim,' Preen said, nudging him with her elbow. 'It's only a snake. You look as though you'd seen a ghost.'

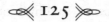

125

The ship's bell clanked, and a squad of smartly-dressed sailors stood to attention on the foredeck, apparently none the worse for their foray into Pera the night before. A belch of black soot drifted from the single stack; its smoke drifted up through the furled shrouds and spars of the mainmast, and slowly vanished into the blue sky.

A fat coachman brought an elegant black-lacquered barouche to a stop on the cobbles. He held the reins firmly in his hand and turned his head to look at the *Ulysse*. No one got out of the barouche.

At the foot of the gangplank a uniformed sailor exchanged glances with two other men, in singlets, waiting on deck.

Amélie Lefèvre put out her hand. 'Goodbye, ambassador.'

Palewski took her hand and stooped over it. '*Au revoir*, Madame.' He nodded to Lefèvre. 'Doctor.'

Now she was looking at Yashim. There was a strange, almost dull, look in her eyes. The sun was in her hair, turning her ringlets to fire. She did not offer him her hand; instead, she placed it on her heart.

'The sultan, Yashim,' she said. 'And the poet. I shan't forget.'

Yashim smiled sadly. 'Perhaps.'

Lefèvre, he noticed, was glancing nervously around the quay. The gangplank screeched as the *Ulysse* rolled lightly in the current.

'I will remember your courage,' Yashim added.

'My courage,' Amélie repeated, tonelessly. 'But I believed in the relics, you see. I thought the myth was real.'

Dr Lefèvre took her elbow. He leaned slightly forwards to catch Yashim's eye, then he raised his cheroot and pointed it at him. 'Pah!' He made a soft explosive sound with his lips, and smiled crookedly. It seemed like a private joke.

Yashim stepped back and frowned.

Palewski raised his eyebrows and glanced at Yashim.

The uniformed sailor put out a protective arm to usher the couple onto the gangplank.

'*Faites attention, monsieur'dame,*' he murmured.

Halfway up the gangplank, Amélie had not looked back.

Lefèvre was slightly ahead of her, his hand beneath her elbow, turning a little, when it all happened.

Perhaps it was the movement of the ship; perhaps the slippers – the slippers which Millingen had bought for her, with their pointed ends. Amélie stumbled. She pitched sideways, stretching out her arms, clutching at her husband for support.

By then it was already too late. With a sudden cry of alarm, Dr Lefèvre flailed his arms through the air, and then he was gone.

Yashim sprang forward. For a second he saw it all frozen, like a tableau at the theatre: Amélie on her knees on the gangplank, staring down; the officer on the quay turning, almost crouched with horror; the two sailors on the deck leaning over the rail, their heads together.

Then he heard Amélie's sob, and the officer was at her side; one of the sailors was shouting something over his shoulder and the other was dropping a rope into the narrow gap between the ship and the quay.

Yashim glanced down. Palewski was at his shoulder, and Yashim heard him murmur: 'I just don't believe it.'

He raised his head. The officer was helping Amélie to her feet, urging her gently up the gangplank. A band of sailors with crowbars in their hands were at the top, waiting to come by.

'Please, madame! Please, just come this way!'

The sailors streamed down the gangplank. They set their muscled arms against the wooden walls of the ship and planted their feet on the quay, and began to heave.

'Loose the stern warps! Give us room!' There were shouts, more orders; other sailors appeared. A man began to slide down a rope, with bare feet.

Amélie, sagging on the officer's arm, passed the ship's rail and turned her head. Yashim felt her glance sweep over him to fix on something further away, and he was about to glance round when Amélie gave a curious little jerk of her head. She was standing

295

against the sun; he blinked, dazzled: for a moment it had looked as though she had smiled, but when he next saw clearly the officer was coaxing her onto the ship and in a few seconds she had disappeared from sight.

Yashim heard a sharp crack behind him, and turned to see the barouche start off. He thought he recognised a face at the window, the face of a woman with strong, dark brows; but it was only a fleeting glimpse, and he could not be sure.

Palewski took him by the elbow. 'How did it happen?' He said, aghast.

Yashim began walking slowly in the carriage's wake. After a few moments he raised his head and spoke to the air.

'Madame Lefèvre thought the myth was real,' he said. Then he nodded sadly, and turned to his friend. 'Until she discovered that the reality was a myth.'

Palewski looked searchingly into Yashim's face. 'It wasn't an accident, was it? She pushed him in.'

Yashim bit his lip. 'Let's just say that Madame Lefèvre was a very determined woman.'

And he began to walk again, uphill through the dusty streets of Pera.

126

'I thought it was you,' Yashim said. 'At first.'

He heard the ticking of the clocks, the rustle of Madame Mavrogordato's silks, the chink of her spoon on the saucer as she laid it down, very slowly.

'It should have been me,' she said. 'Revenge is a dish –'

'Eaten better when cold, yes. I've heard that phrase. I don't believe in it, either.'

Madame Mavrogordato narrowed her eyes and glared at Yashim. 'When I heard that he had died – that he had been killed in the street? I didn't believe it. That was not how it would happen – to him. He had more lives than a cat.'

More skins than a snake, Yashim thought.

Madame Mavrogordato leaned forwards. 'But they said it was him. Why?'

Yashim put his fingers together. 'He was carrying Lefèvre's bag. The dogs had got to him – there was very little left. Except that he had perfect teeth. I wondered about that. Lefèvre spoke with a lisp. Later, I learned that he had lost two teeth in a brawl – at Missolonghi.'

Some expression Yashim could not catch passed across the godlike face.

'Then what happened? Who was he?'

Yashim shrugged. 'He was the man Millingen sent to fetch Lefèvre off the ship. Millingen wanted Lefèvre out of harm's way, so he had him confined in a house somewhere down by the docks.' He hesitated, wondering whether he should say what he suspected: that her supposed son, the impatient Alexander, had been his gaoler. 'Someone else was supposed to bring Lefèvre's bag to the doctor's house,' he said finally. 'A servant. He was unlucky: the killers tracked him down. But they got the wrong man.'

Madame Mavrogordato nodded slightly. 'And Millingen? Why did he want Lefèvre hidden?'

Yashim shifted slightly in his seat, and sighed. 'Dr Millingen learned that Lefèvre's life had been threatened. He, too, believed that axiom about revenge.'

'So he thought I had ordered his death?'

'They were friends, once. And Millingen, of course, was interested in the relics. He expected Lefèvre to tell him what he knew, in return for saving his life. The *Ca d'Oro* is one of your ships, isn't it?'

Madame Mavrogordato gave a brief nod.

'When Millingen's man was killed,' Yashim went on, 'and identified as Lefèvre, Millingen decided to say nothing about it. At first, I suppose, he thought he had diverted you. But later, when other people died, he realised what I had guessed – that it wasn't you at all.'

Madame Mavrogordato's lips moved into a thin smile. 'But when it happened, when it really did happen, it was a woman. It would take a woman, Yashim efendi: Max Meyer was not a man just anyone could kill.'

'Four men died first, on his account.'

Madame Mavrogordato drew back her head. 'Four men, efendi? You think – only four?'

She turned her head, by the neck, to fix him with her dark eyes; and he met them with a jolt of recognition.

'You can believe what you want to,' she almost spat. 'Millingen – what an English gentleman! A bad show, he thinks, Dr Meyer cutting loose like that. Leaving his young wife behind, as well. Shocking behaviour! I don't think Millingen would recommend him to his London club.'

She was almost shaking: Yashim couldn't tell if it was with anger, or contempt.

'But I knew that man. You should have heard what he said to me, the promises he made, the innocence he tore apart with his bare hands like a veil in front of my eyes. He bared me to the world, then spat upon me and turned away.' She lowered her voice, and two tears ran down her cheeks. 'The man who could betray me like that – he could betray anyone. The Turks caught him, I'm sure of that. And he sold them Missolonghi, in return for his own miserable life. He sold us all, Yashim efendi. And you talk of three men dead. Three men!'

She stood up, and went to the windows, wiping her hands across her cheeks.

298

'I'm so glad she killed him, Yashim efendi. I am so very, very grateful.'

She put out a hand, to touch the curtains. Yashim heard a knock at the door of the apartment.

Madame Mavrogordato's fist balled around the silk. 'She must have hated him, very much,' she said.

The knock came again, louder. The woman at the window turned her head. 'Come!'

The footman entered the apartment and bowed. He glanced at Yashim.

'Hanum,' he faltered. 'The sultan is dead.'

Madame Mavrogordato turned her face away. 'Have the shutters drawn at the front of the house, Dmitri.'

'Yes, hanum.'

'The groom will know to put crepe on the carriage. Also the horses' bridles. Ask the cook to see that there is enough for tomorrow, before the markets close. Monsieur Mavrogordato will eat at home. That is all.'

'I will see to it, hanum.'

When the footman had gone, neither of them spoke for several minutes.

'The sultan is dead,' Madame Mavrogordato said at last. 'Long live the sultan.'

Yashim stared at his hands. He caught the irony in her tone, but he was thinking of someone else.

He got to his feet. Madame Mavrogordato had closed her eyes, and between clenched teeth she gave out a strangled moan.

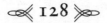

127

Across the Golden Horn, in a dilapidated mansion close to the Grande Rue, a man stood listening at an open window.

'So that's that,' he said at last, so quietly that the girl in the room could only imagine he had spoken. She set the tray down carefully on the desk.

From the windows she heard the distant muezzins calling the prayer for the dead.

Palewski turned. The bottle on the tray was old and squat. Many years ago, a Polish nobleman had ordered it among a few dozen such from one of the best cognac houses in France, to lay down in the cellars on his estate. 'It's good Martell,' Palewski's father would say. 'If in doubt, dump the paintings but hang on to the brandy.'

Palewski pulled out a penknife and slit the wax around the neck. He pulled the cork, and poured a measure into each glass.

Gently he picked up both glasses by the stem.

Marta blushed. 'Lord – I cannot – I –'

Palewski shook his head. 'It's to remember him by,' he said. 'He ruled this empire for as long as I've known Istanbul. All your life, Marta.'

He held the glass to the light. 'To Mahmut!'

'To Mahmut,' Marta echoed, smiling.

128

It was the noise that startled him, even before he saw the crowd: a murmur of voices like the sea. The halberdiers stood to attention in the gate, and in the First Court of the seraglio, where only a few days before he had walked in absolute stillness, Yashim found himself jostled and surrounded on all sides.

Sultan Mahmut was dead. In the faces which surrounded him Yashim saw expressions of anguish and despair; he read fear in one man's eyes, and in the next, expectancy; he heard the murmur of the sutras, and laughter, and the cry of the corncob seller calling his wares. A distinguished pasha walked by in a swirl of cloak and leather, with his horse, a grey, curvetting at the groom's hand on the bridle. An elderly man, bareheaded, lay spread-eagled face down on the ground, as if he had fallen from the sky. A phalanx of small children stood silently against the wall. A yellow dog heaved itself up from the shade of a plane tree and stalked stiffly away, as if disgusted to have its sleep disturbed, while a man in a fez, with an enormous belly, wept openly on the shoulder of another man, dressed like a servant. Many people – Muslim, Armenian – counted their beads, and watched.

The sultan had died at Beşiktaş, like the jewel in a box: but here to Topkapi, to the ancient palace of the sultans, to the great old court of the Empire, the people came with their hopes and their regrets.

Yashim advanced through the crowd to the second gate. The halberdiers did not recognise him at first, and lowered their pikes before the key-holder saw him and nodded him through. They walked in silence to the little door to the harem.

He found Hyacinth sobbing in a little chamber off the corridor.

'Who's with the validé, then?' he demanded.

Hyacinth raised his little red-rimmed eyes to his. 'Oh, Yashim! We are all so very sad!'

'So I see,' Yashim said.

He found her alone and fully dressed, seated on the edge of the sofa with her hands in her lap.

'I hoped it would be you, Yashim. I see that you, too, refrain from weeping.'

Yashim said nothing.

'I've sent the rest of them away. I can't bear to see their faces all crumpled up, the runny noses. Pure chicanery. They have no idea what will happen to me, so they are sorry for themselves. They have hearts like walnuts.'

Yashim suppressed a smile. 'The First Court is full of people, validé. It reminds me of the old days.'

'Yes?' The validé raised her head, as if to listen. Her silver earrings chinked together softly.

'It's a strange thing, Yashim,' she said, in a surprisingly small voice. 'I do nothing at all from day to day, but grow old – yet I find that today of all days, I have nothing to do. I can only sit.'

Yashim rubbed his chin, thoughtfully. Then he knelt at the validé's side. 'I have an idea,' he said.

❧ 129 ❧

The crowd in the First Court was denser than before, and it was only a sufi, with hands upraised and one eye on the second gate, who noticed two figures emerging from the sanctity of the inner court. Perhaps, if the sufi had stopped to think, he might have guessed the identity of the veiled woman who walked slowly, with a stick, supported by her undistinguished companion; but the sufi had deliberately emptied his mind of all thoughts, the better to concentrate on the ninety-nine names of God.

Yashim felt the validé's grip tighten on his arm as they advanced towards the crowd, and took it as a good sign. It was impossible for them to speak over the shouts and murmurs of the mourners thronging that vast space, but he noticed the validé's head turning to and fro as she observed the faces of the men who surrounded them, and now and then she stopped, for a better look. In this way the validé betrayed her particular interest in little children, boiled corn, the traditional ululations of Arab women, and the mount of a long-legged Albanian cavalryman in French trousers.

Yashim wondered, as they walked slowly along, whether they should go as far as the Topkapi gate. He had a daydream, in which he led the validé through the gate and out into the square; by the fountain they picked up a carriage, and rattled down the streets to the Eminönü wharf, where he handed the elderly Frenchwoman into a French ship, and sent her off to enjoy herself in Paris. It was a daydream he had sometimes indulged on his own account, but he startled himself now, as if he had committed a treasonable act. He began to wonder where, indeed, he should lead the validé. She showed no sign of wishing to go back, yet her weight on his arm was growing, and she was evidently beginning to tire.

Yashim began to steer the validé towards the great doors of the old Church of St Irene, at the far end of the great court. As they moved into the shade of the portico she patted his arm, as if she approved of his decision; he tried the little door and – to his surprise – it swung open.

They stepped inside, and as the little door shut behind them with a click the noise of the crowd was abruptly hushed, giving way to an ethereal silence: the silence, Yashim thought, of every consecrated place. Hadn't Lefèvre said that St Irene had never been deconsecrated, never turned into a mosque?

The ancient weapons glinted on the walls.

He found a stone bench under a window, and the validé settled gratefully onto it. She lifted her veil.

'Thank you, Yashim,' she said, smiling. 'I have always wanted to do that. The way the old sultans did – moving amongst their people, in disguise.'

'Selim himself met a baker so wise he raised him next day to the position of Grand Vizier,' Yashim said.

'*Alors*, Yashim, I'm not sure I saw anyone quite so exceptional.' She closed her eyes.

Yashim watched her. He folded his arms and leaned against a pillar. He wondered if she was asleep.

'My son told me an interesting thing, Yashim, just before he died,' the validé said quietly. Yashim jumped. 'It was a secret, passed down the generations from one sultan to the next, and he told it to me because his own son would not come to listen. Do you know why that was?'

'No, validé.'

'Because the boy was afraid. But why should a boy be afraid of death?'

Yashim had no answer. The validé glanced at him. 'The crown prince, Yashim. No longer a boy, perhaps.'

'Abdül Mecid is our sultan now,' Yashim said.

'Yes.' She paused. '*Enfin*, he likes you.'

Yashim lowered his eyes. 'He can barely know me.'

'Come, come. A boy talks to his grandmother. I think you'll find he knows you better than you think.'

Yashim blinked; but the validé did not wait for her remark to sink in. 'At the time of the Conquest,' she continued, 'when the Turks took Istanbul, a priest was saying Mass in the Great Church. He was using the holiest relics of the Byzantine church, the cup and the plate used at the Last Supper, but when the Turks broke in, he disappeared.'

'I've heard that legend myself,' Yashim admitted.

'Legend, Yashim?' The validé looked at him. 'It is what the sultan told me before he died.'

Yashim inclined his head.

304

'Mehmed the Conqueror,' the validé continued, 'had taken the city from the Greeks. But afterwards he needed their support, of course. The Greek Patriarch agreed to treat the sultan as his overlord. But as for the relics, neither of them could accept that the other should possess them. Do you understand?'

'They found a compromise, didn't they? A way of safeguarding the relics, beyond the control of the Church or the Ottoman sultans.'

'Very good, Yashim. I wanted to unburden myself of this secret because – *eh bien*, I am not a church or a line of rulers myself. Someone needs to tell the crown prince, if I cannot.' She opened her eyes, and glanced mischievously at Yashim: 'But I suppose you already know who they found?'

'Yes, validé. And they didn't have far to look. As far as I know, the cup and plate were already hidden in the cisterns, somewhere beneath the Great Church. They were in the safekeeping of the watermen.'

'Bravo! The watermen's guild, yes. They were always Albanians. You know what that means. Some Catholic, some Orthodox. And some, in time, were Muslims, too. But the first religion of the Albanian, as they say, is Albania. They call themselves Sons of the Eagle.'

'And this has been their secret,' Yashim murmured.

He went across the apse to a wooden cupboard hanging on the wall. It was crudely made, its door fastened with a wooden catch. Inside he found a battered-looking copper goblet and a wooden plate, which had split and been repaired with thin iron staples. He'd seen them both before. Water and salt: cup and plate.

'I spent a week with some people who thought they knew exactly where the relics were,' he said, turning towards her. 'They put it together, out of old books.'

The validé sniffed. 'When we get back to the apartments, I

think I shall ask you to read to me a little. Monsieur Stendhal.' She put out her stick, and got to her feet. 'It's cold in here.'

He took her arm, and they went slowly out of the old church. In the shade of the portico, the validé put up her hands to adjust her veil.

'Your friends – I suppose they were very disappointed, *non?*'

Yashim cocked his head. 'Disappointed? I think you could say that. One of them, in fact, wound up dead.'

'Well, well, Yashim. I'm sure you will want to talk about it. It just goes to show that you can't believe everything that you read in books, *n'est-ce pas?*'

She dropped her veil, and they passed out together from the shade into the sun, leaning close together like old friends.

Acknowledgements

I'd like to thank the usual suspects among my family and friends for their encouragement and advice; not least Richard Goodwin, who read the manuscript at an early stage – and hopes that Amélie will make it back to Istanbul one day.

Berrin Torolsan inspires cooks and scholars alike with her writing in *Cornucopia*, that beautiful and indispensable quarterly devoted to all things Turkish. Not only has she generously shared her knowledge of Ottoman cookery and history with me; she has also read the book with a critical eye. I should point out that all its errors, deviations and flagrant misrepresentations are mine alone: fiction, I'm afraid, is no respecter of fact.

Translators, editors, proofreaders and designers around the world brought Yashim's debut in *The Janissary Tree* to life in thirty-two languages. Thanks to Agnieszka Kuc in Poland, Nina van Rossem in Holland, Fortunato Israel and my Italian translator Cristiana Mennella, who made *L'Albero dei Giannezzeri* such a successful *giallo*. I have been grateful for the enthusiasm of, among others, Sylvie Audoly in Paris, and Elena Ramírez in Barcelona.

Sarah Chalfant at the Wylie Agency introduced me to this other world. My thanks to the team, but above all to Charles Buchan for his tireless and good-humoured efforts on Yashim's behalf. I have been lucky to have two superb *editing* editors, Julian Loose at Faber in the UK, and Sarah Crichton at FSG in New York, whose wisdom I have always received gratefully; and generally acted upon.

Much of this book was written far away from the rumpus of

family life, with no interruptions, no battles for control of the computer. My son Izaak has grown tall and learned much. This book is for him.